TITLES BY CHLOE LIESE

THE WILMOT SISTERS

Two Wrongs Make a Right
Better Hate Than Never

THE BERGMAN BROTHERS

Only When It's Us
Always Only You
Ever After Always
With You Forever
Everything for You
If Only You

For those who've lost hope,
and those who've been to hell and back
to find it again.

Dear Reader,

This story features characters with human realities who I believe deserve to be seen more prominently in romance through positive, authentic representation. As a neurodivergent person living with chronic conditions, I am passionate about writing feel-good romances affirming my belief that every one of us is worthy and capable of happily ever after, if that's what our heart desires.

Specifically, this story portrays a character who has a generalized anxiety disorder. No two people's experience of any condition will be the same, but through my own experience and the insight of authenticity readers, I have strived to create a character who honors the nuances of that identity. This story also touches on parental alcoholism and abandonment as well as growing up in poverty.

If any of these are sensitive topics for you, I hope you feel comforted in knowing that loving, affirming relationships—with oneself and others—are championed in this story.

XO,
Chloe

You pierce my soul. I am half agony, half hope. Tell me not that I am too late, that such precious feelings are gone forever.

—JANE AUSTEN,
Persuasion

Ever After
Always

Aiden

Playlist: "Melody Noir," Patrick Watson

The day I met Freya Bergman, I knew I wanted to marry her.

Some mutual friends threw together a pickup soccer game one balmy summer Sunday and invited us both. I'd played in high school, kept up with a recreational soccer league while I went through undergrad. A poor PhD student by that point, I liked the game enough to value the opportunity for fun without a price tag. No awkward outings where I didn't buy an entrée because I'd just paid my rent and emptied my account, no well-meaning buddies insisting—to my humiliation—on treating me. Just a place and time where I could stand tall and feel like I was everyone's equal. A lazy morning under that bright California sun, juggling a ball, goofing off with friends.

But then *she* walked in and goofing off went out the window. Every man on that field froze, backs straight, eyes sharp, and all manner of stupidity vanished as quiet settled over the grass. My eyes scanned the field, then snagged on the tall blonde with a wavy ponytail, wintry blue eyes, and a confident grin tipping her rose-red lips. A shiver rolled down my spine as her cool gaze met mine and her smile vanished.

Then she glanced away.

And I swore to God I'd earn her eyes again if it was the last thing I did.

I watched her trying not to be flashy when she juggled the ball and messed with ridiculous moves that she nailed more than flubbed, how effortlessly she balanced skill and playfulness. I watched her, and all I wanted was closer. More. But when we broke into two sides, I realized with disappointment we'd been placed on separate teams. So I volunteered to defend her, with the arrogant hubris typical of twenty-something men, thinking a guy my size who could still put down some fast miles had a prayer of keeping up with a woman like her.

That was the last time I underestimated Freya.

I all but killed myself on the field, trying to track her fast feet, to anticipate her physicality, to find the same explosive speed when she flew up the sidelines, betraying a fitness I didn't quite match. I remember marveling at the power of her long, muscular legs, which made me daydream about them wrapped around my waist, proving her endurance in a much more enjoyable form of exercise. Already, I knew I wanted her. God, did I want her.

I *may* have been taking defense a bit more intensely than everyone else on that field. I *may* have stuck to her like glue. But Freya radiated the magnetism of someone who knew her worth, and in a flash of desperation, I realized I wanted her to see that I could be worthy, too, that I could keep pace and stick close and never tire of her raw, captivating energy.

In Freya's aura, I forgot every single thing weighing on my mind—money, a job, money, food, money, my mother, oh, and money of course, because there was never enough, and it was an ever-present shadow darkening moments that should be bright. Like the sun ripping a cold, solitary planet into orbit, Freya demanded my presence. *Here. Now.* Just a few dazzling minutes in her gravitational pull and that pervasive darkness dissolved, leaving only her. Beautiful. Bright. Dazzling. I was hooked.

So, in my young male brilliance, I decided to show her my interest by sinking my claws into her shirt, tracking her every move like a bloodhound, and doing anything I could to piss her off.

"God, you're annoying," she muttered. Faking right, she cut left past me and took off.

I caught up to her, set a hand on her waist as she shielded the ball and leaned her long body right against mine. Not romantic, but I remember exactly how it felt when her round ass nestled right in my groin. I felt like an animal, and that was *not* how I worked, at least not before Freya. But she felt right, she smelled right, she *was* right. It was simple as that.

"Don't you have someone else to bother?" she said, even as she glanced over her shoulder and those striking eyes said something entirely different. *Stay. Try. Prove me wrong.*

"Nah," I muttered, my grip tightening in every sense of the word, my desperation for her already too much. Grappling for possession, I met her move for move in a tangle of sweaty limbs and scrappy effort, until finally I won the ball for the briefest moment and did something very stupid. I taunted her.

"Besides," I said, as she came after me. "I'm having fun messing with you."

"Fun, eh?" Freya stole the ball off me too easily, pulled back, and cracked it so hard, straight at my face, she snapped my glasses clean in half.

As soon as I crumpled to the ground, she fell to her knees, brushing shards of the wreckage from my face.

"Shit!" Her hands shook, her finger tracing the bridge of my nose. "I'm *so* sorry. I have a short fuse, and it's like you're hardwired to push every button I have."

I grinned up at her, my eyes watering. "I knew we had a connection."

"I'm really sorry," she whispered, ignoring my line.

"You can make it up to me," I said, with as much Aiden Mac-Cormack panty-melting charm as I could muster. Which was . . . challenging, given I'd just taken a point-blank shot to the face and looked like hell, but if there's one thing I am, it's determined.

Freya knew exactly what I meant. Dropping back on her heels, she arched an eyebrow. "I'm not going on a date with you just to make up for accidentally busting your glasses."

"Um, you intentionally *pulverized* my glasses. And quite possibly my nose." I sat up slowly and leaned on my elbows as the breeze wafted her scent my way—fresh-cut grass and a tall, cool glass of lemonade. I wanted to breathe her in, to run my tongue over every drop of sweat beading her throat, then drag her soft bottom lip between my teeth—to taste her, sweet and tart.

"Just one small kiss." I tapped the bridge of my nose, then winced at the pain, where a bruised cut stung from the impact of my glasses. "Right here."

She palmed my forehead until I flopped back on the grass, then stepped right over me.

"I don't give out kisses, four-eyes," she said over her shoulder. "But I'll buy you an apology beer after this, then we'll see what I'm willing to part with."

To this day, Freya swears she was trying for the goal, which was, ya know, twenty yards to the right of my head, but we both know that's not what happened. The truth is, we both learned a lesson that day:

Aiden can only push so far.

Freya can only take so much.

Before something breaks.

Badly.

ONE

Freya

Playlist: "I Go Crazy," Orla Gartland

I used to sing all the time. In the shower. On road trips. Painting our house. Cooking with Aiden. Because I'm a feeler, and music is a language of emotion.

Then, one week ago, I crawled into bed alone *again*, curled up with my cats, Horseradish and Pickles, and realized I couldn't remember the last time I'd sung. And it just so happened to be when I realized that I was really fucking fed up with my husband. That I had been. For months.

So I kicked him out. And things may have devolved a bit since then.

Hiccupping, I stare at Aiden's closet.

"You still there?" My best friend Mai's voice echoes on speakerphone, where my cell rests on the bed.

"Yep." *Hiccup.* "Still drunkish. Sorry."

"Just no operating any heavy machinery, and you're doing fine."

I hiccup again. "I think there's something wrong with me. I'm so pissed at him that I've fantasized about sticking chocolate pudding in his business shoes—"

"What?" she yells. "Why would you do that?"

"He'd think it's cat shit. Pickles gets diarrhea when she eats my houseplants."

A pause. "You're disturbing sometimes."

"This is true." Coming from a family of seven children, I have some very creative ways to exact revenge. "I definitely have a few wires crossed. I'm thinking about resurrecting some of my most sinister pranks, *and* I'm so horny, I'm staring at his closet, huffing his scent."

Mai sighs sympathetically from my phone. "There's nothing wrong with you. You haven't had a lay in . . . how long, again?"

I grab the bottle of wine sitting on my dresser and take a long swig. "Nine weeks. Four days—" I squint one-eyed at the clock. "Twenty-one hours."

She whistles. "Yeah. So, too long. You're sex starved. And just because you're hurt doesn't mean you can't still want him. Marriage is messier and much more complicated than anyone warned us. You can want to rip off his nuts and miss him so bad, it feels like you can't breathe."

Tears swim in my eyes. "I feel like I can't breathe."

"But you can," Mai says gently. "One breath at a time."

"Why don't they warn us?"

"What?"

"Why doesn't anyone tell you how hard marriage is going to be?" Mai sighs heavily. "Because I'm not sure we'd do it if they did."

Stepping closer to the rack of Aiden's immaculate, wrinkle-free button-ups, I press my nose into the collar of his favorite one.

Winter-skies blue, Freya. The color of your eyes.

I feel a twisty blend of rage and longing as I breathe him in. Ocean water and mint, the warm, familiar scent of his body. I fist the fabric until it crumples, and I watch it relax when I let go, as if I never even touched it. That's how I feel about my husband lately. Like he walks around our house and I could be a ghost for all it matters. Or maybe he's the ghost.

Maybe we both are.

Slapping a palm on the closet door and slamming it shut, I hit the wine bottle again. One last gulp and it's gone. Freya: 1. Wine: 0.

"Take *that*, alcohol," I tell the bottle, setting it on my dresser with a hollow *thunk*.

"Is he still in Washington?" Mai asks, tiptoeing her way around my tipsy rambling.

I stare at his empty side of the bed. "Yep."

My husband is, at my request, one thousand miles north of me, licking his wounds with my brother and duly freaking out because I put my foot down and told him this shit would not stand. I'm home, with the cats, freaking out, too, because I miss my husband, because I want to throttle this imposter and demand the guy I married back.

I want Aiden's ocean-blue eyes sparkling as they settle on me. I want his long, hard hugs and no-bullshit musings on life, the kind of pragmatism born of struggle and resilience. I want his tall frame pressing me against the shower tiles, his rough hands wandering my curves. I want his sighs and groans, his dirty talk filling my ears as he fills me with every inch of him.

Distracted by that vivid mental image, I stub my toe on the bed frame.

"Fuckety shit tits!" Flopping onto the mattress, I stare up at the ceiling and try not to cry.

"You okay?" Mai asks. "I mean I know you're not. But . . . you know what I mean."

"Stubbed my toe," I squeak.

"Aw. Let it out, Frey. Let it *goooo*," she singsongs. "You are, according to my kids, Elsa, Queen of Arendelle, after all."

"But with hips," we say in unison.

I laugh through tears that I furiously wipe away. Crying isn't weak. I know this. Rationally. But I also know the world doesn't reward tears or see emotionality as strength. I'm an empowered, no-nonsense woman who feels *all* her feelings and battles the cultural pressure to contain them, to have my emotional shit in order. Even when all I want to do sometimes is indulge in a teary explosion of hugging my condiment-named cats while cry-singing along to my nineties emo playlist. For example. Like I might have been doing earlier. When I opened and started chugging the wine.

In a world that says feelings like mine are "too much," singing has always helped. In a houseful of mostly stoics who loved my big heart but handled their feelings so differently from me, singing was an outlet for all I felt and couldn't—or wouldn't—hide. That's why, last week, when I realized I'd stopped singing, I got scared. Because that's when I understood how numb I'd become, how dangerously deep I was burying my pain.

"Freya?" Mai says carefully.

"I'm okay," I tell her hoarsely. I wipe my eyes again. "Or . . . I will be. I just wish I knew what to do. Aiden said, whatever it was, he wanted to fix it, but how do you fix something when you don't even know what's broken? Or when it feels so broken, you don't even recognize it anymore? How can he make that promise when he acts like he has no fucking clue why I'm feeling this way?"

Horseradish, ever the empath, senses my upset and jumps onto the bed, meowing loudly, then kneading my boob, which hurts. I shove him away gently, until he moves to my stomach, which feels better. I have cramps like a bitch. Pickles is slower on the uptick but finally jumps and joins her brother, then begins licking my face.

"I don't know, Frey," Mai says. "But what I do know is, you have to talk to him. I understand why you're hurt, why the last thing you want to do is be the initiator when he's been so withdrawn, but you're not going to get answers if you don't talk." She hesitates a beat, then says, "Marriage counseling would be wise to try. If you're willing... if you choose to. You'll have to decide if you want to, even if you think it's too far gone."

And that's when the tears come, no matter how fast I wipe them away. Because I don't know if I have anything left to choose from. I'm scared we *are* too far gone. Crying so hard my throat burns, I feel each jagged sob like it's breaking open my chest.

Because the past six months, I've witnessed the core of my marriage dissolving, and now I don't know how to build it back. Because at some point, critical damage is done, and there's no returning to what it was before. In the human body, it's called "irreversible atrophy." As a physical therapist, I'm no stranger to it, even though I fight it as much as I can, working my patients until they're sweating and crying and cussing me out.

It's not my favorite part of the job, when they hit their low point, shaking and exhausted and spent, but the truth is, that's good pain—pain that precedes healing. Otherwise, muscles that go unchallenged shrink, bones left untested become brittle. Use it or lose it. There are a thousand variations on the fundamental truth of Newton's Third Law: *For every action there is an equal and opposite reaction.* The less you demand of something, the less it gives back, the weaker it becomes, until one day it's a shadow of itself.

"I'm so tired of crying," I tell Mai through the lump in my throat.

"I know, Frey," she says softly.

"I'm so mad at him," I growl through the tears.

Six months of slow, silent decline. It wasn't one big, awful argument. It was a thousand quiet moments that added up until I realized I didn't recognize him or us or, shit, even me.

"You're allowed to be," Mai says. "You're hurting. And you stood up for yourself. That's important. That's big."

"I did. I stood up for myself." I wipe my nose. "And he acted like he had no goddamn clue what was wrong, like nothing was wrong."

"To be fair, a lot of guys are like this," Mai says. "I mean, Pete has gotten better at carrying more of the emotional load of our marriage, but it took time and *work*. You remember two years ago, when I kicked him out?"

"Uh. Yeah. He slept on my sofa."

"That's right. So you're not alone. Guys do this. They mess up, and they're usually clueless at first as to how. Most men aren't taught to introspect on relationships. They're taught to drag race for the girl, then once they have her, to hit cruise control. I mean, not *all* men. But enough of them that there's a precedent."

"Okay, fine, most of them don't tend to introspect. But when things deteriorate like this, how are they happy?"

"I can't say they're *happy*. Complacent, maybe?"

"Complacent," I say, tasting it sour on my tongue. "Fuck that."

"Oh, you know I agree."

There's no way Aiden's happy with this corpse of a marriage, is he? And *complacent*? That's the last word I'd ever use for my husband. Aiden's determined, driven, the most dedicated and hardworking person I've ever met. He doesn't settle for anything. So why would he settle in our marriage? What happened?

Is he content to come home, exchange the same seven lines about our day, shower separately, then go to bed, just to do it all over again? Is he fulfilled by a quick peck on the cheek, satisfied that we haven't had sex in months?

We used to have such fire for each other, such passion. And I know that dims with time, but we went from a blazing roar to a steady, warm glow. I loved that glow. I was happy with it. And then I realized one day it was gone. I was alone. And it was so, so cold.

"This sucks, Mai." I blow my nose and throw the tissue nowhere in particular. I almost wish Aiden were here to cringe at the mess I've turned the house into. I'd watch his left eye start twitching and derive perverse satisfaction from actually eliciting *some* kind of response from him. "This sucks so bad."

"I know, honey. I wish I could fix it. I'd do anything to fix it for you."

Fresh tears streak my cheeks. "I know."

The security system of our Culver City bungalow beeps, telling me someone entered and used the security code.

"Mai, I think he's home. I'm gonna go."

"Okay. Hang in there, Freya. Call anytime."

Sitting up, I dab my eyes. "I will. Thank you. Love you."

"Love you, too."

I tap the button to end our call just as the door shuts quietly. Horseradish and Pickles leap off me, bounding out of the room and down the hall.

"Should have named them Benedict and Arnold," I mutter. "Traitors. I'm the one who feeds you!"

"Freya?" Aiden calls, followed by a *bang*, a *thud*, then a muttered string of curses. I think I left my sneakers right inside the door, which he must have tripped on.

Oops.

The door clicks behind him. "Freya?" he calls again. "It's me." His voice sounds hoarse.

I swallow a fresh stream of tears and try to wipe my face. After a week, you'd think I'd be ready by now, that I'd know what to say, or how to say it. But my pain feels . . . preverbal, tangled, and sharp—a hot barbed-wire knot of emotions, shredding my chest.

Pushing off the mattress, I rush to the attached bathroom and splash my face, hoping a few handfuls of cold water will wash away evidence that I've been crying. Then I glance in the mirror and groan, seeing how I look. My eyes are red-rimmed, which makes my irises appear unnervingly pale. My nose is pink. And my forehead's splotchy. All signs I've had a good cry. Excellent.

Aiden's reflection joins mine in the mirror, and I freeze, like prey who senses the predator's about to pounce. He stands in the threshold of the bathroom, his ocean-blue eyes locked on my face. He has a week-old beard, brown-black like the rest of his hair, which makes him look like a stranger. He's never had facial hair beyond stubble, and I don't know if I like it or hate it. I don't know if I'm glad he's home or miserable.

Silence hangs between us until a drop of water falls from the faucet with an echoing *plink!*

My gaze travels his body, broad and strong. It feels like that first glimpse of home after a vacation that went just a few days too long. I realize I missed him, that my impulse to turn and throw myself in his arms, to bury my nose in his neck and breathe him in, isn't entirely erased. It's subdued but not gone.

Maybe that's a good sign.

Maybe that scares the shit out of me.

Maybe I'm drunk.

God, my brain hurts. I'm so tired of thinking about this, I don't even know what to think about the fact that some part of me wants to be in Aiden's arms, for him to turn his head and kiss that spot behind my ear, then whisper my name as his hands span my waist. That I want that feeling of coming home, I want him to look into my eyes the way he used to, like he *sees* me, like he understands my heart.

"Y—" My voice cracks with phlegm and tears, before another hiccup sneaks out. I clear my throat. "You're back already."

"Sorry, I . . ." He frowns. "Are you drunk?"

I lift my chin. "Plausibly."

"Possibly, you mean?" His frown deepens. "Freya, are you okay?"

"Yep. Grand. I asked you to leave because I'm in seventh fucking heaven, Aiden."

His expression falters. He drops his bag to the floor, and I try not to watch his bicep bunch, the way his shirt hugs his round shoulder muscles. "I know it hasn't been very long. But the janitor kicked me out of my office."

"You were"—another hiccup wracks me—"sleeping in your office?"

"Frankie showed up at the cabin a few days ago. I wasn't sticking around while she and Ren . . ." He coughs behind a fist. "Made up."

My brother, Ren—third-born after me, then Axel—has been at the family A-frame cabin in Washington State for a few weeks, nursing a broken heart. I figured if I sent Aiden there, too, they'd at least have some camaraderie. Ren's gentle and sensitive, and he was hurting over the breakup. Of course I'd hoped that Ren's ex, Frankie, would come around, that they would be able to reconcile. But until then, Aiden might be of some comfort to him.

Seems my hope for their happy ending wasn't for nothing after all.

I smile faintly, picturing my brother's relief, even though in a small, sad corner of my heart, I'm jealous of him. That possibility feels so far for Aiden and me.

"I'm happy for them," I whisper. "That's great."

"Yeah." Aiden stares down at the floor. "I've never seen Ren smiling like that."

Which is saying something. All Ren does is smile. He's a ray of freaking sunshine.

"So," Aiden says. "I came back and made it work, sleeping on the couch in my office, using the gym showers, until the janitor busted me and kicked me out because they're shampooing the carpets. I'm sorry. I'll do my best to give you space. When you're ready . . . we can talk."

I sniffle, blinking away tears.

"I know you said you're not sure if this can be fixed, Freya," Aiden says quietly. "But I'm here to tell you I will do everything I can to make it right. I promise you that."

Nodding, I glance down at the sink.

After a long silence, he says, "I'll sleep on the couch. Give you space—"

"Don't." I wipe my nose, dab my eyes. "It's a big bed. We're tall people, and neither of us are going to sleep well on a couch. Just . . . sleep on your side, and I'll sleep on mine. We can both wear pajamas. We'll get some rest, and in the morning, we can figure out a good sleeping situation for going forward. Maybe we can find a cheap bed for the office."

I blink up and catch Aiden's reflection in the mirror, the emotion tightening his face. "Okay."

I leave the bathroom, rushing past him and biting my cheek as his hand softly brushes my wrist. "Go ahead, have a real shower," I tell him. "I'll give you some privacy."

I leave him alone in our bathroom, silence hanging between us.

Soooo I might have neglected to grocery shop while Aiden was gone. There's a head of cauliflower—*ew*—two eggs, and some questionable apples.

I know myself. I'm good and buzzed, and if I'm going to tiptoe around my husband and try not to blow a fuse the rest of the evening, I need to eat. Taking down our list of take-out places stuck to the fridge, I scour the names that are jumping around.

I squint until the letters settle down and decide pizza sounds good. Then again, Aiden's picky about when he wants pizza. I might want to scream-cry at him, but erasing the ritual of making sure he's up for ordering nauseates me. Or maybe that's the bottle of Cab Franc I had on an empty stomach.

Whatever. Doesn't matter. I can be pissed and still be civil. I can ask the guy if he wants a pizza without it signifying all is forgiven and forgotten.

I blame being tipsy and hungry, relying on muscle memory, for why I walk right into the bathroom without considering that my semi-estranged husband is much more than semi-naked in the shower. Just as I'm about to speak, I hear it—his soft, hungry growl. Every hair on my body stands on end.

He exhales roughly, and a quiet, broken sound punctuates his breath, like a cry he's trying to stifle. My heart trips in my chest, as I peer around the corner, through the glass door of the shower, and freeze.

Aiden's long body. His back to me. The tight muscles of his ass flexing, the divot of his hips deep and shadowed, droplets of water sliding down. One hand splayed on the tiles while the other is hidden, his arm moving.

My cheeks flush as I realize he's masturbating, something I haven't seen Aiden do in years, when we used to be sexually playful and do fun things like get ourselves off while watching each other, seeing who could last the longest until we were jumping on the other and finishing how we really wanted: together, so deeply connected—

Another low growl punctures the quiet, another broken, swallowed sound, and then, "Freya," he whispers.

A flood of tears crests my eyes. My name on his lips echoes around us.

He calls my name quietly again and again, then drops his forehead to the tiles as he groans. His arm flies, the sound of his cock gliding through his hand faster, wetter.

My body responds obediently, remembering what it's like for every tender, sensitive corner to burn awake, for my hands to run down his back, then lower, to pull him close, as I beg him to give me everything.

Desire and resentment smash inside me, a head-on collision of oppositional emotions. He wants me so badly, he's fucking his hand to my name, but he hasn't even tried to make love to me in months? He wants to fix it, but it's on *me* to talk?

Aiden's movement falters. A deep, wounded growl leaves him as he lifts his hand and slams it against the wall.

"Fuck," he groans. Dropping his forehead to the tiles, he starts banging it rhythmically.

And then . . . the groans become steady, jagged, thick. A sound leaves him that I realize I've never heard. Aiden's . . . crying.

I must make some kind of sound, too, because Aiden's head lifts. He's heard me. Slowly, he glances over his shoulder and meets my gaze. His ocean-blue eyes are as red-rimmed as mine, his jaw hard through his dark beard. The shower's turned his hair black, clumped his long lashes. He looks at me in a way he hasn't in a very long time.

Our eyes hold, and somehow I know we're remembering the same thing. The last time we had sex. Here, in the shower. How it started wildly, like we were clawing, flailing for a grip on who we'd once been, doing just what we used to—playing. I rubbed myself to orgasm beneath the water, he worked himself roughly as I stared him down.

I remember how his eyes fluttered, his arm faltered, and his mouth fell open, as one last rush of air left him. How he spilled across the tiles as his eyes never left mine, like always. Then he dragged me out of the shower, dried me off, and knelt at my feet. I came against his mouth again and again. . . . And then we did it once more, so urgently, we never even got beneath the sheets, like a solar flare, burning out bright. Before it became bleak. And cold. An emptiness that much darker without the startling beauty that had just brightened it.

I wipe away my tears, shattering the moment. Aiden blinks away and steps farther under the water.

"I'm sorry," I mutter, staring at anything but his body. "I didn't mean—"

"It's all right, Freya," he says quietly, shampooing his hair. But I can tell he doesn't mean it. I embarrassed him. Invaded his privacy.

Because I guess we need that now. Privacy.

I will my eyes not to stare at him. Not the part of him I know so intimately, not his long legs and powerful quads, whiter at the top, tan from mid-thigh down because the man's a lucky freak of nature who turns golden brown the moment summer comes but has the loveliest alabaster skin in winter. It's more difficult than it should be.

"I came in," I say, steadying my voice, "to ask if you want pizza. I was going to order some because I didn't get groceries."

"I'll go grocery shopping tomorrow."

"Okay. But for tonight, I need to eat, so I'm asking about pizza."

He rinses his hair. "Pizza's fine."

"Fine. Thanks."

I rush out of the bathroom, my heart pounding. And then I feel the salt in my wound—a deepening twinge of cramps that have wracked my stomach all day, the first signs of what I knew was coming but have been dreading all the same: another cycle and no baby. Another twenty-eight days gone with a husband who's barely acknowledged it the past six months since we decided that I'd stop taking the pill. No caring inquiries about how I've felt or if I'm late or what I need. Just another month with a husband who's home from work later and later, who's always on the phone and pauses his calls when I walk into the room. A husband I barely recognize.

I throw the take-out list back on the counter, dial for pizza, and open a fresh bottle of wine. After pouring a fat glass of red, I take a gulp. Then I take another and refill my glass. At this rate, I'll wake up with a nice wine hangover. Tomorrow's going to suck. But my husband came home.

It was going to suck anyway.

TWO

Aiden

Playlist: "What Should I Do," Jaymes Young

"You did *what*?"

I stare up at the sky. Clear blue just moments ago, it's now swarmed by ominous black storm clouds. It feels like my fucking life. "I went back to the house."

"No, man." Pete sighs. "You don't do that. Shit, you told *me* that when Mai kicked my ass out two years ago."

This is true. But mostly because I was worried his wife would actually strangle him. He needed to let her cool down. My problem is the opposite. Freya's already cool, which, despite her pale blonde hair and glacial blue-gray eyes, is not her normal disposition. She's a bit reserved with strangers, but once she's comfortable around you, she's affectionate and expressive, full of warmth and jokes and smoky laughter.

Or she was.

That was how I knew something was very wrong. I came home, and it was like the sun had slipped behind a thick cloud, like every songbird within miles had left the trees. Freya was quiet. Very, very quiet. I realized I couldn't remember the last time I'd heard her sing in the shower or hum softly as she went through the mail.

Then I glanced down at my feet. I saw a bag packed and a ticket with my name on it. That's when I knew my world was falling apart.

"Aiden," Pete says. "Talk to me. What were you thinking?"

"What was I supposed to do? Come enjoy a stay at your place? Your wife would've shish-kebabbed my nuts."

Pete's wife, Mai, is Freya's best friend and undoubtedly knows what's up. She'd murder me in my sleep if I tried to stay at their place.

"What about your buddy you're doing all that secret business shit with? Dave?"

I roll my eyes at the jab. "*Dan* lives too far out from work. Not *Dave*." Pete's pissed that I've been busy with the app and that I won't tell him more than loose details.

Yeah, your wife's none-too-happy, either.

My chest constricts sharply. "Pete, I gotta go. I was already on the phone with Dan, and if I'm out here any longer, I'm pretty sure I'm going to be walking home from the art gallery."

"Go. Call me later."

"Yeah. Bye."

I hang up and stare inside, steeling myself for the crowd and noise, the claustrophobic press of people when my mind's already buzzing with too many thoughts, pulsing with nervous energy that has my body begging for a run that I haven't had time for in too long. My anxiety is fucking terrible today. Not that it's been much better otherwise lately.

I tried explaining it to Pete once, when he asked, like a good friend, what was going on. I told him anxiety is like whack-a-mole. Unpredictable, always waiting beneath the surface. Sometimes it's a trigger that you can pinpoint and deal with, but even then, unexpectedly anxiety rears its head and you're spinning, wishing you could locate that *thing*, for there to be one *thing*, that makes you this way so you can isolate it and smack the shit out of it, or . . . more accurately, fix it. Somehow.

Anxiety isn't always debilitating, and for me, more often than not, it doesn't spiral into depression, because my meds seem to help with that aspect. But anxiety doesn't leave, fully. It's never out of the building. It lurks. It reminds you it's there. Biding its time. At least, for me it does.

It took me a long time—and lots of therapy hours—to accept that my anxiety makes life harder, but it doesn't make me *wrong* or damaged or . . . well, anything bad. It just . . . is. And sometimes it's quiet and sometimes it's loud, and no matter what, I've learned to cope. I'm tough. I push through a lot. And some days, I spend a lot of time wishing there were some silver bullet that would make anxiety vanish from my life for good.

My therapist has encouraged me to be compassionate with myself, instead of wanting to fix myself or change how I am. And listen, I like her. She's good. Shit, I can even admit she's right. But that doesn't mean I like it. Acceptance is not a solution. And I want solutions. I want to be able to fix it.

Because I *love* fixing shit. I love fixing people up—my brother-in-law Ryder and his steady girlfriend, Willa, can tell you that, since I matchmade them expertly. My students will tell you I love applying math to fix their business management challenges so they can plan for success. Freya knows more than anyone else, I love fixing broken objects, putting furniture together, patching our roof, turning messes into tidiness. I get a fucking high from it.

Besides slapping my hand when I have occasionally overreached on my matchmaking endeavors, and that one time I was a little too attached to trying to reglue a total lost cause of a chair, Freya's always made me feel like my fixer impulses that shape our life are something she admires about me. She's never made me doubt she loves me for who I am. And I love her for it.

But even though she's accepting, empathic—so, so empathic—there's a limit to what I'm willing to place on her shoulders. She doesn't know that my anxiety, which is sometimes high but generally managed with a generous dose of Prozac and periodic therapy sessions, is borderline debilitating right now. I've made sure of it.

Yeah, I know. Not talking is a big no-no. But here's the thing. Freya feels for me and other people too much as it is. I know more than anyone how it weighs her down, how when the burden becomes too much, she cries in the shower and sings sad songs when she's working in the yard. How she crawls into my arms at night and sobs silently until her sadness bleeds into her sleep and her dreams are fitful. I know how she hums to the cats and holds them hard after a rough day with patients. Freya holds the world in her heart. All I'm doing is shielding her from the worst of it, compartmentalizing, so she has someone to lean into when we're together.

I thought I was doing a good job.

But I'm starting to wonder, since she drew a line in the proverbial sand, if I've been worse at hiding my struggles than I thought, if I'm not as good at shielding her as I wanted to be. I'm wondering if it's blown up in my face, and I've been wondering that since I came home from work and she literally had a bag packed for me with a round-trip ticket sitting on top of it.

I tried to focus on the fact that it wasn't one-way. That was a good sign, right?

I had to hope so.

Pocketing my phone and bracing myself for the explosion of echoing sound, I step back inside this modern art gallery, a warehouse-style space in the artsy, eclectic LA neighborhood of Fairfax, which is showing my brother-in-law Axel's art. Before the door even shuts behind me, my eyes find Freya, and my system grinds to a halt. There's a guy, grinning at her with unmasked interest. A fiery burst of fear and worry and possessiveness burns through me.

I'm not a jealous man. Freya's my partner, not my possession. That said, when an asshole is staring down the neckline of my wife's dress, and my wife is not—as the past would dictate—either "accidentally" dumping her drink on his expensive-looking boots or giving him her Mrs. Freeze eyes, I feel justified in my response. And I feel my legs moving fast, taking me straight toward her.

I cut through the crowd milling around the gallery, my eyes locked on her. White-blonde waves cut just past her jaw, luminous skin, and mouthwatering curves. Her black dress flutters around her knees, swaying rhythmically because Freya can't help but move when she hears music. She tips her head and sips from her straw as he smiles at her. Shit, is she flirting?

Not that I'm not angry with *her*. No, this is my fault. We're here because I fucked up. Well, I'm lucky we're *here* in the same space tonight, period. Freya didn't express delight when I invited myself to come to Axel's art show, desperate for any time with her, to show her I'm here, committed to *us*, even when I hate noisy, chaotic spaces like this. She barely spoke to me on the drive over or when we arrived, instead chatting with her brothers and Rooney, Willa's best friend from college who's been around so much, she's now an honorary Bergman.

But I'm not letting that deter me. I'm going to fix the shit out of this. And my wife needs to see that—that I'm here, and I'm not going anywhere.

"Freya." I set a hand on her back, sighing with relief when she doesn't arch away from it. In fact, I could swear she even leans in. Just a little. It feels monumental.

"Aiden, this is George Harper. He's showing here as well. George, this is my husband, Aiden MacCormack."

Hah. So there, George. I'm her *husband*.

I extend my hand and accept the guy's grip, reminding myself that squeezing his fingers to a pulp is unreasonable. Freya's a beautiful woman. He'd have to be senseless not to be dazzled. So I let him pass with a slightly too-strong clasp.

"Congratulations," I tell him. "Hell of a show."

"Thank you. It is," he says. "And you're here for whom, again?"

"Axel Bergman." Freya nods toward her brother's corner of the gallery. Ax stands with his back to us, tall and narrow, hands in his pockets, staring at one of his paintings. "Which are yours?" she asks.

Answering her, George gestures over his shoulder, my gaze, then my focus wandering from their conversation to the room around us. First to Freya's brother Ren, a forward for the LA Kings, who's clearly being accosted by a hockey fan while getting us drinks at the gallery bar. Then I spot Rooney as she wanders Axel's section of the gallery.

Axel. Ren. Rooney. Freya. Ren's girlfriend, Frankie, isn't coming. None of Freya's other siblings are coming, so I don't have to look out for them. Ryder and his girlfriend, Willa, are still up in Washington State. Ziggy, the baby of the family, doesn't do crowded spaces like this. Oliver and Viggo, the man cubs, can't be trusted around breakable things. And their parents are, in Axel's words, "not allowed to come" because this show is "too graphic."

They'll visit the gallery and see his work after Axel's flown back to Seattle, where he lives. He makes up an excuse every art show for why they can't come, and they never fight him, because of some kind of unspoken Bergman shit I don't get. Then they visit later when he won't know. That's what they always do.

Locating my people lowers the volume of my brain's calculating buzz to a steady baseline hum. Everyone's accounted for. I take a deep breath and refocus on Freya and George's conversation. I've lost track of who said what, but I'm going to take a wild guess it was mostly George talking about himself.

". . . So that's my approach in a nutshell," he says.

Nailed it.

Freya glances between George's work and her brother's. "That's interesting. Very different from Axel's."

"You can say that again." George glances over his shoulder at Axel, who's being tapped on the shoulder by someone with a camera around their neck and a nervous smile. His stern profile as he stares down at them is so Axel, I could laugh. The poor man hates publicity more than I hate messy closets.

"Axel's . . ." George scrubs the back of his neck and shrugs. "Well . . . he's prolific. I'll give him that."

Freya's eyes turn icy. "Meaning what?" The oldest of her siblings, Freya loves them fiercely, protectively. The moment she catches a whiff of shit thrown their way, she's in mama-bear mode.

George's nervous laughter fades as quickly as it arrived, when he registers her anger. "Well . . ." he says carefully, tiptoeing through a verbal minefield, "meaning he's managed to paint a lot."

"I actually know what the word *prolific* means," Freya says acidly as she clamps the straw between her teeth.

George tugs at his collar, starting to sweat. "I'll be honest. His stuff weirds me out. He weirds me out, too."

Freya grips her glass so hard, I'm waiting for it to shatter in her grip. "Some of the art world's most revered creators—their eccentricities and their visionary work—were misunderstood in their time. Van Gogh being a personal favorite."

George blinks at her, speechless.

"Perhaps you might question your unease about my brother and his art and consider that, when yours and all these other paltry attempts at art are long forgotten, Axel and his work will be immortalized. Good day, sir!"

Freya at her mama-bear finest. She spins, grabs me by the arm, and marches us past him, toward her brother.

"Did you just throw *Willy Wonka* at him?" I ask.

Her mouth quirks, and my heart skips a beat. Freya just almost-smiled for me. It feels like the first drop of rain in a drought.

"He's lucky I didn't throw him a Frankie curse."

Ren's girlfriend, Frankie, has a witchy vibe and a colorful penchant for pointing her cane like a wand at offending parties and tossing hexes their way. I was more expecting Freya to toss her glass of whatever she's drinking right in his face.

"He would have deserved it," I tell her.

"That's the truth. Ax!" Freya says, moving past me.

Axel turns and locks eyes with Freya, wordlessly greeting her. Those two have something I'm ashamed to say I envy—an unspoken understanding. I'd never seen two people bicker in three words and stony glares until them, but then I've seen moments like this, too—silent, pure connection. Freya stands close to him, squeezing his hand once, as she stares at the painting in front of them. Lots of red against a stark white canvas, in a pattern that makes me feel slightly woozy. Shit, now I sound like that asshole George.

"So much emotion, right?" Rooney joins me at one of the narrow bar-height tables placed strategically around the space. Her blue-green eyes drift across the wall where Axel's art is mounted. "Visual art like his says so much, without a single word. I feel like all I do is talk and yet I never convey a smidge of what his art expresses."

Her eyes dance between Freya and Axel, the same envy I feel tightening her expression. I've had a hunch about those two, Ax and Rooney. I have a good sense for chemistry, which is, of course, why I'm a good matchmaker. That's how Ryder and Willa got their start together—I made them project partners when they were students in my business mathematics class. I may have gone a *little* overboard on that, but the point stands. I have good intuition about these things.

"That's what you get with a Bergman," I tell her. "They're pretty economical with their feelings, except for Freya and her dad—"

"And me," Ren says.

I startle and clasp my pounding heart. "You're freakishly stealthy." I'm also jumpy as hell.

"Stealth is the name of the game," he says, raising a ridiculously coordinated collection of cocktails in his big hands. "Take yours and pray they don't fall."

Rooney laughs as she extricates her gin and tonic. I grab my Diet Coke as well as what Ren indicates is Freya's drink, which splashes on my hand. I lap it up, expecting the tang of vodka, but it's . . . just club soda.

Club soda. I nearly drop the glass.

No alcohol. Why? Why no alcohol? The other night, when I came home, she was tipsy. But what if *since* then she's realized . . .

The room rocks beneath me as my gaze lands on Freya and my heart begins to pound. I rack my brain. When's the last time I picked up tampons and pads when I ran errands? When's the last time she complained of cramps and needed the heating pad? My breathing ratchets up.

Shit.

Shit.

The past few months flash before my eyes, nailing me with stunning, convicting clarity. I've been distracted with work, hustling for the app's funding, revising our presentation for potential investors, doing everything I can to make the future feel financially secure, ever since we decided she would go off birth control and we'd stop preventing pregnancy . . .

Six months ago.

It's been six fucking months, and I can't remember the last time we talked about it, the last time I noticed if she'd gotten her period or missed it. I felt the weight of our lives double with the impending promise of a baby—a baby that I want, yes, but that I feel an enormous responsibility to make sure doesn't have the childhood I had—and I've been consumed with what that entails ever since.

Oh God. I have no clue how far along she is, how she feels. Why wouldn't she tell me?

Because you haven't asked, dickhead.

Fucking hell. No wonder she kicked my ass out.

There's more to it than that, and you know it.

I jam that disturbing thought deep into the corners of my mind just as Ren sets a hand on my shoulder. I glance over at my brother-in-law, a gentle ginger giant, his hockey hair floppy, his beard trimmed to a neat auburn scruff now that play-offs are over. He has Freya's striking pale eyes, which scan me with concern. "You okay, Aiden? You look upset."

Ren's the emotionally conversant one. He's the one I spilled my guts to when Freya kicked me out. Granted, he wasn't his most empathic—he and Frankie were struggling to find their footing, which is now solid—but he knows more than the rest of the siblings about what's going on.

"I'm okay," I manage, dabbing my sweaty forehead with the cool condensation dripping down Freya's glass. "I'm, uh . . . contemplating breaking up the sibling lovefest and giving Freya her drink."

Ren smiles. "Good luck. But I'd recommend you wait until it's over."

Rooney sips her cocktail. "I wish I had siblings."

"Not going to lie," Ren says, taking a drink of his own, "I don't know what I'd do without a big family. And I'm really glad Frankie wants a houseful."

I open my mouth to say something cautious like, *You've only been together for a few months. Should you already be planning like that? Aren't you terrified that it could fall apart?* But then I remember how I felt two months into being with Freya, like she was air and sunlight, water and life, like if I lost her, I'd just stop existing. And I've never stopped seeing her that way. I just got better at worrying about losing her—so worried, it started robbing me of the hours I used to devote to soaking her up, basking in her joy, her passion and laughter and kisses.

Sighing, I chug my Diet Coke and, not for the first time, wish I wasn't so uptight about my alcohol policy. I could use a mind-numbing buzz right now. Holy shit, could I.

Rooney grins at Ren. "When you and Frankie have babies, they're going to be so cute. With her big, pretty hazel eyes and your hair. Gah. Have lots so I can snuggle them."

"Have your own!" Ren says playfully. "I'll be hoarding them, inhaling that—"

"New baby smell," they say in unison.

My stomach double knots. A *baby*.

"How is Frankie?" Rooney asks.

Ren smiles a lovesick grin. "She's great. She just felt like tonight would be too much."

Frankie, like the youngest Bergman, Ziggy, is on the autism spectrum—bright, unfiltered, and quickly overwhelmed by busy, loud spaces like the Bergman house or a bustling art gallery.

My anxiety's not a huge fan of those spaces, either.

"Smart lady," I mutter.

Ren nods. "Yep. So she's having a quiet night in at home."

Rooney smooths back her dark blonde hair and smiles gently. "Well, I'm glad she felt comfortable doing what she needed, but I miss seeing her. I really like her, Ren."

Ren grins again. "Yeah. She's the best."

"Who me?" Freya says, inserting herself and sweeping up her drink. "Aw, brother. You're too sweet."

Ren shakes his head and smiles.

"Who's sweet?" Axel says, eyes on Rooney.

"This one, duh," Freya says, looping an arm around Rooney's waist. Rooney smiles, her cheeks pinking as Freya pulls her into a conversation.

When Axel's sharp green eyes finally leave Rooney, they swivel my way, boring into me. It makes me wonder if Freya spilled the dirt while they had their backs to us.

"Aiden," he says, his voice deep and even. It isn't his friendliest expression, but then again, Axel often has a smooth, unreadable look on his face.

I nod. "Ax."

"Thanks for coming." Ax rarely hugs, and when he's up for hugging, he makes that clear. He doesn't this time. So we shake hands.

"As always, well done," I say, gesturing with my glass to his wall of the gallery. "This is incredible."

His eyes are back on Rooney. "Mm-hmm."

I pause, waiting for him to give me his attention. He doesn't. He watches Rooney as she laughs with Freya, as they turn and smile for someone from the gallery asking to take their photo.

"Ax, you're not subtle," I whisper.

"True," he says, still staring at her. "No one's ever called my work subtle."

Freya and Rooney are being photographed. Ren's on his phone, probably texting Frankie. It's just us. So I take a risk and say, "You could let the matchmaker try his hand—"

"Aiden," Ax cuts me off as his eyes meet mine again. There's the tiniest bit of red on his cheekbones.

I fight a grin. "Yes, Axel?"

"Isn't there a proverb along the lines of 'people who live in glass houses shouldn't throw stones'? Deal with your own life before you start trying to orchestrate mine."

My smile fades. She *has* told him.

Freya and Rooney turn back from the photographer, and our group's conversation converges into the usual Bergman family ruckus. I stand quietly and sip my drink, more than ever a stranger to myself, to people who once felt like mine.

THREE

Freya

Playlist: "Alaska," Maggie Rogers

I try not to think too much, let alone get in my feelings that it's my parents' thirty-fifth wedding anniversary dinner. That they look as in love as always—Dad touching Mom whenever he can, Mom leaning into him, a smile warming her face.

And *my* husband is running late.

In the restroom, I check my phone in my purse again, waiting for the ladies to be done. One message:

Sorry, running behind. Unforeseen setback at the office.

"Thank you, Jesus on His Birthday!" Frankie's voice echoes from the bathroom stall. "I finally got my period." Frankie has a flair for creative blasphemes but not even this one can make me laugh. Because while I remember those years, nervously watching the calendar and praying for my period to come, now it's the other way around. Now I hold my breath as the calendar countdown dwindles, praying the dull aching cramps won't come, that my boobs hurt for the right reason.

I'm not concerned from a fertility standpoint. I know things take time and conception is quick for some, not for others. I just want it so badly, it hurts. It's an ache that never leaves my chest, with every mom I see, whether pregnant or with children in arms or running ahead of her, the nagging question in the back of my head, *When will it be me?*

"Me too!" my sister, Ziggy, says from the neighboring stall. "Hey, maybe we're on the same schedule now. Isn't that a thing? I feel like I read somewhere that women who hang around each other somehow get on the same period calendar. Something to do with pheromones or hormones or something. I wish Rooney was here. This is her expertise."

Rooney is an unabashed science whiz who would absolutely be hollering about the transmutability of female hormones if she were here. Even though she came to us through Willa, Ryder's girlfriend, and Willa isn't here, it wouldn't have been strange for Rooney to attend anyway. She's become so ingrained in the family, it feels weird when she *doesn't* come to Bergman functions. But she declined our invite tonight because she's studying for the bar.

Which I found out from *Axel*. Who turned pink in the cheeks when I grinned and asked how he happened to know that. To which he had no reply except to tell me I had lipstick on my teeth. That had me scrambling for my phone's camera to check, but by the time I realized I didn't, he was on the other side of our table, in conversation with Dad.

Asshole. Pranks are unfortunately as common among the Bergman siblings as oxygen is in the air.

Axel's love life is none of my business anyway. But Aiden's an unapologetic matchmaker, and in the decade we've been together, his tendencies have started to rub off on me. I see pairings and chemistry, couples and possibility, all the time now. Unlike Aiden, though, I have the common sense to leave people alone, for the most part, to figure it out themselves.

The toilets flush, then a moment later, the doors unlock. Frankie and Ziggy leave their stalls at the same time, joining me at the sink, where I'm fussing with my hair, which won't quite behave tonight.

Our reflections are like the start of a joke—a blonde, a redhead, and a brunette. Me, then Ziggy, with her willowy body that she got from Mom, red hair like our dad's, and his vivid green eyes, which are the same color as her dress. Frankie scowls at her reflection, long, dark locks and hazel eyes, working her usual color scheme of a black dress and a gray acrylic cane, a mobility aid to help with the pain and instability arthritis has caused in her hips.

"I should have known it was coming," Frankie says, pointing to a small bump on her chin. "The period zit."

"Why are you so worried about pregnancy?" Ziggy asks. "You take the pill, right?"

Frankie laughs emptily. "Yes. But I'm still paranoid that by sheer force of giant ginger will, Ren is going to knock me up. He stares at babies like I stare at burgers—like there's never enough of them and they're vital to existence. The man thinks he's subtle, but he's not."

"Whenever I'm with a guy," Ziggy says. "I'm doubling up. Condoms *and* the pill—"

"Ziggy," I interrupt. "You're not having sex yet, are you?" She's only seventeen, and she's still so young emotionally.

Ziggy turns bright red. "Geez, Freya. No. But I do have a mom already breathing down my neck about abstinence and safe sex, okay?"

I try not to be hurt by how upset she seems that I asked. If we were closer, I'd hope she'd feel comfortable confiding in me, particularly as she grows out of adolescence into womanhood. But she's just a teenager, I'm almost twice her age, and because of that, we've never been close, even though I love her and couldn't get enough of her as a baby. Mom's said I should try to hang out with her more, but Ziggy's always playing soccer and I'm always working. Gelling our schedules is virtually impossible.

Facing the mirror again, Ziggy shuts off the water and dries her hands. "All I was trying to say was that whenever I *do* have sex, I'm not risking my soccer career. I want kids down the line but not until I'm retired."

"So..." Frankie peers up at the ceiling, doing the mental math. "You'll be, what? Mid-thirties? I get it, but I want to be done by then. Done with babies. Done with working."

Ziggy cocks an eyebrow. "You're going to law school to be a sports agent for eight years?"

Frankie cackles. "Okay, fair. Maybe I'll work until forty. After that, I'm making Ren my cabana man and buying an island for all these kids we're apparently having, since the guy already has a minivan to hold them. You're all welcome anytime."

Babies. A minivan. I hold a hand over my stomach, hating that I know for certain it's empty.

These things take time, my mother likes to tell me in her philosophical voice. Easy for her to say. She got pregnant every time my dad *looked* at her.

Be patient, Freya Linn. Be patient.

I'm trying to be patient. I'm really trying. But patience has never been my virtue.

Frankie tosses her paper towel in the garbage and grips her cane. "Let's get out there before the boys clean out the breadbasket again. I only got one roll earlier."

"Right." I pull open the door.

We rejoin the table comprised of all the siblings, only missing Willa, who's traveling for a game, and Aiden, wherever the hell he is. I feel my brothers' eyes on me, their concern and curiosity. I think most, if not all, of them know something's up with Aiden and me. I told Axel at his art show with the understanding we'd keep Mom and Dad out of it, until I could tell them myself. I expected in his short and direct way, he'd tell my brothers, too, with the same expectation of secrecy. And if there's one thing you can count on Bergman siblings for, it's to keep a damn good secret from their parents when necessary.

Even if Axel didn't tell them and they weren't suspicious, they are now. Aiden's as reliable for these family functions as the sun is in the sky. He's always with me. He keeps his promises and shows up.

Until now, it seems.

I clear my throat and smile brightly, telling my emotions to get their shit together. Mom pats my hand and smiles at me as she asks in her soft Swedish accent, "*Sötnos*, where's Aiden?"

"Running late," I mutter into my wineglass, taking a deep drink. "We can order without him."

Dad frowns and leans in closer, wrapping his arm around Mom. "I don't want to leave Aiden out."

"It's okay, Daddy. He'll understand."

My dad's eyebrows rise. He searches me for a moment, and I glance away. He's always read me too easily. "Freya Linn. Is something the matter?"

My throat tightens. "No!" I say too brightly. I school my expression. "No. You know Aiden. He's just busy with work lately."

Mom turns slightly in her chair and inspects me. "Freya."

I peer up at her. "Yes, Mom?"

"Soon, you come to the house for *fika*. I'd like to talk."

I fake a smile and blink at her, scrambling for what to say. She's sniffed trouble. That's why she wants me to come over. And you don't say no to *fika* with Elin Bergman. It's a pause in the day that's a fixture of Swedish life, integral to my mother, who left her home country only when she married my dad. Our traditions, my upbringing, many of my parents' philosophies and rituals are infused with her culture.

Fika is ingrained in us. In Sweden, business pauses, life rests, and just briefly, you have coffee and a treat with friends or coworkers around you. It's about resetting and connecting, refreshing before digging back into the work of your day. And in Mom's house, shit gets dealt with over *fika*.

"Mom," I say apologetically, "I don't know when I'll have time. I have patients—"

"You *make* time. That's what I've taught you. You choose what matters, and the rest follows. Take a lunch break, hm?" she presses, her expression almost a mirror of mine.

Sometimes it's unnerving to look in your mother's face and see what time will bring, not that I fear aging or think my mother is any less beautiful than when she looked younger. It just foregrounds the urgency of the moment, throws each minute between now and then in front of me. When will I be a mother? By the time Mom was my age, she'd had half her children. Will I be sitting next to Aiden, surrounded by a table of kids and their partners? Candlelight and delicious food? Celebrating my marriage not only between the two of us, but with a rousing table of family as well?

"I'll come to you," she presses, after I have nothing to say but silence. "Friday. Ziggy has school, then goes straight to evening training, so I'm free."

"Okay," I sigh.

"If I could have everyone's attention!" Viggo says as he stands and grins, tall and lean, with chocolate hair like Axel's, pale eyes like mine. I can smell the mischief wafting from him. Oliver, my twin in looks, only twelve months younger than Viggo and his partner in crime, sits back in his chair. Grinning my way, he winks at me, then turns back to Viggo.

"Mom and Dad," Viggo continues, "the kids wanted to give you a special gift. You've given us so much, put up with more than you should have ever had to—"

Dad raises his glass to that and grins.

"And our way of saying thanks, our gift to you this year is . . ."

Oliver does a drumroll on the table as Viggo pulls a photo from an envelope and hands it to my parents. A luxurious beachfront home, palm trees, golden sand.

"A family vacation," he says.

My parents are floored. Thankful. Thrilled.

And I had no idea this was coming.

My stomach drops as I stare around at the siblings, none of whom look surprised like me. I glance at Ren, who's usually quick to break down. He's giving Frankie his undivided attention, definitely avoiding my eyes. Ryder's expression is blank, his sharp green eyes inscrutable, his mouth hidden behind a blond beard that hides too much to make him easy to read. Axel looks at me innocently, as if I were in on this, or at least that he thought so. Ziggy's the same, just smiling, probably excited to go on this vacation since she's always stuck at home with Mom and Dad by herself. I don't even try with the man cubs. They delight in antagonizing me.

I turn toward Ryder and lower my voice. "What is this?"

He leans in slightly and says, "It's an anniversary gift. We tend to give our parents one of them each year on the day of their marriage."

"Ryder." I elbow him. "Be serious."

"You were distracted. You've always handled it, and that's not fair to you. So the brothers took care of it."

"And how are we affording this?"

Ryder glances at Ren. I blanch.

"No," I mutter. "He's not paying for everyone—"

"It's decided already," Ryder says. "He's a professional hockey player, Freya. This is a drop in the bucket to him. Besides, Ren's generous, and it makes him happy. The house is his teammate's, and he's opening it to us for the week, free of charge. Ren's contribution—which, I'll acknowledge, is not small—is financing airfare when we settle on a week that everyone can do. We agreed we'll pay for our own food, drinks, and anything else once we're there."

I open my mouth to disagree, but Ryder gives me a look.

"Freya," he says quietly, "you know how blissfully happy it will make Mom and Dad for us all to be there."

Blissfully happy. An entire week in close quarters with Aiden, and I'll have to act like everything's fine to maintain that bliss, even though he and I are falling apart. I don't know how I'll go a day, let alone a week, without losing my shit. And if Aiden doesn't come, it will cause my parents worry and puncture their happiness, which directly defeats the point of this gift.

"I can't go on a family vacation right now," I whisper. "I can barely tolerate sharing the same roof as my husband right now."

Ryder frowns. "That bad?"

Staring at my hands, I sigh. "Yeah. Pretty bad. I'm at the end of my rope, Ry. I can't do this right now."

Ryder passes the breadbasket to Oliver, who's hollering for it. "Well, don't come, then."

"I can't not come, you asshole. That would hurt Mom and Dad."

He gives me a faint grin and sips his beer. "Guess you're going to Hawaii, then."

FOUR

Aiden

Playlist: "Gallipoli," Beirut

I'm late. Really fucking late, without a clear excuse for Freya as to why. But like hell was I going to tell her I'm running massively behind because I shit myself. After that drafty-ass Washington State visit, I got a cold, then a secondary sinus infection, and the antibiotics are trashing my stomach. My stomach was gurgling earlier in the office, and I frankly didn't have time in my day for another trip to the restroom just to have it be a resonant fart, so I gambled.

And I lost.

Pants and boxers trashed, showered and changed into the backups I keep at the office—thank you, my cautious, overly prepared self—I'm now sitting in bumper-to-bumper traffic.

"Dammit!" I slam my hands on the wheel. A text comes in from Freya:

We're leaving.

"No," I groan, tugging at my hair. "No, no, no."

Dialing her number, I hook up my phone to the auxiliary system in the car. It rings. And rings. And rings. Then goes to voice mail.

Of course she's not answering. She doesn't want to talk to me. I don't want to talk to me, either.

She's probably angry. Definitely hurt. I don't blame her. Family's the heart of Freya's life. Her parents mean the world to her—shit, they mean the world to *me*—and I missed their anniversary dinner, which I've always loved because it's a family celebration, not just a celebration between the two of them.

Throwing on a podcast, I try to distract myself, take the first exit I can, and turn back toward our place in Culver City. Going home's easier than making my way to the restaurant from a traffic standpoint, and soon I'm parking in our little driveway and locking the car.

Lights are on inside but not the porch light, which is Freya's hallmark. The woman's damn uptight about conserving energy, and I'm damn uptight about security. The front porch light is a benign battle between us. The light being off, after I turned it on when I left for work this morning, means she's home.

It also means I'm bathed in darkness, my senses attuned to the sounds around me as I start along the walkway up to our house. Halfway to the front door, I feel the hair on the back of my neck stand on end. A twig snaps. Whipping around, I search for the sound I just heard. Yes, my anxiety is high, and my stress about running late, then missing dinner, isn't helping lower my adrenaline levels, but someone's nearby, watching me. I'm positive of that. You don't grow up how I did without learning to look over your shoulder, knowing how to defend yourself.

Suddenly there's a scuffle, then two men are on top of me, their faces unreadable in the darkness. Instinct kicks in, and I leg swipe one of them, but the other gets me in a headlock, dragging me backward.

I don't yell, because the last thing I'd want is Freya running out, getting in the middle of this. After one of the guy's large hands clamps over my mouth, I couldn't yell if I wanted to.

The other guy's at my legs now, knocking me down, and I'm

bodily hoisted across the lawn. A van door slides open before I'm shoved inside, despite trying damn hard to fight against it. The door slams shut with the click of a lock, and the car accelerates rapidly. I blink, urging my eyesight to adjust so I can get my bearings.

Finally, I can see, and if I weren't so damn angry at them, I'd kick myself for not having anticipated something like this. Ren's driving us like heisters in his minivan. Axel's riding shotgun. Oliver sits on my lap, Ryder's in the bucket seat next to me, and Viggo pops up from the third row.

"What the hell is this?" I yell, shoving Oliver off. He lands with an *oof* on the van floor. "Don't answer that until you put on your seat belt." I glare around at them. "Would it have been so hard to say, 'Hey, Aiden, we need to talk to you'?"

Ryder makes a noncommittal grunt. Ren is silent, as is Axel.

"Would you have come?" Viggo asks.

I open my mouth to answer. And realize I can't truthfully tell him yes.

"Precisely," he says.

Oliver slips into the third row and buckles up, then leans in, locking eyes with me. "Viggo and I may have gone a little physically overboard, but we all agreed you'd need to be strongly coerced."

"A little?" I say hotly. "You scared the shit out of me. Jesus, guys. This isn't a Liam Neeson action movie."

Viggo *pff*s. "Please. Ryder talked me down from my original plan."

Ryder grins coldly.

"Ren," I say pleadingly. "I thought I could count on you, man. What is this?"

Ren's eyes meet mine in the rearview mirror, uncharacteristically cool. "I'm giving up a night with my girlfriend, I'll have you know."

"Hey, I didn't ask to be abducted by my brothers-in-law. What is this even about?"

As if you don't know. This is how bad you've fucked up. The Bergman brothers are trying to save you. Oh, how the mighty have fallen.

Oliver says, "When you and Freya started dating, Dad sat us down and made something very clear."

"'*Leave Aiden out of it,*'" Viggo says. "That's what Dad told us. '*None of your brotherly tricks or hazing, no sinister gang-ups. Be kind to him. Most importantly, stay out of his relationship with your sister.*'"

"And?" I ask.

"And that worked," Ryder snaps. "Until you started fucking shit up."

"Je*sus.*" I scrub my face. This is really the last thing I need.

"At which point," Axel says evenly, "we realized an intervention was necessary."

Viggo claps his hands on my shoulders and squeezes. "Welcome to your first Bergman Brothers Summit, Aiden. You're in for a wild ride."

———

"I'm not talking about my marriage to your sister," I tell them. "Not happening."

Ren eases into a chair on his back deck overlooking the Pacific. He has a beautiful home in Manhattan Beach, with a breathtaking view, because his genetics are made for hockey, and he lives and breathes the game. I'm happy for him. No one deserves it more than Ren, who's so generous and levelheaded in his success. But I can't deny I've had moments, envying him and that prodigious athletic ability.

Sure, I'm strong, coordinated. I can hold my own when things descend to wrestling with the Bergman brothers. But I'm nothing beyond average talent with a soccer ball, endurance for running, and some weights. I can't pretend I haven't considered what kind of life I could give Freya if I were like Ren. He makes in a year what I'll make in my lifetime.

Unless this app takes off.

As if he knows I'm thinking about our project, Dan starts blowing up my cell. Talking myself down from anticipating that something catastrophic has happened, I unearth my phone quickly and scan his rapid-fire texts as they pour in. Skimming his messages, I see it's nothing critical. And I breathe a sigh of relief.

"Gimme the phone," Ryder says, hand out.

"It's just my business partner." I flip it over on the table we're seated around. "I'll silence it."

"Listen, Aiden. Believe it or not," Viggo says, "we don't want to know the *details* about your love life with our sister."

The five of them shudder.

Ren pats my shoulder. "We just need the big picture."

"The big picture of what?" I ask.

Axel rubs the bridge of his nose. "Of how Mr. Matchmaker Romance, who brims with confidence and knowledge in this area and has kept our sister seemingly happy for over a decade, managed to bomb it so badly."

"Axel," Ren says out of the side of his mouth. "I thought we talked about a *slightly* gentler lead-in than that."

"Oops," Ax says flatly.

Ren sighs. "What Axel *meant* is that you strike us as a modern man with mature romantic sensibilities. A feminist guy who understands his partner, who supports her."

"Basically," Oliver translates, "you don't have your head up your ass."

"Correction," Viggo says. "You *struck* us as such. Clearly your head is way up your ass. Or something is, because Freya seems miserable. So do you."

I grip my chair until my knuckles ache. "We're not talking about this."

"Even though we can help?" Ryder asks.

"I don't need your help. I don't need anyone's help."

They all give me a look.

"Yeah," Viggo says after a long, heavy silence. "You definitely *don't* need our help, not when you missed a family gathering—"

"Which you never miss," Oliver adds.

"And our sister was on the verge of tears the whole time," Axel says pointedly. "Now, I more than anyone here understand being an independent soul, but there's self-sufficiency and there's stupidity. Don't let your pride get in the way of your good sense. Let us help."

Help.

I glare at them. I'm thirty-six years old. This September, I'm ten years into marriage. Half of the Bergman brothers aren't partnered, and with the exception of Axel, they're in their twenties. What the hell could they tell me that I don't already know? What wisdom could they possibly have?

"How," I say tightly, "do you honestly think you can help?"

"Well." Ryder clears his throat. "We could give you some pointers, seeing as we've known Freya—"

"Twice as long as you," Ren says.

"You guys are freaking me out," I tell them, "completing each other's sentences like that."

Ren shrugs. "We just want to support you. Be here for you. And if, uh . . ."

"If you're screwing up stuff with her, we can point you in the right direction," Ryder says. "Which would be a lot easier if you told us what happened."

I sink into my chair. No fucking way.

"If we know what's going on," Oliver says, popping cheese cubes in his mouth. Looks like he's going for filling his mouth with as many as possible, presumably in competition with Viggo, who's quietly counting cubes as he watches him. "We can help get you two back on track," he says around his mouthful. "Especially when we're on family vacation."

Cue the record scratch. "Family vacation?"

"Yeah," Viggo says, still counting Oliver's cheese cube capacity. "Mom and Dad's anniversary gift. We're putting our calendars together to go to Hawaii for a week of rest and relaxation."

Panic hits me at the prospect of such an out-of-the-blue expense. I can hunt for a bargain flight, but the thought of spending that kind of money right now makes my chest tighten.

"It's a teammate's house," Ren says quietly, as if he's read my mind. "His extended family lives there, but they're traveling through Europe all summer, and he hasn't been able to stay there as much as he planned, so he's happy for us to use it rent-free."

"Great." I massage my temples. Flights will still cost a pretty chunk of change.

"Soon," Viggo says, "we'll all be there, and it would be best if the brothers knew what we're dealing with when it comes to you two."

"I'm not discussing it," I snap. "It doesn't affect you."

"There you're wrong," Ryder says. "Anything that affects you and Freya, affects us. We're family."

Axel stares out at the water, drumming his fingers on the arms of his chair. "Perhaps we should clarify. We aren't without knowledge. I told them what I got from Freya at the art gallery. In an email. Because fuck group calls."

My stomach sinks. "What did she say?"

"Can't say that you deserve my intel when you won't tell *us* anything," Axel says coolly.

"Dammit, Axel."

His sharp green eyes pin me. "You're the one holding back. Trust us, we trust you."

"Aiden," Oliver says, "I know the Liam Neeson angle sort of undercuts this, but you *can* trust us. I love you. We all do. You're our brother."

Bittersweet pain knifes through me. He has no idea how much that means to me, coming from this man who was just a boy when I met him, all white-blond hair and knobby knees and better skills with a soccer ball than me. It's strange, how you can know something cognitively—that the Bergman brothers love me—but how different, how powerful it can be to be *told*, to feel, even in this warped way, how much they care.

I love you. We all do.

"We want you and Freya to be okay," Oliver says. "We just want to help."

"Exactly," Viggo says, around his own mouthful of cheese cubes.

"Do you ever stop eating?" I ask him.

He lobs a cheese cube at me, hitting my shoulder. "I have to get four more to beat him."

Oliver glares at him. "No way you're getting four more in there."

"Try me," Viggo says thickly, looking like a deranged chipmunk.

I sigh and scrub my face, surrendering what I'm willing to. "I've got a lot going on professionally. I've been working more than ever. I think Freya's fed up with how busy I've been."

"Okay," Ren says gently. "That's . . . it?"

Shit, no. It's not just cooler and quieter between us. Intimacy has broken down. And I know it's my fault, but hell if I know how to begin fixing it. Not that I'm telling them any of that.

"Guys, I'm not comfortable saying more. It's between Freya and me."

Viggo leans on one butt cheek and extracts a small book from his back pocket.

"What is that?" I ask.

"A romance novel," Viggo says, chewing thickly. "Ugh. Too much cheese. You owe me twenty bucks," he says to Oliver.

Oliver scowls at him.

"A romance novel," I say incredulously.

He gives me a look. "You heard me. A romance novel. Not that you'd know one if it fell from a bookshelf and smacked your dick."

"I'd remember anything that smacked my dick."

"In that case," Viggo says, lunging toward me.

"Hey!" Ren shoves him back into his seat. "This is a nonviolent home."

That's right—the hockey player is a pacifist. He has yet to get in a brawl in his almost four years with the NHL.

"So," Axel says calmly while Viggo thumbs through his book. "Why are you working so much?"

I stare down at my hands, my stomach twisting as I think about when things began to change. Because it's so horribly unfair. Because I want a baby, too. I want a little person to love and do right by. Even if they're only half as cute as Freya's baby pictures—squishy cheeks and wide pale eyes with a shock of white-blonde chickadee hair—I know I'm going to be ruined for them. Just ruined.

But that's when it all went downhill. That's when it tripped something inside me that I haven't been able to get under control. That's when work became something I couldn't stop fixating on, when preparing financially for a baby became consuming.

"She was cranky at Ziggy's party," Ren offers. "Were things rough then?"

"Yeah. I was an asshole that day. I'd been on a bunch of calls for this"—I clench my jaw—"this *project* that I can't talk about that

I'm working on. We'd hit some roadblocks on financing, and I was upset and discouraged and stuck in my head. I'm sorry, guys. I know I sound suspect as shit, and I know you love Freya, but I just want to get home to my wife and tell her I'm really fucking sorry that I was late."

"And by late, you mean *never showed*," Ryder reminds me.

Oliver leans in. "Why, again, were you late?"

"I'm not divulging that, either."

"That's a lot of secrets, Aiden," Ren says. "Why are you keeping things from us? We're family. You can trust us with anything."

This is what's so hard to articulate to people who haven't grown up like me. When things get difficult, I rely on myself. Because when life's taught you that you're the one person you can count on to survive, the thought of exposing yourself to other people when you're at your most vulnerable feels . . . nearly impossible. That I've been able to do it at all throughout my marriage—admittedly not very well these days—is a testament to how much I love Freya.

I stare out at the ocean, silent. Because I could try to explain it, but how can they understand?

"You're checking out on her emotionally, aren't you?" Viggo asks. "You're keeping all your shit to yourself, stonewalling her. You know that's a relationship death sentence, right?"

That hits too close to home. "I'm working on it," I mutter.

"No, I think you're working on everything *but* that," Viggo says.

"Jesus Christ, Viggo. Who are you? Dr. Phil?"

Undeterred, Viggo clears his throat and reads from his book. "In the words of the inimitable Lisa Kleypas, *'Marriage isn't the end of the story, it's the beginning. And it demands the effort of both partners to make a success of it.'*"

"That's beautiful," Ren says.

"Who the hell is Lisa Kleypas?" I ask.

Viggo scrubs his face and sighs heavily. "The shit I put up with.

She's a *romance* author, Aiden. And her books are dripping with wisdom that you'd benefit from absorbing. '*The effort of both part-ners*,'" he repeats meaningfully.

"I'm making an 'effort,'" I fire back. "But I have only so many hours, so much brain space, so much emotional bandwidth. For a short time, I've directed that to financial success and work, okay? I feel like I have to choose between supporting us so we can be ready for what Freya wants from me and giving Freya what she wants from me. One has to come before the other."

Ryder leans in, elbows on his knees. "What is it you think she wants from you that you're unable to give her while working on this project?"

My heart pounds. I rack my brain for how to say it without say-ing it. "I . . . I . . ." Swallowing nervously, I stare down at my hands. "I've realized the way I've been working in order to provide for us makes her miserable, but she wants a family, and this was neces-sary. I thought I could just bite that bullet and crank it out quickly, then we'd be okay. But that backfired and I hate that. Because this is all for her happiness. All I've ever wanted is to protect her hap-piness."

"And what about your happiness?" Viggo asks. "Does working like this make you happy?"

"Happy? Fuck, I'm just trying to survive." The truth lurches out of me, and God, what I'd give to wrench it back.

"Survive?" Oliver sets his hand on my shoulder. "Aiden, what do you mean? You have a great job. Freya does, too. You're both healthy, with a roof over your heads—"

"You don't get it," I say, shooting up from my chair, my lungs heaving. "Y-y-you don't understand the pressure, the—the weight of this. I didn't grow up with a dad like yours. I didn't *have* one. My mom cleaned houses all day. I went to school, got myself home, made myself dinner, did my homework. Mom came home, tucked me in, then went to work the late shift at the twenty-four-hour diner, had our neighbor across the hall keep an ear out while I slept."

Oliver's eyes tighten with sadness. It makes my skin crawl.

I glance around at the brothers and find some form of it in all of their gazes. "I don't want your pity or your concern or your goddamn meddling. I just need you to understand what I'm up against: I have anxiety. I am a world-class catastrophizer. But I'm also ambitious as hell and determined not to let that hurt the woman I love.

"I'm busting my ass right now because I don't have the safety net you all have to catch me if I fall. I never have. Freya deserves better than that. She deserves solidity and safety, especially if we're going to be parents. I can't compromise on that. My wife and future kids will have what my mother and I didn't. Money in the bank and absolute security. So that if anything happens to me, they won't—"

I pinch the bridge of my nose and try to collect myself. My pulse pounds in my ears.

"Aiden," Ren says quietly. He stands and sets a hand on my shoulder. "You're right. We have no concept of what it was like to grow up how you did, no understanding of how that affects you emotionally. But, Aiden, that family? That safety net? You have it already."

Oliver stands, too, and pats me affectionately on the back. "You have us."

"It's not the same," I mutter.

"No, man. Don't buy that bullshit," Viggo says, slapping his book on the table. "This idea that you're all on your own, that your financial success or failure equates to your success or failure as a man. It's seriously damaging, and it's the lie that an oppressive capitalist patriarchal society wants us to live enslaved to."

All the brothers blink at him.

"Wow, Viggo," Ryder says. "Got some fire in there, don't ya?"

Viggo throws up his hands. "It's true! Life's hard enough without this brutal financial pressure society wields via toxic masculinity. It's even harder for someone who fights the uphill battle with anxiety that Aiden does every fucking day."

He turns back to me. "No matter what life brings, no matter what hardship, you will be surrounded by people who love you and are ready to help you, Aiden. People who know you've done everything you can to make it. Struggling will never make you less of a man or less of a husband to Freya. Struggling means you've been brave. It means you're showing up to life and trying. And that's enough, man. More than enough."

This is always how they talk, people who haven't grown up like me. They think of *their* side of things—charitable solutions, how obviously generous they would be, should the worst happen, because *Of course! That's what family does!* But they don't understand what it is to feel helpless in a system that makes it so easy to fall through the cracks, what it feels like when the lights shut off and you have to scramble for resources, prove your desperation. They've never swiped their SNAP card to buy groceries and had it declined. They don't understand that I'm not only protecting myself from that—more than anyone else, I'm protecting Freya and this baby we want. So they never, *ever* have to worry about facing what I have. Because I promised to love Freya. And love doesn't abandon, love doesn't leave the welfare of its wife and child to the whims of the outside world. Love protects and provides and prepares for the worst, so when and if it comes, they're safe.

I step away from the guys. Running my hands through my hair and sweeping up my phone, I order myself an Uber.

"I have to go," I mumble. "I have to—"

"Aiden," Ryder says.

"What?" I say tightly, eyes on my phone.

"I know we do and say some dumb shit," he says. "But on this, we're right. And I probably more than anyone—maybe barring Ren—have some insight on this: Don't isolate yourself from the people who love you. Don't hide your problems from them. I love someone who's spent a shit ton of therapy hours learning how to be vulnerable because the bridge between loving me and letting me in was almost entirely collapsed by her past pain.

"You have a partner who wants to give you all of herself, who wants all of you, your struggles, included. Don't squander that. Because if you keep that door shut and locked long enough, one day you're going to open it, and then what?"

I stare up at him, swallowing roughly. "There's not going to be anyone on the other side."

"Exactly. So go home. *Talk* to Freya."

A book hits me in the solar plexus. "And read a damn romance novel," Viggo snaps, before he stomps inside and slams the glass door shut behind him.

I slide the book into my back pocket and glance around at the remaining four. "I appreciate the intent of this, but now you need to stay the hell out of my marriage. I know I'm screwing up. I know I've failed my wife. But for us to come out on the other side of this, *I* need to be the one to figure that out, along with her."

They blink at me.

"Respectfully," Ryder says, "I think you're wrong."

"Very wrong," Oliver adds.

"Yeah, well, if I am, it won't be the first time. Not by a long shot."

Turning, I walk the length of Ren's house to wait for the Uber and brace myself for what's next. As much as I want to shove that book down Viggo's throat, he or Lisa Whoever-he-quoted is right. Marriage is so often the end of the story in those feel-good movies, in the books Freya reads and then closes with a dreamy sigh, but in real life, marriage *is* the beginning.

It starts off foreign and thrilling, a roller-coaster ride with your eyes shut, knowing dips and turns and plummeting drops are ahead, but never when or how they're coming. And as you climb that first massive height, then feel the moment when everything changes, when it shifts to a wild, weightless drop, that's when you learn marriage isn't the final destination. It's the ride itself, one moment smooth sailing, the next, jolting and unpredictable. It's the ride that's so upending and life-changing and worth it that we want to stay on and ride it again and again and again.

At least, it should be. For a long time, it was for me. I used to wake up, excited to be a better husband in ways that had nothing to do with savings or tenure or business ventures. I wanted to learn everything about Freya, what made her smile and laugh, what made her light up and sing at the top of her lungs. But then the demands of real life came pressing in, bursting our happy bubble. And time for those moments became a luxury, not a guarantee. Now they're all but gone.

I want them back. I want hours more in every day to watch the sunrise paint her profile, to kiss her awake how I used to, then crawl down her body and wake her up with a patient, teasing come. I want to listen to Freya hum while I make pancakes and she pours coffee. I want to rub her feet, then tickle her until she tackles me off the couch.

But if I do that, minutes, hours, are lost—time I should be spending shoring us up, protecting us, anticipating the worst. Which is exactly what my father never did, for the short time he stuck around, and my mom never recovered from that. I'm not exactly sure I did, either.

I'm stuck between the rock and the hard place, discouraged and defeated. I don't know how to begin repairing what's broken between us. Because this is beyond Freya's healing touch, beyond anything in my fixer-upper arsenal. Freya and I need help. Professional help.

Waiting for my ride, I stare at my wedding band and spin it on my finger, watching it wink in the moonlight. And that's when I realize exactly what has to come next for us to have a chance in hell of coming back from this.

Marriage counseling.

FIVE

Freya

Playlist: "Something's Gotta Give," Camila Cabello

I open the bathroom door connected to our bedroom and shriek.

Aiden glances up from the edge of our bed. "Sorry I scared you."

I tug down my shirt, wishing I was wearing a bra because right now Aiden doesn't deserve to see my nipples, even through a T-shirt. Especially because they're hard. Because I want to wring his neck, but the man is too damn hot for his own good. He sits straighter on the bed and tugs at his tie, eyes on me, the simple movement sending his ocean-water scent rolling my way.

I stare at the dark waves of his hair, his aqua-blue eyes, and the beard he still hasn't shaved, as I step closer, until our toes are touching. He peers up at me and falters with his tie. It's like staring at a stranger.

A really hot stranger.

Shut up, brain.

"Where were you?" I ask.

He swallows roughly. "I, uh . . . work. I was at work. Then I got . . . roped into a meeting . . . of sorts."

I lift an eyebrow. "Yeesh, Aiden. Slow down. I don't think I can handle all the details."

He sighs. "Freya—"

"You know what? Forget it." I spin away, because if I stand there much longer, I might do something insane like grab him by the tie and shake him until it jostles the truth that's so clearly stuck inside. If I just rattle him hard enough—

And that's my problem. I've exhausted myself trying, and nothing has come out. I'm. Not. Trying. Not anymore. I've asked. *How are you? What's up? Anything on your mind? How's work?*

To which I got *Fine. Nothing. Just work. Busy.*

I throw my dirty clothes in the hamper and accidentally encounter my list, which must have fallen from my skirt pocket. My list of feelings and thoughts I've been carrying around. My grievances, itemized. Ink splotched with tears. I stare at the paper, then crumple it until it's balled so tight, I know that when I open it back up, it'll simply disintegrate in my hands.

I made the list because whereas I'm a feeler, Aiden is a thinker, and I've always internalized this pressure in our relationship to handle my emotions more like him. To be "reasonable" when I'm upset. To be "rational" when we argue. Because I want my perspective to be taken seriously, and when I sound cerebral, Aiden seems to listen. If I sound calmer than I feel, I don't risk triggering Aiden's anxiety beyond the point that he can actually hear me out.

Sure, it works, but it's a lie. It's not how I tick. The real me cries and speaks when her feelings aren't tidy but instead a messy mix of emotions. I work out my thoughts as I talk. I'm an emotional, verbal processor who's been biting back that need for a decade, who's only given in sparingly, to the point that I feel so compressed, I'm poised to detonate. No, implode.

Making a list, an itemized bullet point of hurts, confessions, and feeling words, was supposed to give me reprieve, help me feel purged and prepared when the time came to talk it out, then make amends with the man that I love. But writing the list just made me angrier and angrier, festered the hurt. The fact that I needed to make the damn list pissed me off. Where's his list? Where's his discontent? Where's *Aiden*?

Here but not. And I'm so fucking sick of it.

I stare at him, sitting on the edge of our bed staring down at his feet—dark blue tie loose, crisp white shirt, the top two buttons undone. Aiden runs his hands through his hair, turning it messy, then tosses his glasses aside on the bed, rubbing at the shadows under his thick-lashed eyes.

He peers up at me when his hands fall. "I want to go to marriage counseling."

My stomach flips. "What?"

"I said, I want to go to marriage counseling."

"We haven't even talked about what we need counseling for."

"Thus the marriage counseling, Freya," he says, voice raw and low. "I want us to talk through . . . what's happened, with someone's help. Because I don't even know where to begin."

"Beginning with the truth is a good place. Like what you were actually doing tonight."

Horseradish jumps up and meows, rubbing against Aiden. He scratches the cat absently and sighs. "I had an accident at work. I got something on my clothes."

I frown. "What?"

"Then I bumped into some . . . friends who waylaid me. Now I'm home."

"Yeah, not much better."

Aiden's eyes hold mine intensely. "I know," he says quietly. "I know I'm not doing a very good job at . . . any of this right now. Which is why I'm asking: Will you go to marriage counseling with me? I'm trying to tell you what I need to pull my weight here, Freya. I want to fix this."

When I don't answer right away, he stares back down at the ground and rakes both shaking hands through his hair again, sighing heavily. I can taste his anxiety in the air, sharp and painful, pressing in on him.

Not that he's told me. Not that I know lately where his anxiety is, or what's troubling him. The past few months, when I suspected he was having a tough time, he'd smile, falsely bright, then say he had work and disappear into our little home office. The room that's supposed to become a nursery.

I wonder if . . . I wonder if things have been hard—harder than usual—and he hasn't told me. And if so, why? If so much of what's been distant between us is because he's carrying burdens he doesn't want to share, how could I ever honestly say I love him while denying him the chance to talk through it with a counselor? A wave of empathy crests within me, soothing the scorched ache in my heart.

I clear my throat, then tell him, "I'll go, Bear."

Shit. The word's out before I realize I've even said it.

Aiden's head snaps up, and our eyes meet.

Sadness tangles with nostalgia into a sharp, aching knot beneath my ribs. I haven't called him Bear in so long, haven't felt that nickname easy and warm on the tip of my tongue. His nickname that came about when we first started dating, when his black bear hair would tickle me in the morning as he burrowed in close, wrapping me in his arms. When he'd growl into my neck and pin me to the mattress, waking me up with slow, intense sex. That nickname is a vestige of the silly romantic shit we did at first, like couples do when they're newly in love and so sure they'll never break each other's hearts, never fail or fall apart the way *those* couples have.

The fucking hubris.

Fighting tears, I turn away and fuss in my dresser drawers, pointlessly refolding my clothes. It's so obviously a deflection because I never do this. I'm a slob, and we both know it.

Aiden stands, the bed frame creaking as he does. I hear the soft crush of the rug beneath his feet as he stands behind me, the closest we've been in months. "Why'd you call me that?" he says softly.

A tear slides down my cheek. I palm it away angrily. "I don't know. It was an accident."

His hand slips around my waist and pulls me against him. Bold move. Ballsy as hell. Aiden MacCormack in two phrases.

A lesser man could never have won your heart, Freya Linn.

I hear my dad's voice in my head, his toast at our wedding as he raised a glass to us. I cried when he said that. Because I believed it was true.

Aiden buries his nose in my hair, his other hand wrapping around me, too, pinning me to his body, warm and hard behind me. My head falls traitorously back on his shoulder. "Talk to me, Freya," he whispers. One hot kiss right behind my ear—that spot I love, and he knows it. "Tell me what's hurting you. Please."

I suck in a ragged breath and scrunch my eyes shut. "Aiden, I don't know why I know what's wrong and you don't. Why am I hurt and you're fine—"

"I'm not fine," he says roughly, holding me close, his hand caressing my belly. "And I know we're . . . a little distant right now."

An empty laugh leaves me. "*A little* distant. We're beyond that, Aiden. We don't talk. We don't connect. You're secretive, and you're busier than you used to be. We don't . . . have sex."

A fear that I've tried to banish time and again grips me by the throat and bursts out. "Are you cheating on me?" I whisper hoarsely. "Is there someone else?"

Aiden's body goes deathly still. He grips my chin, turning my face to meet his expression, which darkens like a violent storm blackening the sky. "How could you even ask me that?" His voice cracks, and a muscle jumps in his jaw.

I push out of his arms, banging into the dresser behind me. "Y-you act differently. You look different. You got fitter and hotter . . . Wait. I mean. Shit." I cover my face, humiliated by my slip, angry that I can be this hurt by his behavior but I can't deny my body's burning from his touch.

He raises his eyebrows. "Freya, I've been horrible about working out. There's no time. I get so busy, I forget to eat. I've inadvertently lost some weight."

"Exactly!" I latch on to that, thanking my lucky fucking stars he didn't jump on the fact that I called him hot. "You're *busy*. Constantly. And you rush off the phone when I come in the room. It's, like, textbook existential-crisis-turned-cheating signs. And you're not answering me."

"Because it doesn't even deserve a response," he says, dangerously quiet, hurt tingeing in his voice. "Of *course* I'm not cheating on you, Freya!" He leans in, and I shrink back, but our fronts still brush, heat pouring off him, the hard planes of his body sweeping against the soft curves of mine. "You think I could ever want *anyone* but you?"

A tear slips down my cheek. I used to be able to answer that unequivocally. "I don't know."

His brow furrows, pain tightening his face. "Freya, I *love* you. I *want* you. Only you. You're the only woman I notice or desire, and if you think it's escaped me that I haven't had you beneath me, that I haven't been inside you, making you come, in months, you're sorely mistaken."

I swallow thickly.

"*Everything* I do is for you, Freya. For us. And you think because I'm working a little more than I used to that I'm *cheating* on you?"

I shove past him, desperate for space as countless emotions close in on me. "You're doing more than 'working a little more.' Don't downplay what's going on, don't diminish it. You take calls and won't tell me what's up. You've been traveling more, and all you do is throw me some line about 'exploring a business opportunity.' How am I supposed to know? I don't recognize you, Aiden! You're distracted. You're secretive. You don't tell me what's on your mind, what's on your plate. How do I know nothing else has changed?"

"Because you trust me," Aiden says, disbelief lacing his voice. "Because you rely on the twelve years we've known each other, eleven and a half of which we've been a couple, nearly ten of which we've spent married, and you say, *I know my husband. I know he's faithful and he loves me. There must be something else going on.*'"

Anger boils inside me. "You think I haven't thought that? That I haven't tried? Tried talking to you, touching you, connecting with you? And what do I get? Separate bedtimes and short, generic answers. How am I supposed to 'know' this love, Aiden? Where's love when there's no intimacy? No words, no affection. No hands searching for me in the dark."

He blinks away. Guilty.

"Where's love," I press, "when you used to tell me what was weighing on you, used to ask for my ideas and support? Where's love when you don't turn toward me but instead walk down the hall and shut the door, when it's been *months* since we talked about getting pregnant and you never once ask about it?"

He flinches. "I've been preoccupied with work and distracted. I own that. I'm sorry. I should have . . . kept better track—"

"You would have," I say through a stifled sob, "if you cared about it! You have energy and attention, Aiden, for the things that matter to you—work and work."

"That's not fair," he says sharply. "Work is for us. Work is how I love you—" He breaks off, staring at the floor. "I didn't . . . I don't mean that exactly. Work is *one* of the ways that I show you that I love you. By working hard, so we're protected, so we're financially secure."

I sigh and drop to the mattress. This conversation.

Again.

Aiden grew up in extreme poverty. A single mom who struggled to make ends meet. A dad who split when Aiden was a toddler. And I understand this, abstractly at least: Poverty is traumatic. Aiden's worries about money—his exacting need to have all the bills in an Excel spreadsheet, itemized, paid precisely one week before they're due, to tackle loans as soon as financially possible, to work and work and work—are because he grew up not eating some days, wearing shoes and clothes that were too small, taking under-the-table manual labor jobs starting when he was ten years old. How he works and lives now stems from that. That and his anxiety, which . . . those two things are inextricably bound, how he grew up and how his brain simply is.

And I love him for who he is. I would never wish him otherwise. But that doesn't mean I can always understand how deeply his past impacts him. My whole life, I've been safe and comfortable. My dad is an oncologist, a military veteran with a pension. My mom's frugal. Sure, we had a couple tight years when unforeseen expenses stacked up fast, but we were always able to bounce back, unlike so many people in this country for whom one bad turn of luck can mean choosing between lifesaving meds and electricity, facing eviction, food insecurity, complete collapse of their lives.

People like Aiden and his mom.

So I've always tried to honor how he handles the echoes of that in adulthood, to be his biggest supporter, to encourage his dreams to be successful, and I'm wildly proud of him. He's a professor in good standing at an excellent university. He empowers students to be confident and creative business minds and mentors kids like him who're coming from no background of support or financial management.

Aiden is an accomplished, admirable man. He's just become a

shitty husband. And I can't keep saying one is mutually exclusive from the other. He can be both. He can be good for others and bad for me.

"Freya," he says quietly, approaching me like I'm a growling, cornered animal, which is exactly what I feel like.

"What, Aiden?"

He swallows nervously. "The other night, at the art gallery. Your drink wasn't . . . There wasn't any alcohol in it."

I blink at him, trying to piece together what he's asking. Then I realize. He wants to know if I'm pregnant. "Well, we'd have to have sex to make a baby."

He flinches.

"So, no, Aiden. I'm not pregnant." The truth comes burning out, fiery and bitter. But then something happens that makes that hurt double back on itself: Aiden's shoulders drop. Like he's *relieved.*

My mouth falls open. "What was that?"

"What?" Aiden says. "What was what?"

"You just . . . Aiden, you just sighed like you dodged a bullet."

"I . . . did?"

"You did." I spring up from the bed and take a step closer to him. "You just relaxed."

He scrubs his face. "Fine," he grits out, low and tight as his hands drop. "I relaxed. Forgive me for feeling a bit of relief that you're not pregnant while on the brink of leaving me. Forgive me that I'd like shit figured out before we have a baby in the mix—"

"Because it always has to be figured out, before—God forbid!— we do something out of passion or desire or love. Fuck's *sake,* Aiden!" I stomp away, ripping off my shirt with my back to him.

I hear him suck in a breath, feel his response to me from across the room. Screw him. I don't care. He can have blue balls for eternity. I've certainly been suffering enough the past two months.

After tugging on a bra, I pull the shirt back over my head and stomp down the hall. Stepping into my sneakers, I grab my purse.

"Where are you going?" Aiden asks sharply.

My car. Then In-N-Out. Where I will order a large fry and a strawberry milkshake and eat my feelings in the parking lot while cry-singing along to my aptly titled *Allllll the Emotionzz* playlist. It's going to be cathartic as fuck.

"None of your business." I sweep up my keys and charge toward the door.

"Freya," he calls, following me through the foyer, "don't walk out on me. Stay and fight. That's what we do. That's what we've always done."

I freeze, my hand hovering over the door handle. Peering over my shoulder, I meet his eyes. "You're right. We used to. But then you quit. Now I'm quitting, too."

"Freya!"

I drag the door shut and yell over my shoulder, "Don't. Follow me."

"This isn't exactly what I had in mind for *fika*," Mom mutters, browsing swimsuits, "seeing as that was the fastest sit-down coffee and muffin I have ever had, and we barely talked."

I smile sheepishly at her. "I'm sorry. It's just nuts at work right now."

And I knew if I came home and had your cardamom-infused coffee, the kladdkaka *cake that you know I love, I would have bawled my eyes out and told you everything.*

And I'm not telling her shit. Because we've set a date for this anniversary getaway vacation. The one week that worked with everyone's schedule—mostly to fit around Willa's soccer career and my dad's ability to get away from his patients—is a nauseating, all-too-soon one week away. I'm not monopolizing my mom's emotional energy with concern for my marriage this close to her getaway. And I'm certainly not ruining her vacation with it, either.

Aiden and I are going to be the picture of bliss for this trip. Smile, kiss when absolutely necessary, hug, act normal. My brothers are already sworn to secrecy and understand that I don't want to ruin what's supposed to be a gift to our parents with my drama. Everyone's on board with my plan for things to run smoothly.

Is it bad timing? Yes. Is it pretty much the last thing we need? Yes. Since the blowup in our bedroom, things have been stilted and uncomfortable between Aiden and me. We're about to start marriage counseling—which is making me nauseous just thinking about it. Then there's planning for a trip that involves changes in routine, new environments, and additional expense—which exacerbates Aiden's anxiety. On top of all that, when I can barely hold on to hope that my marriage is salvageable, I'll have to spend a week pretending things are infinitely better than they are.

It sucks, but it's what needs to be done.

"And how is Aiden?" Mom asks.

I use sifting through swimsuits to buy myself time. "A bit stressed from work, but okay."

"And you two? How are you?"

My head jerks up. "What?"

"Marriages have their ups and downs, of course," she says, her eyes returning to the rack ahead of me. "Your father's and mine certainly has."

I tell my heart to stop trying to pound out of my chest. "Really? You guys have never seemed anything but . . . perfect."

"Sometimes, Freya, we see what we want to see rather than what's really there. Your papa and I have struggled. But we've tried to handle it in ways that are appropriate for our children. And through our struggles, we've learned how to do better. You see the fruit of that labor."

My stomach knots as I waver, as I come so close to telling her everything. I love my mom. I trust her. And I know she'll have wisdom for me. But I just can't bring myself to dredge up this unhappiness right as we're heading into their celebration. Afterward, when we're back, and things settle down. After that, I'll tell her.

"Hm," Mom says, lifting a sexy black two-piece and holding it toward my body. "This one has you written all over it, Freya. What do you think?"

I open my mouth to answer, but before I can, a saleswoman gathering tried-on clothes from the rack outside the changing rooms says, "Oh, that'll look beautiful on you."

She says it to my *mom*. My mom who has Claudia Schiffer's looks—long and lean, wide eyes, and dramatic cheekbones. While I have my mother's pale eyes and bone structure, her light blonde hair, and the faintest gap between my front teeth, I am absolutely my father's side of the family from the neck down—broad shouldered, muscular, with full breasts and hips and thighs.

A Scandinavian waif, I am not.

Even with increased portrayal of diverse bodies, even with the fact that lingerie and swimsuit shops now feature curvy models working their merchandise, this still happens all the time. Those offhand comments and reminders that people just can't wrap their heads around the fact that I can be full-figured and actually not want to cover myself up. The concept that "someone like me" could wear a *two-piece* is apparently revolutionary. If I wear something that no one would think twice about a skinny person wearing, it automatically makes me a body-positivity warrior, instead of just a woman wearing what she damn well pleases.

Usually, it doesn't bother me, because I'm aware that there are people out there who are simply unaware that they're upholding body-shaming or are otherwise downright assholes. I try not to worry about them. But for some reason, this cuts. I've been here a dozen times. This woman's rung us up before. It's different when it's someone who knows you. It hurts.

"This," my mother says icily, "is for my daughter."

The saleswoman falters, her eyes switching to me, before taking a long sweep of my body. She blinks a few times. "Oh!" she says, nervously. Her cheeks pink. "Silly me. I didn't think we stocked that in her size."

"What?" my mom says. Her voice is subzero.

The saleswoman's color drains faster than I can mutter *Oh shit* under my breath, because I might be a mama bear, but I learned it from the best, and I've got nothing on her. The sight of Elin Bergman provoked when she sees one of her children threatened scares *me*, and I'm the one she's protecting.

"I'm sure it'll look *great!*" the woman says awkwardly, trying—and failing—to cover her tracks.

Mom rolls her eyes and shoves the swimsuit on the rack. "*Come on,*" she tells me in Swedish. "*I'm disgusted with her. We're going somewhere else.*"

The saleswoman's eyes ping-pong between us. My mother is cool and calm as ever, but she has subtle ways for messing with people when they piss her off. Americans can't stand when people speak in different languages around them. It betrays our intrinsic egoism—we're always convinced it's about us. The irony, of course, is that Mom plays right into it.

"*Mom, I don't have time—*"

"*For this, yes, you do,*" she says. "*Besides, it's on the way back to your office.*"

I glance over my shoulder as the door falls shut behind us. It's my mom's favorite boutique. Not too fancy or pricey, just locally owned and stylish. Now that we're out of earshot, I switch to English. "But you love that place."

Mom links our hands together. "I did. Until that. No one makes my beautiful Freya feel like she's anything less." She winks at me and squeezes my hand tight. "Besides, I know just the place."

SIX

Aiden

Playlist: "From the Dining Table," Harry Styles

Freya's barely spoken to me since she came back from wherever she went three nights ago. Then again, I've been quiet myself, even though I know she's still pissed I wouldn't level with her. Yeah, no, I still haven't told her I shit myself and then her brothers abducted me. Sorry for wanting to maintain a sliver of dignity.

"How'd you get an appointment so quickly?" Freya asks, her eyes darting around.

The counselor's office building is fancy. An entire wall of glass windows allows us a view of the water, trees swaying in the summer breeze and evening sunshine bathing everything in buttercup light. It smells like eucalyptus and green tea and world peace. I'm so damn desperate for this to be our solution.

Opening your mouth would be a great solution, too.

Easier said than done. I'm hoping an expert will help me figure out how to do it. Because I don't know how to confess all of this to Freya, how to tell her all my fears and inadequacies and trust that they won't send her packing or giving up before we've even started.

I know I'm not acting like the person I was when I married Freya. To her, I've always been Aiden: ordered, diligent, attentive. Now I'm chaos and pinballing, work-obsessed, and despicably distracted. I feel so fucking broken. And I'm terrified to be broken before my wife.

"Aiden?" she presses.

I snap out of it. "Sorry. Dr. Dietrich is friends with my colleague, who put in a word for us. That's why she made an exception to see us after normal hours."

"What colleague?" Freya asks.

"She's a friend in the department."

"*She?*" Freya stops in her tracks. "Who is she?"

I stop with her, gently taking her by the elbow to the side of the room so we don't block the door. "She, as in the counselor? Or she, as in—"

"Your colleague, Aiden."

"Oh. Luz Herrera."

Freya's eyes narrow. "And you're close enough with *Luz* that you're swapping contacts?"

I open my mouth and pause. Searching Freya's expression, I lean in. "Why are you asking that?"

No answer.

"Are you suspicious?" I ask tentatively. "I told you I'm being faithful to you, Freya."

Freya's jaw tightens. "Of course not."

"Okay." Blinking away in confusion, I gesture us toward Delilah Dietrich's office. Freya walks ahead of me.

"You're not answering me," she says.

I'm still processing her intensity. Even if she isn't suspicious, she's curious. She cares, which is a good thing, isn't it? If she was ready to kick my ass out for good, she wouldn't care who I was "swapping contacts" with.

"We've joint mentored a few students," I tell her. "One of them had some mental health struggles, and when Luz and I were working to support them, Luz was quick to find a recommendation. She explained that it came from Dr. Dietrich, her friend, and that was how she got the student cared for so quickly. At one point in our conversation, Luz mentioned Delilah's an exclusive couples counselor. That's all."

"Hm," Freya says, her eyes slipping away.

Before we even sit in the chairs in Dr. Dietrich's waiting room, our therapist sweeps in, a halo of frizzy silver curls, wire-rimmed glasses significantly magnifying her eyes.

"Good evening, dear ones," Dr. Dietrich says, lacing her hands together. She's wearing a floor-length dress in sage green, ragg wool socks, and Birkenstocks. Clutching her sand-colored knit sweater around her, she waves. "Come on in. Right this way."

Dr. Dietrich steps into her office and putters around her desk, which is a hot mess, lifting a mug of tea from a piece of paper, which sticks and rips when she separates them. The disorder of it makes me wince. Freya, however, is going to feel right at home in this cheerful chaos.

"Comfortable?" Dr. Dietrich asks as we settle in, blinking owlishly through her glasses.

Freya nods. I take off my sweater and try to ignore the shit all over Dr. Dietrich's desk. She seems to notice my attention to it as she sits back and smiles.

"Make you *un*comfortable?" she asks. "My organized disorder?"

I shift on the sofa, wanting to do what I've always done with Freya, which is wrap an arm around her and tug her close. Bury my nose in her hair and breathe her familiar lemony summertime scent. But I can't. Every atom of her body screams, *Don't touch me*.

So I interlace my fingers and shove my hands between my knees.

"A little," I admit.

Freya rolls her eyes. "He's such a neat freak."

"If by 'neat freak,' you mean I keep our house organized so you can actually *find* stuff."

"I find stuff," Freya says defensively.

I cock an eyebrow.

"Most of the time," she amends, glancing away and tilting up her chin a little defiantly. In the past, when she did that, I'd clasp her jaw and kiss her. First, a hard press of lips. Then my tongue, coaxing her mouth to open. Her hands would fist my shirt, and she'd nudge her pelvis against mine. Then I'd push her against the hallway wall, and we'd kiss our way to the bedroom.

My hands itch to do it—touch the line of her jaw, stroke her smooth, warm skin, and bring her soft mouth to mine. Because touch has always bound us together. But that's part of our problem. Even the familiar, loving touch that said so much when I struggled to, not even that knits us together anymore.

We're far past hugging and making up. I know that now.

Dr. Dietrich smiles before sipping her tea. "So you two are quite different personalities?"

"Ohhh yes," Freya says quickly. "Practically opposites."

I frown at her. "Why'd you say it like that?"

Dr. Dietrich sets down her tea. Freya doesn't answer.

"I'm getting ahead of myself," Dr. Dietrich says gently. "First, tell me why you're here."

Quiet hangs between Freya and me. Finally, I tell her, "I asked Freya to come, and she said yes."

"And why did you ask her to come?"

"Because she kicked me out a few weeks ago—"

"I didn't *kick you out*, Aiden," Freya says, her voice tight. "I asked for some space."

I exhale slowly, trying not to be defensive, to betray how much being asked to leave hurt. "You had a bag packed for me, Freya, and an airplane ticket—"

"To my family's cabin, which is like a second home to you," Freya interjects.

"Let's let Aiden finish his thoughts, Freya, *then* you can argue with him," Dr. Dietrich says matter-of-factly.

Freya's jaw drops.

I clear my throat nervously. "Freya asked me to leave so she could have some time and space to think. Since I came back, we've been in a holding pattern that I don't want to stay in. I think we need help to get out of it. *I* at least need help. Freya agreed to come when I told her that."

"Freya," Dr. Dietrich says. "Go ahead. Let's hear from you."

Freya glances away, her eyes searching the view out of the window. "Over the past . . . six months, I guess, I've felt a shift in our marriage, like our connection has been sand slipping through my fingers, and no matter how hard I grasped, I couldn't stop losing it. I tried to ask Aiden what was going on, but he's been evasive. And I just felt . . . defeated. So I asked for space, because I couldn't stand going through the motions anymore.

"If you had asked me when we got married if I could ever see our communication having so fundamentally broken down, that I would be this numb and hopeless, that Aiden could be disengaged and blindsided by my feelings, I would have laughed in your face. Yet here we are."

Dr. Dietrich nods somberly. "Okay. Thank you both. So, Aiden, you said you think you need help getting out of your holding pattern. Can you share what you need help with?"

My heart pounds as Freya's words echo inside my mind. My worst fears are confirmed—all my attempts to keep to myself the worst of my anxiety symptoms, to push and grind through this stressful season, to hide how deeply it's been affecting me and shield Freya, have epically backfired.

But it's not just your anxiety, that voice in my head whispers. *It's what anxiety's done to your body. To your love life. And you're too proud to admit it.*

"I . . ." Glancing over at Freya, I want so badly to hold her hand, to tell her everything. But how? I stare at her, struggling for words.

"Yes?" Dr. Dietrich says gently.

"I mentioned on my intake form that I had a rough upbringing, which brings with it certain triggers. And I have generalized anxiety disorder." The words rush out of me. "Well, the past few months, while things became . . . strained between us, my anxiety's often been high."

I thought I could fix it before she noticed, before she started asking questions and pushing me for answers. I'd managed my anxiety and accompanying symptoms better in the past. I could do it again. I just had to try harder. Fight it harder. Work out. Eat well. Exercise. Keep my sleep schedule. Breathe deep. Meditate on the drive in to work—

Yeah, which went so well when you had that panic attack and had to pull over.

"Why is that?" Dr. Dietrich asks. "What's been elevating your anxiety?"

Sweat creeps over my skin, and my heart pounds harder. "Well, I'm pretty driven at work, trying to solidify my place in the department but I'm also working on developing a business opportunity that will keep us financially secure. And yes, I'm pursuing it, in part, to assuage my money worries, but also because it's simply responsible. It's the right thing to do for my family. Problem is, the risks and possible failure my work presents often trigger my anxiety, so it's sort of a vicious cycle. Then, when it's this bad, it makes . . ."

Fess up. Say it. Tell her planning for a baby sent your anxiety flying through the fucking roof. Tell her your brain is flooded with cortisol and adrenaline, spinning with worries and what-ifs and negative fantasies . . .

My mouth works, my hands fisting until my fingers ache.

Tell her that it's damn near impossible to relax enough to feel aroused or stay aroused or finish, that if you increased your anxiety prescription dosage, it would be even worse.

Tell her.

I bite my cheek until it bleeds, pain and shame tangling inside me. I know I've kept more from her than I ever wanted to, well aware that honesty is gold and communication is key. But God, have I had my reasons. Because I know my wife. If I told Freya about *my* problem, I know exactly what she'd do. She'd shelve her plans, dim her hopes. Go back on the pill, reassure me we could defer pregnancy . . .

Silently, it would crush her. And I'm not in the business of crushing my wife.

Freya peers at me curiously. "Why didn't you tell me, Aiden?"

"Because it's not just my anxiety, Freya. It's . . ." I exhale shakily, flexing my hands, running them through my hair. "It's that my anxiety's . . . affected my sex drive. I didn't know how to talk about one without confessing the other, so I kept it to myself. And I shouldn't have. I'm sorry."

There. A partial truth.

Also known as a lie of omission.

Freya sits back, eyes searching me. I've stunned her.

Dr. Dietrich nods. "Thank you, Aiden, for opening up about that. I'd like to ask something, as a follow-up: Why did you feel unable to tell Freya your anxiety is acute right now, that it's having an impact on your sex life?"

I meet Freya's eyes. "I didn't want to burden her. Freya already supports me so much. I just . . . I tried to focus on taking care of it, rather than placing more on her shoulders."

"You could have told her *and* been working on it," Dr. Dietrich says.

And thick silence hangs in the room.

But then I would have had to admit . . . everything. What anxiety was doing to my body, how far it was taking me from her. "I think . . ." I clear my throat roughly. "I think I was scared to admit it to *myself*, how serious it had gotten, let alone to Freya."

Dr. Dietrich nods slowly. "If we aren't honest with ourselves, we can't be honest with our partners. That's a good insight into yourself. I'm glad to hear it. Now your anxiety is medicated, and you are in counseling, correct?"

"Yes."

"You deserve care and support, Aiden. Please make sure you're keeping up with that."

Yeah. In all my ample spare time.

"*Make* time," Dr. Dietrich says, as if she'd just read my mind. "Freya?" she asks gently. "Thoughts, after hearing that?"

Freya stares at me, her expression wounded. "I wish I'd known, Aiden. You're usually so transparent about your anxiety, and I'm always grateful to know so I can be there for you. Hearing it just *now* . . . that's hard. I feel shut out. Again."

I brush knuckles with Freya. "I'm sorry."

She stares at me for a long moment, then wipes away a tear that's slipped out.

"Well, now that we have some initial feelings before us, now that I have a sense of what we're tackling," Dr. Dietrich says, "let me circle back briefly by saying my company line: There's a lie we've been told in our culture that our romantic partner's attunement to our emotions and thoughts should be nearly psychic, and *that* is the barometer of our intimacy. If we feel like they aren't 'getting' us, we reason that we've stopped having that magical intimate connection.

"But that's not the case. The truth is that we change and grow significantly in our adult years, and to stay close with a committed partner, we have to keep learning them, examining if our growth is compatible or divergent. However, we can't know that until we take action to understand our partner, particularly as they change to the point that we feel we don't recognize them. If we discover that we can engage and appreciate and value their evolution, that they can reciprocate those feelings for us, we've rediscovered intimacy."

"So what does this have to do with us?" I ask. "You're saying we've changed?"

She tips her head. "Haven't you?"

Freya shifts on the couch. "I hadn't really thought about it, but yes. Obviously we've changed since we were in our twenties."

"And perhaps your patterns for practicing and cultivating intimacy haven't changed with you," Dr. Dietrich says. "Haven't accommodated your dreams and your desires, your mental health and your emotional needs."

She glances pointedly between us. We both shrink back.

"But isn't intimacy just . . . there . . . or not?" Freya asks after a moment's silence. "As long as you're still both committed to each other, it should be there, right?"

"Oh, goodness, no." Dr. Dietrich sips her tea, then glances between us. "Intimacy isn't intuition. It isn't even familiarity. Intimacy is *work*. Sometimes it's happy work, like picking sun-ripened apples that drop effortlessly from the tree, and other times, it's like foraging for truffle mushrooms—down on your knees, messy, inefficient; it takes digging up dirt and perhaps coming up empty on your first attempt, before you find the mother lode."

Freya wrinkles her nose. She hates mushrooms.

Dr. Dietrich seems to notice. "Yes, that metaphor tends to break down with my picky eaters. But oh well, we can't be all things for all people!"

Silence hangs in the room. Dr. Dietrich's smile fades softly. "I know this is hard, and I'm putting more in your heads than relieving you, like you think a therapist should. Unfortunately, that's how this starts. Messy and overwhelming and hard to sort out. But guess what? You chose each other today. You set aside your busy schedules, forked over hard-earned money, and said you believe in each other enough to show up and try. So pat yourselves on the back."

When neither of us take her literally, she smiles again. "No, really. Go on."

We awkwardly pat ourselves.

"Excellent," she says. "So marriage counseling is like any new form of intense exercise: We work hard, then we ease up and give our muscles a break, a cooldown. You've done a lot today, so now we're going to switch gears."

I blink at her. "We talked for fifteen minutes."

"Twenty, actually. And what a twenty it's been!" she says brightly.

Freya scrubs her face.

"So," Dr. Dietrich says, reaching behind her. "Without further ado . . ."

A box lands with a *thwack* on the floor.

I stare at the game from my childhood. "Twister?"

"Yes, folks. We're going to limber up—assuming no one feels physically unsafe here or unable to bear touch. Your intake forms said no, but I'm checking in again. Has anything changed for either of you?"

Freya shakes her head. "No. I'm fine," she says.

I nod. "Me too."

"Great. Socks off—oh, well, look at that." Dr. Dietrich bends and unfolds the Twister mat, wiggling her socked feet inside her Birkenstocks. "You're both wearing sandals *without* socks. Interesting."

Freya glances over at me as a smile teases the corners of her lips. I smile back, and for just a moment it's there, the spark in her eyes. The faintest thread of connection.

"On the floor, then," Dr. Dietrich says, scooting her chair back. "Let the games begin!"

SEVEN

Aiden

Playlist: "Train Song," Feist & Ben Gibbard

Dr. Dietrich sips her tea, then spins the dial. "Left hand to red."

Freya's arm slips beneath my chest, brushing my pecs. Her hair, her soft scent of lemons and cut grass, so familiar, always enticing, surrounds me. I breathe her in, feeling her exhale shakily beneath me. I have to make my move next, which sends my pelvis brushing over her ass. We're in an incredibly suggestive position, which doesn't seem to faze Dr. Dietrich. She steals another sip of tea and flicks the dial once more.

"Right foot to green."

"That's cruel," Freya mutters.

"I'm ruthless." Dr. Dietrich evil-laughs. "But it's for your own good."

Freya reaches with her right foot, until she's snug beneath me, tucked against my groin. I close my eyes and picture pressing a kiss to her neck, biting between her shoulder blades. I shift to reach my green circle, wedging my thigh between Freya's. Need tightens my body, a hot ache building low in my stomach, which surprises me as much as it does her.

She sucks in a breath as my weight rests against hers, my breath warm on her neck. I exhale roughly, then draw in a long, slow breath.

Dr. Dietrich flicks the dial again. "Left foot to yellow."

We move accordingly and morph from sexually tense to explicitly uncomfortable. I am not made to bend like this.

"Um, Dr. Dietrich?" Freya says, her voice faint. "Can you spin the dial again?"

Dr. Dietrich frowns at it. "Huh. The dial doesn't seem to be working." She chucks it over her shoulder, where it lands in the haphazard pile on her desk. "I suppose I'll just have to ask you a question, and once I have your answer, I'll pick somewhere new for you to go."

"What?" Freya squeaks.

"Tell me one thing you love about Aiden."

"Besides his ass?"

I frown over at her. "Freya, be serious."

"Aiden, we're playing Twister and in a more adventurous position than we've ever—"

"Freya!"

She clears her throat. "Sorry. Okay. I love Aiden's conviction. Oh my God, my back hurts."

Dr. Dietrich does not care about spinal discomfort. "Conviction for what?"

"That's another question!" Freya yelps.

"Aw, too bad," Dr. Dietrich says. "I happen to be the Twister captain, and I say what goes. You gave me a half answer anyway. Better hope I don't pick right foot to green next."

I glance at that spot. I think Freya would snap in half.

My arms are shaking, my glasses fogging up as sweat drips into my eyes. "Frey, can you just answer her?"

"Jesus, Aiden, I'm thinking."

"You have to *think* about what you admire my conviction for?"

"Pipe down there, big guy," Dr. Dietrich says.

"I love his conviction," Freya blurts out, "about making the most of everything life gives him. He savors life's simple gifts, wrings every drop of meaning and opportunity from them, then he brings that conviction to his students, to his work . . ." Her voice falters. "To *us*. At least he did. Now can you please pick a spot before I slip a disc?"

My heart sinks in my chest. God, how badly I've messed this up. All of this has been for her, and all I've done is made her feel like my last priority.

"Well done," Dr. Dietrich says. "Left hand to blue."

Freya immediately shifts to a comfortable downward dog. I'm so fucking jealous.

"Now you, good sir," Dr. Dietrich says, adjusting her glasses. "One thing you love about your wife."

"She lives out her love, so you can't help but feel it. The moment I knew Freya loved me, I *knew* it. I didn't have to guess. We hadn't been dating too long. I came down with the flu and she stayed with me even when I was contagious. When I was finally not delirious and begging to die—yes, I am a man-child when sick—I asked her what she was doing, risking herself in staying with me. She just smoothed back my hair and said, '*I wouldn't be anywhere else.*'"

I swallow roughly, glancing over at Freya. Her head hangs. She's sniffling.

"I looked into her eyes, and I saw love," I whisper past the knot in my throat. "I *felt* love. And I want that back. I want to *feel* love with Freya again."

Freya crumples to the Twister mat, covering her face as she starts to cry. Before Dr. Dietrich can say anything, before it's a conscious thought, I've tugged Freya into my arms.

Dr. Dietrich crouches down, setting her hand steady and soft on Freya's back.

After a few eternal minutes of her crying, which makes my heart feel like it's being sawed out of my chest, Freya sits up, wiping her eyes. "Sorry I lost it," she whispers.

"Let's call that a game. Have a seat, you two," Dr. Dietrich says, easing back into her chair.

Freya and I stand, then drop back onto the sofa, our bodies landing a little closer than they were when we started. I try not to notice, to place weight in it. If Freya does, she doesn't show it.

Dr. Dietrich says, "Freya, I'm concerned that you just apologized for crying. I'm *proud* of you for doing that. Feeling our feelings is brave and healthy."

Freya gives Dr. Dietrich a watery, faint smile, then blows her nose.

"What are your tears for?" Dr. Dietrich asks her. "What are some feeling words?"

Freya bites her lip. "Hurt. Confused. Angry."

"Good. Go on, if you like."

"I don't understand why we're here. If Aiden wants to feel love with me, why did our communication suffer to begin with? Why did he keep it from me—his work, his anxiety, and its impact on how he felt about physical intimacy? Was it really just because he was figuring that out within himself? He couldn't tell me . . . *any* of that along the way?"

Dr. Dietrich sways in her chair. "Well, I think you should ask him. I think it's also good to ask yourself: Have you withheld thoughts or feelings from Aiden that he should know, too?"

Freya peers down at her hands, then glances up at me, a new kind of vulnerability shining in her eyes. "I . . ." She clears her throat. "Sometimes I sort of bottle up my feelings and try to get them sorted out before I tell him."

"Okay," Dr. Dietrich says softly. "Why?"

Freya glances at me nervously, then away. "I don't want to worry Aiden when my emotions are high. I know it's upsetting to him when I'm a basket case."

"Freya." I clasp her hand. It hurts so badly to hear she would hide herself, hurt herself that way, to shield me.

Breathe through it, Aiden. Breathe.

"Freya," I whisper, "I always want to know what you're feeling."

"That's rich, coming from you," she says through tears.

"Because I'm the one with anxiety, not you! You don't need to carry all that I carry mentally, too. I'm trying to make adjustments to make it fair."

"Ah." Dr. Dietrich lifts her hand. "About that word, *fair* . . . the idea of 'fair' in a marriage, any relationship, I mean it's impossible. No marriage is fair. It's complementary. The idea of 'fair' is absurd at best, ableist at worst."

We both swivel our heads and look at her.

"Ableist?" Freya asks.

"Ableist," Dr. Dietrich says. "Because saying a relationship has to be 'fair' implies that only a certain balance and distribution of skills and aptitudes is valid. It upholds an arbitrary, damaging idea of 'normal' or 'standard' as requisite for a fulfilling partnership. When in reality, all you need is two people who love what the other brings and share the work of love and life together."

Dr. Dietrich smiles kindly between us. "Aiden, you're trying to shield Freya from emotionally carrying 'more' than you think she should. Freya, you're avoiding honesty about feelings and thoughts that you think might make Aiden feel 'more' than you think he should. It's well intentioned, both of you, but it's a terrible idea. And lots of couples do it. Even after, Freya, you vowed to love all of him, and, Aiden, you vowed to give her all of yourself."

Freya blinks up at me, her eyes wet. I stare at her, wanting so badly to hold her and kiss her tears away.

"Freya's just been trying to protect me," I tell Dr. Dietrich, my eyes not leaving Freya's. "And I've been trying to protect her, too."

"Yes," Dr. Dietrich says. "But we protect our spouses from things that cause actual harm—abuse, violence—not our inherent vulnerabilities and needs. Those are there for them to love and complement. If not," she says pointedly, "it comes at the cost of our intimacy, our connection . . . our love."

Freya's eyes search mine. "That makes sense."

"Also, Freya," Dr. Dietrich says, "this is something my female clients often realize in therapy—they hold in their feelings because our culture teaches us that we won't be taken seriously when we're 'emotional,' but I'm going to tell you, your husband needs your feeling words. Aiden, you understand their importance, I hope."

I nod. "I do. But maybe I haven't made that clear to her. I want you to tell me, Freya. I'll do better at showing you that."

Freya peers up at me. "Okay," she says quietly.

Our gazes hold, roaming each other's faces. It feels like wiping away fog from a mirror and truly seeing what's in front of me for the first time in far too long. I wonder if Freya feels that way, too.

"So," Dr. Dietrich says, puncturing the moment. "Your sexual intimacy is impacted by this. Aiden has told you when his anxiety is this high, it's affected his sex drive. How are you doing, Freya? From a sexual standpoint."

Freya's cheeks turn pink. "I've been better."

Heat floods my face, too. It feels like such an ultimate failure.

Dr. Dietrich lifts her eyebrows questioningly. "Would you mind sharing more?"

"Well," Freya says. "It's been . . . months. I'm not sure what came first—my sense that Aiden was working a lot more or that he didn't initiate the way he used to. So I felt rejected. Like he didn't want me. And then *I* didn't want to have sex, either. I didn't want him to be gone from me emotionally but to think he could still have my body."

"That's not how I feel!" I tell her. "I'd never want emotionless sex with you."

Dr. Dietrich glances at me, tipping her head. "So what *do* you feel?"

"That having a baby is no small feat," I admit, before the words can be stopped. "That raising a child in one of the most expensive cities in America with our kind of student loan debt is not insignificant, that it's going to take more than I've been doing. I got a little fixated on working to prepare us for that, and somehow it gets turned into rejecting her, wanting her body but not her heart?"

Fuck, that accusation hurts.

"Aiden, you talk about it like you've been alone in that responsibility," Freya snaps. "And you're not. I'm aware of the cost of living and childcare. I happen to have friends who have children, who've had to make impossibly difficult decisions about their careers and their motherhood. I've carried that with me and mulled it over a lot, considering I work, too, and help pay the bills."

Help? Her last paycheck was bigger than mine, which meant she got that promotion she'd been gunning for after all. And once again, like an asshole, I forgot to say something. I sighed with relief and moved it over to savings, my pulse steadying as I saw that number get a little bit bigger, before an email about the app swallowed up my happiness and dragged me back into the realm of never-ending to-dos.

"I don't mean to imply you don't, Freya," I tell her. "It's just that you approach looming expenses differently, confident we'll weather them. I'm much more familiar with what can happen if you're not financially prepared, and I act accordingly. You *hum* happily while you open bills. I grit my teeth and do mental math about what has to happen to maintain our savings. I'm trying to strike a balance between those two positions, and that means securing extra income, setting us up for stability so that when a baby *is* here, I'm not working constantly. I'll have done that already. And I'll be able to focus on taking care of you both, being a present partner and parent."

"Yep," Freya says, folding her arms. "There it is."

Dr. Dietrich glances between us. "What's the backstory here? And am I to understand you're trying to get pregnant?"

Freya nods tightly. "That was the plan, yes."

Dr. Dietrich glances at me. "Aiden?"

"Yes. That was the plan."

"And?" she presses.

"I grew up poor," I tell Dr. Dietrich. "With a dad who hit the road when I was a baby and a mom who never recovered from that. I've had to work *really* hard my whole life for every bit of financial gain, to finally, for the first time in my life, have healthy savings. Anticipating what having a kid costs is intimidating, so I've been pursuing financial security, and I've been working on a project—"

"Which he hasn't told me about," Freya throws out.

I glance over at her. "I haven't, no. But it's just been a mad rush and constantly moving parts to get where we are, to some semblance of something that might actually succeed. I wasn't going to keep it to myself forever."

"Why keep it to yourself at all, though?" Dr. Dietrich asks. "Trust and openness are fundamental in a marriage."

"Like I said, it was such a pipe dream at first, I just wanted to cultivate it for a while before I shared it with her, once it wasn't at risk of being a total disappointment." I turn toward Freya and tell her, "As soon as I knew we had a prayer of success, I was going to share it with you. A gift, a positive step toward making a better life for our family. The day I came home and you had my bag packed for the cabin, I was ready to tell you."

Freya's face tightens with hurt. "Why haven't you told me since?"

"Because we've barely talked, Freya, and I was pretty sure the last thing you wanted was to hear me talking about work." She glances down and stares at her hands, so I press on, hoping I can reassure her, reach her at least a little bit. "There's no financial risk to us, I'm not sabotaging our funds. It's nothing that affects you—"

"Except that it affects *you*, Aiden, and thus it affects *me*, because I'm your wife, your life partner, who cares about you!" Freya stands and grabs her purse. "This is the shit I can't stand. It's one thing, what we talked about earlier, how we danced around your anxiety and my feelings. I think she has a point. And I can hear that. But this? This shit about money?"

She gestures at me, fuming as she speaks to Dr. Dietrich. "He rationalizes shutting me out, acting like George Bailey, leaving the little wifey home alone while he stumbles around Bedford Fucking Falls and wrings his hands about money."

I love that movie, *It's a Wonderful Life*, but I keep it to myself. Freya might kick down a door if I said that.

"I'm your partner," she says to me angrily. "I should be tripping through the snow *with you*, not stuck in that house we poured everything into, wondering when you're going to come back. You locked yourself out, Aiden Christopher MacCormack—"

Shit. I just got full-named.

"—and now you're upset that I'm staying in there? Well, tough shit. You let yourself back in, or this is it, and I'm done."

Freya storms out and slams the door behind her.

Dr. Dietrich's eyes slide to the door, then to me. "Seems I hit a nerve."

Sighing, I scrub my face. "Yeah."

"Here's the thing, Aiden." Dr. Dietrich leans in. "A relationship is like a body, and without the oxygen of communication, it can only last so long when one person pulls away and deprives it as much as it seems you have. I know it's hard to be vulnerable. I know you wanted to protect Freya. But your protection keeps you at arm's length. If you want to feel close to your wife, you have to draw close, to trust her, even if you're terrified—no, *because* you're terrified. Breathe some life back into this marriage."

As I absorb Dr. Dietrich's words, my mind fixates on Freya,

who's bolted, and adrenaline floods my system. I have to chase after her, make sure she's not fuming so badly, she's marching toward the freeway, crossing Jersey barriers, and getting herself killed on her way to use the Metro, just to stick it to me.

A horrible image of it happening flashes in my mind's eye. I know I'm a creative thinker, and that's a strength, but it doesn't feel like one when I can close my eyes and visualize my wife dying under a bus.

I jump up from the sofa, grab my sweater, and jog to the door. "I'll do it, promise."

"Wait!" she calls.

Cursing under my breath, I swing back around the threshold. "Yes?"

"No sex," she says, grimacing. "Never like telling a couple that, but you two aren't a buy-new-curtains-and-touch-up-the-paint job. You're a down-to-the-studs gut job. No sex for now. It'll help, believe it or not. It's . . . clarifying."

Sweet relief. If there's no expectation of sex, that's one less thing I have to figure out right now. I could kiss Dr. Dietrich. I mean, not really.

Freya, you asshole! Go get your wife!

Dr. Dietrich reads my mind again. "Go get her." She waves me off. "Be gone."

Running out to the parking lot, I see Freya only made it as far as the car, where she's perched angrily on the hood.

I walk slowly toward the Civic, unlocking it with my key remote. She must have forgotten hers. Wouldn't be the first time. A sad smile plays on my lips because there's weird intimacy in those familiar patterns. Freya loses her keys weekly, but I've privately always liked that she felt safe enough to misplace her keys in the first place. It meant she trusted me to be the one who found them.

"Freya—"

She lifts a hand. "I don't want to talk right now."

"Is there a point at which you will?"

"You," she says, standing and stomping toward me. Her finger pokes my chest. "You have *no* goddamn room to talk. You started this silent mess. Don't even blame me for it. Now get in the car and drive me home or give me the keys, Aiden."

I walk toward her side and open the door. Freya drops down and yanks it out of my grip. I thought things couldn't feel worse between us. I was so sure we'd hit rock bottom.

I was wrong.

EIGHT

Aiden

Playlist: "Sleep on the Floor," The Lumineers

After counseling, Freya disappears into the bathroom the moment we get inside the house, the lock sliding with a loud, poignant *click*.

I tell myself I should stay, wait until she comes out showered off and cooled down, and try to talk to her. But I can't. Not when I have no idea what I'd say, no clue how to reassure her when I can hardly reassure myself. I can't stay in this house a second longer. So I scribble a note, leave it on the kitchen counter for Freya to see, and pack up a duffel bag of workout clothes and tennis shoes.

Once I'm parked at campus, I use the sports facility's indoor track and run. I run and run, until my legs are jelly and my lungs burn. I haven't run in too long because I've been so busy, but I should—I always feel better after a run, after a rush of endorphins and other potent feel-good chemicals flooding my brain. Chemicals that help with anxiety and everything else that feels like it's strangling me when I walk inside our door.

After I've run myself to exhaustion and showered in the locker room, I throw back on the clothes I wore to counseling, then hide in my office while I lose my shit. Being a college professor who's not at the absolute bottom rung of the department, I have a decent little space—couch, desk, a wall of books, an actual window, and air-conditioning. And while it's far from home, it's a safe space for me. If I'm honest, it's where I've hidden when I haven't known how to be the husband I want to be to Freya.

Which is why I'm here, once again. Because I don't know what to do. How to go home and face her, what I can promise, after what her brothers put before me at Ren's the other night, after what Dr. Dietrich said at counseling this evening.

I know her brothers meant well. I know in their way they wanted me to understand how much they're behind me, how much they care about seeing Freya and me through this difficult moment. But shit. It just heaped on the pressure. Pressure and more pressure. To function like they do—to emote and reach out and feel and argue and get messy in all those ways that Freya's fluent in and I'm a novice.

And Dr. Dietrich's admonition, that I've been suffocating our relationship with my behavior, when all I've wanted was to protect us from the outside world's indiscriminate cruelty and threats— it's so fucking defeating. Because her insight made it clear, how warped I am. My mind sabotages me, always seeing the worst in a situation. My heart's this traitorous asshole who beats too hard for the wrong things like money and security and order, when it loves a woman who could give a shit less about material comforts, whose heart thrills for wildness and passion and thrives in the untidy present moments of life.

I have never felt so fundamentally wrong for Freya, so ill equipped to love her how she deserves. And as I flop onto my office sofa and stare at the ceiling, my heart beating like a bird against its too-small cage, I know this is a turning point:

Stay and fight for her. Fight to bring myself back to a place in which I know in my soul how much she and I—despite our deep differences—belong together. Fight to feel once again close and intimate with the woman I love with every fiber of my being . . .

Or finally give in to that voice that lies and whispers horrible things. That I'll fail her, that I'll break her heart, that I'll sabotage us and ruin what we've built together, even the future we haven't yet built.

I want to be strong. I want to be courageous for Freya. Because she deserves to be fought for, her forgiveness earned, her trust won again. I want to go home and say sorry and tell her I'll make it right. But can I promise her that, when I have no idea what fixing us looks like?

My eyes dart around the room, full of books crammed into built-in shelves, my desk brimming with tidy piles of folders. All this knowledge and order. And none of it has the answers I need.

Groaning, I scrub my face. "Fuck."

"Like that, is it?"

I nearly fall off the couch, startled by the voice behind me. Craning my neck, I see it's Tom Ryan, our building's janitor. As always, he wears a faded black ball cap pulled low, his gray janitor's uniform, and a bushy salt-and-pepper beard. Tall and lean, he cuts an imposing figure, yet his body language is hunched, deferential. He never looks anyone in the eye, always keeps his gaze down, his voice low and quiet. For months, we'd cross paths when I was here for evening classes and office hours, and he never said a word. But then one night I stayed late and, on a whim, made conversation with him, then he made some crack I can't even remember, and I realized he has a great bone-dry sense of humor.

Now . . . well, now I'd call him a friend of sorts. One of those people who comes into your life unexpectedly and clicks. Now we talk regularly, anytime I work late in the office and he comes in to empty trash cans, vacuum, and straighten up.

He's good company, a laid-back-uncle type—not that I have any of those. I'm not upset to see him right now. I just prefer not to be ambushed and startled so violently, my heart feels like it's beating right out of my chest.

"Did I catch you off guard?" he asks as he walks in.

I slump back on the sofa and exhale, hand over my racing heart. "You scared the shit out of me."

"Better not have," he says, bending over to the garbage and emptying it into the big bin that he pushes on casters. "I'm too old to clean up shit. Sorry I startled you, though. I thought you heard me coming."

"No, man, you have spy-level stealth."

He drops the garbage can, then steadies it. I notice his hand has a tremor, and because my brain's a prodigy at imagining worst-case scenarios, I start worrying if he's unwell, if he's getting frail, if one day this janitor who I feel oddly bonded to won't be there and—

Tom pulls out the cord for the vacuum with sure, swift movement, snapping me out of my spiraling negative thoughts.

"What are you doing, still here?" he says. "Awfully late to be in the office."

"Just . . . thinking." I stand from the couch, running my fingers through my hair. I should leave. I always feel bad sitting around while he works, especially when someone his age should be retired, not vacuuming carpets, polishing floors, and bending over garbage cans. "I'll get out of your hair," I tell him.

"Please do. You should be gone for the night. I already kicked you out once."

"Yeah." I scratch the back of my neck. "Well. Sometimes a guy's wife needs space. And this is where I can give it to her."

Tom shakes his head. "Nope. That's no good. Go home and stay there." He walks over to my desk, grabs my workout duffel bag, and chucks it at my feet. "When a woman says to leave her alone, when she pulls away from you and acts like she wants you miles away, that's the last thing she wants."

"Well, see, that's actually pretty dangerous thinking—"

"I'm not talking about forcing yourself on her. Jesus. I'm saying when your wife acts like she wants you to be gone, she's asking you to prove that you want her bad enough to stay and fight."

I stare at the duffel bag, wordless, so fucking lost. Because part of me thinks Tom's right. And part of me is scared Freya truly finds my epic head-up-my-ass-ery unforgivable, that her anger in counseling isn't going to fade but only build and deepen.

"I've been in your shoes," Tom says. "And I learned it the hard way. Get home."

"Tom, I appreciate it, but everyone's marriage is different."

"Maybe, but marriage's dangers are the same." Turning away, he lifts things off the floor, clearing it to vacuum. "Complacency. That's what kills them. Dispassion. Resignation. Days become weeks. Weeks become months. Months become years."

He points at an old copy of Aristotle's *Poetics,* which I've carted around since I was an undergrad. "You read that, presumably, years ago. Remember what Aristotle said about tragedy?"

"Yes," I say slowly, confused as to where he's going.

"This is the moment he talks about—*peripeteia*, the turning point, and *anagnorisis*, the point of recognition—when your wife tells you to go, when you finally see your relationship and her feelings in a way you hadn't before. '*A change from ignorance to knowledge, producing love or hate between the persons destined . . . for good or bad fortune*,'" he quotes. "What comes next?"

I swallow roughly. "The scene of suffering."

"The scene of suffering," he says. "That's right. '*A destructive or painful action, such as death on the stage, bodily agony, wounds*.'"

"Well, now I'm psyched."

He sighs. "Of course you're not. Because you're human. And I am, too. What's more human than wanting to avoid pain? I figured, if I stayed away for a while, I could avoid it, let it blow over, then come back when the tension had died down. It didn't seem so dangerous, wanting to shy away from the pain of facing what had fallen apart between us."

He tugs his ball cap lower and says, "But it's like a drug, avoidance. And each day that goes by without tension or worry or disappointment, lulls you with the promise of peace and ease. You give her time, tell yourself things will quiet down, and before you know it, things have gotten *too* quiet, then you have papers in your office, and not the kind you grade."

Pain knifes through me at the mere thought of that. "No. Freya's not divorcing me."

Not yet. She can't. She has to give me a chance. She *has* to.

"Trust me," he says, "when a woman tells you she's at her breaking point, she's been past it for a while. Now's your moment, like Aristotle says. Now you have to make the leap and do whatever it takes to make it better. That's the only way. You just told me."

"Tom, those are Aristotle's thoughts on *tragedy*."

"Exactly. At some point, every love is a tragedy. It just doesn't have to stay that way. We choose our endings. That's Aristotle's point. Tragedy is *built*—it has a structure. And if that's not the ending you want, then you get out of that trajectory. You change the narrative."

I stand there, stunned.

I've just had the best lecture of my life on Aristotle from the janitor. Not that I'm surprised. Tom's sharp, and I know more than anyone that having a low-income job is no indication of a person's intellect or wisdom. I just . . . wasn't expecting his explanation to make so much sense.

It's an epiphany that flashes like lightning against the dark backdrop of my hopelessness—Freya and I can't go back to what we were, but we can lean into this painful moment, learn from it, and become something stronger, something better, together.

Tragedy is built, Tom said.

Which means I can change course and find a way forward that doesn't keep pulling us apart but instead brings us close again. I'm a business and numbers guy. I understand changing trajectories. I understand that when one approach doesn't work, you tweak the formula, then try another.

If that's not the ending you want, then you get out of that trajectory. You change the narrative.

Tom's words echo in my head, morphing into a whisper of hope. Hope that beyond the necessary work of counseling, I can go back home and tackle my fucked-up head. I can grip our disintegration and drag it away from the arc of tragedy, back to the path we started on. The path of long, hot nights and quiet afternoons, touching, talking, confiding in each other; the road paved with laughter and playfulness and hard fucking work. I can *show* Freya what I haven't in too long—how much she means to me, how much I love her.

"Now get out," Tom gruffs.

Before I can answer him, let alone thank him for his advice, he turns on the vacuum. I take the hint. Conversation ended. So I scoop up my duffel bag and leave.

Outside, it's one of those rare nights when you can actually see the stars in the night sky, past the city's light pollution. I stare up at that bowl of velvet black, flecked with diamond stars, remembering our honeymoon. We couldn't afford much, so we'd planned to make the most of it up at her family's Washington State A-frame. But her parents surprised us with a weeklong all-inclusive stay in Playa del Carmen.

I can see Freya in my mind's eye, in her sheer white nightgown fluttering over tan skin, blonde hair long and beachy from the ocean air, like an exotic, night-blooming flower unfurling in its native environment. She spun outside our secluded waterfront bungalow, the waves sloshing softly just beyond us. Then she stopped and held out her hand.

"Look, Bear," she said, the warm affection of her nickname for me filling her voice. I took her hand and wrapped her in my arms, felt the overwhelming, beautiful weight of responsibility for this woman that I still couldn't believe had somehow chosen me. She smelled like salt air and the flower garland she'd worn in her hair that morning, and I hugged her so tight, she squeaked. "Aiden, look."

There were stars. So many stars. And they meant nothing to me—no, that isn't true, not nothing. It was simply that at the moment, my wife on our wedding night held all my attention, and unlike Freya, I didn't grow up sitting on my dad's knee, staring up at the constellations and learning their stories.

"Stunning," I whispered against her neck.

She smiled. I felt it against my temple. "You're humoring me."

"I like listening to you. I'm just a little distracted by this very lovely woman in my arms."

Freya sighed. That sweet, breathy sigh that meant I was winning her over. My lips trailed her neck, softer than starlight kissing her skin, and she shivered happily. "It's Lyra," she whispered, pointing up at a cluster of stars, "the harp—well, the *lyre*—of Orpheus, the great musician."

"Hm." One strap down, her shoulder bare and tan. I kissed it, savored the heat of her skin, the flesh and blood vitality of her body, safe and warm against mine.

"Well, Orpheus was very popular, sort of like the ancient Greek version of a hot rock star," she said. "And he fell for Eurydice, who was your classic plain Jane. A mere mortal. One day when Orpheus was on the road, doing his rock star thing, Eurydice was caught in the crosshairs of war, which, when you were a woman back then, was dangerous business. So she fled for her life. As she did, she stepped on a venomous snake, who bit her. Then she died."

I stopped and peered up at her. "Jesus, Freya. Where's this going?"

She turned, slid her nose against mine, and stole a quick, too-short kiss. "Orpheus went to the Underworld to save Eurydice, and played his lyre, wowing Hades with his mad shredding skills."

I snorted against her skin but felt my laughter fading quickly. "What happened?"

Her eyes, pale as moonlight, searched mine. "Hades told Orpheus he could have Eurydice and bring her back to life, on one condition: He must never look back as they left the Underworld."

My grip on her tightened. "What happened? He didn't look back, did he?"

Freya nodded.

"What?" I heard myself half yell, sounding much more invested than I had when we started, but that's Freya, just like her dad. She speaks, and you listen. She shares, and you want to be a part of it. She had me enthralled. "I mean, how hard is it," I asked her, "not to do the one thing that ruins everything? All he had to do was not look over his shoulder and keep his eyes forward, to protect the person he loved."

Freya smiled sadly. "I think that's the lesson. It's harder than we think. Eurydice was tired from her time in the Underworld, and she was slow behind him. Orpheus struggled to trust she would follow him all the way. His love wasn't enough to overcome his fear. And so at the very end of their journey, Orpheus faltered and glanced back, dooming Eurydice to the Underworld forever.

"Then he spent the rest of his life, playing the lyre . . ." She pointed to a smattering of stars that looked nothing like a harp to me. "Wandering directionless, refusing to marry another."

I remember holding her tight, staring into her eyes as she bit her lip and said, "Sorry. I forgot how sad that story was. I just remember it moved me."

Then I turned her in my arms and held her close. "I promise I'll keep my eyes ahead, Freya."

She smiled as she said, "I know you will." Then she sealed my promise and her belief with a deep, long kiss.

My chest aches as I stop in the parking lot, next to our old, beat-up Civic. I drop my bag onto the hood and yank out the chain that holds a stamped metal pendant, warm against my skin, hidden beneath my shirt. My gift from Freya on our wedding night.

To Aiden—

Thank you for this happily ever after beyond my wildest dreams.

—Love, Freya

From "happily ever after" to this. God, how did it happen?

Sharp, tight pangs of guilt stab my chest. I did what I said I wouldn't. Like Orpheus, I looked back. I looked back at the hell I knew as a kid and felt the flames lick higher, fear grabbing me by both hands. And I dragged Freya there with me.

But this isn't some ancient story, some doomed, grim tale. Tom said it—this doesn't have to end in tragedy. We get to choose our endings, and I choose mine.

I choose Freya.

I grab my bag, slide into the car, and turn the engine. I'm going home. And I'm not looking back.

Not anymore.

NINE

Freya

Playlist: "Hide and Seek," Imogen Heap

"Freya?" Cassie, our front desk admin, pops her head into the break room.

I glance up from the cup of tea I'm sipping. "Yes?"

She smiles, flashing her braces. "There's someone out front for you."

"What? Didn't you say my last patient—"

"Canceled. Yes. It's not a patient. Why are you still here, anyway?"

I stare down at my cup. "Nick's my ride."

Cassie peers at me in confusion but doesn't ask why I didn't call Aiden.

I'm glad she doesn't. Because I wouldn't know what to tell her. I would never tell her I was scared to ask my husband to pick me up instead of waiting to carpool with my coworker, Nick. I would never confess I was scared that Aiden would be running late, or he'd say he couldn't, any whiff of a brush-off that would be too much for me when I'm so raw from counseling, from sobbing in the shower afterward, then coming out to a quiet kitchen and a note in his tidy scrawl, saying he went for a run.

A run that lasted long enough for him to come home hours later, after I'd crawled into bed. I felt the mattress dip, and my traitorous lungs breathed him in, ocean-water clean. For just the faintest moment, my hand slid across the bed, toward the warmth radiating from his body, from the broad expanse of his back stretching a soft white undershirt. And then I remembered. How much he's hurt me. How long I've felt alone. I snatched my hand back, turned, and faced the wall.

It took me hours to fall asleep.

My head's a mess. My heart hurts. I feel like one wrong move from either Aiden or me, and I'll collapse. Which is why I've been hiding in the break room, waiting for Nick to be done with his patient.

"Who is it?" I ask.

Cassie smiles. "See for yourself."

I narrow my eyes at her. "Some front desk receptionist you are."

"I'm a receptionist," she says on a wink. "Not a bouncer."

Sighing, I stand and follow her out to the lobby, then falter. "Aiden?"

He smiles hesitantly. "Hey."

"Gotta go check the fax machine!" Cassie says. "Don't mind me."

I stare down at my tennis shoes, peering up when Cassie slips into the back room. Aiden sets his hands in his pockets and tips his head. "Senior physical therapist. You wear it well."

My heart tumbles. He saw my pay stub, then; he knows I got the promotion. I hate myself for devouring that crumb, the faintest hint of considerate awareness.

"Same scrubs," I say evenly. "But thanks."

He hesitates for a moment, then steps closer, brushing knuckles with me.

I shut my eyes.

Stay strong, Freya. Don't you dare give in. One knowing compliment. His hand touching yours. Fingers brushing is not romantic or sensual or tempting or emotional.

Well, you try reading *Persuasion* on a ten-week celibate streak and see if you can honestly say that. Three hundred pages of longing and loaded silences, days spent in each other's company, so vulnerable and wounded, neither of them is willing to face what they mean to each other, let alone admit it to themselves.

I'm drowning in need and loneliness. I can't help that Aiden's warm, rough fingers tangling with mine makes heat simmer beneath my skin. So I pull my hand away.

But Aiden's Aiden, which means he has balls of steel. He slides his hand up my arm, and tugs me against his chest, into a hug. "I'm proud of you. I didn't tell you. And I should have. Forgive me."

I wrap my arms around his solid waist before I can stop myself. I need hugs like I need air. I'm overflowing with unspent love and affection that haven't gone into my intimate life in months, and I bite back tears because this feels dangerously good. Sighing unsteadily as Aiden squeezes me to him, I soak up his presence, warm and clean, the soft scent of his ocean-water cologne, a mint tucked inside his cheek. I bury my face in his collar.

"Thanks," I whisper.

Clasping the nape of my neck, he presses a kiss to my hair, then steps back.

"What's the occasion?" I ask, blinking away sudden tears, hoping they're not obvious. "What are you doing here?"

"I wondered if you'd want to—" He clears his throat. "Whenever you're done, that is. With your patients. I wondered if you'd want to get ice cream—that is, have an ice cream date . . . with me."

My stomach swoops. "Ice cream?" Our first date was at an ice cream place near campus.

"Yeah." He scrubs his neck. "Then I thought we could order pizza to have once we're back."

"Why?"

He stares at me unblinkingly. "You know why."

"I need the words," I whisper.

"Because I miss you. Because I know dessert for dinner makes you happy and—" His voice catches. He stares down at his shoes. "And I just want you to be happy, Freya."

My heart flies in my chest as his words sink in, as I try to battle how weak I feel, how readily I want to throw myself at him and trust that this means we're on our way and we'll be okay.

But then I remember so many late nights. Quiet dinners. Short answers. The loneliness that settled in, a bone-chilling ache that slowly turned to hypothermic numbness.

He's trying. Give him a chance.

"My last patient canceled, actually," I tell him after a long silent moment. "So I can leave now. And . . . I'd like ice cream."

A wide smile I haven't seen in so long brightens his face, before it dims, like Aiden's trying to hide his relief as much as I'm trying to bury my hope. "Great."

After grabbing my bag and paying a visit in back to say goodbye to a grinning Cassie, I walk with Aiden out to our car. Like always, he gets my door.

Like always.

That makes me pause. "Like always" is something you start to think when you've been together for a while. Certain behaviors become predictable, taken for granted. Even a gesture as kind as opening the car door for me.

I make myself stop and savor it, the feeling of him standing close, the evening air whispering around us. Peering up, I watch the low sun bathe Aiden in its golden light, making his dark waves sparkle, glancing off the strong line of his nose, the tight set of his mouth. A mouth I used to slide my finger across, then kiss until it was soft and smiling.

Staring at him, I recognize that familiarity dulls the shine of your partner's mystery, but it doesn't make them any less of a puzzle. We just . . . stop seeing them that way. We stop exploring, stop wondering with the wide-eyed fascination of new lovers. I'm afraid to admit that somewhere along the way, I stopped seeing the mystery in Aiden, and I think maybe he stopped seeing the mystery in me.

I wish we wouldn't have. And I wonder if we'd be here if we'd done it differently. If we hadn't decided we knew everything there was to know about each other and began to act accordingly, one predictive step ahead of each other. If we hadn't let that take us so far from the other person, from the ways that we'd changed, from the truth that we still had needs and hurts and wonders and fears…

"You okay?" Aiden asks quietly. His hand settles low on my back, the heat of his palm seeping through my scrubs. Longing unfurls inside me, a soft, deep ache for something I haven't felt with him in so long.

"I'm okay," I whisper.

He smiles gently.

After I lower into my seat, Aiden shuts the door behind me. He strolls around the front of the car, and I watch him walk, his long purposeful stride, the way he bites his lip in thought as he pulls out his keys, then slides into the driver's seat. With the windows halfway down, our drive's breezy and quiet, but I don't mind. We're both in our thoughts, sadly unused to time like this, time in which we're *trying* this consciously to be present to each other.

I feel a pinch of nerves like I did on our first date. But I shove that feeling away. I can't let the past get mixed with the present. Young, twenty-year-old Freya had no clue what was ahead. Thirty-two-year-old Freya knows all too well, and she'd do well not to forget.

We pull up to the ice cream shop, which is in its lull after the post-dinner rush. Once Aiden throws the car into park, I let myself out and he comes around. Shutting the door behind me, he sets his hand gently on my back as he hits the key fob to lock up.

"Hm." I stare at the massive ice cream menu, frowning.

Aiden crosses his arms and frowns at it, too. "Hm."

I glance over at him, and my stomach does a somersault as I read the tentative playfulness in his expression. "Making fun of me, are we?"

"I would never." He gives me a quick sideways glance, before refocusing on the menu. "I'm just doing some mental math."

"What kind of mental math?"

He leans in slightly, his shoulder brushing mine.

He's flirting with me. Aiden is . . . despicably good at flirting. He wears his charm like he wears his clothes—with a genetically predetermined comfort and grace. And when he leans close and drops his voice, when his sea-blue eyes glitter and a dark, rakish lock of hair falls onto his forehead, he turns me into a big, gooey, doe-eyed puddle. Always has.

I try to straighten my spine and snap out of it, but it's so damn genuine, and he's so clearly feeling bashful, a splash of pink warming his cheekbones. When the wind picks up and bathes me in his scent, I have to stop myself from shoving my nose into his solid arm, breathing him in.

His eyes dip to my mouth.

"The mental math?" I remind him, curling my fingers to a fist until crescent-moon indents sting my palms.

"Well . . ." He leans even closer, his mouth a warm whisper away from my ear. Goose bumps dance across my skin. "It's a very complex equation that allows me to calculate how long it'll take you to pick two flavors for your ice-cream cone, before you decide you like mine better."

I shove him half-heartedly. "I don't do that anymore."

A huff of laughter leaves him as he guides me forward when the line moves up. I peer at the menu again and sigh heavily. "There are too many choices," I mutter.

Aiden bites his lip.

"Stop laughing at me," I tell him.

He lifts his eyebrows and looks at me. "I'm not laughing!"

"You want to."

"But I'm not."

Turning, I face him. "So what's this equation? And how accurate is it?"

"It's highly complex math," he says, pushing his glasses up his nose. "Let's just say if I could monetize it, I would. It's pretty damn accurate."

I stare up at him, fighting a smile. "You're such a nerd."

"Mm-hmm." He grins. "You are, too, though."

"Not like you. I'm just overly competitive at Trivial Pursuit."

"You? Overly competitive?" He shakes his head. "No way. Never noticed."

The line moves, making us next to order after the group in front of us. "Stop flirting with me. I need to pick my flavors."

There's a pause, before Aiden's knuckles brush mine. "That's what you said on our first date."

I glance up at him quickly. "I did? How do you even remember that?"

His eyes hold mine. "I remember *everything* about that date, Freya. You wore a strapless yellow sundress and gold sandals, and your toes were painted hot pink. Your hair was down in these sexy beachy waves before you threw it up in a bun because it was sweltering hot. And you were so fucking pretty, I could barely remember my own name, let alone order ice cream. So I got—"

"Two scoops of vanilla," I whisper. "You said you liked vanilla."

"It's fine," he says as his eyes travel my face. "What I liked was what *happened* when I got vanilla."

A blush stains my cheeks. "I ate it."

"*Licked* it." He bites back a smile. "While your chocolate peanut butter swirl and salted caramel melted in your hands."

"So we switched."

He nods. "And then we shared. And it felt so . . . intimate. I was out with you, Freya Bergman, this knockout of a woman who was *radiant*—passion and vitality lighting you up from a place so deep within that I wanted desperately to know. A woman who painted her toes electric pink and sang along to music blasting from the outdoor speakers and stole my vanilla ice cream." His eyes search mine. "You felt like the missing part of my life."

Tears sting my eyes.

"W-what—" He clears his throat. "What do you remember from that night?"

I stare at him, warring with myself as his fingers dance along my palms, coaxing them to clasp his. Finally, I slide my hand inside Aiden's. His grip clamps around mine like a vise. "I don't remember what you wore or the precise date. I just remember standing next to you, looking into your eyes and knowing I was . . . exactly where I was supposed to be."

Our gazes hold as our fingers lock together.

"What can I get ya?" the server behind the glass says, startling us apart.

I blink up at the menu, indecision swarming me. I glance over at Aiden helplessly.

He smiles, then turns toward the cashier and says, "Two scoops of vanilla in a cup, please, then chocolate peanut butter swirl and salted caramel on a waffle cone."

Our fingers thread tighter as he says, soft enough for only me to hear, "For old times' sake."

TEN

Freya

Playlist: "when the party's over," Billie Eilish

Back at home, Aiden thanks the pizza guy. I find myself staring at the wave in his dark hair, the taper from his strong shoulders to his waist and that round, solid ass. My chest feels like a blender, a sharp, whirring mash of emotions—desire, sadness, longing, fear— observing this man who remembers what ice cream I got and what I was wearing on our first date, yet holds a part of himself in such profound secrecy, I had no idea it was suffering until our foundation was crumbling beneath us. I want to run out of the house, just as much as I want to throw myself on his lap and kiss him senseless.

I feel like I'm fraying at the edges.

Food in hand, Aiden shuts the door with his foot, and nearly trips over my shoes. On a hop and spin he saves himself, then straightens out and gives me that *I can't believe I live with a slob like you* look that's so habitual, it sends a pang of bittersweetness tearing through me.

"Jesus, Freya. My life insurance policy isn't *that* good."

It actually makes me laugh. "All part of my grand plan to become a wealthy widowed cat lady."

That makes him laugh, too.

As Aiden sets down the pizza box, I pour myself a glass of red wine without offering him any. Aiden rarely joins me, and if he wants to, he tells me. He barely drinks, and when he does, it's typically in social settings, something low-ABV that he seldom finishes. He says it's because it clashes with his anxiety meds and makes him incredibly sleepy, but even before he was on Prozac, he never drank. I've always had a hunch it's equally because his dad was an alcoholic; at least that's what his mom says. Aiden doesn't remember anything about his dad. He just knows enough never to want to be like him.

A few times we've shared a bottle of wine. Got a little buzzed and horny together. And I loved it—sharing wine in your veins, clumsy couch sex. But it's been a long time. Which is why I nearly drop the bottle when Aiden gets himself a glass and sets it in front of me.

"Half a glass, please," he says, focused on serving us food.

I pour carefully as Aiden selects two artichoke and olive slices for me, scoops some tossed salad from the bowl, sets it on my plate, then slides it my way.

He lifts his wine. I lift mine. Our glasses clang quietly in the kitchen. When he takes a sip, Aiden's eyes don't leave mine. The kitchen feels warm, and when I set down my glass, my hand's trembling.

"Hold still," Aiden says, his hand gently cradling my jaw. His thumb slides along the corner of my mouth, catching a drip of wine. He brings it to his lips and sucks with a soft *pop*.

Shit. It's hot in here.

Blinking away, I scoop up the pizza and take a bite. "Thanks for this. It smells great."

"'Course," he says quietly. "Congratulations again on your promotion, Freya. You should be proud."

I peer up at him, swallowing the pizza that lodged in my throat. "Thank you. I am."

He nods. "Good."

Just as I'm about to have another bite of pizza, he blurts out, "I'm working on an app."

Horseradish and Pickles choose this moment to start tangling beneath our feet, meowing loudly because I've raised monsters who expect cheese from my favorite artisanal woodfired pizzeria. "I'm sorry?"

"I'm . . ." He runs an unsteady hand through his hair, ignoring Pickles, who puts her paws on his knee and meows. He clears his throat. "It's an app. It's . . . it's hopefully going to help equalize the higher learning experience for business and economics students."

Halfway through her *meow*, I pick up Pickles and set her in my lap. I need something to hold and ground me. Because the world feels like it's tipping sideways. "What? How?"

"We've recorded tutorials on initial high-level topics, started beta testing, creating an app interface. If it does well, if we can secure a major investor, we'll reach out to more academics to record tutorials. The brightest business minds out there, experts on every business economics and management concept out there, available to any kid who can afford ten dollars a month, not just those who can pay for an Ivy League education. The hardest part has been up to this point, Freya. We've begun pitching to prospective angel investors. Once we have one, I'm . . . free. Well, I'll be freer. Much freer. Able to relax."

I blink at him in complete shock, and Aiden presses on.

"I'm working on selling prospective investors on apportioning funding so people without financial means can apply for relief when months are short. It could change . . . everything. For us, for students like I was, struggling so much to get the opportunities they deserve. So . . . that's what the private phone calls have been. I'm sorry I worried you, that I weirded you out with being so secretive."

An app. He's designed an app to help kids kick college's ass and get where they dream of going in business, regardless of their backgrounds or resources. I almost want to laugh with relief. But hurt chases my surprise and swallows it up whole. "Why wouldn't you talk to me about this, Aiden?"

Becoming a bit of a refrain, that question. Isn't it?

"Because, like I said in counseling, I was trying to keep one more thing off of your plate. It was an idea, a dream, and I had no idea if it was going to amount to anything." He holds my eyes intensely. "What if I put it on your mind, showed you how invested I was, then I failed?"

"Then you'd have pursued a dream and tried and failed and learned something, and I'd be there for you."

"Watching me fail," he mutters. "Burdened by that."

I roll my eyes. "Aiden, come on. You've failed at shit before. It hasn't scared me off or worn me out, has it?"

He rips off a tiny piece of cheese from our pizza and bends to feed Horseradish, cocking an eyebrow. "What have I failed at?"

Ugh. Male arrogance.

"Well . . . You've failed at hanging pictures. Hardcore. And I had that huge wall of photos I wanted. You can't play charades to save your life, like, you are the worst at it. Ever. You're way too literal, and no one ever knows what you're doing with your hands. You've failed at getting roses to grow—every year you try and they keep dying—"

"Okay." He throws back his water like he wishes it were instead the wine he's been responsibly sipping. "Thank you for enumerating my random personal flaws. I meant big stuff. Work stuff. Provision stuff."

"Ah. This is about your dick—I mean your job."

His face blanks. Silence rings in the kitchen.

"What?" I ask, picking up my pizza and stealing a bite. Pickles stares at it longingly.

"Saying my job is about my dick is reducing it to being about my ego, Freya. Like I've got something to prove."

"Don't you?"

He exhales roughly, like I punched him.

"Aiden, it was a joke." Which, like most jokes that sting, is a little too close to the truth. Men's ego in their work has frequently struck me as poisoned with the need for masculine validation.

"Yeah, I get it, Freya." His voice is flat. "I just didn't find it funny. You know what work means for me."

"Oh, do I ever, honey. It's been the third member of this marriage since Day Fucking One."

His jaw tics. "I know I take work too seriously. I know I fixate, okay? I feel like shit about it as it is. I don't need anyone else making me feel worse."

I throw my arms up, making Pickles startle and jump off my lap. "Gee, wonder why we haven't been talking? The moment I open my mouth, I make you feel like shit."

"Fuck." He shuts his eyes and breathes deeply. "Okay. I'm sorry. Let's just . . . table jokes about work. And dicks. And yes, I'll acknowledge I'm sensitive about them."

I take a viciously large bite of pizza, chew, and swallow. Aiden opens the box, serving himself another slice and then a scoop of salad. And our recent companion, stilted silence, is with us once again.

After a few more bites of food, my ears no longer ringing with defensive anger, I can see I didn't help us with that jab.

Groaning, I rub my forehead. "Aiden, I'm sorry. I was out of line. I've been . . . I've felt replaced by your work, and I dug at you about that. It's been hard not to take it personally. Like you want to work instead of wanting me."

Aiden stares at me, for a long moment, then drops his fork. "I need you to understand this."

He steps between the gap in my legs and tilts my head so I'm looking at him, my face held firmly in his hands. "*How* I've gone about work lately has made you feel like you're less than the center of my world. That's wrong, and that's what I'm going to fix. Because you have to know, Freya, that *everything* I do is for you. I want to give you everything you deserve. I want to lay the world at your feet."

I bring my hands to his wrists, stroking his pounding pulse with my thumbs. "But I never wanted the world, Aiden. I just wanted you."

He stares at me with such earnest confusion, it makes my heart ache. "Want*ed?*" he whispers.

I blink back tears. I can't even begin to know what I want, except for Aiden to know this, to get the truth through his thick skull, because if this doesn't stick, then we really have no hope, and my husband knows me much less than I ever thought he did. "I would have lived in a flimsy cardboard box," I tell him, tears thickening my throat. "Under a shitty run-down bridge, with nothing but the clothes on my back, so long as it was with you."

His eyes dim. "Spoken like a woman who's never been poor."

"No, I haven't." I swallow my tears. "But I've had a roof over my head these past six months. I've had a soft bed and heat and water and food in my stomach, and I haven't felt comfort or warmth or satisfaction. I've felt empty and cold and lonely because you weren't here, not really, Aiden."

His eyes glitter with unshed tears as he stares down at me. "Freya. Life's not that simple."

"But my love is," I say hoarsely, squeezing his wrists. "And you don't get to say otherwise. It's my heart. I know it. I can see now that it's not the case for you, even if I don't understand. So I'm telling you right now, the only reason I care about this app of yours is because it does something good for others, and because it means something to *you.*

"I've never cared if you made us gazillionaires. I don't want fancier clothes or a second car. I don't need a bigger house or a new fridge. I've needed hugs and trust and kisses and laughter and that *us against the world* feeling I knew in my bones the day I stood in my parents' backyard and held your hand in mine and said *I do*." Searching his eyes, I whisper, "What is it you need, more than that?"

He swallows roughly. "To keep you safe, and when there's a baby, to keep them safe, too. I need that, Freya."

My hands slide up his arms. "I just wish it didn't cost you so deeply. I wish it hadn't drawn us apart."

Aiden's eyes dance between mine. His hands slip in my hair. "I wish that, too," he whispers, his eyes searching mine. "Please know, Freya, I'm trying. Trying to do better. I know it's not great. It's not nearly enough. But I am trying." He pulls me from the stool and holds me close, burying his face in my neck. "I just need some time. Please don't give up. Not yet."

I swallow tears, heart aching, wishing I had more to promise him than the truth. "I'm trying my best, too."

He sighs roughly, holding me tight. I press my nose to his hair and breathe him in, cool and crisp as the ocean, a whisper of mint because he brushes his teeth three times a day, without fail after breakfast, lunch, and dinner. Because his mom taught him to as a kid, since they couldn't afford the dentist, and it's a habit he says he can't quit for the life of him.

I still remember the first time I stayed over at his apartment for the weekend and I caught him brushing after lunch. He blushed and glanced down at the sink as he told me why. I wrapped my arms around his waist, hugged him hard. Then I picked up my toothbrush and brushed with him.

My hands slide up his chest and freeze. I feel it beneath my fingers, warm and smooth, the rounded rectangle. My fingers drift higher, tracing the chain beneath his shirt. The pendant I gave him on our wedding night.

Tears burn my eyes as I remember *his* gift, a gift that told me how deeply he knew me: a song. A song he wrote and sang softly in my ear as we danced under moonlight. A song that he couldn't play on the guitar like he'd planned, because Mom and Dad sprung a destination honeymoon on us, and all our cool-weather Washington State clothes and his guitar were left in place of haphazardly packed shorts and tank tops that never got worn. Because we never even left our tiny little bungalow on the water.

"You're still wearing it?" I whisper through tears.

Aiden's hand rests over mine. "I never took it off."

I peer up as he bends closer and our noses brush, then our lips. A shower of sparks dances beneath my skin, as Aiden holds me in his arms, as his grip tightens around me and he lets out a slow, ragged breath. I lean in and feel him, so solid and heavy and warm. Cupping his face, I smooth his cheeks with my thumbs.

And then he kisses me.

Our kiss sings in my body, from my lips, through the hum of my throat, to the tender ache that builds in my heart and soars through my veins.

Slow down. Be careful.

I don't want to. I'm lost in his touch. His taste. In the strength of being held and the thrill of being wanted. Our kiss feels like magic—like shooting stars and blue moons and meteor showers—and I'm enthralled by its power, its rare, blinding beauty. I close my eyes, weightless, lost to something so precious in its familiarity and so exciting because, somehow, it's new. He tastes like Aiden, and I sigh when he does what he always has, pushes that little bit. His tongue breaches my mouth and coaxes mine, a faint teasing touch that floods my body with warmth.

Aiden groans into my mouth as I drag his bottom lip softly between my teeth. My hands slide over his shoulders, his strong, thick arms, the breadth of his chest and his heavy muscles tightening as he holds me close.

He feels like the man who climbed up on our roof and patched it for years, when a new roof would have wiped out our savings. He feels like the man who rescued Pickles from the filthy attic even though he hates small, dark spaces, who drove a sick Horseradish to the 24-hour emergency vet clinic like a Formula One racer, even though he's a firm believer in observing the speed limit. He feels like the man I painted walls with, muscles flexing, shoulders rolling as he worked next to me, then went back and neatly cut in with a hand brush because I was too impatient, too messy to do it well.

Touching him reminds me of the man I married, the man I love. I feel like he's really *here*, kissing me, wanting me, and I'm delirious with the satisfaction of it.

"Freya," he says against my lips.

I'm climbing him, my body ignoring my brain that's blaring *Pump the brakes!* I'm getting ahead of myself, and I don't care. I want this. I want him.

"Baby, slow down," he whispers. He wraps his arms tight around me, spins, and with my hop, lifts me onto the counter, settling between my wide-open thighs. "God, I want you. But we can't."

"Why?" I'm sex-crazed, tugging at his shirt, trying to get it over his head.

"Because Dr. Dietrich said we can't."

"She *what?*" I freeze, dropping my hands and his shirt. "That Birkenstock-wearing Twister sadist is cockblocking me?"

Aiden drops his forehead to mine, exhaling slowly. "That's what she said after you left the office. She told me we're an overhaul, not a redecoration."

His words sink in, dragging me back to reality from my lust-soaked fugue. I clutch my arms around my waist and fight a shiver. Embarrassment heats my cheeks, and Aiden sees it immediately.

He steps closer. "Freya, I—" He cups my face, forcing my eyes to meet his. "Freya, I *want* you. Please don't doubt that."

"No," I whisper as tears slip down my cheeks. "Why would I ever doubt that? I've felt so wanted."

Aiden's eyes fall shut as he presses his forehead to mine again. "I want to show you. I want you to know, but I don't want to do something that hurts us right now."

"I understand," I whisper. "I'm fine."

"You're not. I can tell." He wraps his arms around my waist, before his touch drifts down, cupping my ass and hoisting me closer. "I hate when you're sad," he whispers. "It feels like I'm being gutted. All I want to do is take that sadness away, Freya. For you to smile and sing and be happy."

Aiden slides his nose along mine, gives me a faint, worshipful kiss. My hands fist his shirt reflexively, tugging him close, before they drift beneath the soft cotton of his T-shirt. Dancing along his hard stomach, my touch finds the soft hairs that lead to what I want deep inside me.

His breath hitches, then he groans softly and leans his hips into mine. His breathing is rough and fast as his mouth claims mine. One kiss. Another. His hips nudge mine harder, and our mouths open, sharing air and soft, hungry sounds.

But then he pulls back and kisses the corner of my mouth, scrunching his eyes shut. Desire looms, thick and crackling between us, like ozone filling the air before a storm.

"Some couples therapist," I mutter, burying my face in the crook of his neck and shoulder, hiding my messy emotions, my fear of what comes next. "Telling us not to get our freak on."

Aiden laughs softly. "I think she's concerned that sex might do more damage than good. Maybe it's like with your therapy clients. Walking too soon on a broken bone could set back healing."

"And sometimes it's that first painful step that helps them remember that healing *is* painful, and that's okay," I counter, trailing my lips down his throat.

He smiles softly as his head tips back, dark lashes fanned and casting shadows across his cheekbones. "You could have been a lawyer," he whispers.

A reflexive smile tips my mouth as I lick his Adam's apple. His hips lurch into mine. "Law school was too sedentary."

Aiden's hands dive into my hair, and he tips my head until our mouths are crushed together again, his chest pressed to mine. He gives over, unraveling under my touch, and it feels so good, to be wanted like this—passionately, recklessly.

He groans as I palm him over his jeans. "Freya—" He kisses me harder, his hands slipping beneath my shirt, tenderly tracing my belly, then my breasts. I gasp as his palms rough my nipples.

Hooking my legs around his hips, I nudge Aiden closer as he eases me back on the counter. He clasps my chin and drags his teeth down the length of my throat, his pelvis grinding into mine. I gasp as he shifts my hips until I'm beneath him, as he leans over me, giving me the weight of his body. His hands frame my face, his tongue coaxing mine in a rhythm that I want our bodies sharing, not just our mouths.

"Please," I whisper.

He doesn't answer me, and I know he's torn. In the rational corner of my mind, I'm torn, too. But it's been so long since we slowed down and felt each other like this, played and petted and kissed each other. Why did we stop? *When* did we stop? What if we lose it before we've even fully found it again?

Aiden's hands wander beneath my shirt again, his thumbs circling my nipples until they're hard and so deliriously sensitive. An ache builds between my thighs as he rubs himself against me, and my hips start rolling into his. Cupping my breasts, he teases my nipples more, kisses me deeply. The ache builds, urgency growing. I throw my head back and gasp and then—

The blare of Aiden's phone shatters the moment.

No, that's not quite right. It's not the phone that shatters it. It's the immediacy with which Aiden pulls away and dives for his phone in his pocket.

Humiliation burns through me, red hot and staggeringly painful. I sit up slowly and tug down my shirt as he stares at his screen, his fingers flying as he answers whatever message he got.

"I'm sorry about this," he mutters to his phone. He can't even look at me and apologize.

And every faint, delicate, good thing I felt this evening, the tiny flame of hope that flickered to life as he swept me away with ice cream and pizza, as he told me he loves me and confided in me about his dreams, his fears, is snuffed out.

A new creeping desolation settles beneath my skin as I stare at him. Even if Aiden and I survive this, even if he opens up to me the way he used to, will it really be better, *knowing* what he's working on, if he's still married to his work instead of me? Or will it only be a different kind of pain? A new way of feeling alone, second best, runner-up to the god of his smartphone and professional success calling him away from me.

I don't dignify his actions with a response. And Aiden doesn't seem to notice.

Slipping off the counter, I grab my pizza, snag a bottle of wine, and call the cats, who run and follow me to the bedroom.

At least someone still finds me worth chasing after.

ELEVEN

Aiden

Playlist: "Bad Things," Rayland Baxter

It's one of those days, when the weight of my anxiety is a vise grip around my ribs, when I can hear my pulse pounding in my ears and my heart feels like one big palpitation. There's nothing to pinpoint, no particular reason.

Except that you were two seconds away from going down on your wife in the kitchen, then Dan texted you, and you jumped off of her like her skin had caught fire.

Fuck. *Fuck*. I just keep replaying it, like many things I've screwed up throughout my life. Moments I made an ass of myself or felt embarrassed. When my clothes were worn out or too small. When I was so tired from the landscaping work I did on the weekends in middle school that I fell asleep during homeroom, then woke up with drool on my desk and a dick on my face that someone drew with Sharpie. Which I noticed in the bathroom mirror during *fifth* period.

It plays on a loop in my brain.

Sometimes it keeps me from sleep. Other times, I wake up and I'll fixate on that one time I messed up explaining a term in lecture and had to email my entire 300-person class, telling them what I'd gotten wrong. Another time when I found a typo in my section of a coauthored academic journal article, and I spiraled into worry that it was somehow going to get me fired.

It makes my skin crawl. Sometimes it gets me on the verge of throwing up.

And today is one of those days. Fuckups front and center in my brain. On the razor's edge of a panic attack. I can't lie, I feel the tug of despair. That choking, tear-out-my-hair anger that I'm stuck. That anxiety is managing my life, instead of me managing it.

So when I have a break between classes that doesn't involve office hours, I walk, trying to breathe and distract and steady myself. Squeezing my hands, then flexing my fingers, breathing through my nose, out of my mouth. There's a small, less-trafficked bit of green space outside my building that I walk like a track, probably looking like any professor around here, strolling while working out an idea.

On my way back from another lap, I slow as I spot Tom sitting on a nearby bench. Ready for work in his gray janitor's uniform, he sets down a small Igloo cooler, probably packed with his dinner, and sips from a thermos. When my path takes me a few yards from his bench, he peers up through dark sunglasses beneath his usual faded black ball cap, and waves politely.

I slow to a stop. "Hey, Tom."

"Afternoon," he says, lifting his thermos. "Doing all right?"

My expression falters. "Sorry?"

He sips from his thermos, then sets it between his legs. "You look like you're trying to win the power-walking Olympics. Thought maybe you're stressed. But I could be projecting. I walk when I'm worked up."

"Oh. Well . . . yeah. With anxiety, sometimes walking helps."

"Ah, that it does." He says it like he gets it. I wonder if he does. If maybe that's why he puts me at ease. Because he's unfazed by me, because we're a little more alike than I thought. "Well, I don't want to keep you if you need to keep walking," he says.

"Actually..." I find myself eyeing the spot on the bench next to him. "Mind if I—"

"Please," he says, scooting down to give me ample room.

Once I sit, my legs start bouncing. And it makes me miss Freya. She never sets her hands on my thigh or tries to make me stop. Her fingers simply slip through mine, followed by a hard, reassuring squeeze.

Fuck, I love her.

I scrub my face and sigh. "Sorry. I'm in my head today."

"Doesn't bother me." Tom rolls his shoulders back and folds his arms across his chest. I catch the faint whiff of menthol cigarettes on him now that we're this close.

"You smoke?"

He nods. "Yup. Not on campus, of course. I like getting my paycheck."

I knot my hands tightly between my knees, breathing against the tightness in my chest. "You shouldn't."

He shifts on the bench. "I'm aware. I've been doing it since I was thirteen, though, so it's a little late to clean up the act."

"What? How'd you get that past your parents?"

He half glances my way, before staring straight ahead again, and saying, "Well, uh . . . they weren't around much. And when they were, they reckoned I was trouble and there was no changing me."

"Stubborn?" My legs bounce steadily but my heart's started slowing down. I suck in another breath through my nose and focus on listening to Tom.

"Yep," he says. "I was and am incorrigibly stubborn. Well, until I met a girl who made me straighten things out. She was the first person I ever wanted to bend my life around. And I did. But, of course, eventually I screwed that up real bad."

"How?" I ask, shutting my eyes, focusing on my breathing.

He shifts on the bench and coughs wetly, then says, "I drank. I was addicted. And I chose it over her. Over . . . everything."

Those words send a chill over my skin. *I chose it over her. Over everything.*

"But uh . . . for the past three years, I've been sober," he says, "so that's something I try to celebrate. Well—" He laughs, husky and thick. I can hear the tar coating his lungs. "'Celebrate' might be a stretch. I remind myself when I walk by the bar I used to get lit in every night that I don't *actually* want that drink; my brain just wants the calm that alcohol gave me. And then I go home and read instead." He sips from his thermos. "That's when I celebrate."

Maybe it's because he looks about the same age I imagine my dad would be. Maybe it's because my mom says Dad was one of those people who was brimming with potential but who could never slip out from under addiction's thumb pinning him down, but it makes me grateful that I get to see *someone* who did. Someone who made it.

"Sorry," he says, scratching his beard, "for dumping my sobriety story on you."

"I don't mind hearing it at all. It's something to be proud of."

He shrugs and tugs at his ear, hurtling me into whatever place that is where we experience *déjà vu*. I do that, too, when I'm feeling self-conscious. Tom's hand drops from his ear, and I'm yanked back to the present.

"Mind my asking how you ended up in academics?" he says, picking at his work-hardened hands. He catches a cuticle and tears it sharply. A thin streak of blood wells to the surface.

Blinking away, I ease back on the bench and draw in a deep breath. "I was good at math in school, and I was pretty much obsessed with how successful businesses operated, how people got rich, and how wealth worked."

"Why was that?"

"I grew up without much. When I learned there were formulas to apply, logical steps I could take so I wouldn't have to live how I'd grown up, it appealed to me for obvious reasons. And then I realized I could *teach* people, help them learn about it, too." I shrug. "Just sort of went from there."

"So you . . . didn't have much growing up. Yet you got here? How?"

"Classic underdog story. Hustled. Took under-the-table jobs. Worked my ass off. Had enough smarts to snag some scholarships. Met a woman way out of my league who, for some reason, wanted me, who believed in my goals and supported every one of them. And now here I am, on the cusp of a huge success, with all my baggage about to drag me down and pull us apart before I can even share it with her."

Well. That last bit wasn't supposed to come out.

Tom frowns. "Your baggage . . . You mean your past."

"I've always been really fixated on work and climbing the ladder here. People can say I'm just living as a slave to my past, that I'm caught up in some toxic capitalist lie that you're nothing if you don't earn, but those people can kiss my ass, because they have *not* known what I've known, and neither has my wife. And it's going to stay that way."

Tom clears his throat. He peers over at me, then away. "I'm sorry . . . I'm sorry it was hard when you were young, that it's bled into your adult life. I—" He scrubs his beard. "That's damn unfair."

Self-consciousness tugs at me. I just verbally vomited on the janitor. I just cornered him on a bench, while I was brimming with anxiety, then blabbed about my childhood. I stare down at my fingers, tugging and knotting them between my knees. "That's okay."

"No," he says firmly. "It's not. But you can't change it. You can just move forward as best you can and tell yourself you'll give your kid better." After a beat he says, "You got any kids? Not yet, do I remember right?"

I shake my head. "We've been trying, but I've been having a tough time—"

Christ. I almost said it. What is *wrong* with me? Even though I didn't finish my sentence, it shouldn't be difficult for Tom to intuit what I meant. A flush of embarrassment heats my cheeks.

Tom tips his head, and as the sun jumps out from behind the heavy clouds, I see the faint outline of his eyes through his dark lenses. But before I can process what they look like, he peers down.

After a quiet moment, Tom says, "You talked to your wife about it?"

"Freya?" I shake my head. "Hell no."

Tom laughs faintly. "Can't say I blame you. But, uh . . . sorry, if this is overstepping, it's more common than you think. It's just part of life. So maybe she should—Freya," he says, like he's trying out her name. "She should know."

I stare down at my feet. "Yeah. She should." Sighing, I rake a hand through my hair. "We're about to go on vacation with all of her family, though, and she's pretty desperate to keep up appearances in front of them, doesn't want to worry her parents since it's their celebration. So now's not a good time."

Who're you kidding? There'll never be a good time.

Tom tugs his ball cap down as the sun grows even brighter and bathes us in hot, glaring light. "That sounds stressful."

"It will be."

"Just flying itself." He shudders. "I hate those tin-can death traps."

I peer over at him. "Yeah. That's . . . how I feel."

"But you're going," he says. "For her."

"I'm going, yes. For her. And I do like her family. I love them, actually. They feel as close to family as I'll ever get."

"Because it's just you and your mom?"

I glance up at him, a prick of unease tingling along my neck.

Easy, Aiden. Your anxiety's high. And when it is, you're suspicious and jumpy.

But I still ask, "How do you know I don't have siblings or a dad in the picture?"

Tom shrugs, then glances away. "You don't have any pictures in your office besides your wife and your mother. Not that I'm looking, but I do clean in there, you know. And I read between the lines. That underdog story has 'deadbeat dad' written all over it."

My stomach drops. "That obvious, huh?"

Tom stands abruptly, glancing at his wristwatch. "Shit. Lost track of the time. Gotta clock in." Thermos in one hand, Igloo in the other, he turns as if he's going to leave, but then he stops and turns back my way. "I didn't mean offense when I said that. When I said it was *obvious*, I meant it's clear that you had the odds stacked against you, because the man who should have been there for you wasn't. *Obvious*, as in, you've achieved incredible things despite struggling against the quicksand of poverty and a rough start in life."

My throat tightens. "Oh. Well . . . thanks."

"Your old man failed you," Tom says, staring down at his work boots. "That caused you to struggle. Which is wrong. But . . . well, if it means anything to you, I'd say you can be sure he's somewhere struggling, too."

"Can't say I care, Tom."

He nods, like he was expecting that. "Yeah, and I don't blame you. He's paying his penance now, though. Mark my words."

I join Tom in standing, slipping my hands into my pockets. We're almost the same height. I have maybe an inch on him. He keeps his eyes down, shifts with his cooler and thermos. "How so?" I ask.

"Because he's spent every day since he hit the road missing out on you. He's got to live with the consequences of his choices. He didn't get to see you grow up or take pride in how great you turned out or witness how strong you are. He won't get to recognize himself in you or meet your wife or hold his grandbabies."

"That's only fair, I'd say."

"Yeah," Tom says. "Me too."

Then without another word, he touches his ball cap in goodbye, turns, and walks off.

I stare after him, feeling weird and unsettled. I've told the janitor more about my current predicament than I've told my own wife. What does that say about me? What am I doing?

I turn toward my building, pissed at myself, when my phone buzzes. Extracting it from my pocket, I peer down at the screen. A text from Dan:

That investor who's been sniffing around
asked for the full deck of slides. Fingers
crossed. She might be it.

I quickly answer him, and when I close out of my messages, I'm left with my background photo. Freya, head tipped to the sun, wide smile, her wavy blonde hair wild in the breeze.

I grasp my phone and the sight of my once-happy wife. I hold it over the pendant beneath my shirt. A promise and hope, clutched to my chest.

TWELVE

Aiden

Playlist: "Begin Again," Nick Mulvey

Jesus, keep me strong. First my mother in my house, then hurtling three thousand miles in an airborne tin can over the fathomless depths of the Pacific Ocean.

I barely slept last night, thinking about it. I'm going to need the world's longest nap when we touch down.

"So where's the cat food again?" Mom says. She frowns between Horseradish and Pickles, who meow and twine around her legs. "Hi, babies." She bends and scratches Pickles. "Relish. Aren't you cute."

Freya smiles like she's not remotely concerned my mom can't remember these cats' names to save her life. "I'll show you, Marie," she says. "I went too fast through everything, I'm sorry."

Mom tugs her sweater tighter as she straightens. "That's okay. A second walk-through sounds good, though."

"Thanks, Frey," I say distractedly, rechecking our suitcases.

Freya's hand lands softly on Mom's shoulder, guiding my mother ahead of her. "Right, Marie, so here's the list of the daily routine, and here are our neighbors Mark and Jim's number if you have any problems . . ."

They drift down the hallway toward the office, where we keep the cat supplies, my mom asking which house is Jim and Mark's again. I sigh.

Mom doesn't have the greatest memory. I keep track of her finances since she started slipping up on her bills, which was also when Freya and I gently asked her if we could please pay her rent so she could retire. She said *hell no*. And that led to a massive fight after I told her the request was not a request, because my mother was not cleaning houses and breaking her body one more day after Freya and I realized we could afford to make retirement possible for her. Even if it made things tighter. Even if it meant more hustling to be where *we* needed to be financially. I owe my mother everything. Paying her rent so she can ease up on her tired body and spare her scattered mind is the least I want to do for her.

She was pretty pissed at first, but now she only acts mildly annoyed with me when Freya and I make the hour drive north once a month. We help her clean, sort through mail and odds and ends that have accumulated, make sure everything around her place is taken care of and the landlord hasn't been blowing her off. Eventually, if her memory continues to decline, she'll need to move in with us. Or we'll have to find an assisted-living community she doesn't hate. Another thing I budget and save and work for.

I carry Mom with me all the time, and the worry that her memory is bad keeps me up at night sometimes. What if she leaves something on the burner? What if she forgets where she is when she's out running errands?

So on top of that constant concern, now I'm leaving her alone with said not-great memory in the keeping of the house that I've poured my blood, sweat, and tears into.

Deep breaths, Aiden. Deep breaths.

Down the hall, Mom laughs at something in the wake of Freya's murmur. Freya's bright laughter follows, and a shiver runs up my spine. She's laughed so little lately. I savor the sound the way I used to savor the rare hot fudge sundae Mom would let me get from McDonald's.

I still get myself a hot fudge sundae, on those days when it's all just too damn much. I sit and eat it in the car and remind myself how far I've come, every hurdle I've surmounted. I tell myself, if I made it through that, I can make it now, too.

"Well, kids," Mom says as they reenter the foyer, "I hope you have lots of fun. You work too hard, Aiden. A vacation is good for you."

"Ah, I'm okay. But I am looking forward to some time off."

I smile at Mom—bird bones, soft gray-green eyes, silvery hair cut sensibly to her chin—and accept her hug, gently wrapping my arms around her. She smells like fresh laundry and cinnamon mints, like always, and it makes a bittersweet wave of memories wash through me. The rare Sunday morning coloring at the table. The few times she had a good pay month and we got donuts, then went shopping for clothes that fit and sneakers that made me feel like I was walking on a cloud. I clung to those bright moments between so many nights watching her from behind the crack in my bedroom door with a view to the kitchen, where she stood, head hung, shoulders shaking in silent sobs.

I was seven the first time I caught her crying like that. And that's when I swore the moment I could, I'd make life better. For her. And me. For anyone I ever loved.

"You two go on," Mom says, shooing us. "Get out of here. Mustard and Relish and I will hold down the fort."

Freya smiles as she lifts the handle of her suitcase. "Right kind of food, Marie, but they're Horseradish and Pickles."

"Whatever." Mom waves her hand. "Cats are dumb as doornails. They'll know I'm feeding them and scooping their shit."

I massage the bridge of my nose.

"Thanks again," Freya says, hugging her goodbye. "Remember, the list is on the fridge, and there's a copy in our room. Fresh sheets are on the bed, and please help yourself to any and everything."

Mom nods. "Great. I've got the male strippers coming at ten, and I'll make sure to buy lots of on-demand porn."

My hand drops. "Mother!"

She laughs and slaps her knee. "Just trying to loosen you up." Bringing her hands to my shoulders, she squeezes them as her eyes search mine. Her fingers drift up to my face and comb through my beard, which for some reason, I still haven't gotten rid of since Washington.

"What is it?" I ask.

She shakes her head. "You look like him with this," she says quietly.

Disgust rolls through me. I hate that I've already deduced I look like him. I look nothing like my mom. But still, I never want to hear that there's anything like my dad in me. As usual, she reads between the lines.

"I said you *look* like him, that's all, Aiden. He was very handsome. You think I would have gone for anything less than a hunk? I was hot stuff in my day."

Freya's eyes crinkle with a deep smile. "You still are. I have no idea why you don't date, Marie."

Mom doesn't answer her as she stares at me, hands cupping my face, until she says, "Love you. Be safe."

I bring a hand to rest over hers. "I will. Love you, too."

Pulling her close, I hug my mom hard, until she starts grumbling and pushes away. When I let go, she dabs her eyes and shoos us out.

Freya, of course, hugs and kisses the cats goodbye, too, before we're off, bags in the car, windows down, a mellow playlist she made meeting the breeze. Not needing to save face in front of my mom, Freya's warmth fades like the sun behind thick, gray clouds. She leans against the car door, staring out the window in chilly silence.

I grip the wheel harder, take a deep breath, and drive.

It's beautiful here. So beautiful, it almost justifies nearly dying for five hours on a plane.

Okay, I wasn't *actually* nearly dying, but I could have been for how miserable I was. I'm way too well read in plane crash statistics and mortality rates, which pretty much takes the fun out of flying first class. I triple-checked Freya's seat belt, made sure all our emergency necessities were identified, and asked her if she was okay upwards of five times.

But Freya knows me. Even still clearly pissed, she answered me patiently every time, even humored me with a detailed breakdown of what to do in case of an emergency so I could be confident we wouldn't be *that* couple who didn't know our floaties' location when the plane started nose-diving into the Pacific.

She also packed a book, which she extracted and disappeared behind. I shoved one of those donut pillows around my neck, tugged my sunglasses down, and told myself to try to sleep, which I didn't, of course. I closed my eyes and visualized calming things for about four seconds before I thought about that one part of the app's interface that felt glitchy and I didn't tell Dan about. Dammit.

After a quiet deplaning and ride to the house, I stand, showering off the plane ride—because I'm me, and I'm a germaphobe—enjoying a beachfront view of this breathtaking place from our bathroom. Swaying palms. Turquoise waves. Pale, golden sand, and a sapphire-blue sky that stretches low and rich against the ocean. I take a deep breath, only to feel it rush out of me when Freya walks into the bathroom.

She's wearing a red cover-up that pops against her lightly tanned skin. It's short enough to earn my immediate interest but opaque enough to drive my mind wild with possibilities of what's beneath. I want to slip that flimsy fabric off her shoulders and watch it travel down her decadent curves. I want to squeeze her soft, round ass and rub myself against her, remind Freya what she does to me, how desperate she makes me to be inside her, to feel as close as possible.

But I can't. Because I'm terrified that as soon as I get underway, the swarm of thoughts and worries will crowd my brain, draining my body of that hungry edge that makes me reach for her, that makes my body hard and desperate.

And even if I wanted to, Dr. Dietrich said no sex.

There are other ways than your cock to make your wife scream in ecstasy, Aiden.

Oh, there are. And I want to use every single one of them. But nothing about Freya's body says, *Seduce me*, right now. It says, *Touch me, and you'll lose a nut.*

My gaze drifts up her body and freezes. She must have put it in before we left, but it's the first that I've noticed. She's wearing her septum ring again. She took it out a few weeks ago, mumbling something about being taken seriously for the promotion she was up for. I mourned it, because with that delicate silver nose ring, her short, messy waves, and gorgeous face, she looked hot and badass and beautiful. She looked like Freya. And when she slipped it off, it felt like she was setting aside the part of herself that made her happiest. The free-spirited, karaoke-belting, no-bullshit woman inside her.

Now the ring's back in. And I wonder if that part of her she's felt she had to subdue is back, too. I hope so.

Freya finishes rubbing in sunblock across her face and notices me staring at her. Our eyes meet in the mirror. "See you out there," she says shortly.

Then she's gone. I drop my forehead to the shower stall and turn the water ice cold.

Dried off and in swim trunks, I head down the stairs and take in the place. I was single-mindedly focused on getting clean when we got here and didn't absorb too much about the house, but now

I can see it's stunning. Expansive yet homey, open windows and a cross-breeze. Cool white walls, dark-stained wood beams and floors. Fabrics and paintings in warm and inviting earth tones, midcentury furniture, bursting with luscious plants that have vibrant petals and glossy deep green leaves. I eye the massive caramel-colored L-sofa longingly and soak up the quiet in here. I want a nap. But I should go be social on the shore. And I can always nap in the sun.

As I finish my inspection of the living room, I turn toward the open-concept dining room and kitchen area, starting to make my way, when a long catcalling whistle pierces the air.

I freeze, then slowly glance over my shoulder.

There's a parrot in a dark corner at the far end of the living room that I somehow missed, dancing side to side on its bar. A *big* green parrot that cocks its head sharply and stares at me.

I glance around, waiting for one of the Bergmans to jump out and laugh at their funny prank. *Ha-ha. Let's freak out Aiden with the catcalling parrot.*

This bird doesn't really come with the house, does it? If it does, I feel like someone should have told me an oversize, objectifying parrot lives here.

"Dat ass," it squawks.

My eyebrows shoot up. "Excuse me?"

Swiveling its head, the parrot lays down a beat, then says, "Pussy tight, hit it right—"

Holy shit.

I start toward it, not sure exactly what I can do, as it just keeps going.

"—Booty slappin', make it happen—"

I clap my hands at it. "You can't say that here. This is a-a-a family vacation."

The parrot does not care. "Make it cream, pussy supreme, love it, lick it, make me scream!"

"Hey!" I'm close enough that the parrot startles at my next clap, then cocks its head before giving me another long whistle.

I set my hands on my hips. "Honestly."

"Hey, hot stuff," it squawks.

"Hey yourself," I say. "No more . . . of whatever that was, okay?"

The parrot ruffles its wings, then spins on the bar, so its back is to me. At least it's quiet.

Turning, I head toward the side of the house that leads to the beach. I'm almost at the door when the parrot says, "Tight-ass," followed by a cackle.

I take the moral high ground and shut the door behind me.

All of Hawaii's beaches are public property, making this luxury around me feel somewhat less overwhelming. As I walk toward the Bergmans, I see kids playing nearby in the surf, another family not too far off laughing and building a sandcastle.

And the Bergmans fit right into that domestic picture. Ziggy reads under an umbrella she's sharing with Axel, both of them stretched out on chaises and wearing T-shirts and shorts. Ren's behind Frankie, rubbing sunscreen on her back and saying something in her ear that makes her laugh.

My in-laws wave from over their shoulders, chairs wedged into the soft sand as the waves lap at their legs. I wave back. A few chairs are vacant, so I wander down and drape my towel over one of them. "Has anyone else talked to the parrot?" I ask.

They all glance up at me.

Ziggy smiles and lowers her book. "Yep. She was so cute—said, '*Hiya, toots!*'"

"Really? Huh." Dropping into the chair, I crack open my water bottle and take a long drink.

Ren tips his head. "Esmerelda was pretty quiet when I was in the kitchen earlier. Tyler said she's on the old side and tends to sleep a lot. I called him because I was concerned she'd fly away with the windows open, but he said we don't have to worry, she's a homebody."

"My kind of gal," Frankie says.

Ren rubs in her sunblock and squeezes her shoulders affectionately. "Why do you ask? Did she say something funny?"

Apparently I'm the only one who got harassed by *Esmerelda*. I'm keeping that to myself unless I hear otherwise. "Just curious."

"Gotcha," he says. "Good flight?"

"As good as flights can be."

He squints against the sun and grins. "Yeah, figured you'd say that."

"Thank you," I say, swallowing my pride. "That was incredibly generous, Ren."

He blushes tomato red, and peers down at Frankie, who's smiling at him over her shoulder.

"Aw," she says. "You made Zenzero blush."

Zenzero is Italian for *ginger* and Frankie's nickname for him, given Ren's copper hair. Playfully glaring at her, Ren blushes deeper, then clears his throat before he directs himself to me. "You're welcome. It's . . . I honestly think what professional athletes make is unconscionable. Paying for flights made my bank account feel less offensive."

Frankie snorts and pats his thigh. "I don't get it. Load me up. Call me Scrooge. Then again, I grew up in a shoebox in Queens, wearing hand-me-downs and extreme couponing."

Something eases inside me hearing that, knowing I'm not the only one who grew up without much. Frankie gives me a sharp stare. "I get a very Alexander Hamilton vibe from you, Aiden."

"Don't you dare start singing it," Ren says. "Not until Oliver's here. It would crush him."

Frankie laughs. "I would never. That kid's more obsessed than me. Now's not the time anyway. I'm having a heart-to-heart with Ocean Eyes, here."

"Hey." Ren pokes her side. "No compliments to the studly brother-in-law. Or heart-to-hearts."

"Relax, Zenzero," she says affectionately, glancing up at Ren. "He's got great eyes, but as you know, I'm a sucker for redheads." Turning back to me, she says, "So am I right?"

"Yep. I grew up similarly, and I have no plans to live that way again."

Saying it out loud feels liberating. Generally, I tiptoe around my childhood with the Bergmans, not because I'm ashamed, but because it's such a marked contrast to their lives, and, well, nobody wants to be the poor kid at Christmas sitting around saying, *Hey, this is the stuff of movies I watched and only ever dreamed of having. I can't believe I'm sitting here, having a real celebratory feast!*

It's a buzzkill. Especially when my mom refuses to come. She orders Chinese at her apartment and watches Christmas movies and swears she couldn't be happier. I still force a morning-of-Christmas-Eve visit on her, which I can tell she privately enjoys.

"I knew it," Frankie says, shaking me out of my thoughts. "I'm the same way. I mean, I don't plan on hoarding if I'm ever filthy rich, but it's nice not to have to worry about money."

"Absolutely," I tell her. "If I'm ever loaded, I won't sit on it and not share, but I won't mind having a fat bottom line."

She raises her water bottle. "Cheers to that."

Ren smiles between us, then glances around. "Where's Freya?"

"I don't know." I peer around, too. "Where's . . . the rest of your siblings?"

"Present and accounted for," Viggo says from somewhere over my shoulder.

I startle in my chair. "Jesus. Will you ever make a normal entrance?"

"Pff." Viggo plops onto the seat next to me. "Where's the fun in that?"

When I turn back, Ren's rubbing zinc oxide onto the bridge of his nose.

Viggo snorts a laugh. "You do know you could try not staying paper white, right, Ren?"

Ren arches a russet eyebrow. "Does this look like skin that ever sees the sun?"

"No," we all say.

Frankie grabs the big tube of open sunblock and squirts it in her hands. "Don't listen to them, Zenzero." She rubs the sunblock between her hands, turning and straddling the chaise as she smiles at him. "You need sunblock. Lots. All over you."

Ren laughs as she slathers it down his chest and pushes him back on the chaise.

"Ugh," Oliver says, startling me just as badly as Viggo. Goddammit, these two. "We always knew he'd be like this once he had a girlfriend, but geez. Get a room!" he says through cupped hands.

Frankie flips him the bird. "Public beach, bitches. Avert your eyes if you don't like what you see."

Oliver grumbles to himself, then steals my water bottle and chugs half of it.

"You know, Ollie," I tell him, "you could actually drink your own beverage one of these days."

He does this. Constantly. Nabs a bite of food from your plate, tastes your wine. Chugs your water if he's been running around and your glass happens to be there.

Oliver gives me a *What are you smoking?* look. "You try being the bottom of five brothers and see if you don't form survival tactics. If I didn't eat or drink other people's sustenance, I didn't get any."

"Oh, please," Viggo says, rolling his eyes. "I'm twelve whopping months older than you and I'm not a kleptomaniac with other people's food."

"You were always twelve months developmentally ahead of me, too," Oliver argues. "Just that little bit bigger and better."

Viggo smirks. "And that still holds today. Just that little bit *bigger*. And *better*."

Oliver glares at him. "Yeah. That's what I was doing. Comparing dicks."

"Okay." I throw my hands up. "I'm not sitting in the crosshairs of your incessant sibling spat. Don't you two ever just relax and get along?"

They both look at me like I have four heads, then say, "No."

All right, then. I open my book, the romance novel Viggo gave me, hidden in my lap, and change the subject. "Where's Ryder?"

And my wife?

"Arriving tomorrow morning," Viggo says, adjusting his chair so he's reclined farther and opening his own book, which features half-naked people entwined on the cover. "Willa wasn't going to be back from a traveling game until this evening. She told Ryder to go ahead but he said—" Viggo drops his voice and tries for sounding like his brother, "'*No way. I don't come until you come.*' Which is generally a very good principle for a relationship," he says, turning the page of his book.

"Come on," Oliver says. "Choreographed orgasms are the stuff of your bullshit romance novels."

"You watch your mouth!" Viggo snaps, and sits upright. "Sometimes, yes, romance has reinforced unrealistic expectations of sexual intimacy and pleasure—*however*," he says, making big, *I'm saying something important* eyes at us. "At least it's put on the page. At

least it foregrounds human intimacy and sexual freedom and passion, not just staring into the abyss, waxing philosophical about
our inevitable mortality."

"Here we go." Oliver sighs.

Viggo is undeterred. "Romance is about the centrality of loving
relationships, and it reminds us that human connection is vital to
existence, rather than glorifying egoism or violence or greed. So
excuse my genre for not being perfect, but let's back the fuck up
from hypocritically critiquing books that have done a lot more for
humanity than slashers and circle-jerk, five-hundred-page, nihilis-
tic tomes."

A slow clap echoes from behind us, snapping my attention over
my shoulder. And then my mouth falls open. Because Freya's unty-
ing her red wrap, and then it's fluttering to her feet by my chair, and
then she's walking—no, strutting—in a tiny red bikini, straight
down to the water.

THIRTEEN

Freya

Playlist: "Breakaway," Lennon Stella

The water's perfect, but the feeling of Aiden's eyes on me makes it even better.

Try jumping off that *for your stupid phone.*

I dive beneath a wave, feeling the ocean wrap me in that magnificent silence that greets you when you're underwater. It's so peaceful, so quiet beneath the waves, and for as long as my lungs can take it, I let myself hang below the water's surface, feeling the rhythm of a fresh wave crashing down.

Then a strong arm is drawing me up, crushing me to a hard, solid chest.

"Freya!" Aiden's voice is raw, his eyes searching me wildly as I gasp in surprise. "Holy *shit*! Don't do that."

I gape at him. "Wha—"

He kisses me. Hard. Frantically. "Holy shit," he mutters, crushing me to him again. His arms are so tight around me, I can barely breathe. "You scared me, Freya. You didn't come up."

"I was just enjoying the water," I whisper against his shoulder, reeling from his intensity. Tenderly, his hands drift along my arms, as if he's reassuring himself I'm really there. Then he cradles my head against his chest, where I feel his heart pounding. "I'm okay, Aiden."

"I'm not," he says honestly.

For just a moment, I bask in his attention, his concern, the urgency in his touch. I bite my lip, remembering the warmth of his mouth on mine. But then the water slaps between us, snapping me out of it. I pull back the little that I can in his tight grip, hating how easily I respond to his touch.

Aiden still holds me close, everything soft of mine crushed against the hard planes of him. I look away, trying to numb myself to how good it feels. "I didn't mean to scare you," I tell him. "I didn't even think you'd notice."

"Not notice," he mutters, cupping my jaw and tipping back my head until our eyes lock. "Freya, of course I did."

I swallow slowly as his thumb slides along my throat.

"Of course I did," he whispers. His eyes are as aqua blue as the ocean waves around us, sparkling under the sun, and not for the first time do I notice how mesmerizing they are, how beautiful he is. Sometimes I wish I wasn't so attracted to him, that when I met his eyes, I wasn't swept into their turquoise depths, that I didn't fall deep and just keep falling.

Aiden exhales slowly, steadying himself. "I'm sorry I mauled your face. It was half CPR, half *Oh, thank fuck you're alive.*"

Before I can answer, his head whips sharply toward an incoming wave. In unspoken understanding we fill our lungs with air, then drop under the water together as it crashes overhead. The sounds of the ocean wrap around us as Aiden holds me close, and when the wave clears, we rush to the surface.

Our chests bump, then our noses, as we're both thrown off-balance and clasping each other to steady ourselves. Steady again, I squint against the sun and the saltwater on my lashes as Aiden peers down at me. His thumbs wipe beneath my eyes gently, his body warm against mine.

I start to pull away again, but he stops me, hands wrapping around my shoulders. "Freya."

"Aiden."

He swallows roughly. "I'm sorry. The other night, when I answered my phone was . . . I feel terrible. I'm sorry."

Pushing off the sand, we swim through a building wave and let it roll past us to shore. "So you've said."

"But clearly you're still angry."

And hurt. Embarrassed. Humiliated.

"Well, Aiden, you took a call when my shirt was halfway off and I was about to orgasm on the kitchen counter, so, yeah, not great for self-esteem."

"Freya, I said I was sorry, and I meant it. That had *nothing* to do with your desirability."

I laugh emptily. "Okay. Except your actions didn't say that. They haven't for months. It's one thing to tell me that your sex drive is affected, but does your sex drive include hugs, Aiden? A real warm hug? A kiss good night? Just a little bit of affection and honesty? That's all I wanted. I didn't need to be ravished, but I don't think the most basic sense of being the woman you want was too much to ask for."

He sighs, running his hand over his mouth and beard. I stare at him, this man who somehow looks everything and nothing like the person I married.

How does this happen? How do you swear your life to someone, knowing you'll both change? How do you promise each other *'til death do us part* and *happily ever after*, knowing that more marriages end than survive?

You tell yourself you're different. *We're* different.

But we're not. We're just Freya and Aiden, floating in the Pacific, with no damn clue how our story will end. And I hate it. I hate not knowing. I hate wanting him and fearing what will happen if I give in. I'm so tired down to my bones, tired of hurting and existing in this ambiguous, shitty marital purgatory.

As if he senses my readiness to bolt, Aiden gently tugs me through the water until it's deeper, and the waves are rolling instead of crashing toward the shore.

His eyes search mine. "Freya, I messed up. Work got away from me. I let it suck me in too far. I admit that. And I have a knee-jerk response to my phone going off because I worry I'll miss something time-sensitive from Dan for the app. It was not at all about not wanting you. Though I hear you. I understand what you're saying. That my behavior didn't demonstrate that. That it hasn't in too long. And I'm sorry."

I roll onto my back and float gently now that we're in a calmer part of the water. Aiden's eyes dart down my body, and he swallows roughly. I barely bite back a smile of vengeful satisfaction. "I already accepted your apology."

"But I'm still suffering the consequences."

God, men really don't get it sometimes. They want apologies to wipe away the pain. But pain takes time to heal. You can forgive *and* hurt as you recover from the wound.

"Guess so," I tell him. "And your penance continues tomorrow."

"What's tomorrow?" he asks warily.

"The boys have plans for you guys, soon as Willa and Ryder get in."

He groans. "Oh no."

"Oh yes."

"Dammit," he mutters, dunking under the water, then coming back up.

My eyes traitorously drift to Aiden, to water sluicing down his hard chest, as the sea breeze wraps around us and his flat, dark nipples tighten. It reminds me of how he shudders when my tongue traces them, when my hand drifts down his stomach—

The water rolls beneath me like an admonition. *Snap out of it.*

"You could always not join them," I tell him, making sure my tone comes across even and unaffected. "I'm sure you have work to do."

"Can you let up on the jabs about work, Freya? Christ."

I give him an icy sidelong glance. "You're right. Whyever did I think you'd plan on working?"

His left eye twitches. Telltale for when I really get to him. He presses a finger to it. "I told Dan I'd be available sparingly."

"*Sparingly*," I repeat skeptically. "Hm. Well, as long as you wear a smile around my parents, that's all I need."

"I wasn't planning on being privately miserable," he says testily. *Makes one of us.*

I shut my eyes and focus on floating. "No. I assumed you were planning on being privately busy. Working."

He sighs. "You're seriously holding this over me?"

I stop floating, dropping into the water as I glare up at him. "*Holding* this over you? Your tendency for work to eclipse every other part of your life, including your wife? The work that constantly preoccupies you, that vastly contributed to our marriage imploding because you kept it to yourself and kept me out of it? Oh man. You're right. What am I thinking, 'holding this over you'?"

Aiden stares down at the water, his face tight, eyes lowered. And a stab of empathy cuts through me.

"Aiden, as I've said, while it hurts, I understand why you didn't talk about your anxiety, how it affected our intimate life. You were coming to grips with it yourself. But this shit with your work and success? No, Aiden. It's prideful and egoic, and I don't have time for it. What you did the other night just cements its priority in your life."

He opens his mouth, but we're interrupted by Viggo hollering from the sand. "Pickup! Get over here!"

Not waiting for Aiden's response, I swim away and catch a wave in.

When I walk up the sand toward my parents, my mom squints up from beneath her straw hat and smiles. "What do you think of the water?" she asks.

"It's great. Have you gone in?"

"We have." Dad pats her thigh affectionately. "And she only dunked me twice."

Mom's smile deepens as she picks up her book. "You deserved it."

Dad slides his sunglasses onto his head, glancing over his shoulder to where my brothers and Ziggy are setting up for pickup soccer. "You going to show those punks how the old folks play, Freya?"

"Excuse me! Old folks?"

Dad laughs as I ruffle his hair in retribution.

"Freya!" Ziggy yells. "No goalies, right?"

I wrinkle my nose. "Of course not."

The guys all throw their hands up in protest.

"One-on-one, winner decides if we play goalies," Oliver calls, crooking his finger at me in challenge.

I point to my chest. "Who? Me? Are you sure? This hardly seems fair. I'm quite old and delicate these days."

Oliver flashes a cocky smile. "Which is why we'll have this settled nice and quick."

Viggo massages his forehead. "Shouldn't have said that."

"Yep," Ren says. "She's gonna whoop your butt now."

Axel slides his shades down onto his nose and sets his hands behind his head. "And I'm going to enjoy watching."

I rush toward Oliver and pull the ball off him, but soon he's right on my tail. He's twelve years younger than me, in prime fitness, plays soccer at UCLA, so I'm probably not going to win, but confidence sometimes goes a long way, and for a moment, I have him scrambling, trying unsuccessfully to gain possession.

"Geez, Frey!" He laughs when I throw a hip. "Like that, is it?"

I laugh, too, as I spin, then go for a shot, which he blocks with his foot. When Oliver pulls the ball back and tries for a shot himself, I turn and take his shot straight to the ass, sending all of them into hysterics, including Oliver. Which makes it easy to steal the ball, then kick it right through the makeshift goal.

Ziggy squeals as she runs at me, throwing her arms around my neck. "My heroine! No goalies!"

"Of course there's no keeps," a new voice says.

I jolt, turning to face Aiden, and feel my knees go wobbly.

He stands, the sun behind him, casting his tall frame in sharp backlit shadow. He tips his head and shakes water out of his ear, making all the muscles in his torso flex and bunch. I barely swallow a hum as my eyes trail his body.

Strong but not shredded. Solid and heavy and hard. Round shoulders, big pecs, water glistening down his taut stomach and dark hair arrowing beneath his swim shorts' waistband. A rush of air leaves me as my eyes wander down and lock on the thick outline of him inside his wet swim trunks, plastered to his muscular thighs—

Dammit. I'm angry at him. And I am on the longest no-sex streak I've been on for the better part of a decade. It is not a nice combination.

Aiden's eyes meet mine and flicker like he knows what I'm thinking. I shut my eyes as he walks right by me toward my brothers.

I will not look over my shoulder and check out his ass.

I will not look over my shoulder and—

I look and bite my lip as I stare. Aiden says he's hardly had time for working out, but it's very obvious he hasn't been skipping deadlifts.

At all.

Ziggy clears her throat.

"What?" I blurt out.

She smiles. "I didn't say anything."

"Right. Okay. C'mon, Zigs. Let's show those boys how to play."

I glance over at Aiden, my stomach twisting when he smiles at something Ren says. It jars my memory, reminding me of when we used to play on a co-ed soccer team, when Aiden and I would make a date out of it.

Riding in the car, we'd sing along to each other's playlists. Then when we were there, we'd watch each other in a sea of other people, high on that fizzy delight of observing your person out in the wild, realizing how much you liked them and wanted them, how special they were to you, how much you knew about them that no one else did.

I'd watch his bright smile, the deep groove of a dimple bracketing his mouth, as he offered someone that easy charm that lights up a room. I'd notice as he shifted his weight and his big thighs flexed. My eyes would travel and settle on his bright blue eyes and the kindness in his face. And I'd want him. So deeply, from the core of my body to my fingertips. I'd want him with my heart and my body and this inexplicable thing I still can't name except belonging. Undeniable, soul-deep belonging.

That same fierce sensation coils inside me as I watch him chugging water, giving Viggo shit about the width of the makeshift goals.

And my stomach does this unsettling flip-flop, like it did the first time I saw him, staring at me across the field. He was tall and lanky and beautiful, almost too beautiful. An angular face that I felt like I could stare at for lifetimes and still not fully appreciate. Thick dark lashes, those vivid blue eyes pinning me. It felt like a strike of lightning, straight down my spine, and I looked away, terrified. No one had ever made me feel that.

Just how he did twelve years ago, Aiden glances my way and

holds my gaze for a long moment. Electricity zips through me as his eyes flick down my body once, hungrily, like he can't help himself, before he turns back to the guys, tossing his water bottle aside.

"Look at you, muscles," Oliver says, poking Aiden's round bicep. "What's Freya been feeding you?"

Aiden grabs his towel and brings it to his hair, rubbing it fiercely. "Feeding me?" he says, running his hands through his hair to fix it as he tosses the towel aside. "I cook most nights. Freya's the breadwinner now."

Surprise jolts me. The last thing I expected in all his I-must-work-to-provide urgency would be for him to announce that I now make more than him, especially in front of my father and brothers.

Our eyes lock. His smile is tentative yet brimming with pride. My heart twists sharply.

"Freya Linn!" Dad yells from his chair. "Why didn't I know this?"

I blush and drag my foot through the sand. "I don't know. It's no big deal."

"It's a big deal!" Mom says, beaming at me. "Congratulations, Freya. Champagne with dinner tonight, to celebrate."

"Thanks, Mom." Turning back to my brothers, I say, "Now can I kick your asses at soccer?"

Ziggy scoops up the ball and juggles, before sending it to Viggo. "I'm with Frey. Let's play ball."

Decades of playing for most of us has us splitting intuitively across our sandy field—Viggo joining Ziggy and me against Ren, Aiden, and Oliver, which is pretty fair. Axel sets himself in the middle. He'll play a central position and switch to offense with whatever team has possession, to even it up.

Frankie presses a button on her phone, making a whistle noise for kickoff.

And it becomes clear very quickly that Aiden's either feeling extra sporty or looking for a brawl, because immediately he's there, hands on my waist, fighting me for possession. His intensity, the heat of his body hard on mine, feels like coming full circle. Just like the first time we met, he's on my ass.

Literally.

And now I'm reminded how much he can piss me off when we're playing on opposite teams. We're much, *much* better when we're on the same side, going after the same goal.

"You're awfully handsy," I tell him.

"It's called defense," he says, reaching for the ball.

"Some of us manage to play defense without groping others," I mutter. "Kissing me like that in the ocean, now this. I should break your glasses again." Spinning, I try to cut around him.

But Aiden's faster than he once was, or maybe he's stronger, or maybe I'm slower, or maybe we're just so connected in that odd way long-term couples are that he anticipates my every move. His hands grip my waist, and for just a moment, I want to lean into him, to feel every bit of his big body snug against mine.

"It was a habit," he grunts when I throw my butt into his groin. "Sorry I'm used to kissing my wife."

"Because we've been kissing so much lately," I say sarcastically.

Aiden grips my hip harder. "I've been—"

"Working. Trust me, I remember."

His breath falls on my sweat-soaked skin, and the fiery snap of desire floods my body. I pass Ziggy the ball and take off, trying to get open for a give-and-go, but Aiden's still on me. "Dammit, Freya, I don't want to do this."

"Makes two of us."

The ball comes back my way, but Aiden steps in and takes it, dribbling along the sand. When I catch up with him and reach for the ball, Aiden passes it to Oliver before I can stop him.

Time slows as Aiden's eyes widen, and he grips me roughly. I watch fear play across his face, a hard determination in his eyes, before the world lurches forward at warp speed and he throws me behind him.

And then I watch my husband take a close-range power strike straight to the nuts.

FOURTEEN

Aiden

Playlist: "Varieties of Exile," Beirut

Holy God. My balls.

"Aiden!" Freya drops next to me. At least I think it's Freya, based on the sound of her voice and the familiar, summertime scent of her skin. I can't see for shit. Having my nuts murdered by a soccer ball has blinded me.

"Damn, Aiden." That's Oliver. "I'm so sorry, man." He sounds *zero* percent sorry. "I was in beast mode and got all turned around. I wasn't even shooting at the goal. I'm just glad I didn't hurt Freya. Thankfully, you protected her."

I crack open an eye, glaring at him, before my gaze travels over the brothers and suspicion dawns. They didn't do it . . . on purpose, did they?

But then I think back to the moment that Viggo interrupted us when Freya and I were in the ocean, when I was about to lose my cool and dig myself deeper in our argument. Now this . . .

Shit. They're meddling again. Or, as I'm sure they think of it, helping. Helping crush my balls. At this rate, Freya and I will be lucky if we can ever have kids.

Freya's hands slip through my hair. "You stepped in front of me."

"You sound surprised," I wheeze as my eyes lock on hers.

She doesn't say anything, and I won't lie, that crushes me. She should never doubt that I'd put myself between her and anything that could hurt her.

What if that anything *hurting her is* you?

The truth seeps in, a poison that shoots straight to my heart and makes it seize. I feel sick.

Freya runs her fingers through my hair again, smoothing it off my forehead, looking at me how she hasn't in so long. She looks like she almost took me for a stranger, and now she's second-guessing herself. As if finally, she's seeing *me* again.

Ten seconds ago I'd say nothing would make this pain worth it, but now I know that's wrong. I'd take a nut-shot a thousand times for this moment all over again, to see just a sliver of recognition in her eyes.

Viggo smirks over Freya's shoulder. I take a deep centering breath as dread sours my stomach. Because if this is how this week is going to go, and this is the Bergman brothers just getting started, I'm honestly scared of how it's going to end.

My eyes crack open to faint violet light pouring through the billowing curtains before they shut again. For a second, I'm not sure where I am. The bed feels different, but I could swear Horseradish or Pickles is kneading my chest with their paws—a light, alternating pressure walking up my ribs.

"Hey, hot stuff," the parrot squawks.

My eyes snap open. She ruffles her feathers and lays a beat, swaying her head.

"Esmerelda," I hiss. "Don't even—"

"Bounce on that dick! But first you gotta lick. Lick it gooood."

Freya moans in irritation and elbows me in her sleep. I sit up, making Esmerelda hop back and ruffle her feathers in annoyance.

"Asshole!" she squawks.

"*You're* the asshole," I whisper. "You're going to wake up Freya."

Suddenly the door to my bedroom bursts open. Esmerelda sees herself out, flying past Viggo, to whom she offers a polite, "Top o' the morning!"

I slump back on the bed and flip onto my stomach, burying my face under a pillow. Esmerelda *and* Viggo are too much to ask of anyone before they've had coffee.

"Is my sister naked?" he asks. "Knock twice on the headboard if I can open my eyes."

Before I can answer, my face drops to the mattress. I hear the thump of a pillow connecting with a human body.

"Oof," Viggo says.

Peering up, I see Freya's now burrowed under her pillow and blankets. Based on the bare space where my pillow was, she hit Viggo with *my* pillow.

How nice.

A second later, Freya starts snoring.

Viggo's eyes widen. "Is she *snoring*?"

"She's snored for years, since the last time she broke her nose at Sunday pickup soccer. If you even think about teasing her, I'll twist your nipple until you cry. She's self-conscious."

"Look at you," he says. "Very husbandly of you to defend her."

"Viggo," I mutter tiredly, "what are you doing here? And what the *hell* are you wearing?"

He flashes a smile and strikes a model pose, then another. "Bike shorts. Spandex. You like? I bought them right before the trip, and I'm obsessed. Breathable. Flexible. They're like a second skin."

I shudder as I shut my eyes. "I really didn't want to know that much about your anatomy."

"I understand if you're jealous. Bergmans are notoriously well endowed—"

"Viggo," I groan. "Shut up. And go away."

"I'm not going anywhere. This is your wake-up call for Brother Bonding Day. Let's go. Mush-mush, up you get."

I glare at him. "I don't remember agreeing to this."

"You did," he says.

"Nope. Definitely didn't."

"In spirit you did." He claps his hands quietly, rightly wary of waking Freya, who continues to snore beneath the blankets. "C'mon. The women have their own plans. Ryder and Willa got in about an hour ago, so Willa's sleeping, but Ryder's wide awake and grumpy as ever, so best not keep the mountain man waiting."

"I'm wide awake and grumpy, too," I mutter, scrubbing my face. The pillow connects with my head. I drop my hands and death-stare at Viggo. "There better be coffee."

He grins. "There is. Report to the kitchen in five. Coffee and granola bars provided."

Then he's gone, and I'm very tempted to flop back and burrow under the covers. But I don't. Because I'm sure Viggo would pull some retributive prank if I played hooky. And maybe, even more than that, I'm curious to see what these Bergman brothers have cooked up.

Easing out of bed, I pull on clothes quietly, then slip downstairs.

And twenty minutes later, I'm in a *very* uncomfortable position on the deck, feeling *very* positive this was not worth waking up for.

"Ow." My leg is not supposed to bend like that. Makanui, our visiting yoga instructor, heartily disagrees.

"Breathe," he reminds me, like it's not an autonomic process.

"Can't really help but keep doing that," I mutter, trying not to groan in pain.

Oliver glares at me, mid-*chaturanga*. "Aiden, I don't feel like you're invested in this. You're not the only one who would have liked to sleep in this morning, but you don't see me being a smart-ass, now do you?"

Makanui smiles at me calmly and pushes my leg farther. "Your pelvis is very tight," he says. "Breathe from your pelvis."

I stare up at this guy. "Um. What?"

"I think what he's inviting you to do," Ren offers, looking annoyingly serene, "is to connect your awareness of that part of your body to your breath. Often it helps us release tension and welcome our bodies into deeper openness and receptivity. Flexibility isn't just in the body, Aiden. It's in the soul."

What the actual *fuck*?

Makanui nods. "Exactly."

I know Ren and Frankie do their own yoga routine every morning, but come on. *Flexibility is in the soul?* Also, I cannot understand voluntarily starting your day suffering this kind of pain. I stare over pleadingly at Axel, who I feel like I can count on to call this for what it is—torture—but he's staring at the sunrise, hands behind his head, looking blissed. I would be, too, if Makanui wasn't giving me his undivided attention.

Makanui *tsks*. "Your neck, too. Breathe, Aiden. Breathe."

"I'm breathing!"

"Shh!" Ryder says, eyes shut. "For once I don't want to throttle a single one of you ass-hats. Let me enjoy it."

I frown at Ryder, surprised by his calm expression as he holds the pose Makanui showed us. The pose I stoutly said my body did not do.

Well. Makanui proved me (painfully) wrong.

Then there's Viggo and Oliver, shirtless and in their matching bike shorts, doing what appears to be a *chaturanga* competition, going through the motions of the flow Makanui showed us as fast as possible, in some frenetic, yoga-meets-push-up challenge.

"Aren't you concerned about those two?" I ask, hoping it'll get Makanui off my case.

He shakes his head. "Some men are still boys. They cannot be helped."

A laugh jumps out of me. "Fair enough."

After another moment, Makanui decides he's put me through enough. We transition to another flow sequence that I manage to get into, before we move on to a cooldown that's surprisingly relaxing. Lying on my back in *shavasana*, I peer at the glowing sunrise and take a deep breath. My heart isn't pounding, my thoughts don't feel like they're pinging around my pinball machine brain. And even though I know it won't last, for just a moment, I savor it—the rare quiet in my head, the heavy calm weighing my limbs to the deck.

Makanui invites us to sit up slowly and conclude.

Namaste.

I stand, running my hands through my hair and stretching my arms over my head. I feel loose everywhere, including my pelvis. It's one of those places I didn't realize held so much tension. But as I think about it, with a sick, sinking feeling in my stomach, I probably should have.

After saying our thanks to Makanui, we roll up our yoga mats.

"Good job, Aiden," Ren says, clapping me gently on the back. "You eventually got into it."

"Thanks. Wasn't so bad after a while. Well, okay, kids. This has been fun—"

"Whoa, whoa, whoa," Oliver says, wrapping an arm around my neck, which is so foul. He's dripping with sweat.

"Get off." I shove him away. "You're soaked."

"You thought you got to do yoga, then call it a day?" Viggo shakes his head and sighs. "Aiden. Aiden, Aiden, Aiden."

Ryder sips his water, unsuccessfully hiding a smile.

"What's going on?" I ask.

"We," Viggo says, turning and spinning me away from the house, "are on an *all-day* brother bonding adventure."

I stop in my tracks, causing a collision of Bergman brothers, domino-effect style.

"Idiots," Ax grumbles from the back. "I'm surrounded by idiots."

I turn and face them. "I'm not your brother. Don't you want to do this stuff, you know . . . without me?"

They all fold their arms across their chests and tip their heads the same direction. It's beyond weird. And also . . . shit, it's kind of endearing.

"So that right there," Oliver says, "is exactly why we need today."

Viggo pins me with his sharp stare. "Somewhere along the way, you forgot the day you became Freya's, you became ours, too."

Ah, man. My eyes blur with tears. I stare down at my feet and blink them away as I clear my throat.

"So to answer your question," Ryder says. "No. We don't want to do this without you."

Ren grins. "Today's for all six of us. Brother time."

"You're in this for good," Ax tells me. "You don't get to act like you're somehow outside this merry-fucking-go-round that is being a Bergman. If I have to deal with this madness, so do you."

And before I can say anything—not that I even know what I'd say, because words are stuck in my tear-thick throat—Viggo lets out an earsplitting Tarzan shriek and takes off along the wooded path beside the house.

A sigh of resignation leaves my chest. "I'm supposed to follow him, aren't I?"

"Yep," they all say.

After a moment's pause, I suck in a breath. And as my own Tarzan bellow leaves my lungs, I take off after him.

FIFTEEN

Aiden

Playlist: "Olympians," Andrew Bird

"Everything hurts," Oliver whines.

"Now you understand how I've been feeling since Makanui went at my groin like a drill sergeant." I throw a marshmallow at Oliver. It bounces off his chest, but he catches it and pops it in his mouth.

Chewing, then swallowing, Oliver cranes his neck and stares up as daylight fades, a watercolor sky painted in streaks of forget-me-not blue, tangerine, and lavender. "Sometimes hurting like hell is worth it, though," he says. "If it's the right kind of hurt. Like conditioning. That blows. But I wouldn't be game-ready, I wouldn't get better at soccer, if I didn't do sprints until I puke and lift weights regularly, which I will *always* hate."

"True that." Ryder lifts his thermos. "Well, except I like weights. And running. But to your point, yes, pain can have a purpose."

The flames pop and snap, drawing us close to the firepit, huddled against the impending darkness. As a sea breeze whips around us, I glance among the Bergman brothers. Axel, pensively staring into the fire. Ren, smiling as he crunches on a s'more. Ryder, lost in thought, poking the fire. Oliver, searching the sky. And Viggo, whose pale Bergman eyes are locked on me.

"How are *you* doing, Aiden?" he asks.

I ease back in my chair, propping one foot on my knee. "Sore as hell. Between mountain biking and the swim to our trust fall."

"I'm still mad about that," Oliver grumbles.

Viggo's mouth twitches as he fights a smile. "I got sidetracked. A bird made a noise, and you know how distractible I am."

"*Oh,* do I ever. So does my bruised ass, from dropping like a sack of potatoes to the ground instead of being caught." Oliver scowls. "I can't believe I entrusted this priceless body of soccer glory to you."

Ryder coughs a laugh into his arm, then straightens his expression. "Sorry. I'm sorry. Viggo, that was shitty."

Viggo's not paying attention. "I want to hear from Aiden."

One by one, their eyes fix on me.

"I told you, I'm sore. Otherwise, I'm . . . I'm fine. And, uh . . ." I glance away and swallow the unexpected emotion tightening my throat. "This has been a good day. So. Yeah. Thanks."

Ren leans forward and pats my knee. "Good. We love you, Aiden."

A brotherly echo of that wraps around me, making it impossible not to smile back at them. Ryder claps me on the back as Oliver spins in his chair, then sets his feet in my lap.

"Gross, man." I shove them off. "Too far."

Oliver howls. "I'm so sore! I just need somewhere to stretch my legs that won't burn the soles of my feet."

"The drama," Viggo says, rolling his eyes, but he traipses over and lifts Oliver's legs, then spins Ollie until his feet are resting on his thighs. "So let's talk strategy."

I blink at him. "Excuse me?"

The brothers exchange glances before Viggo starts ticking off fingers. "You were bickering in the ocean. Big no-no. You don't bicker with Freya when she's pissed. You let her get it all out."

My left eye twitches. I press a finger to it. "Please. Lecture me more about my wife of nearly ten years."

"Emphasis on *nearly*," he says. "Let's not get ahead of ourselves."

I contemplate how good it would feel to throttle him.

"Next." Viggo ticks off another finger. "You're still being an arrogant asshole who can't be taught. Has it ever occurred to you that maybe just because Freya put up with a certain dynamic for nine years, she was never *thrilled* about it? Maybe she just wants you to shut your yap and listen to her."

"Like a teakettle," Oliver says, as if imparting some deep wisdom, "instead of making it whistle, just lift the lid and let it . . . steam."

Ryder snorts.

"I think what Oliver means," Ren says diplomatically, "is that getting defensive with Freya when she has emotions and thoughts to voice isn't in your best interest. It'll backfire. Best to hear her out without arguing point by point."

"Yeah," Oliver says. "That."

Viggo gives his brothers a withering glare. "If I may? As the one guy here who spends a decent amount of time in books that are literally designed for men to understand the female romantic perspective."

The guys raise their hands.

"Nicholas Sparks has the microphone," Ryder says.

Viggo exhales deeply and shuts his eyes like he's trying to talk himself down from violence. His eyes snap open, then lock on me, piercing and pale. "Ollie's nut-shot seemed to earn you a few points, but clearly we need to work on something else. Something that makes her feel . . ."

"Loved," Ren offers. "Loved *by* you. Is there something special she doesn't get to do very often? Something meaningful that she hasn't done in a while, that you could offer as a gesture? It shows her you're thinking about her and what makes *her* feel loved, not *your* idea of showing love."

I drum my fingers on the armchair. "I took her on an ice cream date, just like our first date. She liked that."

Viggo nods. "Good, that's smart. Drawing parallels to when you fell in love. Great. So how'd it go?"

I deflate. "Oh. Well . . . Started off strong. Ended really badly."

Viggo sighs and buries his face in his hands.

"Okay, then it's too soon for another date," Ryder says. "She needs a buffer. Something to mentally wipe her RAM."

"Karaoke?" I offer. "She hasn't sung in a while."

They all suck in their breaths.

"Shit," Ryder exhales. "That's bad."

"Definitely bad," Axel says. "That woman never stops with her damn singing and humming. The humming!" Clearly, this is a grievance from childhood that I don't understand, because Axel looks like he's reliving torture. "If she's not singing, this is serious."

"You guys are not helping me feel better," I mutter.

Viggo shakes his head. "Not our job. Our job is to help you not botch this any more than you have. Let's circle back. I need to know where you are mentally. How's the book reading going?"

I swallow nervously. "You mean the one you gave me?"

"Yes," he says, sounding like he's calling on the patience of a saint. "The book I gave you. The one where the guy's fucking up epically by compartmentalizing his feelings and expecting his wife's intimacy in return."

"Um." Feeling my cheeks heat slightly, I glance around. "It's . . . good. So far."

Viggo nods. "Go on."

"What is this, a book report?"

"Easy," Ryder says. "He's just trying to help."

True, but the pressure and expectation that weighed me down the night Viggo hurled the book my way suddenly feels like it's collapsing my chest.

Of all people, Axel breaks in at the most unexpected time and buys me a reprieve. "I'm reading another one of hers, actually."

Viggo blinks at Axel like he's short-circuiting. "I'm sorry, you're what? You actually read it?"

"You keep shoving them in my suitcase every time I visit. What else am I supposed to do, open a romance bookshop in Seattle?" Ax sniffs and picks at his nails. "I started one about a guy who's a workaholic. Aiden should read that one."

I narrow my eyes. "Thanks for the brotherly love."

"Just saying, you'd probably pick up some tips. So far I've learned he believes himself incapable of love, but the author's begun foreshadowing that he *says* he's incapable of love because he actually faced a previous painful rejection and thus heads off anyone else having the opportunity to make him feel unlovable again."

Well, shit. My chest tightens as I try to take a deep breath. Axel's words bring back the cutting pain I felt when Freya told me to leave, the panic that gripped me when she stormed out of the house not long ago. Isn't that what everyone feels? Fear of being left? Unloved?

Not everyone's father left them. Not everyone's questioned how lovable they are if their own flesh and blood couldn't be bothered to stick around.

Maybe I will read that book Axel has. After I survive the one I'm reading currently.

Ryder sips from his thermos and frowns in thought. "So how does he learn his lesson? How does he grow? That's the point of a story, right—how the character evolves?"

"I haven't read it, but knowing it's a romance, I'd guess that he learns his lesson as he falls in love," Ren says, handing Ryder a s'more.

"Hey." Oliver pouts. "I want a s'more, too."

Ren smiles. "I'm coming, Ollie."

"So." Ryder nudges Axel. "What Ren said, is that what happens?"

"I haven't gotten that far," Ax says. "But I imagine it'll have something to do with a woman showing up and infiltrating his brain until all he does is think about her, worry about her, draw her, dream about her, until he's miserable and his tidy plans to enjoy a long, uneventful bachelorhood are completely upended." Axel stares into the fire and mutters darkly, "In other words, rampant chaos ensues."

A thick, heavy silence hangs between the brothers as they trade glances around Axel.

Until Ren cheerily says, "But at least it's rampant *romantic* chaos."

Viggo blinks at his oldest brother in bewilderment. "Axel. I'm so proud of you."

"I'm chucking that book in the fire," Ax grumbles.

"Excuse me!" Viggo bellows.

"No," Axel says, more to himself than anyone else. "I'll give it to Aiden. That's a better call. He needs it."

"Sounds like *you* need it," Ryder mutters.

Axel says nothing as he stares into the fire.

Then Viggo's attention is back on me. "Well. We got all the emotion Ax is willing to part with for the month. So back to you, Aiden."

"I'm going to be honest, I'm not too far in."

"Read. It," Viggo says. "Because so far, you're not inspiring my optimism."

Oliver crunches on his fresh s'more. "Freya's low. Like, really low. What'd you do before you guys left? She's worse than she was at the restaurant."

Shame slithers through my veins. I rub my forehead. "I fucked up."

"No shit," Ryder says around his own s'more. "But *how*?"

"For the love of God, no graphic details," Axel warns.

I don't know if it's because I'm exhausted from how active we've been for the past twelve hours, being forced into weird bonding shit all day with them, or because after talking to this many people this long, my filter's simply shot, but I blurt out the truth. "I was pretty well into seducing her. Then my phone blew up, and I took the message."

Their jaws drop.

Oliver squirms. "Ew. I don't want to picture that. Ew. Ew."

Viggo smacks him upside the head. "Get out of middle school, Oliver. Jesus."

"You took a *phone* call," Ren says, horror painting his face, "while you were . . . Christ, Aiden! That's—"

"Horrible," Ryder says, blinking at me in disbelief.

Axel shakes his head, his mouth a grim slash of disapproval.

"I said I was sorry," I mutter miserably. "Many times."

"Yeah." Viggo sighs, rubbing his temples. "So, *sorry* isn't going to fix that one, and you know it. Women need to be *shown* they're desirable. You made her feel like second best. You put her in an incredibly vulnerable position, and then you abandoned her."

"I didn't abandon her," I say defensively. "Freya knows I find her desirable."

"How?" Ren asks. "Not by what you did. And that's what counts."

He's right. I just have no idea what else to do except not do it again.

"Seriously," Viggo says, snapping me out of my thoughts. "Why are we telling you this, when you literally helped me plan my first date, when you gave Ren the courage to ask his high school crush to senior prom? What happened to you? You're thirty-six years old. You've given all of us insight into romantic gestures and dating."

"Not me," Axel points out, like this is a badge of honor.

I glare at him.

"Aiden's expertise is seduction," Ryder explains. "He could charm the panties off a nun. That's what he taught us. Groveling, however, is not in his repertoire."

Viggo rounds on me, eyes narrowing. "Wait. *Wait.*" He leans in. "Holy shit. You've never groveled."

My cheeks heat.

"How?" Oliver asks. "How have you never groveled?"

"Because before Freya, no one was worth groveling for," I mumble.

Ryder bats his eyelashes. "*Awww.*"

"I'm going to punch you in the dick," I tell him.

Viggo ignores us. "Okay. You need to grovel. Legitimately *grovel*. I can't believe I'm honestly spending my Hawaiian vacation saving your sorry ass."

"I didn't ask for your help! In fact, I remember explicitly saying just a few weeks ago how much I *didn't* want your help. Yet here we are."

"Focus," Viggo says, clapping his hands and disregarding me. "First things first. From now on, Aiden, your phone does not stay in the same room as Freya when you're—" He shudders. "When you're together like that."

"But with my work—"

"Aiden," Ren says, leaning, elbows on knees. "I think we all understand better now how pressing your work is for you at the moment. We didn't get that before, and I can only imagine that trying to develop whatever this business venture is, while your marriage is strained is . . . well, a lot. Too much. So for now, you're going to have to make a choice: devote your energy to making it up to Freya or keep trying to hedge your bets, dividing your time."

"And I think we've seen how well that's been going," Ryder says, raising his eyebrows.

Axel shifts and peers at me. "You have a partner in this, don't you? That guy who was blowing up your phone at Ren's. Why can't he cover for you for a week?"

My legs start bouncing nervously. Theoretically, Dan *could*. But . . . what if he messed up something while I was off the grid? What if everything I've worked for is ruined?

"If you trust this guy enough to collaborate," Ryder says like he's read my thoughts, "you would think you'd trust him not to implode your work while you're unavailable for a few days. In fact, I seem to remember this very rationale being used in a highly manipulative situation when you were Willa's and my professor."

"Wait, what?" Oliver asks.

Ryder shakes his head at me. "He said business partners need to be tight, trusting, and on the same page, then used that to force Willa and me into a team-building outing, also known as 'the waterfall hike that shall live in infamy.' I had blue balls for fucking *months* after that."

Ren frowns. "But wasn't that a good day? Didn't you realize you were falling for her after that trip?"

Ryder gives Ren a sidelong glance. "Yes," he says slowly. "But that's not my point."

"Why don't you get to that, then," Axel says flatly, rubbing his eyes like he's about done with this circus. That would make two of us.

"My *point*," Ryder says tersely, "was that Aiden preaches the gospel of trusting business partnerships, and unless he wants to expose himself as a giant fucking hypocrite, he better take his own advice, trust his partner, and focus the rest of this vacation on his crumbling marriage instead of micromanaging the business venture he's working on."

"Damn," Oliver says.

I hate that he's right. I clutch my phone in my pocket.

Viggo's gaze tracks my movement, then narrows. His fingers drum on his sides. "Okay. So we're agreed. Aiden needs to lose the phone. Grovel to Freya. And keep reading that romance," he says directly to me. "Think long and hard about what she's trying to get through your thick skull."

"Long and hard." Oliver smirks. "And thick. Heh. That's the perk of a romance novel, all right."

Ren coughs as his cheeks pink. Ryder snorts.

"Wait, what?" I ask. "What are you talking about?"

Ax sighs. "Book boners, dude."

"Book *what*?"

A book? Could make me *hard*? What is this sorcery?

Viggo douses the fire. "You'll see, Aiden. Just keep reading, and you'll see."

Ryder swears suddenly, staring at his phone.

"What?" we all ask.

He flattens his phone against his chest and clears his throat, a hint of pink on his cheeks above his beard. "Nothing. I mean, it's something, but none of you are seeing it."

Ren wrinkles his nose. "What are you talking about?"

"You're so naïve," Viggo says. "She sent him a nudie."

Ryder neither confirms nor denies. "The women are getting massages," he says, fingers tapping his phone. "Then grabbing drinks and a late dinner. I think we should clean up, then get ready to crash a ladies' night out."

I groan. I'm so damn tired, the thought of going out sounds miserable. Bright lights, crowded space, loud music . . .

Wait.

A light bulb goes off, and I dive for my phone.

"What are you doing?" Oliver asks.

My internet search turns up two places with karaoke, but only one with a live band. Freya will love it. I AirDrop it to Ryder's phone, and his eyebrows rise as he opens his browser. "Look at you, Aiden."

I can picture it. The smile on her face when she sings, the way her cheeks flush and her skin glows and she just comes alive. Even if I'm only a fly on the wall, out of her sight watching her sing, seeing her happy will be enough.

Viggo cranes and reads my phone. "Karaoke? You're sending them there?" He pats my cheek. "See, you're not entirely hopeless."

I shove off his hand. "Thanks a lot."

"Telling Willa now," Ryder says, thumbs flying. "She'll make sure they get there."

Ren sets a hand on my shoulder in reassurance. "You've got this. Time for grand gesture number one."

They all smile my way. Then I realize what they're suggesting.

I am *not* singing in front of an entire restaurant. I have a decent voice. I can play guitar okay. But I am not making an ass out of myself in front of a hundred strangers.

"Guys. No."

Viggo grabs me by the front of the shirt and hoists me up. "Groveling, Aiden. Yes."

SIXTEEN

Freya

Playlist: "Rolling in the Deep," The Ukuleles

An ungodly groan rolls out of Willa through her face cushion on the massage table.

"Hey," Frankie grumbles. "Some of us like getting massaged without your animal noises."

Willa laughs. "Sorry. I'm. So. Sore. I can't help it."

"Get Ryder to give you massages," I tell her.

"Heh." Willa sighs audibly as her massage therapist glides his hands up her oil-slicked back. "Ryder's why I'm so sore."

Now it's my turn to groan.

Frankie cackles. "If I could high-five you right now, I would."

"I want a new room," Ziggy mumbles into her face cushion. "A quiet one. And could you please do it harder?" she asks her therapist. "Just brutalize my muscles, and then hands off when you switch things. Light touch is uncomfortable for me."

Her therapist nods. "Absolutely."

I have a tiny moment of pride in Ziggy because I couldn't see her having done that just a few months ago. But now she's getting more confident in voicing her sensory needs, whether it's how to be touched in a massage or explaining what she needs for a group outing to work for her.

"Whereas you?" Frankie says to her therapist.

The therapist working her shoulders smiles wryly, as if there's some shared joke between the two of them. "Keep my hands off your hips," he says, "or be prepared for some involuntary blasphemous swearing."

Frankie sighs in contentment as he slides his hands up her neck. "You're the best."

"How's *yours* feeling?" my therapist asks gently.

"Fine, thank you," I tell her. "Just keep doing what you're doing, please."

After finishing our evening massages, we shower off and slip into comfy sundresses, then catch an Uber to a late dinner and drinks. Mellow and relaxed, I'm looking forward to winding down with authentic Hawaiian food and a good cocktail, enjoying a beachfront view.

"I feel so loose," Ziggy says, waving her limbs like Gumby as we walk up to the restaurant.

Willa laughs.

"I'm starving," Frankie says. "I need a burger in me, then bed. I know I got a nap, but kayaking took it out of me."

"The sun took it out of me," I tell them. "I feel radioactive."

Ziggy tests her nose. "Yeah. I got sunburned."

We went for a kayak and snorkel trip this morning because it was something we were all interested in and wasn't too hard on Frankie's body. Then we came back, napped—well, everyone else napped; I read more *Persuasion* and soaked up the late-afternoon sun—before we packed bags for our evening massages and girls' night out.

It was a strategic effort on the siblings' part to—*ahem*—give our parents the house to themselves for most of the day. It is their anniversary vacation after all.

I glance out at the restaurant's tall copper torches burning in the night, listening to the roar of the ocean. There's a sensual, unending warmth to the air here. And something about the island—whether the kindness of its people, the abundance of natural beauty, the constant pouring sunshine and breathtaking ocean—makes me feel alive, hopeful.

And now? Firelight and crashing waves, shadows and warm, sultry air, I can't deny it's also incredibly romantic. Of course, Aiden and I are here at the low point in our marriage.

Sigh.

"So," Frankie says, setting her cane between her legs and stretching her arms along the back of her chair. "Let's talk about the elephant in the room."

Ziggy peers up from her Kindle. "What elephant?" She glances around. "Oh. Proverbial elephant. Got it. I'm listening."

Willa sets her elbows on her knees and tips her head, caramel curls dancing in the sea breeze, eyes tight with concern. Frankie frowns softly, focused on me, too, and nerves tighten my stomach. It's one thing to have told my best friend, Mai, who knows all my dirt, but it's another to open up to these women who only know the tough-big-sister, has-all-her-shit-together Freya.

"Hey," Willa says gently, setting her hand on mine and squeezing. "No pressure. You tell us when and how is best for you."

"How about alcohol?" Frankie says, raising a hand for a server.

"Not too much," Ziggy says, eyes back on her Kindle. "After a massage you sweat a lot, so you need to rehydrate. Two glasses of water to one alcoholic beverage."

"Ugh," Frankie says. "Kids these days. So responsible."

Ziggy smiles, still reading, and doesn't say anything else.

"Yeah," I admit. "I'm going to need a drink for this."

Frankie summons service remarkably quickly with one crook of her finger and a magnetic look she gives a helpless server, making sure we get some food ordered, too. Within a few short minutes, we're clinking mai tais and Ziggy's lemonade. Settling deeper into our low, comfy chairs around a similarly low, circular table, we stretch out our legs and collectively sigh in contentment.

"All right," I say after a long drink of mai tai. "Aiden and I are in a pretty rough patch. I'm leaving Mom and Dad out of it for now, so please keep this between us and my brothers. I didn't want to put a damper on my parents' celebration."

Ziggy glances up. "Are you guys going to be okay?"

I take another sip of my mai tai. "I don't know, Ziggy."

It was one thing to sense abstractly, over the months, how distracted Aiden was by work. It was another, that night in the kitchen, to viscerally experience being rejected because of it. His emotional absence has been painful. But his thoughtless presence hurt even worse. And that wound keeps festering.

"Sorry," I mutter, dabbing my eyes.

Willa sets her hand on my back. "I don't have anything to say that will fix what you're going through. But just know, I think you're brave and badass. I have so much admiration for the work it takes to sustain long-term partnerships. Since I met you, I've looked up to you and your marriage to Aiden, and that hasn't changed, knowing this. If anything, I admire you even more."

"Thank you," I tell her. "That 'work' of long-term relationships, as you said, I think I'm just wrapping my head around how deep that runs. It's not just compromising about where you buy a house or how much you spend on takeout. I thought it was surface-level work if you found the right person. Because I grew up seeing my parents' happiness and assuming it was effortless. Does that make sense? And that held water—being with Aiden felt effortless, or at least like happy work, the good kind, for a long time. Until . . . until it wasn't. Now it's just hard. All of it."

Frankie says, "Obviously, I haven't known you or Aiden for

long, but Ren told me that when they were at the cabin, he'd never seen Aiden so dejected. As someone whose personal stuff came between them and the person they love, I can speak to the fact that sometimes people do a crap job of showing how much the people they love mean to them. Not an excuse, just a reminder. I think your husband loves you deeply. But I hope he'll do a better job of showing you. You deserve better."

"Thanks, Frankie," I whisper.

Ziggy reaches over and hugs me hard. "Hang in there, Frey. I love you."

I squeeze her back, swallowing a knot of tears in my throat as we pull away. "Thank you. Love you, too."

"These men," Frankie mutters around her straw. "Making us fall in love with them. Ruining our grand plans for spinsterhood. Troublemakers."

It makes me laugh.

"Good thing he has an amazing dong," Willa says.

"Ay!" Ziggy claps her hands over her ears. "Stop it. Yuck."

"Party foul," I groan. Making a face, I suck down a lot more mai tai.

"My apologies," Willa says. "Okay, no more boy talk. Now it's time to get drunk and do karaoke."

"What?" My eyes widen. "Karaoke?"

Frankie tips her head and sips her mai tai. "A little birdie named Aiden told us you adore live karaoke."

My heart pinches. "He told you that?"

"Well, he told Ryder to tell me," Willa says. "And I told Frankie and Ziggy. And then I strong-armed them into coming here. So, in a roundabout way, yes."

I glance over nervously at the band setting up, the microphone, waiting for someone to rip it out of the stand and fill it with their voice. The Freya who'd dash up there and belt anything feels like a ghost from a former life. Realizing that, sadness tugs at the edges of my heart.

"I haven't sung in . . . months. Haven't karaoked in *years*."

"Well, let's fix that," Willa says. "Starting with a round of shots."

Ziggy sighs and draws up her knees. "At least I brought my Kindle."

―――

When Ryder was little, he was fascinated with wildlife. We'd go to the library, and he'd make me read book after book about monkeys, livestock, butterflies, and birds. I learned about mating patterns and migration, about which animal was the largest *this* and which was the smallest *that*. I learned so much, reading to him. But what I remember most vividly was learning about animals' instincts to move toward safety before humans have the slightest clue that catastrophe is coming.

There's no hard science to prove it, but the theory is that animals feel the earth's vibrations before an earthquake is even underway, that when pressure systems shift and violent storms are coming, they sense it in the air, and so they seek shelter and higher ground. I thought that was incredible—the wisdom of animals to anticipate calamity before dumb old humans have an inkling their world is about to be inverted.

But tonight, right now, I feel like one of those animals—my senses honed, my perception heightened. Maybe it's because I'm that perfect level of tipsy, before words get mushed and limbs become lazy. I'm calm yet aware, relaxed but focused. And something in the air shifts as I sip my drink and watch the band finish setting up.

"Whoa," Ziggy says, lowering her Kindle. "I didn't catch that they had a *live* band. That's so much better than those prerecorded versions." After a beat, she mutters, "The drummer's kind of hot."

Frankie wiggles her eyebrows. "Into bad boys, are we?"

Ziggy blushes spectacularly. "I think I like tattoos."

"You're a woman," Willa says sagely. "Of course you like tattoos. It's in our DNA."

"Huh?" Ziggy wrinkles her nose. "How?"

"I mean—" Willa sips her mai tai. "Not *literally*. I'm stretching the truth because Rooney's not here to give me hell for scientific inaccuracy, but it's . . ." She turns pleadingly to Frankie.

"She means," Frankie says, "that you're not the first woman to look at a guy like that and feel hot and bothered. Guys with tatts emit a certain sense of danger and intensity. And there's an animal part of our brains that likes that. Though, I will say, don't judge a book by its cover. Often the roughest-looking ones are secretly big softies." She grins and swirls her cocktail straw. "And the strait-laced good boys are the ones you have to watch out for."

I bite my lip to swallow my emphatic agreement. I don't want to scar Ziggy. But I vividly remember the first time Aiden and I had sex, how shocked I was as this impeccably polite, not-a-wrinkle-in-his-clothes PhD nerd flipped me over on the mattress, threw my leg over his shoulder, and whispered the filthiest thing I'd ever heard from a lover.

It was the hardest come of my life so far. After that, there was no looking back.

Ziggy narrows her eyes. "Is this . . . Are we talking about . . ."

Frankie's sinister grin deepens.

"Oh my gosh." Ziggy sinks lower in her chair and lifts her Kindle. "I'm gonna puke."

"Harsh, Frankie," Willa says.

"What? I was subtle. You're the one who said her brother had a big schlong!"

Ziggy stands and drops the Kindle on her chair. "I'm going to the restroom to splash off my face, which is on fire because you two somehow have less of a filter than me. And when I come back, no further references will be made to my brothers' anatomy, not anymore."

"S-sorry, Ziggy," Willa says, trying to hold back a laugh.

Frankie salutes her. "Aye, aye, Captain."

My awareness of Willa and Frankie's conversation fades as my gaze travels the open restaurant. Nighttime turns the world magical, with glowing lights and copper-domed tiki torches. The air feels warmer, sweeter, full of heat and night-blooming flowers, and when the bassist strikes an experimental chord, a frisson of excitement rolls up my spine.

It's loud and the threat of feedback whistles through the speakers briefly before it cuts out. The bassist glances up and smiles apologetically as people startle. "Sorry about that, folks."

He looks around the space as he sets down his bass and switches over to a ukulele that he tests, too, before his eyes stop on me. Another jolt of awareness travels my body. An echo of something I haven't felt directed my way in months—pure, animal interest.

Hi, he mouths.

I give him a polite, closemouthed smile back, before I glance away and focus on my poke bowl.

"Someone brave enough to come help us check the balance against a voice?" he asks in the mic.

Willa nails me with her knee. "He's staring at you. Go on. Go for it."

I sip my mai tai. "No."

"Why not?" Frankie asks.

"That guy's staring at me like I'm dinner. I don't feel like being the main meal."

"Ah, he's harmless," Willa says. "You said yourself you haven't sung or done karaoke in so long. Singing makes you *happy*, Freya. So, get that joy, ignore the flirt, and open the set!"

The guy strikes a sultry chord. "No one?" he says. "Not even a pretty blonde in a blood-red sundress?"

Heat floods my cheeks. I tuck a hand over my forehead like a visor, shielding me. "I told you this dress was a bad idea."

Willa wiggles her eyebrows. "And I told you that dress was the *best* idea. Red is sinful on you."

"It's the neckline. The tatas," Frankie says, making a chef's kiss. "*Magnifique!*"

"I'm murdering you both after this," I mutter before I drop my hand and meet the guy's eyes again.

He grins triumphantly, changing his strum to a well-known love song.

Men. The subtlety of a bull in a china shop.

"There she is," he says.

I stand and sweep up my cocktail, then wend my way to the front.

When I'm close, the guy steps around the mic and smiles at me. He's about my height, and closer up, I have to admit he's handsome. Eyebrow piercing. Sharp hazel eyes. Deep bronze skin and dark hair spun into a bun at the nape of his neck. Tatts winding up his right arm.

I set my mai tai on the closest table with my left hand. My ring catches the light, drawing his eye.

He sighs. "The good ones are always hitched."

A smile leaves me, now that I know we're in more comfortable territory. "Was I badgered up here for my marital status, or did I give you a *she's-got-pipes* vibe?"

He laughs. "I was hopeful on the first count and confident on the second. Name's Marc."

"Hi, Marc. Freya. What's it going to be?"

"What do you sing?" he asks, strumming and taking a step back.

"Anything, really."

"Hm." He bites his lip. "Your voice is smoky. Alto?"

"Not trying to brag, but my voice goes where I want. So don't worry about me."

He laughs, throwing his head back. "Shit, I'm in trouble. Okay, Adele," he says, winking at me as he takes the ukulele into a fast strum. "You ready?"

"Yep."

As he kicks up his volume and repeats the intro, I grab the mic, fill my lungs, and hit the first note, warm and rich as sunlight pouring from my throat. Tears prick my eyes as I feel the power in my voice. It's an earthquake in my chest, a warning that shakes me from the core of my body outward.

Never forget me like this again.

How did I let it slip away? How did I become so numb that I buried this need to sing like the need to breathe, the need to *feel*?

I know, in some corner of my mind, that I numbed my feelings when I numbed my pain. Because you can't pick which emotions you feel—you're in touch with them and you experience them or you're not and you don't. And I chose numbness to survive the pain of my marriage.

Not anymore. My heart—its depth and wildness—isn't meant to be buried. It's meant to power my life. To fuel my work, my relationships, my pursuit of joy. And I reclaim that power as each note punches through my lungs and carries through the space around me. I make myself a promise: I won't abandon myself like this again. I will never again deny a vital part of who I am.

As Marc ramps up the tempo, then joins me in a harmony, the rest of the band comes in. I close my eyes and belt out the chorus. For the first time in too long, I feel alive.

Wildly, beautifully alive.

SEVENTEEN

Freya

Playlist: "Whole Wide World (Unpeeled),"
Cage the Elephant

Buzzing with adrenaline, I plop back into my chair, breathless and sweaty. I feel like the pilot light inside me is burning once again, hot and incandescent, as I sigh with relief.

"That was *incredible*," Willa says, sliding a fresh cocktail my way.

I pluck the hibiscus flower from it, licking the stem clean before I nestle it behind my ear. "Thank you. It *felt* incredible."

"You killed it, sis."

Recognizing my youngest brother's voice, I automatically reply, "Thanks, Ollie." Then I do a double take to the long-limbed blond standing next to me. "*Ollie?*"

My head snaps up, my focus widening like a panoramic zoom as I take in two broad figures leaning against the column next to our table. Ryder. Ren.

I glance behind me. Axel. To my right. Viggo. He grins. "Hiya, sis."

"Hi," I say carefully, peering between all of them. "What are you guys doing here?"

Oliver leans past me and nabs a bite of smoked pork. "Heard there was live band karaoke."

"So we figured we'd pop by," Viggo says.

I glance at Ren. Pure of heart, terrible at lying. But he's in a stare-down with Frankie, whose tongue is doing things to her mai tai straw that make even *me* blush.

Ryder's impossible to read. Axel, too. Dammit.

"Where's Aiden?" I ask.

Ax lifts a hand from his pocket and points toward the karaoke band. "There."

My head snaps to the front so fast, something in my neck pops, then burns.

Holy. Shit.

Aiden's taking an electric guitar from Marc, torchlight painting his dark hair with flecks of gold, slipping down his strong profile. Short-sleeved button-ups have never *ever* looked good on a single soul except for him, and tonight is no exception. It's a cambric blue, one of my favorites because it makes his vibrant ocean-blue eyes even bluer. Soft and worn, it's cuffed casually and strains against his arm muscles as he lifts the strap and slides it over his shoulder.

Khaki shorts. Long, tan legs speckled with dark hair. I remember their feel, brushing against mine in bed last night, the zip of longing that shot through me when he turned and sighed in his sleep.

When his fingers slide down the frets, I cross my legs against the ache between them.

I'm drunk. That has to be it.

"I'm seeing things," I mutter.

"Why do you say that?" Ryder asks casually. Somewhere in my silent freak-out as I spotted Aiden, Ryder ended up next to Willa on her chair, his finger toying idly with one of her curls.

"Because Aiden can lecture in front of eleven thousand people about progressive business practices and microloans, but the last time I tried to drag him up to sing karaoke with me, he practically crawled out of his skin. He's self-conscious, performing in front of other people."

Even though he has a beautiful voice. And when he plays guitar, I feel like I see a part of him that only comes out when we share music.

Viggo rests his butt on the back of my chair and fixes the hibiscus in my hair. "When did that happen?"

I swallow, my eyes dancing to the front of the room, where Aiden stands with his back to us, talking to the band. "Years ago."

"Hm," Viggo says. "That's a long time. Maybe he's overcome that fear."

"Or maybe—" Oliver looks up from my poke bowl, which he stole, and takes another bite. "Maybe he still *does* get stage fright, and he's a nervous wreck, but he's doing it anyway."

"Why would he do that?"

Viggo tips his head. "I wonder."

The low rhythmic chords to a song I know that I know but don't yet recognize cut through the air. I peer up just as Aiden's voice hits the microphone, and our eyes meet, two live wires once again connected, arcing in a band of surging current. The visceral sensation that I can *feel* Aiden again—his nerves, his intensity, his *love*—bursts, white hot and crackling, a straight shot through that connection rocketing beneath my skin.

He has a beautiful voice—rich and low, a little gravelly. When we dated and were first married, he used to fool around on his guitar, and we'd sing for hours. When we had no money to go out, just a fixer-upper falling down around us, two rescue cats, and all the time in the world for the two of us, we'd get projects done, then sit in the backyard, overrun with wildflowers and a lemon tree dripping with sunshine-yellow fruit.

I made so much lemonade, we got sores in our mouths.

And Aiden sang this song.

I recognize it as the drummer comes in, my heart pounding just as hard and fast. Aiden's eyes hold mine as he strums and plays from memory. And when he hits the chorus, singing a promise that nothing will stop him from finding the woman he loves, I feel the earth tip beneath me.

Everything but Aiden disappears. The world becomes soft and unfocused, a blur of night sky and warm wind and torchlight. Each breath I take is hot and sharp, tinged with tears. It feels like the pain of what's broken slowly knitting back together. It hurts like the first tender, terrifying step toward healing.

Aiden's eyes still hold mine as the softest smile tips his mouth.

I smile back. And a small bud of hope blossoms in my chest.

The song's done, but it reverberates through my body as Aiden's eyes remain locked with mine, even when he lifts the guitar strap from his shoulder and hands it to Marc. Faced with a dense gathering of people who've clustered to be close to the band, a few women leaning toward him in interest, Aiden glances down only momentarily to sidestep them. I hope they see the thick wedding band on his hand. I hope they know he's *mine*.

Mine. The intensity of my response unnerves me, and my stomach swoops as a memory fills my thoughts: the saleswoman ignoring me, shamelessly flirting with him. While he was *wedding band* shopping. Because everyone flirts with Aiden. It's my cross to bear, marrying a charming, beautiful man.

"What can I help you find today?" she'd asked.

She batted her eyelashes and leaned on the jewelry display. But Aiden was staring at the bands beneath the glass. He didn't look up once, his hand holding mine, thumb sliding in slow circles around my palm. A habit that soothed him as much as me.

"Something," he'd said, "that screams '*taken.*'"

He chose a wide, flat band. A band that my eyes find now, brushed white gold, stark against his tan, work-worn skin, flashing in the warm lights as Aiden's fingers glide through his hair, pushing sweat-soaked waves off his forehead. From here I can see his hands are shaking.

He was nervous to sing in front of all those people. But he did it anyway. For me.

"You pressured him," I tell Viggo, even though my eyes hold Aiden's.

At the edge of my vision, I see Viggo lift his hands. "He's the one who went up there—"

"But you told him he should. You all did, I'm sure." Protectiveness wooshes through me. I want to grab my brothers and knock their hard heads together until they finally listen to me when I say to keep their noses out of my business. "He doesn't have to make himself sick to his stomach to show me what I mean to him."

Viggo folds his arms and glowers. "No one *made* him do anything."

I don't answer him. I watch Aiden, whose eyes hold mine as he makes his way toward me, knifing through the crowd, which dies down when Marc hits the ukulele and picks up a reggae tune. My heart thunders in time with the drummer as Aiden draws closer like a big cat stalking through the jungle grass. And when he's only a few feet away, I shoot out of my chair, take an instinctive step back, prepared for him to crash down on me.

Except as he does, it's gentle, tempered. A wave built to a daunting height that breaks unexpectedly into a soft, lulling crest.

"Freya," he says quietly. Rough, unsteady hands cup my face as his body brushes against mine. The softest kiss sweeps over my lips, warm and gentle, the whisper of mint leaves and rum. It's reverent. Careful. Like our first kiss, which I still remember because he kissed me like he couldn't believe it was happening.

Tears spring to my eyes as I clasp my hands over his, then slide my touch along his forearms. Aiden slowly walks us back into the shadows. Glossy dark leaves whisper over my skin as he presses me against a column hidden from eyes and tiki lights. It's cooler in the moonlight, and I shiver.

"Why did you do that?" I whisper. "You hate singing in front of people."

His hands drift down my neck, his thumb softly tracing my throat. A shower of sparks bursts inside me. "It's called grand gesturing. And groveling."

A surprised laugh jumps out of me. "What?"

"Music speaks to you, Freya. It makes you feel. And it's something we used to share, a way we connected. I wanted . . . I wanted to show you what you mean to me. I wanted you to *feel* that again."

"I did," I whisper. "I did feel it."

Aiden steals another soft kiss, then pulls away, his expression growing serious. "Yesterday, you said something that was hard to hear. But . . . I needed to hear it. That my actions haven't shown you that I desire you, for too long. I hate that I haven't shown you what you mean to me, Freya. I've been trying, but in *my* way, I realized, not yours. All my work *has* been for us, but it came at the cost of doing what makes you feel loved. I'm sorry it's taken me so long to get that. I want to fix it, to do better."

Hot tears blur my eyes. "Then what, Aiden?"

His face tightens in confusion. "What do you mean?"

"You'll reel me in with your . . . way that you know you have, and I'll fall for it, and then I'll want it from you, Aiden. And, sure, that'll be possible here, while we're in paradise, but when we're home, the phone will ring, and the emails will come, and what if you're just as busy and—"

"It'll be different," he whispers. "I promise. I'm talking to Dan tonight. Soon as we're home. I'm going to figure out how to release some responsibilities. And yeah, that'll stress me out at first, and no, it won't be an overnight success. I'm sure I'll screw up again somehow, but I *get* it now, Freya. I'm committed to changing it."

Tears blur my eyes. God. It's every word I wanted. Everything I hoped I'd hear. But how can I know? How can I trust that he won't hurt me again?

I search his eyes and bite back tears. My stomach's in knots. I'm so scared, as I teeter on the edge of free-falling. Because that's what trust is—a free fall of belief that your faith is not misplaced, that the rope you're relying on will catch you, and the precipitous drop won't crush you but instead end in a rush of relief, a stronger capacity to be brave and fearless.

I have to see past what Aiden's done and believe what he says he *will* do. I have to choose him, to take a risk, not because of what the recent past dictates, but because of who I believe Aiden is, truly, at his core—his best self.

I stare up at him, moonlight painting the angular beauty of his face, his eyes glowing a fathomless, starlit blue. And my heart thunders against my ribs.

Aiden's eyes search mine and read me too well. "Please, Freya."

I can't explain why I do it, what makes me brave enough to wade into waters that already nearly drowned me once. Except that I look into his eyes and there's a glimpse of the man I married as much as the promise of a man who's grown and changed, who I've barely begun to understand. Our vows echo inside me, and I clutch them tightly for courage.

I promise to hope all things, believe all things . . .

"Yes," I whisper.

Air rushes out of Aiden as he carefully wraps me in his arms. His mouth is soft, his words punctuated with caressing kisses. "Thank you. Thank you, thank you, thank you."

EIGHTEEN

Aiden

Playlist: "August (Acoustic)," flipturn

Freya's stretched along her towel on her stomach, reading, chin propped on her hands.

I can't stop staring at her, at the soles of her feet swinging as she flips the page, at the bows at her hips that flutter in the wind. The fine blonde hairs on her body glittering in the sun. I want to do filthy, worshipful things to my wife's body, and none of them are possible right now. At least beyond my mind, where they stay, building in detail and creativity.

Which means, much as I'd like to be reading the book Viggo gave me, I've read the same line ten times now.

My mother-in-law shifts in her beach chair and smiles over at me. "You're reading a romance, Aiden?"

Freya tips her head and peers up at me.

I slap the book shut, caught red-handed—minded?—as a blush heats my cheeks.

"Yep. Viggo lent it to me."

Alex, my father-in-law, glances up from his book, too, and squints at the cover. "Ah. Kleypas. She's good."

My eyebrows lift in surprise. "You've read her?"

He grins. "I read romance to Elin every night."

She smacks his arm. "You'll scar them."

"What?" he says. "I said I *read* to you, not that I—"

"Alexander," Elin says, clasping his jaw and kissing him. "You need a swim. You're being naughty."

"Am I?" he asks, leaning in for another kiss.

Freya drops her head to her book and groans.

It makes them both laugh as Alex stands and drags Elin to her feet. And not for the first time, I marvel at them. Seven kids. A life-changing injury. Three decades together. And they still look at each other like they hung the moon.

I swallow the acrid taste of disappointment crawling up my throat. Because I feel that way about Freya, and when I think about growing old with her, having built a life, I imagine still wanting her, desiring her, treasuring her like that. Yet somehow, a rough bout of high anxiety, the pressure of planning a family, and I nearly ruined our marriage for good.

I kick that defeatist line of thought to the curb. I can't even let it make a pit stop in my brain. Freya's giving me a chance to make it right. She told me so. I have to hold on to that.

"I need the restroom, Alex," Elin says, gently stepping out of his arms. "I'll swim later."

"Aiden," my father-in-law says briskly.

I fumble with my book. "Yes."

"C'mon, son." He smiles warmly. "Let's have a swim."

I couldn't say no to him when he calls me *son* if I tried, and he knows it. Standing, I set down my book and join him, watching his careful steps on the soft sand as we approach the water. Alex has a cutting-edge, water-friendly prosthetic for his left leg, which was amputated just above the knee back when Freya was little and he was an active military field physician. I watch him walk—spine straight, the slight lag in his left leg as he negotiates the sand—praying he doesn't trip.

"I'm all right, Aiden," he says.

My gaze snaps up. "I'm sorry. I didn't mean to make it seem like I thought otherwise."

His sharp green eyes search me for a moment, the sea breeze rustling his copper hair that he gave Ren and Ziggy, streaked with luminous white, the color of crisp paper pressed over a fresh penny. He sets a hand on my shoulder and squeezes. "Your worries run deep because you love deeply, Aiden. I don't mind your concern. I just wanted to reassure you."

"I appreciate that." My throat feels thick as I swallow. "But I'm aware it can get overbearing."

"So can a plant that hasn't been pruned. Doesn't mean the roots are bad. It just needs help staying in check. I've always thought that was an important similarity between you and Freya."

I glance over at him. "What?" Freya and I are such opposites, the remark catches me completely off guard. "How are we similar?"

Alex grins at me. "You both love deeply and live out your convictions from that. Yours braids with pragmatism, and of course, yes, your anxiety. Freya's tangles with her need to please, her desire to heal. It's just like the flower and leaf of a plant can be entirely different but grow from the same soil, the same root system. That's how I see you two."

"I . . . never thought of it that way. But that's the deepest compliment, that you think I'm like Freya in any way."

We ease into the water, and Alex dives fluidly into an oncoming wave. I follow him just in time before we come up on the other side of it, wiping water from our faces. He rolls onto his back and floats the way Freya did the first time we came into the ocean. Even though she's a dead ringer for her mother, for a moment I see her in his smile.

"The boys say you're undertaking quite the business venture," he says. "No details, just that it's making you burn the candle at both ends. How are you holding up?"

"Oh." I brush my hair out of my face. "I've held up better."

Alex glances over at me. "Feeling stressed."

"I am. It's my own fault. I'm micromanaging when I shouldn't be. But I called my business partner last night and talked through some plans to help me delegate more responsibilities. And he also updated me on our financing. If all things go well within the next few weeks, we'll have an angel investor secured, and then I'll be able to really relax."

"You get some breathing room at that point, once you have financial backing."

"Absolutely."

"But until then, pretty tense?" he asks.

I nod. "Yeah. The past few months haven't been the easiest from that standpoint."

Alex swims out a bit farther, and I follow, my limbs knifing through the turquoise water.

"After my surgery . . ." He nods to his left leg and the black prosthesis pointing up in the water. "I went through a tough time. It was all I could do to keep my head above water for months. I was transitioning to civilian life, being home with two children—a newborn no less, who came not three months after my surgery. Then Elin had a bout of postpartum depression. Did you know that?"

I shake my head.

"Not sure any of the kids do, come to think of it. Just not something I've thought to discuss, but when you and Freya have children, you'll need to watch for that."

"I will."

"Good. Now, what was I saying? Oh. Yes. So here I was, back into practicing medicine in a hospital rather than in war zones, with Axel, who was doing his hellish newborn thing; Freya, who was an impossible toddler; Elin, who was a shadow of herself; and me desperate for everything to feel normal when *nothing* was like it had been.

"And suddenly the pressure of it all felt . . . insurmountable. I woke up one morning feeling like I was drowning."

"What did you do?"

Alex peers over at me and squints against the sun. "I accepted help."

My stomach knots. "From who?"

"Friends. My mother. Therapists. Mom took Freya two mornings a week to give Elin a break. Elin started on antidepressants and went to counseling. I came clean with my supervisor at the hospital that I'd bitten off more than I could chew, so we reduced my hours. And then I made sure I protected time for my family, cut out what was too much for us, and slowly built back from there. Even then, it wasn't an easy time. It was rough. And when Elin asked about a third baby, I told her she was barking up the wrong tree."

I grin. "How long did that last?"

"Oh, I held her off for a good while. Told her we needed time to catch our breath. That's why Freya and Axel are so close in age and there's a bigger gap until Ren. I have a theory that's why he was such a peaceful kid. He was born into peace. We were rested and balanced, in a good place when he was born."

"What explains Ryder's grumpiness?"

Alex's laugh booms across the water. "Oh, that's just Ryder. Grumpy and stubborn as an ox, born when and how he wanted, which was inconveniently three weeks early and at the Washington cabin. Very on-brand for Mr. Woodsman. And then Chaos One and Two came along in the quest for another girl." He scans the shore and spots Ziggy, his twin in looks, with her striking green eyes and copper hair. She sits, knees up, a Kindle obscuring her face. "And then we got her," he says softly. "And that's when I told Elin that even though a big family had been *my* grand idea, she was the one who fell in love with it, and if she so much as looked at me like she wanted more, I'd go hiking in the woods and not come back."

A laugh jumps out of me as my gaze catches Freya, eased back on her hands, watching us.

"Life's hard, Aiden," he says. "Kids make it incredibly beautiful, but they don't make it any easier. Make sure . . . make sure you're both ready for that, before you dive into parenthood. There's no shame in taking your time and taking care of you first."

I nod and swallow roughly, trying to hold in what I want to say because I know how much Freya wants her parents shielded from our mess.

My mess.

The one I made for us.

But if I could ask him, I think I would.

How do you do it? How do you love so openly? How do you do it without fear tainting . . . everything? How do you work so hard and love so hard and juggle it all? How did you learn to do that? Can I?

Alex drops from floating in the water and closes the gap between us, breaking me from my thoughts. He clasps my shoulders and holds my eyes, then says, "It sounds like you're carrying a lot, Aiden, but you don't have to carry it alone. I'm always here. While I know I'm not your father, I love you like you're my own. I'm proud to call you son."

My throat catches before I finally manage to say in a hoarse whisper, "Thank you."

"C'mere." He pulls me against him, a hug like he gives his sons, held close, his hand clasping the back of my head.

I might cry. And through his example, I know that wouldn't

make me weak or wrecked. Because I've seen Alex tear up and kiss his sons' foreheads. He's shown me that strength lies in how openly you bare your heart, not how deeply you guard it. I just never thought that I could do it, that I was capable of such vulnerability.

I'm starting to realize I am. And that hiding from that vulnerability cost not only me but Freya. And our marriage. I can't fix how much work there is to do, or how many dollars aren't yet in the bank. But I can fix this. How much I bare of myself, how much I entrust to her.

A hot tear slips down my cheek as Alex pats my back, then gently pulls us apart, still holding my shoulders. I palm away a tear and clear my throat.

"There's one more thing I forgot to mention," he says quietly, "that I relied on very much in those difficult months."

"What was that?"

His eyes crease at the corners as he grins. "Laughter."

In unspoken understanding, we both disappear under the water one more time before surfacing, then catching a wave in. Alex starts up the packed sand, earning everyone's attention when he says something I can't hear, because I'm knocking water out of my ear. And then he yells as he trips and faceplants right in the sand.

I rush onto the shore, instinct driving me to help, to cover him and shield him from embarrassment. But I'm not even halfway to Alex when his booming laughter rings in the air. He pushes up on his elbows, turns, then flops onto his back as Elin beats me to him and drops down. When I get closer, I see she's laughing, too—no, not just laughing, howling. In fact, when I glance around, I realize they're *all* laughing. Well, except Axel, who just stares over his sketchbook, one eyebrow arched.

"What the hell is wrong with you people?" I ask.

Alex lifts his head and catches my eyes, a grin widening his face. Tears glisten at the corners of his eyes before he laughs even harder. Elin takes his hands as he tries to stand, but he just keeps laughing and yanks her down until she flops on top of him in the sand. Gently she cradles his face in her hands, kissing him between bursts of laughter.

Before I can turn to Freya and ask for an explanation—not that I'd get one, because she's laughing so hard, she's crying—Oliver pops up beside me out of thin air, like a creepy blond poltergeist.

"Hey, Aiden," he says. He sets a pointer finger at each corner of my mouth and drags up until I'm smiling unnaturally. "Why so serious?"

I swat his hands away. "Your dad just humiliated himself, and you all laughed at him."

Oliver frowns and blinks at me in confusion, before his expression clears. "Bud, it's a joke. He does this every time we're on a beach vacation. He lives to do it. How do you not know this by now?"

"What?" I sputter. "He purposefully eats sand?"

Oliver laughs. "Yeah."

"Why?" I'm starting to think I'm the most reasonable person in this family. That's a very scary thought.

"Because." Oliver shrugs. "It's funny. Well, and it has a history. It started when he actually didn't mean to biff it, but he did. This was back when we were little—no, actually I was only a twinkle in my dad's eye—and prosthetics weren't what they are today. He had some clunker that didn't work well on the sand, but what was he going to do? I think Ryder was a baby, so there were four of them by then, and just like any other dad, he was going to get their shit down to the shore and play with his kids. I guess he was pulling one of those wagons with the older kids in it, and he just ate it, epically. Freya laughed so hard, she threw up her ice cream."

It makes my heart twist fondly. "Sounds like Freya."

"And Dad said he learned a lesson that day. Well, two. One, don't fall in front of Freya, because she *will* laugh in your face."

I glance over at Freya and catch her eyes as she fights another fit of laughter. "True."

"And two, we can choose how to live—miserable about what we've lost or grateful for what we still have. Dad chooses gratitude. And now he commemorates that with an epic sand biff every family vacation and never at the same point in the trip, so it keeps us guessing. My favorite was the year he did it right before we got on the road to go home. Mom was pissed because he was covered in sand and there was no outdoor shower. I loved it because he had us all convinced it wasn't going to happen, then he surprised us, and it made it that much better."

When I glance up, Alex is walking steadily across the sand, his hand tight with Elin's, until she stops him, cups his neck, and brings him in for a kiss.

And that's when something clicks inside me. This is what Freya grew up seeing. This is what she expects from the man she loves. Someone like her dad, who's figured out how to struggle and surpass feelings of inadequacy, a man who's learned to love fearlessly, or perhaps more accurately, to love and be loved even when he's afraid.

Dr. Dietrich's words ring in my head. *"If you want to feel close to your wife, you have to draw close, to trust her, even if you're terrified— no, because you're terrified. Breathe some life back into this marriage."*

As if she's heard my thoughts, Freya glances my way. I walk toward her and jerk my head toward the water. "Race ya."

Her face transforms from guarded curiosity to interest. Then she bursts out of her chair and flies past me toward the water.

NINETEEN

Freya

Playlist: "Wonder," Jamie Drake

I beat him. Handily.

And when he bursts from the ocean, Aiden has the nerve to look like a swimsuit model, running his hands through his dark hair, his aqua-blue eyes sparkling as he gives me a knowing grin. "Like what you see, Bergman?"

I splash him. "You're well aware there isn't a woman on this beach who hasn't noticed you and liked what she's seen."

"I don't care who noticed me," he says, yanking me by the ankle across the water and into his arms. "Unless it's my wife." My cheeks heat as Aiden stares at me intensely, his hand gentling my back. "Don't make plans tomorrow night."

I frown. "What?"

"I have something for us to do. Just the two of us."

I try to swallow the happiness bubbling up inside me.

Honestly, Freya. All excited for one measly date. Your first in months.

Besides the ice cream date. And we all know how badly that ended.

Aiden seems to read my mind. "That is . . . if you want that."

I shift in the water and my leg brushes his, making both of us jolt, then I lean in that little bit closer. "Does it involve food?"

"What do you take me for?" He smooths back my hair.

"Seafood?"

"Of course."

"Yes," I whisper as he draws me in tight.

Aiden searches my eyes, then presses one gentle kiss to my forehead. His hand cups my cheek tenderly as more kisses feather across my face, before finally his lips meet mine.

I hold his face, too, smoothing his jaw, curling my fingers in his hair as I bring our mouths together, coaxing his tongue softly with mine. It's a tentative kiss, a cautious one that opens to something deeper as he meets me and sighs against my mouth. It feels honest and real. It feels precious and delicate and daunting, like waking up to a new world that's inarguably beautiful but what was up is down, and my bearings are hard to find.

Gently, we break apart at the same time. Aiden's eyes dart down my body, darkening as his hands caress my arms and waist.

"I'll take it that you like the swimsuit?"

"Like?" He groans, pulling me into his arms again. "When you wore it the first day we were here, my jaw dropped. You're so beautiful."

I wrap my arms around his neck and rest my head on his shoulder, feeling the sting of bittersweet emotion. "Thank you," I whisper.

"You don't even have to ask that," he says against my hair. "You know I'm wild for your body, Freya. Let alone in a sexy red bikini."

I swallow roughly. "I think maybe I was struggling to know that, Aiden."

His grip tightens. After a beat of silence, he says, "Because we haven't . . ." He clears his throat. "Because it's been a while?"

"Because even once we were past the honeymoon phase, I still felt wanted. And I thought maybe we were going to be that couple that kept the spark. Mai said it. Amanda said it. Cristina said it. Heat dims in a marriage, kids douse it, and I was worried that before we even had babies, the novelty of me had worn off, or with you getting leaner, you wanted me to look how I did when we met—"

"Hey." He pulls back, staring into my eyes. His hand cups my cheek, and his thumb slips along my lips. "Where's this coming from? You know I love your body. *You* love your body."

"Not always," I admit. "I tend to oversell the body love a bit."

He frowns at me in bewilderment. "What? Why?"

"I don't know how to explain it. It just feels like I can't simply eat and exercise and look how I look. I have to *love* that I'm this way and make sure other people know, too. Otherwise, they think I'm trying to lose weight, that I'm not happy with how I am."

His eyes search mine. "Frey. Why am I just hearing this?"

I shrug, trying not to cry. "I try not to think a lot about it. I've got lots of other things to do besides worry about how preoccupied people are with women's appearances."

"Freya. I'm sorry. I should have . . . I should have paid better attention." Sighing, Aiden presses a kiss to my temple. "I've had my head so far up my ass," he mutters.

"I didn't tell you, either. I could have."

"We've both done that." He nuzzles my hair. "And we're both going to do better."

I nod.

After a moment's silence, he whispers, "I want you to know how beautiful you are."

"Sometimes I feel beautiful. Sometimes I don't. I'm always grateful for my body. That's enough."

"I'm grateful for your body, too," he says, holding me close and drawing a lazy smile from me. "Very grateful."

The water's rhythmic and gentle, the sun's hot, already drying salt water on Aiden's skin. And the unexpected closeness of this moment, the quiet and calm, softens something inside me, makes me feel brave. Tracing my fingers along his shoulders, down his back, I press a kiss to the base of his throat, swirl my tongue, and taste him.

Aiden draws in a ragged breath, his grip tightening on my waist before it drifts down. His palms round my backside, kneading, squeezing, as he pulls me against him. More kisses along his shoulder, his hands moving me against him. I feel his length, not wildly hard, nothing aggressive, just close. Intimate. Us.

"Hi," I whisper.

He exhales roughly. "Hi."

"It's like college again, sneaking like this."

I feel his smile against my temple. "*You* were in college. *I* was a very cool PhD student. And by 'cool,' I mean ridiculously nerdy."

"You were so cute. Do you remember how we used to make out for—"

"Hours?" He grunts as my teeth sink gently into his skin. "Vividly."

I chase the bite with a kiss. "And how we used to go down on each other and—"

"Shit," he says, tugging me close.

"What?"

Aiden clears his throat. "Ziggy's coming."

I sigh.

Ziggy waves, lanky limbs and skin as pale as Ren's, wearing a sensible one-piece Speedo and stubborn streaks of sunblock on her face. Pulling apart from Aiden, I wave back. And just like that, our moment's gone.

Aiden glances away, wipes his face. "I'm going to head out and read, give you two some time."

Before I can even say *okay*, he plunges under the water.

"Hi, Frey!" Ziggy says, teeth chattering as she gets closer.

"Hey, Zigs."

Ziggy clears her throat. "Sorry if I crashed the party. I got too hot, and the sand bugs me, and I'm trying not to be rude and sit inside the whole time reading."

It makes me smile. "No one would blame you."

"Probably not," she admits. "But Mom and Dad . . . I don't want them to worry about me."

Ziggy went through a rough season before her autism diagnosis made sense of what she was struggling with. My parents have stuck to her like glue since then, and I think it's been extra intense for her since Oliver left for UCLA and she became the last kid home.

Even though our situations are very different, I empathize with her desire not to worry them. "Yeah, I get that."

She tips her head. "You do?"

"You know what's going on with Aiden and me, and I'm shielding them from that just like you're out here freezing your butt off to avoid going inside. We all want to please Mom and Dad in our way."

"I guess I just thought you always do."

"Ziggy, I'm far from perfect, and Mom and Dad know that."

"Yeah, except you aren't home hearing, '*When Freya was your age . . .*' and '*Freya always used to . . .*' Mom says it kindly, but I can hear an uneasy pitch hiding beneath the surface."

"I think all parents are guilty of that. I'm no better than you or any of our brothers, Ziggy. I just came first."

Her eyes meet mine, revealing her doubt. And then I feel guilty. Really guilty that I haven't made more time for my only sister, the other bookend girl in a house of wild boys. "I'm sorry I haven't been around more," I tell her quietly.

"You're grown up," she says. "There's fifteen years between us. I never expected you to be."

"Yeah, but I should have been better. I should have known when you were hurting."

Ziggy splays her hands over the water, seeming to revel in the surface tension. "Sometimes, Freya, no matter how hard you try, you won't know how much a person you love is hurting because that person doesn't want to hurt the people who love them."

"But they shouldn't hide that pain."

"Easy for you to say," she mutters. "It's hard to be brave and say you're not okay when you grow up struggling to explain your feelings, when it feels like mental health issues are a shameful thing to own up to."

I stand there, stunned.

Bobbing under the water, then rushing up, Ziggy gasps for air. Her eyes meet mine as she rubs the water from her eyes. "Sorry. That was blunt, wasn't it?"

"No . . . I mean, yes. But it's okay. You make a good point." My eyes drift to Aiden leaving the water. He runs his hands through his dark hair, down his beard, then turns and squints into the sun, his eyes finding me. Then he lifts his hand tentatively.

I smile at him, despite the threat of tears, and lift my hand, too.

As I turn over Ziggy's confession, as I watch Aiden settle into his chair, my heart aches. Aches for the people I can't shield the way I want to, whose pain I can't erase by loving them as deeply as possible. I want love to heal all wounds. But I'm starting to understand just how much it doesn't. Sometimes love is a splint, an arm to take, a shoulder to cry on—helpful but not the healer itself.

That's when it hits me, how much I've wanted loving Aiden to work *my* way, rather than the way he needs. I've wanted him to tell me everything, to own his pain and fear, because in my mind, love's all you need to feel safe to do that. But it's not that easy for Aiden. It's harder. Maybe it wasn't once, when the stakes were lower and pressures were fewer, when we were younger and less rested on his shoulders. But that changed along the way. And my understanding, my expectations, didn't.

Regret knots my stomach. But before I can even start to think about swimming toward shore, telling him, Viggo and Oliver burst up from the water, startling us.

"Chicken time!" Oliver yells.

Ziggy squeals. "Yes! I call Viggo."

"Fine by me," Oliver says. He jumps onto my back, then scrambles up my shoulders, lean and wiry in that twenty-year-old way. "Let's take them down, Frey."

I grab my brother's legs and roll my eyes. "One game, then I'm going in."

Ziggy smiles as she crawls onto Viggo, who's crouched in the water. "Deal."

"Freya." Ollie clasps my face and peers at me, upside down from my vantage point. "What could possibly be more important than playing endless rounds of chicken?"

My eyes find Aiden, reading his book, and my heart skips a beat. "So much, Ollie. So, so much."

———

Dinner's how it always is when the Bergmans are together. Loud, messy, and delicious.

Up to my elbows in soapy water, because the guys cooked, so the women are cleaning up, I wipe my forehead, warm from doing dishes and taking some sun.

My brothers fill the deck behind me, sprawling, long-limbed, beers in hand, everyone a little sun-pink, except Aiden, whose golden skin glows. His linen shirt's unbuttoned one more than usual, his hair's extra wavy from the saltwater air, and when he brings his one beer for the night to his lips and takes a long pull, the outdoor lights flash off his wedding ring.

Longing floods me, molten hot. I drop a plate clumsily in the water, splashing Willa, Ziggy, Frankie, and me.

"Sorry," I mutter.

"Ugh," Ziggy says. "I can't stand half-wet clothes. Be right back."

"Don't worry about it, Zigs," Frankie says. "We'll take it from here."

Ziggy shrugs. "Don't have to tell me twice. I have a book calling my name."

Turning back to the water, I focus on the dishes, rinsing them, then handing them to Willa. When I glance up, she's smiling at me, drying a bowl. But she doesn't say anything.

"Well?" Mom asks, coming back from the bathroom. "Can I help?"

"Get outta here," I tell her as Frankie hands me another plate scraped clean of food.

Mom smiles as she presses a kiss to my cheek. Then she strolls out to the porch and slips onto Dad's lap. I turn back to the dishes, my thoughts wandering.

But then the door shuts again behind us and I glance over my shoulder. "Aiden," I say quietly.

He smiles, setting his beer on the counter. "Ladies, go ahead and relax. I'll finish these up."

Willa and Frankie make noises of protest until Aiden all but shoos them out, demonstrating the quiet yet intimidating way he has that I've seen on the rare times I could sneak in and watch him lecture. Soon, they're outside, joining the growing noise of my family, and we're left alone in the quiet.

That is, until the parrot catcalls him. He glares at her over his shoulder. "Behave yourself."

Esmerelda ruffles her feathers, then turns away on her stand.

I bite my lip. "You're the only one she does it to."

"Tell me something I don't know," he mutters, wiping down the counter, which is covered with water. "That's not all she says, either."

"Really?"

His cheeks pink. "She's got a mouth on her; let's leave it at that."

Setting the towel aside, Aiden steps up next to me, heat pouring off him. He smells even more ocean-water wonderful than normal. I squeeze the sponge beneath the dishwater to rein myself in, so I don't bury my nose in his shirt and huff him.

"When I told them to go relax, I meant you, too," he says quietly, peering down at me.

I meet his eyes, so vivid blue against the tan of his skin. I feel about to fall into them and never surface. "I know." I nudge his hip. "You shouldn't be here. You helped cook."

"I needed a break," he says, rolling his sleeves higher. "I love your brothers, but damn, can they talk."

Oh Lord. The sleeve rolling. The forearms. Veins. Tendons. It's all my catnip. I shut my eyes, so I don't get any more flustered than I am.

"Freya, I think the plate is clean."

"Hm?" My eyes snap open. "Yep. Right."

Aiden smiles softly. "You okay?"

"Totally." I nod. I'm so far from okay. I'm a top, whirring with so many emotional facets, they're one wild blur. I feel dizzy and hot, about to spin out of control.

"Here." Aiden's hands wrap around my waist, making air rush out of me. Gently, he guides me to the right. "I'll take a turn washing. You dry, okay?"

"Okay," I whisper.

Quietly, we stand, side by side, washing dishes. Our elbows bump. Aiden's fingers brush mine when he hands me each plate. On the last platter, we almost drop it between us, but Aiden catches it, steadying it in my grip.

"Sorry," he says, meeting my eyes. "I was distracted."

"That's okay," I tell him hoarsely. "Me too."

Aiden stares down at the water, pulling the plug. "Did you know you were humming?"

I freeze, halfway done drying the plate. "I was?"

Aiden nods, smiling faintly as he steps closer. "You were."

And somehow, I know we *both* know what it means. This tiny thing that I've always done, that drifted away when we were at our lowest, has found its way back. I realize, to him, to me . . . it's not just humming. It's hope.

"Forgot these!" Viggo says, bounding in with a fresh pile of glasses and dessert plates, then dumping them in the half-drained sink. "Man, that sucks that someone forgot to run the dishwasher earlier. Happy washing!"

I give Viggo the stink eye as he strolls out, whistling cheerfully.

Aiden turns on the water again and adds more soap. "Personally, I'm not too broken up about staying in here with you, enjoying the quiet, but you can go out if you want."

"No." I shake my head. "I'll stay." Peering up at him, I feel us lean, closer . . . closer . . . Aiden's eyes flick to my mouth, and then he closes the distance and presses one deep kiss to my lips.

When he pulls away, we both turn back to our tasks, side by side. The water runs. Aiden scrubs. Quietly, I rinse and dry. Then my hum returns, steadier, louder.

As Aiden wipes down the sink and the water drains in a slow, lazy spiral, it dawns on me—

Somewhere along the way, he started humming, too.

TWENTY

Aiden

Playlist: "Heaven," Brandi Carlile

"Where are we?" Freya asks.

"See for yourself." I uncover her eyes, watching them widen and adjust to the darkness. She peers around, quiet, taking in our surroundings.

"What is this?"

"Dinner," I tell her.

Freya glances up at me. "This is not just *dinner.*"

I smile and shrug. "Well, no."

She narrows her eyes playfully. "Is this more grand gesturing and groveling?"

"Is it working?"

Turning toward the picnic spread on the sand, tiny tea lights in lanterns circling it and hibiscus flowers strewn across the blanket, she sighs dreamily. "Yes."

"Good. Then, yes. I am an unabashed grand-gesturing groveler."

Her laugh is bright, and the sound makes every hair on my body stand on end. I set my hand on her back, guiding her toward the blanket.

"Why did we drive here?" she asks. "Couldn't we have just done this outside the house?"

I give her a look. "You honestly think we would have had a moment's peace there? Your brothers would have built suggestive sand sculptures, then serenaded us with every Disney song that precedes the couple's first kiss."

Freya laughs so hard, she snorts. "It's like you know them or something."

"Oh, do I. More than I ever thought I would, after Brother Bonding Day."

Freya smiles up at me as she lowers to the blanket and stretches out her legs. "You said it was good, being with them. But a long day?"

I follow, and slip behind her, bracing Freya inside my legs. "Lean back," I whisper against her ear. She hesitates, then glances over her shoulder, meeting my eyes. I run a hand along her shoulder, down to her fingertips.

Slowly, she relaxes inside my arms, then sets her hands on my thighs.

I press a kiss to the soft skin behind her ear, then reach and scoop up the first dish, popping off the lid. Spearing a piece of fish, I bring it to her mouth. Freya takes a bite, then settles in against my chest, nestling her head beneath my chin. It feels so good, so right, holding her how I used to, feeling her lean into me and sigh contentedly.

"Brother Bonding Day was fun," I tell her, answering her earlier question. "And exhausting. There's a difference between twenty-six and thirty-six. I'm not in shape like I once was. Haven't made time for exercise."

Freya glances back. "Do you miss it?"

"I miss soccer most."

She nods. "Me too."

"Would you . . ." I clear my throat, setting down the first container, then opening another. "Would you want to play with me on a co-ed team again? It would need to be once I get everything up and running on the app, if this investor comes through, but—"

"Yes," she says, her hand landing warm over mine. She squeezes gently, then tangles her fingers with mine. "Whenever you're ready. I'd like that. But there's no rush. I'll probably start back up with my old women's league, too."

I smile down at her. "I'm glad. That league always made you happy. Seemed like a good time." Offering her a new taste of food, I watch Freya's soft mouth slide over the fork. My skin feels hot, too tight, and I lean into the feeling—longing, hunger. It's been so long since I could savor her, that I could savor *wanting* her.

"Aiden," she says. "This is all so good. Where did you get it?"

"A restaurant nearby. There's a Blue Hawaiian, too." I open the cooler next to me. "Here." Pulling out the to-go Mason jar, I add a straw, a tiny tiki umbrella, then last but not least, a pink hibiscus flower. Then I set it to her lips. "Voilà."

"Fancy. Thank you." She takes a long sip and smiles. "Where's yours?"

I lift a seltzer, knocking it with her glass. "Yours truly is driving."

Humming to herself, Freya gently takes the fork, tasting from each container that's left. She stabs a piece of fish and turns in my arms, lifting it to my mouth. "Try it."

Emotion tightens my chest as I stare at her, so quick to share what brings her joy. It's so Freya. So absolutely her.

Her expression falters. "What is it?"

I grasp her wrist, before she can lower it. "I just . . . the look on your face. I've missed it." She tips her head, searching my expression. "Happiness."

Her eyes fill and she quickly wipes the tears away as they spill over. "Sorry," she whispers.

"I'm the one who's sorry, Freya." I wrap an arm around her and press a kiss to the crown of her head. "So very sorry."

For long quiet moments, she lets me hold her as I kiss her tears away. When I loosen my grip, she gives me a watery smile, then peers out at our picnic. "This is . . . so lovely, Aiden. Thank you."

"Thank you for trusting me when I told you to shut your eyes and drove you across the island."

She laughs faintly and sips her cocktail. "Of course I trusted you."

Cupping her cheek, I give her one soft kiss. "I don't take your trust for granted. The past few months, they haven't made trust easy. They haven't made any of this easy. I'm sorry for that."

Peering down, Freya traces a finger through the sand along the edge of our blanket. "Ziggy said something yesterday that stuck with me."

"What was that?"

She wrinkles her forehead in thought. "She said it's easy to tell someone they should be open about when they're hurting, but it's hard to do that when your pain feels shameful, or . . . daunting. It got me thinking about how scary failure is for you. How costly it was when you were young. Failure for you and failure for me mean very different things. I wanted you to act how *I* act when faced with risk, to trust me with those fears. But in the past, in your life, when you've felt threatened or vulnerable, you turned to yourself, to survive. Rather than remembering that, I took it personally."

My heart thuds against my ribs. I slide my palm against hers and grip her hand. "I'm glad failure doesn't mean for you what it means for me, Freya."

She meets my eyes, blinking away fresh tears. "I wish you hadn't grown up like that, Aiden. I hate it."

"I know. But it's done. And now look what we have. Look at all that's before us." I press a kiss to her temple. "I'd go through it a thousand times."

"Why?" she asks.

"Because it was part of what led me to you. You're worth all of that."

She drops her forehead to my chest, rolling it back and forth as she wraps her arms around my waist. "I wish I'd understood. I pulled away when I felt like *you'd* pulled away, instead of coming after you. I should have."

"You were hurting, Freya," I say quietly. "You shouldn't have had to chase me down."

A heavy silence holds between us, but for the sound of an ocean breeze whooshing through palm leaves, threatening our tiny lights in their lanterns.

"Still. We'll both do better," Freya says resolutely. She lifts a pinkie as I pull her closer. "Promise?"

I curve my pinkie around hers and kiss where our fingers meet. "Promise."

"I'm so full," I groan.

Freya sighs contentedly. "Me too. That was incredible."

We lie on the blanket, staring up at the night sky, glittering with stars. "I can't get over how clear the sky is here," she says quietly. "How much you can see. It's stunning."

I peer down at her, the breathtaking beauty of her face—that long straight nose sparkling with its silver hoop, the sharp line of her cheekbones, which I've traced with my finger countless times, those soft, full lips pursed in thought. "It is," I tell her. "Stunning."

Glancing up, she realizes I'm staring at her. A soft blush pinks her cheeks.

"It reminds me of our honeymoon," I tell her.

She smiles faintly. "I loved our honeymoon."

"Oh, me too." I can't stop the grin that tugs at my mouth.

Freya swats me half-heartedly on the stomach and wraps her arm tighter around my waist. "Wipe that self-satisfied smirk off of your face, Aiden MacCormack."

I laugh. "Freya, allow a man to glory in happy memories of how deeply he enjoyed his wife being a nudist for a week on a secluded beach."

"Oh God," she mutters, thumping her forehead softly against my chest. "I was so horny."

"Because you made us wait *weeks* before the wedding."

"I wanted our wedding night to be special!" she says.

My fingertips whisper along her arm, reveling in the satin softness of her skin. "It was."

"Yeah." Her eyes search mine as her hand settles over my heart. "It really was."

"And you sang."

She tips her head, confusion tightening her features. "What?"

"On our honeymoon. You sang constantly. You sang in the shower, in the ocean, in bed, over breakfast, wrapped in my arms. I loved that . . . that I knew, by how you sang and what you sang . . . I loved that it told me what you felt. That so often it told me you were happy."

Freya's eyes shine, wet with unshed tears, sparkling like the stars reflected in them. "I loved when you played guitar," she says. "It felt how you talk about my singing—like it showed me feelings you didn't always say, it showed me your happiness with us, together. Sitting in the backyard, making music together . . . those are some of my best memories."

My heart twists at her bittersweet words, the beauty of remembering simpler times.

"That's why it was so emotional," she says. "When you played and sang the other night at karaoke."

I smile down at her. "I know what you mean. That's how I felt, watching you sing, too."

"You saw me?" She bites her lip. "I wasn't sure if you were there yet when I was up at the mic."

"I was." Tucking a pale blonde wave behind her ear, I trace the curve of her jaw with my thumb, gentling her delicate skin. "It gave me chills. You looked so *alive*, Freya. Like something inside you that I hadn't seen in so long was burning bright again. Such unbridled joy."

She exhales roughly and palms away a tear that slips out. "That's how I felt."

"That's how I *always* want you to feel."

Nestling in, Freya drapes her leg over mine. I pull her close and savor the feel of her lush body tucked against mine. "That's what I want for you, too," she whispers. "For both of us."

I glance up at the sky, drinking in its dark, beautiful vastness. "When we go home, I want to do that again. Sit outside, make music."

Freya sighs and rests her head on my shoulder. "I'd like that, too."

Tearing my gaze from the stars, I nuzzle her hair and breathe her in, a whisper of lemons and cut grass, the sweetness of the flower she stuck in her hair. "We'll quit our jobs. Start a band."

She laughs, knowing how completely unserious I'm being. "You'd never."

"You're right. I wouldn't. Maybe in my next life."

"You'd never abandon your students," she says. "You love them too much. Just like I love my patients."

I press a kiss to her hair. "I know. They're headaches sometimes, but mostly they're just young people trying to find their way, and I like that I get to help them. I remember how hard it was. I empathize with that."

Her smoky laugh jumps out. "Unless they're DI athletes."

"Entitled little shits."

Freya peers up at me, searching my eyes. "But you've learned your lesson, after you messed with Willa, haven't you, Aiden Christopher?"

I smile at her guiltily. "Yes. That was not my finest moment."

She shakes her head. "You're lucky they turned out happy together."

"Oh. About that. I have a confession."

"What kind of confession?" she asks warily.

"The kind of confession that I'm only confessing because I think it's outside the statute of wifely wrath limitations."

She lifts an eyebrow. "That so?"

I fight a blush. "So, when your brother and Willa were my students and I sent them on that team-building outing?"

"Yes," she says slowly. "The one I gave you hell for."

"That one, yep. Well, I gave them a questionnaire they had to use that day, too. It borrowed a bit from corporate workshop material that I had, but it also relied heavily on . . . couples bonding questions, too."

Freya bites her lips, very clearly trying not to laugh. "What were you *thinking*?"

"You didn't see them pining over each other in my classroom. They just needed a little nudge."

"A little nudge."

"Freya, I saw it. They were so perfect for each other. And the thought that a few communication barriers and crappy attitudes could keep them from ever realizing that . . ." I sigh, feeling the real weight of my words. "I couldn't take the thought of them missing the love of their lifetime. Because I have that. And I can't imagine a world without her."

Her eyes soften. "Aiden." She wraps her arms tighter around me.

I squeeze her back and kiss her temple, soaking up the feel of her in my arms. Then I pull away and sit up. "C'mon."

She frowns at me as I offer a hand and pull her upright. "What are we doing?" she asks.

I tap my phone, selecting the first song from one of her many playlists. This one's titled, *Dancing on the Beach*. The perfect sound-track, on a silver platter.

Freya knows it, too, when I draw her close and start us swaying. She laughs. "Well done."

"How could I turn down the perfectly titled playlist?"

"I don't know," she says, planting a kiss on my cheek. "But I'm glad you didn't."

Holding her close, I move us to the rhythm of the music, breathing in Freya, who smells like sunshine and flowers, the always sweet-tart lemon scent on her skin, so soft and warm in my arms. She feels like heaven.

"Why are we dancing?" she asks.

I press a kiss to her temple. "Because you love to dance, and I love to hold you."

"Well, those are nice reasons."

Smiling, I tug her closer and set my mouth to the shell of her ear. "And because I want to tell you things I don't know how to tell you otherwise, and it's easier when you're in my arms."

"Like what?" she whispers.

"Every day, I wake up scared that I won't love you how you deserve to be loved. When I'm nervous before I speak at a conference, I hold your pendant in my palm until it's hot, and then I press it hard to my chest, so it's warm against my skin when I speak; I tell myself that you're with me, and it makes me braver."

She pulls back and meets my gaze.

"Performance high is no joke," I tell her quietly. "I almost threw up before I sang for you at karaoke, but afterward, I loved it. I love that you make me want to be brave and try things I other-wise wouldn't. Oh, and I had my first hard liquor drink—or at least three sips of it—for Dutch courage before I played. Those zombie cocktails are high alcohol proof, in case you didn't know. Tread carefully."

A smoky laugh jumps out of her. "Yeesh, Aiden! A zombie?"

I place a kiss behind her ear and trail more down her neck. "It's vacation. The perfect place to bend my own rules."

"I knew I tasted mint *and* rum."

My laugh is soft as I kiss her shoulder. "I've always struggled to admit my fears and my failures to you because I never ever want to disappoint you, Freya."

She holds my eyes, slipping her fingers through my hair. "You don't, Aiden. You could never disappoint me. Because you would never do anything that compromised your integrity, your goodness. You hurt me when you pulled away, yes. But you never disappointed me."

"Tell that to my brain. He's a lying asshole."

"I will," she whispers. "Let me know when he's talking shit, so I can tell him off."

Tears tighten my throat. "I will."

Setting her cheek on my shoulder, Freya sighs as I sway us in soft, mesmerizing circles. "Aiden?"

"Hm?"

"Thank you. I needed this."

My lips meet hers as I whisper, "I needed it, too."

TWENTY-ONE

Aiden

Playlist: "I'm with You," Vance Joy

Birds chirp quietly outside. Sunlight spills through our sliding glass door and paints Freya's profile in shades of gold and bronze, slipping down the line of her nose to her lips, pursed in sleep. Someone bangs down the hallway—my money's on one of the man cubs—and startles her out of her deep sleep.

On a soft, quiet stretch, Freya squeaks, and her eyes blink open. Sleepily, she glances toward me, where I lie next to her in bed, propped up on one elbow. I smile at her, and she smiles back, warmer than the sunshine brightening her face.

"Morning," she says quietly.

"Morning," I whisper. Staring at her, I brush my hand against hers. She slides her palm tentatively along mine until I tangle our fingers tight.

Her eyes dance between mine, and her smile deepens. "Your hair's wild."

"I know." I slip my thumb along her palm, soothing myself how I have countless times, touching her this way. "I need a haircut. I've just been too busy."

Too busy. God, Aiden. Very wrong thing to say.

Her expression falters as she glances down to our hands. "What time is it?"

"Early."

"How early?"

I shrug. "Don't know."

She frowns. "Can't you check your phone?"

"I don't have it."

Her eyes widen comically. "What?"

I'd be offended by how shocked she is, but I have practically had the thing glued to me for months. It was hard not to worry I'd miss something, but I did it, left my phone downstairs for the second night in a row. And I still haven't checked it. Instead, I woke up early and did some of Makanui's yoga flow on our small private deck. Much as I resented the guy for almost dislocating my groin the other day, what he taught us helps me breathe deeper and loosen up my body from all the points that it holds tension.

"It's in the kitchen charging," I tell her quietly, feathering my fingers along the inside of her arm.

"Color me surprised," she whispers. "Speaking of the kitchen, I should get up," she murmurs, glancing past me at the bright morning sky. "If I don't make breakfast, Mom does."

"Ren and Axel are handling it today."

She tips her head. "They are?"

"The guys made a calendar for the rest of the week so it wouldn't all fall to you. And . . ." I glance past her shoulder at the tray I have waiting. "Your breakfast is here, today."

She peers over her shoulder, then meets my eyes, biting back a smile. "Wow."

I smile at her. "Come on. Before your coffee gets cold. And Ryder finds out where his Yeti thermos got to."

"Oh, you'll be a dead man for stealing that."

"That's why he's not going to know, wife." I give her a look. "What he doesn't know doesn't hurt him. Or me."

Freya laughs softly as she scooches up in bed and I set the tray over her lap. "This is really nice, Aiden," she says. "You didn't have to do this."

I smooth back her bed head hair and kiss her cheek. "I wanted to."

When I reach for her nightstand and grab her water to set it on her tray, I notice the book she had beside it. "*Persuasion*?" I ask.

She pauses with her coffee halfway to her mouth. "I watched the movie a few weeks ago and loved it. I decided to read the book, too."

Settling next to her in bed, I cross my legs at the ankles and lean in, straightening her silverware on the tray. Freya smiles at me over her cup.

"When did you watch the movie?" I ask quietly.

"When you were in Washington," Freya says as she sets down her coffee. "I cried. A lot."

I peer up at her. "Why?"

She smiles faintly. "Because it's about waiting for the one you love for a long time, after they've hurt you and you've hurt them. It's about deciding the outside world doesn't get to dictate your happiness, about forgiveness and second chances and love that grows with people as they grow, too."

"Sounds pretty damn good."

She nods. "It is. I actually like the book better, so far."

I lean into her hand, which hasn't left my hair. "Can I read it?"

"Only if you read it aloud to me. In a British accent."

I nip her shoulder. "I'm as bad at accents as I am at charades, and you know it."

She kisses my cheek. "I love your accents." Her lips move to my jaw, and I feel her hesitation, her warm breath soft against my skin. "And I love you."

Those words. I haven't heard them in too, too long. *I love you.*

My heart feels like a drum solo, rolls and pops, percussive rhythm that's an explosive relief. She said it. She *loves me*.

Still.

I turn and catch her lips, stealing another kiss. "I love you, Freya. So much." Fighting the urge to sweep her tray right off the bed and break every rule Dr. Dietrich gave us, I sit back and take a deep breath. Now's not the time to push past what we're building, let alone test my body and risk disappointing both of us.

That's a conversation we'll have at home, when the pressure of being "okay" for her parents is behind us. When we've shored up what leads to that physical intimacy: our emotions, our trust, our connection.

Freya sits back and smiles at me, tossing a piece of fruit in her mouth. Then another. I watch the sun brighten our room, Freya delighting in every morsel of breakfast, each lick of the tips of her fingers, each happy sigh and soft hum of contentment.

Finally, she sets the napkin on her plate and smiles. "Thank you again. Why didn't you eat?"

I shake my head. "Not hungry yet."

"Hm," she says, narrowing her eyes at me. "Make sure you do. Need energy for when I kick your butt at sand volleyball later."

"Psh. Please." I pick up the tray and set it on the floor near me.

She snuggles down into the bed again. "But not before I go back to sleep. What a breakfast! Now I need a nap. Axel and Ren made it?"

"Excuse me, *I* did. It's not groveling if you outsource it."

"Mm. Grovel breakfast."

"Indeed." I press a kiss to her head. "They're cooking for everyone else now. Your meal was made with love."

She smiles. "Even better. So who's on breakfast duty tomorrow?"

I sit back on the bed and twirl one of her white-blonde waves around my finger. "Oliver and Viggo."

"Oh, God, no. They'll kill each other. There'll be scrambled eggs stuck to the wall and waffle batter dumped on each other's heads."

"They'll be okay, I think. They love to eat too much to waste food, even if they bicker like an . . ."

Freya lifts an eyebrow. "Like an old married couple?"

"Shh." I set a finger playfully over her soft lips. "You're supposed to let my gaffs slide."

"Am I?" she says, before playfully nipping my finger.

I suck in a breath as her eyes lock with mine. My body heats and tenses as I stare at her mouth, as Freya lifts a tentative hand and slips it through my hair, smoothing my bed head waves off my face.

Watching her, I drag the sheet away. Sheer white panties and a tank top that shows her tight, pebbled nipples. Such pure beauty. I stare at her for a moment, drinking her in.

"Can I touch you, Freya?"

She blushes prettily. "How?"

I press my lips gently to her throat and breathe her in. "I want to kiss you."

"Better brush your teeth, then—*oh*." She shivers as I kiss my way down her chest.

"That kind of kissing," I tell her.

She exhales shakily, her hands threading through my hair. "Why?"

"Because I miss you," I whisper against the soft curve of her stomach, lifting her tank top. "Because I want you to feel good." One gentle kiss, as I nuzzle the satin-smooth skin between her hips. "Because I love you."

Freya's hips roll toward mine. Her fingers trail my shoulders delicately, until they curl into my hair again and pull me closer.

"I need your words, Freya."

"Yes," she says faintly. "Yes, you can kiss me."

I hook her panties off and drag them down her legs. She's so beautiful, wet and flushed. I tease her gently, parting her delicately, blowing cool breaths.

"Aiden," she whispers, restless beneath me.

I drift my other hand beneath her shirt and cup her breast, thumbing her nipple. "Did you wake up aching, Freya?"

She bites her lip, then nods faintly.

"What were you dreaming about?"

Her blush deepens. "How do you know I was dreaming?"

I rub her clit, then lower, stroking that soft, velvety skin. Each flick of my thumb, every coaxing touch, makes her sigh. "Because I can tell. You were restless in your sleep. These gave you away, too." Cupping her breast, I roll her nipple beneath my fingers, shifting to tease them both. "They always do."

I kiss my way up her thighs until I'm so close to where she wants me. "And I know my wife's body," I whisper. "I know when she needs to come."

I trail my fingers over her stomach and watch goose bumps rise in their wake as Freya tips her head back, biting her lip. Her eyes flutter shut as I crawl up her body and suck her nipples through the fabric of her tank top, stroking her rhythmically.

"Touch yourself, Freya." My voice is gravel, and my dick juts up, hard and pulsing. My balls tighten harshly as I toy with her nipple. "Show me."

Her hand slides down her body, stroking where she's wet and flushed and so fucking pretty. I prop myself higher on one elbow, my touch whispering over her thigh. She shuts her eyes and exhales slowly, then begins circling her clit.

"Freya," I whisper against her skin. "Tell me your dream."

Freya's a very sensual person, and yet she's shy in bed. I figured out early on in our sex life that making her say what she wanted turned her on almost as much as when I gave it to her.

"You were . . ." She swallows. "You used your tongue."

I reward her with a deep teasing suck of her nipple. She bows off the bed. "Where?"

"Here."

Her fingers slide farther down, and an animal grunt leaves me as I watch her. My grip sinks into her thigh. "Tell me exactly. Where was my tongue?"

"My pussy," she whispers, rubbing herself in tight circles. I watch her move, the sensual way her foot slides along the sheets, the soft jagged breaths she takes as her desire builds.

One soft kiss to her lips, my hands kneading her, I watch her writhe and chase release. "Is your pussy wet for me, Freya?"

"Oh, God, yes." Freya sighs shakily. "Aiden, I'm so clo—"

Someone bangs on the door. "C'mon, lazy asses. Breakfast!"

That would be Oliver. Who I'm going to murder.

Freya gasps, arching into my touch. "T-tell him to go away."

"Why can't you?" I ask her playfully. I stop her hand's movement and earn a sharp glare.

"Swear to God, Aiden," she says. "Now is *not* the time for edging. I haven't come in weeks."

"It's always time for edging." I nip her bottom lip with my teeth and chase it with a kiss, then begin to crawl my way down her body again. "You come so hard when I do it, Freya. You shake and cry, and it's so fucking beautiful."

She moans faintly.

"Hello?" Oliver calls.

I swear, he's twenty going on twelve. We're not answering. We're in our bedroom. What does he think we're doing?

Holding Freya's eyes, I lower my mouth, flicking her swollen little nub softly with my tongue. "Better answer him," I whisper, slipping two fingers inside her and stroking her steadily.

"What?" Oliver asks through the door.

"I mean it, Freya. Pretty sure we didn't lock the door."

She shudders as she rides my hand. "I'm g-going to dunk you in the ocean for torturing me."

I still my fingers and feel her legs tremor around my touch before I resume pumping them into her. "And I'll deserve it."

"F-fuck off, Oliver!" she yells as I bring my mouth to her body once more and tongue her roughly. Burying her face in her pillow, she comes, crying out in relief.

"Geez," he mutters. "Somebody woke up on the wrong side of the bed." His footsteps lumber off, then die away.

Freya gasps for air as I coax wave after rhythmic wave of her release. Finally, I press one slow kiss to her thigh, then her stomach.

She glares at me. "You think you're funny?"

I grin and steal another kiss where she's so impossibly beautiful and sensitive. It makes her gasp and shut her legs around my shoulders. I shove them open and crawl up her body. "I *think* you came spectacularly. And if I had to piss you off a little to accomplish that, then I'll pay that price."

Her eyes narrow as she tries not to smile. "I should torture you back," she says darkly.

"You can dunk me in the ocean. Just like you promised." I press a kiss to her chest before I push off the bed. "C'mon."

TWENTY-TWO

Freya

Playlist: "Over the Rainbow," Israel Kamakawiwo'ole

"Okay!" Ryder calls. The living room grows quiet. "Everyone who's coming on the hike is here, yes?"

"No," Axel says evenly, before he turns toward the stairs, cups his mouth, and shouts, "Viggo! Oliver! Get your asses down here!"

The man cubs thunder down the stairs a moment later, gear bags swaying heavily on their backs.

"What the hell are you packing for?" Dad asks. "Planning to camp out in the jungle?"

"Snacks," Viggo mumbles.

I believe it. All those two do is eat.

Oliver starts past Ryder toward the front door. "Yeah. Snacks."

Ryder grabs his bag, stopping Oliver in his tracks, then spinning him around. "*Now* do we have everyone going on the hike? Everyone has their water and some food to tide them over?"

To a chorus of affirmatives, Ryder turns and opens the front door, ushering us out.

Frankie wiggles deeper into the couch cushions with her blanket and flashes a self-satisfied grin. "The couch *and* the TV. All to myself."

I playfully narrow my eyes at her. "No gloating. Some of us got strong-armed into this."

"That's your problem," Frankie says, brandishing the remote at

me. "You're too nice. You've got to learn my favorite word. *No.
N.O.* I've been working on Zenzero, but look, there he is, suited up
for this hike even though he's going to end up looking like a lob-
ster impersonator."

"Hey." Ren leans over the sofa and kisses her. "I have a hat and
SPF 100 on, head to toe."

She kisses him again. "Be smart and drink your water. Love
you."

"Love you," he whispers.

I follow Ren, Aiden behind me, as we load into our massive
rental van that'll take us the thirty-minute drive to Ka'au Crater
Trail. I'm nervous to see Dad pile into the driver's seat, not because
I don't trust him behind the wheel, but because I feel like a hike
that Ryder says is fairly technical could tax him.

"Freya Linn," he says, adjusting his mirrors. "Stop worrying
about me. I'll be fine."

Busted.

My cheeks heat. "Okay, Daddy."

"*Okay, Daddy*," Viggo and Oliver mockingly singsong.

Aiden jerks back and swats each of them on the head. "Knock
it off."

They sink down in their seats, looking like sad puppies.

I glance over at Aiden for a heartbeat. He smiles, then cups my
neck, massaging gently. My fingers curl into the upholstery, and
my heart beats hard beneath my ribs.

"Shouldn't have done that," Ren tells Viggo and Oliver. "Mocked
the bride of Frankenstein."

Ryder snorts.

Axel coughs.

Mom wheezes.

And Aiden scowls at Ren. "That was the most obvious Frankenstein ever. And you all know it. You were trolling me."

Dad's deep laugh echoes as he turns on the engine. "I just didn't want it to end."

I bite my lip and set my hand on his thigh. Aiden tried his best at charades last night, but he's still so terrible. It was one of those familiarities that made my heart sing. Because even though we struggled guessing and the parrot kept calling him "hot stuff" as he lumbered around the living room, he gave it his all. I watched him, clueless, as he looked at me so pleadingly, like I just *had* to know. And then he laughed at himself, collapsing into my arms as time ended. And I laughed, too. I laughed so hard, I woke up with my ab muscles sore from it.

"I got it," I remind him.

"Yeah." Aiden smiles, nudging me. "Right at the end of my time."

I squeeze his leg before he slips his palm beneath mine and tangles our fingers. He meets my eyes for the briefest moment, before his gaze flicks to my mouth, then forward, on the road as Dad pulls out.

Quiet chatter fills the van as Kailua disappears behind us and Dad merges onto 61-S. Willa laughs at something Ryder says while Ren and Ziggy discuss the information guide Ryder brought for our hike. Axel cranes forward, answering my mom as she turns back and asks something I miss, too lost in the feel of Aiden's hand wrapped around mine, the warmth of our bodies next to each other.

I press my forehead to the glass and watch the beauty of inland Hawaii unfold before my eyes. To my right, a kaleidoscopic blur of beauty bursts to life as Dad takes the turn, then slows a little so we can appreciate the view. Moss-green mountains scrape the sapphire sky as we pass rich marshland that's the same vibrant color as the mountains above it.

Having spent my life in the Pacific Northwest and then Southern California, I'm no stranger to lush landscape and ocean views, but this is so far beyond that. It's like the moment Dorothy stepped onto the yellow brick road and Oz became a Technicolor world of jewel tones and sun-drenched surfaces. Otherworldly lovely.

"So," Ryder says, clearing his throat.

"Prepare yourselves," Willa tells us. "The mountain man is in his element."

"Shut it," he says before clasping her jaw and planting a hard kiss right on her lips. "This is Kawainui Marsh to our right. *Kawainui* means 'the big water,' likely because once long ago this was one big estuarine—"

"God bless you," Oliver deadpans.

Ryder throws him a death glare. "An *estuary* is a partially closed-off coastal body of brackish water with at least one fresh water source as well as a connection to the open ocean."

"Thanks," Oliver says tartly. "Not that I asked."

"No," Ryder concedes, "you didn't. You made a crack about it instead of saying what you really wanted, which was to know what I was talking about. Consider yourself educated in spite of your overblown pride."

"*Burnnnnn*," Viggo says.

Oliver elbows him sharply, and to no one's surprise, they start pummeling each other in the back row, where, wisely, no one else joined them.

"Anyways," Willa says. "Go on, Lumberjack."

Ryder clears his throat. "So *Kawainui* was most likely an estuarine body of water at the time when the area was first settled. Nowadays, the marsh is floating on water or possibly growing on a mat of peat floating on water—which is super cool—and in the higher-up parts of the marsh, it's essentially a soggy meadow."

Ren snaps a photo with his phone, then starts typing. I bet anything he's texting it to Frankie. "It's beautiful. Why aren't we hiking there?"

"Because the views will be much better on the Ka'au Crater

Trail," Ryder tells him. "Multiple waterfalls, killer views of Kaneohe, Kailua—which is where our house is—Diamond Head, and of course, the Ka'au Crater."

Dad says, "As Ryder told us, it's a pretty tough trail, and there's no pressure to do all of it. We'll check in with each other periodically, and if someone's getting tired, we're experienced enough hikers that we can break into groups. Anyone who's ready to go home will head back with me and Mom, and I'll drive them, while Ryder takes the rest of you for the full hike. It's only a thirty-minute trip to the house, and I'm happy to be shuttle driver."

Mom cups his neck and smiles at him as Dad sets his hand on her thigh. A lump forms in my throat as I realize each day that passes here, my hope grows but my question is still: *Will we have that? Will we make it?*

I glance away, out the window, taking a slow deep breath. Aiden's hand squeezes mine, and I could swear I hear his voice, soft as a whisper: *Yes.*

———

Well. If I doubted whether or not I was in shape, this hike confirms it.

I am a badass motherfucker with muscles of steel. I mean, I know my job's physically demanding, but even *I'm* surprising myself with how well I'm making my way through this.

Ahead of everyone except Ryder, who leads, I grip a stabilizing rope when I hit a slippery patch, bumping into yet another guava on the trail. Viggo's already eaten two.

The sounds of wildlife, the vitality of the jungle all around us, are breathtaking. Our hike is also breathtaking. As in taking our breath. Except for me. Because I'm a beast.

"Damn, Frey," Ryder puffs, glancing over his shoulder. "You're pushing my pace."

I wipe my forehead, which is dripping with sweat. It's in the mid-eighties, but with the humidity, it feels well into the nineties. My clothes are soaked with sweat. I smell like a barn animal.

It's fucking glorious.

"She always was an endorphin chaser," Dad huffs, his momentum starting to wane. We all glance back and subtly drop pace, too, until we come to a natural stop at a wide stretch of the trail. "When she was three, she'd make me time her doing sprints across the yard and count her push-ups. I'd do my physical therapy routine, and she did them right with me. Saying, *'Come on, Papa, don't give up!'*" Dad laughs quietly as he dabs his forehead. "I couldn't skip my PT exercises if I wanted to."

I feel myself blushing.

"And that's how Freya fell in love with physical therapy," Aiden says quietly, brushing his knuckles against mine.

"Ugh," Willa groans. "What's happened to me? I just teared up." She turns to Ryder. "Am I officially a softie now?"

Ryder grins and strokes her cheek. "You have been for a while."

"Dammit," she gripes.

Mom smiles and sets her hands on her hips, taking deep tugs of air. "She'd say, *'I want to be strong, just like Papa.'* He was very fit then."

Dad frowns. "Excuse me, wife. *Was?*"

Mom laughs, her smoky voice like mine, popping against the quiet of the trail. "I'm so sorry. Was. Is. Always will be."

"That's more like it." Dad unscrews his water lid and hands the canteen to her, watching her drink, signaling to keep going. "More, Elin."

She rolls her eyes and gulps more. Lowering the bottle, Mom dabs her mouth and sighs. "Well. Your father is up to this hike, but that prosthesis isn't. And I'm getting tired. Ready to go back, Alex?"

Dad smiles. "Sure, sweetheart. Anyone else who's ready to go back?"

Axel's eyes leave the tree canopy that he's been watching in silence. "Yeah, I am."

"Same here," Ren says, hand inside his pocket around his phone. "I'm out of cell reception, and it's making me antsy. I want to get back to Frankie."

Mom blows all of us a kiss. "I love you, every one of you. Be safe," she says to us, before she and Dad turn and start down the path.

After they're on their way down the trail, Willa turns and says, "Okay, keep it moving. This is fun and all, but I've got a beach calling my name."

Ryder holds out his hand, which she takes. "C'mon, Sunshine."

As I turn to join in, too, my foot slips. Before I can even shriek or grab the stabilizing rope, Aiden's hands are on my waist, clutching me hard and steadying me. "Okay?" he asks quietly.

Heat soars through my skin at his hard grip. I swallow thickly. "Y-yes."

Ziggy jogs past us, before Oliver and Viggo follow her, bickering about something as usual.

I'm on a knife's edge of longing. Because after charades went on for hours and we all got a little tipsy, Aiden and I blearily brushed our teeth and fell asleep kissing, tangled close in bed. And then I woke up, very much expecting to pick up where we'd left off, but no, Ryder was banging on doors telling people to get up and get going so we weren't hiking in prime-time heat.

"You seem distracted," he says. "What's wrong?"

"Nothing hiking with my brothers will cure," I mutter.

Aiden coughs behind a fist. "I can't believe we fell asleep last night."

"Right? How old are we?"

"Well, you have no excuse. I, however, am in my late thirties," he says.

"Oh, please. Thirty-six is not late thirties."

"Pretty sure math is my wheelhouse, Bergman." He softly swats my butt and walks by, giving me a dazzling smile. "Thirty-six rounds up to forty."

I jog to catch him. "I hate when you do that."

He leans in and drops his voice. "Generally not what your panties report afterward."

"Aiden!" I hiss, jerking my head toward Ziggy, who's not far in front of us.

"What? I was quiet."

"Not *that* quiet."

Aiden suddenly yanks me by the elbow and pins me against a tree, its wet bark digging into my back, dark leaves making a secret canopy around us.

His mouth is warm on mine, firm and hungry. I thread my fingers through his hair, the waves so tight from Hawaii's humidity, they're almost curls. He groans and pulls me close when I drag my nails along his scalp, melding our hot, sweat-soaked bodies together.

"We're going to lose them," Aiden mutters.

"It's a well-marked path," I say between kisses, tugging him even closer. "We're stopping at the first waterfall. We'll be fine."

Aiden's hands sink into my hair as our kisses grow hotter, slower, tongues dancing. My touch wanders the planes of his chest, down his stomach. He shudders and pulls back to press a kiss to my temple, then down my cheek. His tongue darts out, tastes the sweat of my skin, and Aiden groans, rocking his pelvis against mine. I'm exactly seven seconds away from dragging us behind this tree and telling Dr. Dietrich her no-sex rule can go take a hike instead of us.

"Guys?" Viggo calls from up the path. "Coming?"

Aiden bites my neck in frustration and groans before he turns back and pins me with one more hard kiss.

Emerging from beneath the tree, we catch up quickly to Viggo, who's peeling *another* guava fruit. He cocks an eyebrow. "Behaving yourself, children?"

"I hope you choke," Aiden mutters, dragging us past him.

Viggo smirks and falls into step behind me as we make a turn in the path.

A prickling sensation crawls up my spine as we turn the bend. Ziggy's leaning against a tree—long legs crossed at the ankles as she stares at the guidebook.

"Where are Willa and Ryder?" Aiden asks.

Ziggy glances up. "I'm not the most astute observer of human behavior but even *I* could tell they wanted a little alone time. I let them go ahead a bit."

Aiden grins and peers down at me. "See. Hikes are sentimental for them. Because yours truly meddled and set them on the path to bliss."

I roll my eyes. "I'd almost find it tolerable if you didn't *gloat* about it."

His smile deepens as he laughs, making so many moments from our early years flash through my mind—when we were young, even with so little, somehow so much happier and closer. I try to push away my worries about when we're home and life's busy and our professional demands drag us a dozen different directions. I try to stay in the here and now, grateful for what this week has given us. Because I know that getting away forced us to face each other in a way that being home never would have. And yet part of

me is scared that going home will shake what we've tentatively begun, isolated from the outside world and its countless pressures.

As if he senses my spiraling thoughts, Aiden's thumb circles my
palm. "Watch your footing, Frey," he says gently.

When I glance up and focus on the trail, I realize we aren't just
missing Willa and Ryder, either. "Where's Oliver?"

Viggo tosses the guava peel and pockets the Swiss Army Knife
he lifted from the house. "Hm?"

"Oliver," I say tightly. "Twelve months younger than you? Looks
like you but with blond hair and an even worse penchant for mischief? Ringing any bells?"

"Oh," Viggo says casually, glancing around. "I'm sure he's up
ahead harassing Willa and Ryder."

Ziggy pockets her guidebook and pushes off the tree. "He said
he had to pee."

"Ah." I peer around. "Shouldn't take that long, though."

Aiden releases my hand and quickens his pace. "I'll poke around
up ahead on the trail."

"Wait, Aiden." I jog after him, feeling uneasy about something,
but not knowing what. I don't want him out of my sight.

He peers over his shoulder and frowns. "Freya, stay back and
keep an eye on Ziggy and Viggo."

"Ziggy is a fair point but Viggo is twenty-one years of hellish
trouble. He'll handle himself." I turn back and call for Ziggy.
"C'mon, Zigs."

She lengthens her stride, giving me a long-suffering look. "Yes,
Mother."

I gently tweak her long red braid. "Don't sass me. We're in the
jungle. And I care about you."

Smiling, she falls into step with me. "Well, when you put it
that way."

We find ourselves in a dip in the trail that has us rushing down ffort235

a small hill, then climbing its other side, toward a blind turn along a narrow point in the path that overlooks a steep drop. I hug closer to the wooded edge and drag Ziggy with me, so she's tucked safely away from the ledge.

Halfway up the hill, Aiden catches his foot and swears under his breath. Dropping to one knee, he ties his unlaced boot. "Go ahead," he says. "I'm coming."

Ziggy and I jog up the last of the hill, huffing and puffing as we turn the bend, then come face-to-face with the last thing I'd ever expect in the middle of a Hawaiian jungle: a tall man in full-on circus gear, complete with a horrific clown face.

It scares the ever-living *shit* out of me.

Shrieking in tandem, we startle violently. But while Ziggy falls safely toward the trees, where I purposefully set her, I stumble toward the ledge, tripping over a root.

And then I'm hurtling backward, with nothing but the terrifying silence of falling whirling around me.

TWENTY-THREE

Aiden

Playlist: "Video Games," Trixie Mattel

My head snaps up the moment I hear Freya scream. Then I realize Ziggy is screaming, too. And then my heart lurches as a guy in clown gear flies toward Freya, desperately trying to catch her—Freya, who's falling, stumbling toward the edge of a drop whose height I have no time to calculate but only know I can't risk.

I can't explain it. How in the blink of an eye, I explode up the last of the hill, lunging toward Freya as her arms pinwheel and she starts to pitch off the ledge. The clown catches her hand, enough to slow her fall, before I grasp a solid fistful of her shirt and use all my strength to hurl her toward me, throwing myself forward as a counterweight. I hear Freya's body connect with the earth, a collective gasp of relief around us.

And then the piercing sound of my wife screaming as I fly into the air.

They say falling happens in an instant. But for me, it happens in merciful slow motion. My head jerks back as I realize there's another ledge below me. Maybe twenty feet. I can land there and not career farther into the jungle below. Hopefully.

It's instinctive, my muscles calling to mind what I've learned, because I'm *that* guy who has actually studied how to fall safely. You never know when you'll have to jump out of a multistory building and try not to die. I know to bend my legs and hold them together to prepare for impact so that I won't fracture my spine or split my head. You bet your ass I've made sure I'm prepared.

Even though the ledge is approaching, it's narrow, and there's a chance I'll flip off it and fall to . . . well, my death, probably. I have to slow myself down, decrease momentum, so I reach out, clawing for anything I can, and find a sapling that my hand somehow catches.

Freya screams again. I hear it, far off, yet close. I want to yell back that I'm okay, tell her she doesn't have to worry, but as I grab the sapling with my other hand, and the weak branch starts to bend, then snap, I realize I shouldn't make promises I can't keep.

That's when my grip fails, and I drop, for a terrifying moment, inverted, until I tuck myself so I can land feet first. And I do, with a sickening crack that sends white-hot pain burning up my left arm.

Viggo yells something overhead, but I can't process it. All I know is that I landed and I'm safe. For now.

Voices blend, a wild mix of urgent speech that I still can't make sense of. My body's flooded with adrenaline, my ears ringing. I can't catch a breath, whether it's panic or the wind was knocked out of me, or both.

"I got you, Aiden!" Ryder yells, landing beside me with a complex arrangement of rope linked to his waist, anchored in his grip. "Hey. Can you feel your hands and feet?"

"Unfortunately," I wheeze. "My left arm. Don't touch it."

Ryder exhales roughly. "Okay. I'm going to chance moving you. Hold on with your right arm, locked around me."

Viggo's voice follows him. "Go slow."

Somehow we're hoisted up along the ledge, Ryder holding my not-busted arm hard over his shoulder, coaching me to walk my way up the path's steep face as he anchors us with rope, until more hands than I can count are dragging me onto the trail.

"Aiden!" Freya mutters. Her voice is thin and fragile, like glass blown too far.

"M'okay," I mumble thickly. My eyes are slammed shut, my heart flying out of my chest. I'm not entirely sure I'm not dead. My head hurts. My back hurts. My arm *really* hurts. With my good hand, I wander the earth until I feel her. "Are you all right?" I ask.

A sob jumps out of Freya. "Aiden, I'm fine. Y-you nearly killed yourself."

"You or me," I mutter. "Easy choice." My hand wanders my body, as I try to orient myself. And that's when I feel its absence from my neck. "My chain!" I yell hoarsely. My eyes snap open as I visually search the ground.

"Aiden, easy." Freya sets her hand on my chest, calming me. "It's gone."

"No." My heart pounds. That chain . . . I can't lose it.

She searches my eyes. "It means that much to you?"

I stare at her, wounded fury tingeing my expression. "Of course it does, Freya. I told you I've never taken it off. I touch it every day. It means a *fuck* ton to me."

"What is he talking about?" Ryder asks.

Freya shakes her head. "It was . . . it was my wedding gift to him. It was just a pendant with a little inscription."

"It wasn't *just* a pendant," I tell Ryder. "Can you look? See if it's there?"

Ryder stands. "I'll try, Aiden."

My head flops back to the earth, throbbing painfully. "I lost it," I whisper.

"What do we do?" Ziggy's voice cuts through, shaky and quiet. "Should I call Dad?"

"No, not yet," Freya says. "Just give me a second to think and figure out his injuries." Her hands are warm against my face, and I sigh. She bends over me, leaning close. "Bear, I know you're upset about the chain, but right now I need you to tell me what's painful."

"Um," I say roughly, swallowing and licking my lips. My mouth feels like it's stuffed with cotton. "Ribs hurt. Left arm's the worst."

"That's it?"

"Hurts *a lot*."

"Oh, Aiden, that's good." I feel Freya's hands shaking. "Thank God."

I feel the man cubs' silence.

Until one of them has the idiocy to open their mouths.

Oliver yanks off his red clown nose and says, "Freya—"

"Don't talk!" she snaps, her hands examining my left arm. "Just shut your mouths and be glad you didn't just kill my husband."

Absolute silence.

I wince when she hits the tender point, before she slowly starts to flex it.

"Fuck." I wrench it away. My stomach churns with nausea from the pain.

"Broken," she mutters.

"Badly broken?" Ryder asks.

Freya doesn't say anything. Which means yes.

"I'm okay, Freya." I stare up and see her, really see her. Beautiful Freya, her white-blonde hair a halo around her head, reflecting late-morning sunlight. Pale blue-gray eyes wet with unshed tears.

She bends over me again, kissing me and kissing me. I feel her tears, wet against her cheeks. "Aiden."

"Shh." I clasp her to me with my not-throbbing arm. "It's all right."

She's okay. That's all that matters. I'm just going to be haunted by that nightmarish image of her teetering on the edge of the drop for the rest of my life.

"I'm okay." Slowly, I sit up, to prove to everyone—including myself—that I'm not wrecked. Pain slices through my ribs and left arm. "Just kidding. Might vomit."

Ryder crouches next to me and sets a hand on my back. "Take some slow breaths. Willa's grabbing your water."

Freya stands and points her finger at Viggo and Oliver. "What the *fuck* were you thinking?"

Viggo stares at the ground. Because even though he didn't wear the mask and clown gear, fifty bucks says he helped pack them. That must be why their bags were so big.

Oliver drops down next to us and clasps my good hand. He looks to Freya, then me. "I'm so, *so* sorry. I—" His hand is shaking, his eyes wet with tears. "I thought Freya, then you, were going to die because of me, and I never ever meant—"

Freya sighs. "Ollie, no one died."

"They could have!"

I pat his shoulder gently. "I'm okay, bud. So's Freya."

Viggo stands over us, staring up through his lashes at Freya, like a puppy who got caught pissing on the rug. "It was a shitty get-back for your clown prank on us."

"*Ohhh*," Willa says, eyes widening. "You mean the one she pulled at your joint birthday party? Yeah, that was good."

"Actually, it was horrifying," Viggo says.

"That was a *year* ago!" Freya yells.

"I know," Viggo snaps. "Okay? It was juvenile. Clearly, we regret it."

"It was my idea," Oliver blurts out, staring miserably at her. "To do something to help you guys. And Viggo pointed out it had the added bonus of settling the score on the clown front."

We both frown at Oliver. "What?"

Ollie sighs. "In my human psychology course this spring, they taught us about how trauma bonds people. You both hate clowns—"

"*Everyone* hates clowns," Freya and I yell.

"Fair," he concedes. "I mean not everyone, but that's neither here nor there. So I thought a good jump scare might help things along with you two. I was even ready to take a right hook from Aiden for it. *Viggo* was supposed to make sure you were together on the trail."

Viggo throws up his hands. "I was trying, okay? You didn't wait for my whistle."

"Oh, right. This is all *my* fault."

"Seeing as you're the asshole who jumped out prematurely on a narrow part of the trail, I'd say yes, Oliver, it is—"

"Enough!" I don't yell, but it's my professor voice. The one that carries and commands attention. Silent, Viggo's and Oliver's eyes snap to me. "No use pointing fingers. It was dumb. You shouldn't have done it. But it's over with."

Willa crouches down and sets my water bottle in my good hand. "You okay, Mac?"

I nod, then manage a short chug of water.

Ryder takes the bottle from me and screws on the cap, glowering at Oliver and Viggo. "You know, at some point you two have to actually grow the fuck up, right?"

They both give him petulant glares.

"I said I'm sorry," Oliver growls.

Viggo narrows his eyes. "You're one to lecture about pranks."

Freya bends over me in physical therapist mode as I clumsily work my way up, hoisting me easily to my feet.

"Let it be, Ryder," I manage roughly.

Viggo's face flashes with a grateful smile before he tucks it away under Freya's severe glare.

Freya's arm is solid around my waist, anchoring me against her. "I love you both," she tells the man cubs. "Nothing changes that. That said, you need to know what you did was over the line. I understand why you're going to such great lengths." Her gaze drifts between them. "Because you want us to pull through this. Because while Aiden and I aren't Mom and Dad, we're important to you—*us*, as a couple. Aiden is your family, a brother to you, and you love him. You're scared of any of that changing. But this isn't how things get fixed, guys. Aiden and I are working on us. We're committed to that. Let us be, already."

My throat thickens as her hand clasps my side. It's the first time I've heard her say that. When she told me she loved me, I held on to that like a lifeline. But this?

Aiden and I are working on us. We're committed to that.

It feels like finally making it to dry land, safe and sure, after too long barely holding my head above water.

I watch Freya still lecturing them, and I feel so lucky. No, not lucky. Chance isn't at play here. It's a choice. Freya chose me. And I feel so grateful. So, so grateful.

The man cubs stare at the ground guiltily, scuffing their feet into the dirt path.

Oliver peers up and bites his bottom lip again. "I can't say enough how sorry I am."

Viggo looks up next and nods. "Me too."

"Forgiven," I tell them. "Maybe, though . . . Maybe this is a learning moment. Maybe it's time to put aside pranks. At least, pranks like this. Stick to whoopie cushions and toothpaste-filled Oreos. But no more meddling or dangerous moves. Not like this, guys."

They both nod miserably.

As I stand longer, the world starts to dance with stars. When I try to take a step to steady myself, reflexively moving my hurt arm for balance, pain rips through me, so excruciating that I wobble, then my knees buckle. And, yes, I'm secure enough in my masculinity to admit what comes next.

I faint.

Waking up from sleep, I'm sore and disoriented. Freya's lips, soft and gentle, trace my face. "Freya."

She smiles against my skin. "Aiden. I brought you more ibuprofen."

I groan. "Doesn't work."

"I know," she says sympathetically. "Compound fractures hurt like a bitch. But that's why I'm here."

My eyes open blearily and take her in. They widen. Because all she's wearing is one of my undershirts. No bra. No panties. The fabric stretched tight across her tits.

Air rushes out of me. "Freya, I want to do so many things to you right now, but I can't."

"You don't have to do anything," she whispers. "You know how you run your fingers through my hair, massage my legs after a long day with patients? How you kiss me everywhere except *those* places, and it drives me wild?"

I search her eyes. "Yes."

She smiles, luminous, dazzling in the moonlight filling our bedroom. "I want to do that to you."

Her touch wanders my chest, soft swirls of her fingertips that make my skin crackle with awareness. I shut my eyes, my heart pounding anxiously in my chest. A hive of worries, buzzing and angry, swarms my thoughts.

"Aiden?" she says quietly. "I want to distract you, help you relax."

My eyes blink open. I peer down at her. "How?"

She strokes my cheek. "I'll just touch you. Kiss you. Make you feel good. There are lots of places on your body to do that." Pressing her lips to my pec, she breathes deeply and sinks her teeth into my skin. I suck in a breath, as heat rushes down my stomach. Her eyes meet mine again.

"What do you think?" she whispers.

After a long silence, I draw her close and give her a soft kiss. "Okay."

Freya leans in as her hand wanders my stomach.

"Close your eyes," she says.

"Why can't I look?"

She leans closer, her taut nipples brushing my chest through her shirt. I groan as she kisses me. "Because I said so. Now, close your eyes."

I listen to her, shutting my eyes. The world becomes dark and quiet, the only sound, Freya shifting off the bed. A drawer opens, then shuts, before she crawls across the mattress and straddles me again. My hand wanders up her thigh, but her grip clamps down on it. Pointedly, she presses my uninjured wrist against the mattress.

"Behave yourself," she says briskly, swatting the side of my ass.

A bolt of lust slams through me. "Jesus, Freya."

She laughs to herself. "There's a new boss in town, MacCormack. Now take a deep breath."

As I do, her hands slide up my stomach, slick and warm with oil. She works my shoulders, my arms, every single fingertip. Next, my thighs, then calves which she rubs slowly, deep, strong kneads of her fingers. I feel the strength in her touch, the power in her body.

And I feel her love.

"If anything hurts or you're just tired of it," she says, "tell me. Okay? We can stop whenever."

I shake my head. My body is heavy, my mind blank. It feels like *shavasana* on the deck the other morning. "Feels great."

"Good." I hear the smile in her voice. Her touch moves to my feet, kneading my arches, stretching my toes, until she moves back up my legs. She stops at my hips, her palms rubbing in deep circles around my groin. I tense against them at first, so self-consciously aware of that part of my body, how frustrated I've become with it. But Freya's touch melts that tension away, and my hips respond instinctively, pushing up against her, the familiar ache building in my cock.

Even so, I don't think about it beyond a fleeting observation. I'm not fixated on whether I'm ready for her, not preoccupied with performing, anticipating how to make it good for us. I'm just . . . feeling. Next, her palms flatten, sliding up my chest. Her thumbs circle my nipples, but it's not a teasing glance. They stay there, circling hypnotically, building sensation I had no idea I could feel.

"You like that?" she asks quietly.

I nod. "So much."

Slowly, Freya straddles higher on my stomach, her hands never leaving me. She bends over me, soft teasing flicks of her tongue against the sensitive peaks she's coaxed under her thumbs. She's relentless, as minutes tick by and she does things to my chest and nipples I've never felt before. Nips and bites, long, torturous strokes of her tongue. A moan rolls out of me. I'm hot and agitated, hungry for something I can't even name except *more, harder, longer*.

Her hands sweep down my waist, which feels like it's lit up with a thousand more points of sensation than it ever has. My skin is electric, my breathing taut. And when her touch wanders lower, cupping my ass, kneading it, I realize I'm rocking beneath her, the familiar build of release close, lightning bright, hot and urgent. Long, hard kisses trail up my neck. Feeling her tits brush my oversensitive chest is an incredibly pleasurable agony.

"Freya." I draw my knees up, desperate, chasing release.

"Yes, Aiden," she whispers.

I drag her mouth to mine, burying my sounds as I come unexpectedly, roughly, spilling in long, hard juts that paint my stomach. Freya's touch soothes me as she murmurs softly against my neck and plants one last kiss. Panting, I drop my head to the pillow.

Freya smiles and brushes my hair off my face. "See. Distracted you, didn't I?"

I stare at her in wonder. "What was that?" I ask hoarsely. Freya and I are fairly adventurous, but this is a first. I've never come without touching myself.

She kisses me again. "You'd think for how often you like to do it to me, you'd know." Her eyes search mine as her smile deepens. "You just had your first nipple-induced orgasm, my friend. Welcome. It's a wonderful world, isn't it?"

Dazed, thrilled, relieved, I draw her close to me. "I don't know for sure," I whisper, dragging the shirt up her body and giving one of her full soft breasts a tender kiss. "Better corroborate the evidence with you, too."

TWENTY-FOUR

Freya

Playlist: "1234," Feist

Hot, relaxed, I lie with my face to the sun, soaking up Aiden's voice as he reads *Persuasion*. No British accent—party pooper—but deep and warm. Goose bumps dance on my skin as he reads Wentworth's letter to Anne. His delivery is urgent and moving, his voice soft, for only my ears. Tears prick my eyes.

"*'I can listen no longer in silence. I must speak to you by such means as are within my reach. You pierce my soul. I am half agony, half hope. Tell me not that I am too late, that such precious feelings are gone for ever—'*"

When Aiden pauses, I crack open my eyes. He bites his lip. "Shit," he mutters, pinching the bridge of his nose. "She's wrecking me."

I squeeze his hand, then run my hand along his forearm. "It's a beautiful moment."

"If by beautiful, you mean ripping my heart to shreds and making me cry on a public beach, then yes."

A laugh jumps out of me. "Bear." I bring his hand to my mouth and kiss it. Aiden clears his throat and adjusts his sunglasses. "Okay," he says. "Continuing. *'I offer myself to you again with a heart even more your own, than when you almost broke it, eight years and a half ago. Dare not say that man forgets sooner than woman, that his love has an earlier death. I have loved none but you. Unjust*

I may have been, weak and resentful I have been, but never inconstant.'"

As Aiden finishes Wentworth's letter, I stare at him, seeing a glimpse of what we're becoming—individually, together. Something newer, paradoxically softer, after all that we've sustained and weathered. I never knew I could love him differently, that something that felt total and complete the day I married him could evolve into a deeper, more complex expression. But I realize as he shuts my book and presses a kiss to my lips—I do.

"Now," he says, pulling out his own reading. "Back to *my* book. Which so far has not made me cry, thank you very much."

I lean in and steal one more kiss. "How is it?"

Aiden peers at me, dark sunglasses shielding his eyes as he wiggles his eyebrows. "Good. I think they're finally about to get down."

Our gazes tangle. My grip on my beach chair nearly crushes the handles.

The past few nights have been the kind of torture I only remember from the two weeks leading up to our wedding, when I had this brilliant idea for us to be celibate and wipe our sexual RAM. I wanted Aiden to look at me in a different way when he peeled off my dress. I wanted there to be an edge of need and longing that I'd already felt shifting as we'd settled into living together, establishing a routine that mellowed our desperation.

Our wedding night was explosive. And just like the night of the rehearsal dinner, I feel like I'm about to detonate. Slow, deep kisses. Touch wandering each other's body, teasing, coaxing sensation and desire from parts of me I've forgotten could be so exquisitely sensitive.

"Well." I clear my throat and sip from my water bottle. "Good. At least someone's getting some."

Aiden huffs a laugh and sets his hand over mine, sliding our fingers together. "Home tomorrow."

And we have a marriage counseling appointment the next day with Dr. Dietrich. Who just might give us the green light for sex again.

"Yeah," I whisper.

He lifts my hand to his mouth and kisses my knuckles softly, one by one. Lowering my hand, he slips his finger over my ring, spinning it and revealing the tan line I've earned after a week in the Hawaiian sun. "Impressive," he murmurs.

"Well, not all of us can have a beard tan."

His eyes widen. "Shit. I didn't even think about that. Man, now I'm committed."

"Hardly. You could shave it, spend one afternoon working in the yard, and it would be evened out." I look him over, practically bronze now, sweat glistening on his skin, and swallow a sigh.

"Not that I'll be doing any of that," he says, returning to his book.

"That's right. You'll have the man cubs to delegate to." Viggo and Oliver's penance for their prank gone wrong is doing our yard work until Aiden's fractured arm has healed.

Aiden grins evilly and flips the page of his book. "That's going to be so gratifying."

A laugh jumps out of me but quickly fades when Viggo walks by, searing my retinas. He's wearing a Speedo, and holy shit, I wish I'd never seen that.

"Christ, Viggo," Axel mutters, shaking his head. "The lengths people will go for attention."

Ziggy slaps a hand over her eyes. "I can't unsee it," she groans.

Everyone else in the family is either doing their own thing elsewhere or blissfully preoccupied. Lucky them.

Oliver hoots and scrambles for his phone as Viggo struts down to the water, glorying in our horrified reactions. Just as he gets to the water's edge, Oliver's phone starts blasting. Viggo spins, faces us, and starts busting surprisingly good moves that I'm too scared to watch any longer in case the Speedo doesn't hold up to his hip thrusts.

Aiden's laugh bursts beside me like a firework in the night sky, so bright and rich that it stuns me. "I knew it!" he says. "Oh man, that kid is dead meat."

"Oliver," he barks.

Ollie peers over his shoulder, looking wary. "What's up, Aiden?"

"You and the parrot haven't by chance been spending any time together, have you? Particularly on the first day when you and your parents arrived bright and early, before everyone else?"

"Um." Oliver's cheeks pink. "Why would you ask that?"

"Oh, I don't know," Aiden says casually, slipping the bookmark into his book. "She seems to have quite the vocabulary. In fact, verbatim the vocabulary of that song you're playing."

"What are you talking about?" I ask him.

Aiden narrows his eyes at Oliver. "The parrot keeps harassing me with explicit lyrics."

I frown at him. "Esmerelda? The polite old lady parrot that says *'Top o' the morning!'* And *'Hiya, toots!'*"

"To *you* she says that." Aiden drums his fingers on his chair. "You've heard her call me *'hot stuff.'*"

"I mean, she's not wrong."

He gives me a look. "She's not saying it because she actually thinks that about me. She's saying it because someone *taught* her."

I frown at him. "Is that possible?"

"Seems so." Aiden throws down his book and stands, as Oliver scrambles upright. "I might only have one good arm, Oliver Abram, but I know your weakness."

Oliver blanches. "No tickling, Aiden. You know I can't take that shit."

"Should have thought of that before you sicced the Lil Wayne of parrots on me for a week straight. You know how disturbing it is to shower with a giant green parrot sitting on the counter nearby telling you '*Li-li-li-lick, lick that cream, make her scream*'?"

As Aiden stalks toward him, Oliver backs away, hands up. "It was just some harmless fun!"

"Harmless?" Aiden's mouth twitches, suppressing a smile. "Possibly. But was it also aggravating? Bizarre? Uncalled for? Absolutely."

Oliver stumbles on a beach chair, glancing over his shoulder. "Aiden. Your arm," he says pleadingly. "You shouldn't run. You need to be cautious of it."

"Unfortunately for you," Aiden says, throwing his sunglasses onto his chair behind him, "I'm experiencing an uncharacteristically reckless moment."

Realizing he's screwed, Oliver takes off down the shore, Aiden streaking after him. And when my troublemaking brother gets tackled to the sand, his screaming laugh is swept up in the sun-warmed wind.

―――――

"Well." Dr. Dietrich smiles at us over her glasses. "That sounds like quite the trip."

Aiden squeezes my hand gently, his thumb circling my palm. I squeeze back.

"It was," he tells her. "I had a good conversation with my business partner about more evenly distributing responsibilities. I stayed off my phone and prioritized being present, relaxing as much as possible."

I smile at him. "Aiden planned an incredibly romantic date, and we had lots of good downtime together. It felt like we made some strides, talking and reconnecting."

"And how did that come about?" Dr. Dietrich asks.

Aiden peers over at me, his vivid blue eyes holding mine. "We had honest conversations. We talked a good bit about what you said before we left—about how we've changed and how we want to better understand what that means for loving each other."

I squeeze his hand again.

"How do you feel, being home now?" Dr. Dietrich asks.

My smile falters slightly as I meet her eyes. "I'm a bit nervous to be back in the real world, with its pressures bearing down on us again, but I feel . . . hopeful. I feel excited, too. Like there's so much to figure out and learn together."

Aiden's grip tightens. "I'm nervous, too. I don't want to get sucked into work the way I was. But I feel like we're in a better place, that it's less likely to be something that comes between us. Freya knows all there is to know about the project. There are no secrets."

Dr. Dietrich smiles between us. "Well, dare I say, I was apprehensive about you two disappearing on me so early into our work together, and I'm certainly not saying you're done with therapy, but this time away served you."

Aiden turns toward her. "How do you think?"

"What you both just told me demonstrates that you've arrived at an important milestone in reconciliation: building back trust. You've made peace with the very unsettling truth that people who love each other can hurt each other deeply, often without meaning to. It's like knocking over a lamp. One rogue elbow when you weren't looking, and the glass is shattered, the shade irrevocably bent. It's so easy to break something, and so paradoxically hard to put it back together. Even when we do, it never looks the same."

Aiden's eyes hold mine as we share a brief moment of unspoken recognition.

"What you've decided," Dr. Dietrich says, "is that you can see the beauty in those stitched-up, glued-together places, that you're willing to learn for the future. To watch that wily elbow while acknowledging the possibility that hurt will come again, hoping this time it will be gentler, that this time the glue of forgiveness can mend the cracks that come."

I lean into Aiden. "I love that."

He wraps an arm around me. "I do, too."

"Good," she says brightly. "So on to the next order of business. Sex."

Aiden chokes on air and blinks away. I pat his thigh gently.

Dr. Dietrich shrugs, wearing a warm smile. "Let's talk about how you're doing on that front. I'm going to take a gander that *something* happened intimately between you two. Because this"—she points to our bodies, wedged against each other on the couch—"screams, *We might have bent the rules a little bit.*"

I blush. Aiden clears his throat and says hoarsely, "Yes. The rules were a tiny bit bent."

My blush deepens as I stare at my hands.

"Well, that's good. I approve. In fact, I'm lifting the ban. With one contingency." She stares at Aiden, then glances toward me. "Complete communicative transparency. Sex is vulnerable. If you're ready for that intimacy, I want the conversation and dialogue flowing honestly and trustingly. When you're hitting a roadblock, back up, regroup, talk. Then reattempt physical intimacy. Okay?"

Aiden's face is grim, his eyes tight. Which . . . I have no idea what to make of that. I'd guess it's a matter of his anxiety and how it's impacted his sex drive, but it seems like that was obsolete in Hawaii. If it's not that, what is it?

"Okay," I tell her.

"Yes," he whispers. "Okay."

"Great," Dr. Dietrich says, spinning in her chair and scooping up a remote from the pile of papers that even *I* can say I find disturbingly messy. "Now the fun part."

She presses a button, startling us both when a screen pops up from the thin side table next to her desk. Riffling through one of her desk drawers, she pulls out two controllers and tosses them our way. "Time to kill some zombies."

Aiden frowns at her. "Are you actually telling us to play video games?"

Dr. Dietrich sighs. "It's the pedagogist in you, constantly questioning my methods."

Aiden blushes. "Sorry."

I set the remote in my hand and peer over at Aiden. "He broke his arm, Dr. Dietrich. That gives me an unfair advantage."

She grins. "Good thing you're playing together. You two against the world. How's that sound?"

Aiden's thigh nudges mine as he holds my eyes. His smile is dazzling. "I like the sound of that a lot."

TWENTY-FIVE

Freya

Playlist: "Ready Now," dodie

"Do you think it's weird that my mom wasn't here when we got back?" Aiden asks.

I shut the tea drawer with my hip and drop the sachet in my mug. "It hadn't struck me as weird, no. I mean, she knew we'd be home shortly, and she said she had a brunch she'd forgotten about. Seems like a good reason not to stick around to give us the report on how many times Horseradish tried to eat your shoelaces."

Aiden drums his fingers on his laptop, with his back to me. I can't see his face, but I notice the tense set of his shoulders.

"Are you worried about her?" I ask him.

"I can't quite put my finger on it. I just . . . had a feeling something was up." He shakes his head. "I'm overanalyzing."

"You could text her, ask her if everything's okay. Maybe she'll tell you if something's going on."

Aiden snorts, his fingers back to typing. "Yeah, 'cause Mom's an open book."

"I know she can be hard to get to open up."

"Understatement of the year. Then again, who am I to talk?"

"Aiden, don't shortchange yourself." Adding a spoonful of honey to my mug, I screw on the lid and stare at the back of his sweet, stubborn head. "You've been in talk therapy since I've known you.

You are a hell of a lot better at articulating your emotions than almost all men I know, barring my brothers, and God, do I wish they articulated less."

He laughs drily. "Yeah, but I still have a ways to go."

"And you're working on that. We both are."

Aiden glances over his shoulder and meets my eyes. "Yeah. We are."

The kettle starts to whistle. I grab it off the heat before it screeches. "Need anything while I'm in here?"

Narrowing his eyes playfully, Aiden says, "I need to recover from the fact that all these years we haven't played video games because my wife said, and I quote, '*I'm not that into them*,' and then here you went and slayed the zombie game at counseling."

I grin from behind the counter, pouring hot water into my mug. "I didn't say I wasn't *good* at them, just that I'm not that into them. Because I'm not. It was something Ax and Ren and I did sometimes, and I got good at it."

He shakes his head. "I'm not even sure if I really know you anymore."

A warm laugh leaves me as I cross back into the living room and plop on the other end of the sofa. Sipping my tea, I peer at Aiden over my mug, watching him struggle with typing, given the cast. His fingers can still move fine, but he's clearly hurting.

"Do you want to dictate to me?" I ask.

He glances my way. "Sorry?"

"I offered to let you dictate." I nod toward his computer. "Looks like typing hurts. I can help you crank out some emails more efficiently, get you caught up, and then you don't have to be uncomfortable."

His expression is unreadable as our eyes hold each other's. Finally, he blinks away. "Yeah. That . . . that would be great. Thank you." Carefully, he lifts the laptop with one hand and sets it on my lap.

I spin it around, then stash my mug on the coffee table. "Ready when you are."

Aiden props a pillow under his cast arm but then grabs my feet and sets them on his lap. Slowly, he drags his thumb up my arch. "Okay," he says.

I nod. "Dictate away."

"Wait. Let me savor you saying that for a moment."

Kicking him gently, I earn his *oof*, followed by a laugh. "The only place you get to boss me is in that room at the end of the hall. And it's staying that way."

Our eyes meet. Aiden swallows roughly. His hand wraps around my ankle, whispering up my calf. Soft. Sensual. My toes curl against the sofa cushion.

Aiden's eyes search mine, as his hand drifts even higher. Gripping the laptop, he lifts it away, then sets it on the coffee table.

"What are you doing?" I ask quietly.

"Work can wait."

"It can?"

He smiles softly and clasps my hand, tugging me until we're side by side, my legs bent over his lap, his good arm wrapped around my waist. One soft kiss to my lips, before he pulls away and meets my eyes. "Come with me?" he asks.

I tip my head, curious. "Okay."

Slowly, he stands from the sofa and tugs me along with him.

Horseradish and Pickles scamper along with us, tripping me up, so I bump into Aiden. He catches me on a laugh and lands with his back to the wall, my body tucked against his. Spinning, he leans into me and plants another gentle kiss to my lips, before dragging me the rest of the way into our bedroom.

"What are we doing?" I ask.

His expression dims, careful, guarded. "Shower with me?" He frowns, lifting his cast. "I'm tired of baths. And . . . I miss showering with you."

A lump catches in my throat. As I step closer, I cradle his face and press a kiss to his cheek. "You have to wrap it."

"Damn. I thought I could just lean dashingly half out of the shower and protect my arm."

I laugh. "I'll grab some plastic wrap and tape. You'll still make it very dashing, have no worries."

When I come back, Aiden's sitting on the edge of the bed, staring down at his feet. I walk toward him until we're toe to toe. He doesn't look up.

"Aiden?"

Suddenly, he wraps his arm around me and tugs me close, his head resting against my stomach. Stunned, I blink down at him, then carefully slip my fingers through his hair, hoping I can soothe whatever's troubling him. "What is it?"

He sighs heavily, pressing a kiss to my stomach and resting his head against me, squeezing me to him tighter. "I have something I need to tell you."

My pulse starts pounding as apprehension washes through me. He sounds so dejected. What could it possibly be?

"I'm listening," I tell him.

"I'm going to tell you this way," he says, still clutching me, head pressed to my stomach. "Because it's easier for me."

"Okay, Bear."

"I said at marriage counseling that my anxiety was affecting my sex drive."

I stare down at the crown of his head, willing myself to stay calm, to hear him and not imagine the worst, not that I can even imagine what that would be. "I remember."

"I said that after you pointed out the physical distance between us, I'd stopped initiating."

I swallow the threat of tears. "Yes."

"That was true." He exhales slowly. "But it wasn't all of the truth."

My grip on him tightens as I wait for him to find the words. "It's more than that," he whispers. "It has been. And it's not you, not about you *at all*," he says roughly. "It's . . . me. It's my—" Scrunching his eyes shut, he presses his forehead to my hip, thumping it there softly.

"It's my fucking brain, Freya. My anxiety's been so goddamn bad that it messed with my ability to respond to you, and I felt broken and ashamed. And I didn't know how to tell you without dashing your hopes for a baby. So I kept it to myself, because I hoped I could fix it before you noticed, before I'd have to try to explain . . . *everything* that was going so wrong. All the ways I felt I was failing you, our dreams, our plans.

"And then we were on vacation, trying to keep it together for your parents, and I couldn't risk upsetting you, when I knew how much it meant to be a positive front around them. I'm sorry I kept it to myself for so long. I promise, you know it all now. Everything that I held in, everything I've been struggling with."

I stand, reeling as his words sink in, as countless moments in our recent sex life flash before my eyes.

How often Aiden gave but didn't ask, how frequently he gently redirected me when I reached for him. How many times I was given three incredible orgasms, and as I was drifting off in his arms, I sleepily noticed he hadn't had one. And the seed of doubt had burrowed inside me, painful and foreign. What if he wasn't attracted to me anymore? What if he wanted someone else? What if he didn't want me, but he was . . . placating me?

Now I understand that wasn't it. That wasn't it at all.

I hold him in stunned silence, my ears ringing so loudly, I'm shocked I can hear him when he whispers, "I'm sorry, Freya. I'm sorry I kept it from you. I'm sorry it's my reality right now. But I already saw a doctor, and it's not physical. It's psychological. I mean you saw what happened the other night, what we were able to share when we were on vacation. It's possible, but more often than not, it takes some time and relaxing and—" He sighs heavily, pressing a soft kiss to my stomach. "I won't let this stop us from having a family, I promise—"

"Aiden." I lower to my knees and cup his face, holding his eyes. "I love you."

He blinks down, and I grip his face harder.

"Look at me," I whisper. Slowly, he meets my eyes. "We'll find our way through this. As lovers. As a family. Please, *please* know, my only sadness right now is that you've held this in, all on your own, when I could have held it with you."

"I want a family with you, Freya. I promise."

I smile. "You already have a family with me."

"You know what I mean," he says. "I didn't want to disappoint you, because I knew what you would have done. You would have said we could wait for a baby, even when I knew how badly you wanted a baby—*I* wanted a baby. It was so confusing. Sometimes I just felt numb, like I couldn't respond, even when I wanted you, even when all I wanted was to be close. Other times, I'd start and then some shitty thought would hijack my thoughts. And sometimes, I just couldn't . . . finish."

He buries his face in his hands. "And all of that made the possibility of a baby impossible. So I focused on doing everything *else* that would have us ready for a baby, and I hoped I'd find some way to fix it. I couldn't figure out how to tell you the truth *and* protect you from how it hurt you."

I wrap my arms around him, and press a kiss to his cheek, wet from my tears, from his. "I'm so sorry, Aiden."

"Why?" he says roughly. "It's not your fault."

"Aiden, we did this, both of us. This twisted dance of always trying to fix ourselves and protecting each other from the parts that we couldn't. We both did that. You hid your anxiety, your frustration with your body. I numbed myself, kept my pain from you. It takes two to play that game, and we did. But not anymore."

His eyes hold mine. "I wish it wasn't like this."

"I know. But we'll find our way through it together." I press our foreheads together. "Promise."

I don't tell him we'll fix it. Or that it doesn't matter. Because I won't make promises or diminish what this means for him or for us. Because I know better now. I've learned that's not how love works.

I've learned that the measure of your love isn't how "okay" you both are or how quickly you hit the curveballs that life throws at you. Love's true test, the measure of its strength, is its bravery to be honest, its willingness to face the hardest moments and say, *Even though there's nothing to be done, at least I have you.*

"Come here." I interlace my fingers with his and get up from my knees. Aiden stands with me, looking uncertain and so beautiful—his wild, dark hair, fathomless ocean-blue eyes; the strong line of his nose, and a soft, full mouth hidden by his beard.

Eyes locked with his, I grip the hem of his shirt and lift it up, smoothing my hands along his chest. Stopping at his pecs, I rub my thumbs over his nipples, earning a rush of air from his lungs. Aiden's hand dives into my hair and brings our mouths a whisper apart. Tipping my head, he nudges my nose with his, then whispers, "Freya . . . I want you so badly, but I don't know . . ." He sighs roughly. "I don't know what will happen."

"Neither do I," I whisper. "I just know that I want *you*. Only you, that's all. Just like you want me."

"But if I can't . . ."

"If you can't?" I say quietly. "We'll enjoy everything that *can* happen. Then we'll figure out the rest together."

He stares into my eyes. "I love you."

I smile softly and kiss him—a faint brush of lips. His grip in my hair tightens, and I lean into him, wrapping my arms around his waist, gentling the hard planes of his back, that smooth warm skin. "I love you, too, Aiden."

Groaning, he leans out of my arms, yanks his shirt over his head, and drops it behind him.

I gape. "You just threw an article of clothing. Not a fold in sight. Not even placed on the bed."

"Stop it." He grins. "I can prioritize passion over tidiness . . . sometimes."

My smile echoes Aiden's as he tugs at my shirt and I help him, lifting it over my head. Aiden's eyes darken as he drinks me in, then, before I can reach back, his good hand finds my bra and unsnaps it in one effortless flick of his fingers.

"Impressive."

"Oh, trust me," he mutters against my lips. "There's lots I can do one-handed."

His kiss is deep and long as he tucks me against him, as I unbuckle his belt and slip my hands inside his jeans, tracing his hips, the firm curve of his backside.

"Undress," he says between kisses. "Please."

We clumsily strip each other, tripping on clothes, stumbling into the bathroom through messy kisses and desperate hugs. Skin to skin feels like heaven, like coming home and the first sign of spring after a long, cold winter. I plant soft open-mouthed kisses over his chest. Aiden kisses my neck, my jaw, the corner of my mouth, the tip of my nose.

"I love you," he whispers. "I can't stop saying it."

I kiss him again and stare into his eyes. "I love you, too."

Backing away, I lean into the shower and turn on the water. Aiden steps behind me, his hand gliding up my back, gentling the curve of my spine. Faint kisses travel my vertebrae, until he nips my neck, then my earlobe. I shiver as I straighten and turn toward him.

Guiding him to the sink, I set up my supplies and quickly wrap his arm. When I'm satisfied with my handiwork, I touch his bicep, above the plastic and tape, curling my hand along the rounded muscle. I kiss his shoulder, his collarbone, the hollow at the base of his throat.

Our bodies touch intimately, and we jolt, Aiden angling his head and meeting my mouth hungrily, a kiss that feels like the first spark of a bone-melting blaze. Backing into the shower, he slides the glass shut behind us and presses me against the tiles. Steam floats around us, curling a lock of his hair against his forehead. I look into his eyes, feeling us, close—not just our bodies, but *us*—and soak it up like rain after a drought.

"You're so beautiful, Freya." Aiden weighs my breast in his hand, thumbing my nipple until it's hard and so sensitive, sparks dance through me, hot and warm between my thighs, in my belly, deep within me. His mouth teases my other breast, soft rolls of his tongue, nips of his teeth that make my moans echo around us.

I touch him everywhere—the curve of his strong back, his hard backside flexing as he moves against me instinctively, his powerful thighs bracketing my body. Our tongues tangle, hotter, faster, until Aiden pins me against the shower.

"The night you saw me," he whispers. "When I came home."

"Yes?"

He parts my legs, his hand wandering up my thigh, before he slowly sinks to his knees. "This was what I touched myself to the thought of. Kissing you, feeling you, tasting you until you were begging to come."

I exhale shakily as his hand parts me gently, finally strokes me—*there*—so perfectly, so tenderly I could cry.

"I love teasing you, but tonight I can't make you wait, Freya." He plants a soft kiss to my hip, before one finger, then two ease inside.

"Oh God." My hands dive into his hair as he lifts one of my legs and guides it over his shoulder. I'm exposed so intimately, spread before him as his kisses brand my skin, trailing up and down my thigh, everywhere except where I'm dying for him as each thrust of his fingers unravels me.

Aiden peers up, eyes hooded, breath coming in jagged pulls of air. "I missed this so much. I missed *you*."

Then his mouth closes on me, decadent sweeps and swirls of his tongue that make me gasp and rock against him.

There are men who go down on a woman because they know it gets her off. Then there are men who use their mouth like it's worship, like every single moment that their face is buried between her thighs is their idea of heaven. Aiden is like that, and he's always made me feel like a goddess when he does this.

I watch him, the soft rhythmic thrust of his mouth, his hand gentling my body, slipping around my hip and caressing my every curve. He traces the stretch marks at my hips, the dimples of my thighs, his grip tightening, betraying his desperation just as much as the hard jut of his erection shows me how much he loves making me come this way.

My heel digs into his back, my hands clutching his hair, as I pant, barely able to breathe against the need to come. Molten heat smolders through my limbs and breasts, pooling deep inside my body as Aiden groans against me.

I close my eyes, lost to the expert stroke of his tongue, the growing desperation building inside me. Suddenly he stands and crushes my mouth with a kiss. I taste him and me as my arms wrap around him, and my knees nearly buckle.

"Freya. Touch me. Touch me, please."

He grabs my hand and wraps it around his length, throbbing and thick. I stroke him, velvet soft, every hot, rigid inch pulsing under my hand.

"I want you," he says, low and quiet against my ear. "I want you, wet and begging for it. I want you writhing on my cock."

His words unfurl a new depth of need, a hot desperation to be as close to him as I can.

"Freya," he whispers. With the grip of his uninjured hand, he lifts my leg and sets it on the built-in bench, rubbing me as he grinds against my hips. "Tell me."

"I want your cock," I gasp, my hands whispering down his chest, his length, the tightness of his balls, earning his breathless groan.

"Take it, then," he says, easing himself inside me, painstakingly slow. I claw at his shoulders, tortured, so ready for all of him.

Air rushes out of me as he draws back, then thrusts deeper. As he lowers his mouth to my breasts, Aiden gives them tender, singular focus, making my nipples peak and throb.

He's so hard, and I'm so desperately close already. I slip my hand down my stomach and rub my clit, feeling the first whisper of release.

"I feel you," he whispers. "God, I *feel* you, Freya. Come, baby. Come all over me."

Our mouths crash together. Deep, slow plunges of his tongue that keep pace with the steady drive of his hips. I pant against his mouth. My toes curl. My veins simmer, liquid gold, dazzling. Release builds, hot and weighty, an ache so sweet and harsh, I hear myself crying out, echoing around us as I beg him for everything.

"Everything," I gasp.

"You have it, Freya." As Aiden holds my eyes and thrusts deep, I come on a gasping sob. A sob that doesn't end with one pent-up cry of release. A sob that becomes weeping, weeping for joy and relief and bittersweet feelings that don't have names, only the shape and shadow of what we've missed and what we've gained as we've battled our way to this place. A place in which water pours over us and I don't hide my tears. A place in which I trust my husband, who kisses my tears—every single one—and holds me tight.

TWENTY-SIX

Aiden

Playlist: "Stoned on You," Jaymes Young

Freya lies in my arms, damp from the shower, her breath soft and even. "I'm not sleeping," she murmurs.

I press a kiss to her hair, running my hand down her back. "It would be okay if you were."

"I don't want to sleep," she whispers. Her hand drifts down my body, wrapping appreciatively around my length. "I want to touch you."

I didn't come after she did. I didn't hide it. Part of it was because she was sobbing, and there's always something about Freya crying that sends adrenaline flooding my body. At first I was afraid, for just a moment, that somehow I'd hurt her or upset her, but I realized she was just . . . feeling. And I loved that the woman who'd walked in on me in that shower just a month ago, eyes cold, body closed off, a thousand unspoken words between us, felt safe to cry in my arms simply because she needed to.

After that, every trace of my body's response was gone. Freya kissed me, whispered she loved me. Then we washed each other, stole kisses, and held each other until the hot water ran out.

I knew this might happen, that we'd climb into bed and she'd try to pick up where we left off. As I contemplated that, the fears and worries of what might go wrong grew louder and noisier in my head.

As her hand strokes me, I don't know what to do. I just know that a cold wave of anxiety washes through me, like our second morning in Hawaii when I forgot the number one rule—never stand with your back to the ocean—and got slammed to the sand. And like swimming against a riptide, each second I try to fight the building power of my thoughts, my panic just pulls me farther from her.

Freya's touch shifts, roaming lovingly across my body, but the crush of defeat drags me down, a vicious undertow I can't escape.

She bends over me and presses soft kisses to my mouth. "Stay with me."

"It's . . ." I scrunch my eyes shut. "I'm trying."

"Aiden."

Slowly, I open my eyes and meet hers.

"You know how sometimes I don't come?" she whispers.

I narrow my eyes, hating where she's going with this. "Yes."

She smiles softly. "What do you tell me when that happens?"

"'*It's okay, baby,*'" I tell her through the thickness in my voice. "'*Just let me hold you.*'"

"That's right," she says, before a gentle kiss to my lips. "Do you know how safe that made me feel? For my partner to normalize that and make me feel loved? Because it *is* normal."

A rough sigh leaves me. "Yes."

Freya tucks herself tight against my body, her thigh draped over mine, and wanders her hand along my stomach and chest. Her lips meet mine in a soft, long kiss. "Just stay with me. We'll find our way, Aiden. Together, okay?"

Our eyes meet as I turn toward her, tucking her close to me. Skin to skin. Quiet in the darkness. I wade into the unfamiliar waters of acceptance as she touches me, kisses me. I bathe in the weight of Freya's love as I kiss her back.

Her kisses fade. Her touch slows. I hold her tight long after she's fast asleep.

———————

I can't sleep. And when Freya rolls off me, warm with sweat and sighing, I watch her, so beautiful, so desirable to me. Tired but wide awake in that awful way adrenaline has of fucking with my brain, I pick up the romance from Viggo that I've been working through. I haven't read since we got back from Hawaii, and things were about to get steamy.

Could be a nice way to make my eyes tired.

A quiet, optimistic voice inside me whispers, *Or get a "book boner."*

Yeah. Not getting my hopes up after that train wreck earlier.

I open to where I was, locating the small clip-on book light I've had for years. Freya's one of those heavy sleepers for whom light isn't a problem, a gift I wish I had. The plus is that it's made my insomniac bouts less of a wedge between us. I've always just read in bed, listening to the comforting sounds of her breathing. I flick on the tiny lamp, settling in beneath the sheets and the coziness of our room, dark but for the light's faint yellow glow.

The story gets hot. Fast.

The guy finally, *finally* bares his soul to her, and holy shit, it's explosive. *Tongue. Taste. Thrust. Wet. Desire. Heat.* It's a sea of words that builds to a sensual tsunami, each line a concerted step toward such an incredibly subtle yet hot climax—in every sense of the word—that when it ends, my hand is white-knuckling the page, my breath tight and ragged.

I close my eyes, clumsily shutting off the light and setting it on the nightstand. I stare up at the ceiling, stunned. This is . . .

Madness.

Really fucking magical madness.

Holy *shit*, I'm reading romance forever.

Not because I'm actually deluding myself it will always work like this—and by "this," I mean make me rock-fucking-hard—or because it guarantees anything, but because that was . . . beautiful. The vulnerability, the tenderness, the give and receive. I've spent so little of my adult life thinking about it, and why is that? Because I was raised to think men shouldn't?

Shit, are men missing out, and it doesn't just hurt us—it hurts our partners. At least men like me are missing out, and I think there's a lot of us, unfortunately. Men who don't spend time digging into how we want to be close to our partners. It leaves us despicably unprepared.

Why would I expect myself to just be able to flip on a switch for this space inside myself when I've barely cultivated it? For years, I relied on my marriage's emotional ease to pave the way for our sexual intimacy. But when things became difficult, I had no road map for how to move forward, how to stay close with Freya, even while I was struggling.

Yes, I love my wife. Yes, I'm deeply attracted to her. But that doesn't mean I miraculously knew how to find intimacy with her when the landscape around us shifted so drastically, when we changed, and life became much more complicated than working hard and chasing our dreams together.

Like the projects I've developed, the lectures I've taught, the physical exercises I do, I need to learn and practice this. And yes, maybe I'll need a little bit more help being comfortable with sex when it dredges up difficult emotions, compared with someone who doesn't have anxiety or a past like mine, but so the fuck what? There's no shame in it. Freya loves me for exactly who I am. She'll be patient with me, believe in me, desire me, in all my imperfection.

She's shown me that, time and again. Now I get to show her I trust that.

"Shit," I mutter, palming my eyes, wet with tears. I've cried more in the past week than I have in my entire life. And if that's part of what I take away from this nightmare season, I'm glad of it. Because it means I've grown as a person. A man. A husband.

Freya sighs in her sleep and rolls toward me, as if somehow she knows how much I need her.

She mutters nonsense as she settles in, her mouth brushing my shoulder. Air rushes out of me when her hand sleepily wanders my stomach and wraps around my waist. Heat builds beneath my skin, everywhere her body brushes mine, and before I can think about what I'm doing, I wrap my hand around hers, guiding it lower. Lower.

She sighs again, stirring a little from sleep. "Aiden," she murmurs.

I swallow roughly when she touches me, slow and lazy. When I drag her hand over my aching cock, every inch of me that's so heavy and hard, it's almost painful, her breath hitches. Her eyes spring open. Waking, she lifts her head and peers up at me.

"Hi," she whispers.

"Freya." It's all I can say, but our eyes hold, and she sees . . . everything I need her to.

Wordlessly, she moves closer, sliding her leg along mine, and her hands are finally on me. We kiss and I breathe her in, pull her close, our tongues tangling, her mouth soft and searching. I can't touch her enough, can't feel enough of her beautiful body, every lush, decadent curve. My hand traces her hip, her full, soft ass, the swell of her breasts, and her tight nipples.

"Aiden." She chokes as I feel her, as my mouth opens with hers, and we breathe, ragged and shallow. Her hands dive into my hair as I move against her, not yet inside, but so damn close. Each fast,

firm stroke of my cock against her soft body makes light pop behind my eyelids like fireworks against an ink-black sky.

"Touch me," I beg her. Her hands roam my skin, gentle sweeps
over my legs, kneading my ass, rubbing my arms, my chest. Our
kisses deepen, and I draw her closer to me, sucking her tongue,
tasting her, needing every part of my wife, every single corner
of her.

I move against Freya with an urgency I haven't known in so
long, different from anything I've ever felt. The desire to come, to
be close to her, isn't just caught in one intense part of me. It's . . .
everywhere. In my palms and my throat, the backs of my knees,
the breadth of my chest, coursing like a shower of sparks that radi-
ates outward along my spine.

"I have to be inside you," I whisper against her lips. "I have to."

Freya nods frantically as I drag her leg over my hip. Gently, her
mouth meets mine. I breathe her in, wrapping her tight inside my
grasp as we lie side to side, our bodies aligned so easily, so perfectly,
that with a roll of her hips she's gliding over me, wet, hot, and
so, so soft.

Reaching between us, Freya guides me inside her, and a pained,
hoarse cry rips from my chest. The sudden wet blur of tears behind
my eyes shocks me as I drag in a breath and meet her gaze.

"I love you," she whispers.

"God, I love you." I crush her body against mine and thrust
home, earning her breathless gasp that I know so well, the sound
of her pleasure, her beautiful body responding to mine.

"Aiden," she cries.

I press deeper, burying myself within her, tight and warm, so
exquisitely familiar and precious to me. Connected, moving, steady,
urgent, we stare into each other's eyes until Freya's begin to drift
shut, her hand fisting my hair.

"Oh," she says faintly. Her cries build, the sounds of our bodies, the hoarse rush of air that leaves me with each frantic drive, echoing around us.

"Touch yourself, Freya."

She slides her hand between us and rubs herself where we're joined. It drives me wild, watching her. Her moans fill my ears as her leg tightens around me, and her body clenches mine, drawing me in.

"So close," she whispers. "I'm so . . ."

Blinding heat tightens, coils deep inside me as Freya's body unfurls, sweeping and rhythmic, and she cries against my mouth.

I do everything I can to slow down, to stop myself and give her time, but she bites my bottom lip and rides me, urging me on. "Don't you dare stop for me," she pants.

Savoring her every breath, the soft, undulating waves of her release around me, I kiss her, let my senses drown in *her*. Only her.

Freya hitches her leg higher over my hip, burying me deep, and it's all I need. I spill inside her so long and hard, it's seconds until I can finally breathe. Jagged pulls of air, lips meeting tenderly, we fall into each other. I whisper my fingers along her back, then whip the blanket over us both, wrapping us in a canopy of soft cotton that glows like clouds in a moonlit sky. Another kiss to the corner of her mouth, and I pull back so I can see her better, so I can bask in her satisfied beauty.

"That was . . ." I inhale roughly, trying to catch my breath. "Wow."

She smiles and nestles closer to me, her eyes drifting shut as an expression of pure contentment smooths her face. "It was, Aiden. It was really 'wow.'"

We both laugh softly, sharing gentle touches, a faint, reverent kiss.

"Thank you," I whisper against her lips, before I steal another kiss, a gentle bite of her bottom lip.

Freya smiles, eyes still shut. "For what?"

"For loving me." I press my lips to hers again and breathe her in, my wife and love, friend and partner. The woman who loves all of me, who I love beyond words and understanding.

Dragging my thumb over her lip, I kiss her again and again and again. "I love you."

She opens her eyes, bright and luminous as a glittering canopy of stars.

"My Aiden." As she wraps her arms around me, Freya whispers in the darkness, "I love you, too."

TWENTY-SEVEN

Freya

Playlist: "SUPERBLOOM," MisterWives

"Look at you!" Mai belts. A few people glance over their shoulders at her volume and my equally loud laugh. She hugs me hard, and I hug her hard right back. Used to our over-the-top reunions, Pete and Aiden leave us to our girl crushes, heading inside the restaurant to grab us drinks.

Mai pulls back, holding me by the shoulders as she looks me over. "Vacation looks good on you."

"Stop it." I fluff my waves and smile at her.

"You put your septum piercing back in, too. Yes. Yes. I approve of this." Then Mai squeezes my boobs. In plain sight. Because this is our friendship. "Mm. And the titties are lush and up."

"Thank you!" I fondle them myself, admiring my cleavage. "It's the dress. It makes them look like a million bucks. I got it in Hawaii."

"I think you got more than a dress in Hawaii," she says under her breath.

"Not exactly." Dropping my hands, I smooth the front of my blue sundress.

Mai tips her head and assesses me. "But Hawaii *agreed* with you?"

"Yeah," I admit happily. "It did. You look incredible, too. You're glowing. Like you swallowed a bottle of sunshine."

"Thank you! The kids slept through the night last night. It

does wonders for my skin. Now stop trying to distract me. Talk about Hawaii. Did it . . ." She wiggles her eyebrows. "Y'know, *really* agree with you? You and Aiden?"

A blush warms my cheeks. "*Agreement* of the highest order was reached once we were home."

She squeals. "Freya, that's good. I mean, that is, if he groveled epically and promised to make you his Nordic Snow Queen Goddess again and thus commenced hot-as-hell *we're making up and fixing shit* kind of 'agreement,' not the hate-banging kind of 'agreement.'"

"It was the former," I say, tucking my hair behind my ears. My gaze finds Aiden at the bar, shoulder to shoulder with Pete. He laughs at something Pete says, then glances back, meeting my eyes. I smile softly. He smiles, too. And the butterflies in my stomach beat their wings furiously.

"So . . . things are good since you came home?" she asks, giving me a knowing look.

"Two weeks of being back to reality and so far, so, *so* good." I lean against the wall of the restaurant's outdoor patio, where we're waiting for our table, and buy myself a reprieve from the sharp evening sun. "We had another counseling session together and talked about being more intentional about our time together when we *are* together, and also balancing it with solo time. Time when Aiden can work for hours in a row and not feel guilty or pulled in two directions, time when I can get out and do things that make me happy."

Mai nods. "It's weird isn't it? How easy it is to sort of collapse into each other and get so stuck in that. Every couple needs to share plenty of life, but both people need their independence, too. I'm so much happier since we set up our schedule where Pete gets his night out for trivia and I get out for soccer."

"Exactly. I let my life get small. I was sad when things got hard with Aiden, and then instead of turning to the things that brought me joy, I just got miserable. I stopped playing our women's league, I worked later, I didn't feel like going out or doing karaoke . . . I don't know. I just let a part of myself fade, and I don't ever want to do that again. Especially now, while so much is in flux. Aiden's working on this project, and it's not going anywhere anytime soon. Rather than sitting home and stewing, I'm going to do what I like. Get back into soccer or at least some kind of fun workout, have nights out with you and the ladies again."

Mai smiles at me. "There are seasons like that. Pete and I've had them. You just have to take care of you and take care of each other and make it through, then you enjoy the hell out of each other when life calms down."

"Exactly." I smile back at her. "Do you have any spots on the team next session, actually? I've been meaning to text you, but I've been a bit *distracted* since we got home."

Clearing her throat, Mai peers down at her feet. "Um, yeah, we do."

I read her body language. She looks nervous. "What's wrong?"

She scrapes the soles of her sandals against the patio tiles. "Well, we're going to need another person on the team, because someone's pregnant again."

The pain in my chest isn't as sharp as it once was, but it's still there. Yes, I'm grateful I didn't go through this marriage crisis with Aiden while in the throes of hormonal overhaul and growing a baby, but it's bittersweet. Especially since my period came two days ago. And I surprised myself by feeling . . . relief. Massive relief.

"Who is it?" I ask. "Unless they're keeping it under wraps. I don't want to pry."

Mai sighs and meets my eyes, pain tightening her face. "It's me."

My throat knots. "Oh!" I blink at her, biting my lip against the impulse to cry. "Oh my God, Mai. I'm so happy for you!" I wrap my arms around her, my friend who's tall and curvy and strong like me, so that her chin easily sits on my shoulder.

"I feel like shit," she says hoarsely. "I wanted us to share this, and I know how much you've wanted a baby. Now I'm hurting you, and you're the last person I want to hurt. I swear it was an accident, Freya—"

"Mai." I pull back and hold her eyes. "Stop it right now. This is such good news, only good news. A baby!"

She searches my eyes. "You sure? You're okay?"

I nod. "Yeah, I am. I . . . I actually started back up on the pill."

Mai's eyes widen. "What?"

"Shh." I glance over, seeing Aiden and Pete sweep up our drinks from the bar. "I haven't told Aiden."

"You *what*?" She lifts an eyebrow. "Freya, are you trying to fuck shit up, just when it got good?"

I fidget under her intense stare. "Mai, listen. I just want to have a little time with him before things get complicated by a baby *because* it got good."

"Then why haven't you told him?"

"Because I'm nervous about how he'll take it. Planning for a baby and our marriage problems had a lot of overlap, and I just want to be thoughtful about how I approach it with him. It's only been two days."

She gives me a skeptical look. "Two days is two days too long, my friend."

"Mai," I groan. "He feels guilty that we haven't gotten pregnant yet, and I don't want to hurt him. I'm going to tell him tonight, I swear. It's hard, okay? I've been struggling to find the right words."

"You better find them fast, lady," she says, shaking her head. "I do not approve—"

The guys throw open the door, and I yank her to me in a hug. "Please don't say anything," I whisper, squeezing Mai's arms as I smile over her shoulder at Aiden and Pete, hoping I've saved face. "Congrats," I tell her again. "I get to cuddle another of your beautiful babies and drink for you!"

"Oh, ha-ha, so funny," she says, taking from Pete what I now know is a virgin cocktail.

"Hey," Pete says to us, "I meant to text. Can you watch the kids for us two weeks from now? Her brother's getting married at his fiancée's childhood home in Sacramento, and it's no kids. He *just* told us that."

Mai rolls her eyes. "You don't have to watch them. In fact, I forbid you. You watch them way too much for us as it is."

Aiden joins us, kissing me softly behind my ear. He hands me my seltzer with lime, then sets his hand on my back. "We haven't watched them in weeks. We don't mind."

"Says the guy who brings his laptop," Mai says pointedly. "Your wife's the one who wrangles the rug rats to bed."

"Excuse me." Aiden levels her with an indignant look. "*I* am the one who makes a mean grilled cheese *and* reads to them. Your son says my Dad Tiger voice is better than Pete's."

Pete scowls. "Ungrateful spawn."

Mai laughs. "Fine. I take that back. You still don't have to watch them, though. I can find a sitter for the day. Seriously."

"But they've only ever done overnights with us," I tell her. "How are you going to go up to Sacramento for a wedding and not stay over? You'll be exhausted."

"It's only a five-hour drive, or a quick flight."

"That you'd be catching late in the evening, after the wedding," Aiden says.

"We'd figure something out," Mai mutters, poking her straw around her drink.

"But it would be tiring," I remind her. "And you just need to take care of yourself."

Pete wraps an arm around Mai. "You told her."

"Yeah." She meets my eyes and smiles faintly.

"Yes," I tell Pete. "Yes, she did. And I'm so happy for you both."

Aiden peers between Pete and Mai. "Told who what? Why are we happy?"

"You're going to be an honorary uncle, *thrice* now," I say, beaming at my friend. "Mai's pregnant."

"What? Congratulations!" Aiden hugs Mai and Pete, then glances back at me, his smile deepening. And I have the unsettling sensation that Aiden thinks soon Mai won't be the only one.

———

Halfway through dinner, Aiden reaches into his pocket and extracts his phone. "I swear to God, I'm going to kill him."

"Kill who?" Pete asks.

Aiden sighs as he unlocks his phone screen. "Dan."

"Dan," Pete says darkly.

Mai elbows him. "You are so jealous of him. He's his *business* partner."

"He's butting into my bromance." Pete meets my eyes sympathetically. "You're not the only one he's too busy for."

"Pete!" Mai hisses, elbowing him sharply again.

"Sorry," he mutters into his glass.

Aiden glares up at him. "Remind me to spit in your beer after I take this call." He turns toward me. "Sorry, Frey. Can I sneak out? Dan's messaged me a bunch."

I glance at his phone, seeing a voice mail pop up. "You've got a voice mail, too."

"A number I don't recognize. Probably spam, but I'll check it when I give Dan a call back real quick. He's flying solo for the first time with our investor."

I blink at him in shock. "Aiden, are you sure you shouldn't be there?"

"Yes," he says evenly, typing back to Dan, then pocketing his phone. "I needed to get out with our friends, and Dan needs to fly the nest. I've done my part. I sold our investor on this, answered her every email. I wrote the damn presentation. Dan is more than capable of pulling his weight on a follow-up meeting. I trust him."

"But is it stressing you out?" I ask.

He smiles softly. "A bit. But that's okay. I'm doing all right."

I fidget on the bench, guilt tugging at me. "We should have discussed this."

Mai gives me a look and does her best-friend telepathic talking. *You're really going to lecture him about transparency right now?*

I glare back at her.

I said I'd tell him tonight.

Arched eyebrow. Pursed lips. *Mm-hmm*, her expression says. *Sure.*

Aiden's hand drifts over my thigh under the table. "*I* didn't want to miss our night out. That was my choice."

"But Dan's messaging."

Aiden shrugs. "But Dan's messaging. So I'm going to call him."

"And if it's a crisis, if it makes or breaks this project, I want you to go to the meeting. I'll drive you myself."

He wraps his hand around mine and squeezes gently. "I will, Freya. Thank you."

I kiss his cheek, then scoot out of our bench, watching him, tall and broad, strolling smoothly out of the restaurant. I plop back down on a sigh.

"Watch out." Mai laughs. "I think you drooled."

"Sue me, I like my husband's ass."

Pete sighs and throws his arm around Mai. "You used to look at me like that."

"I still do. After you put the kids to bed and load up the dishwasher. When you bend over and put that detergent in—" She shivers. "Mm-hmm."

I shake my head. "You two."

Mai sucks down half of her nojito and grins at me around her straw. Pete takes the conversation and runs with it, in that easy way he has, talking and making us laugh. I'm so engrossed in Pete's antics that it's not until Aiden's almost the whole way to our table that I notice him, his face grim.

"What is it?" I ask.

"Dan's fine. I mean, I handled his questions. But checked that voice mail. It's . . . Tom," he says, bewildered.

"Tom?" I wrinkle my nose. "Who's Tom?"

"The janitor in my building that I have . . . I don't know what I'd call it. I suppose a friendship is fair. He works when I'm there late."

My stomach sinks a little, remembering what he said the night he first came home. "He's the one who sent you home."

Aiden nods. But he doesn't sit.

"What's wrong?" I ask.

"I don't know. He just asked me to please meet him at the building this evening. Said he needed to talk to me urgently."

"When?" I ask.

"Didn't say when. Just tonight, that he'd be at work." Aiden drops onto the bench finally. He looks upset.

I slide my hand inside his and squeeze. "We can swing by there, let you two talk, if you think you should?"

"I . . . guess. I'm just . . ." He shakes his head. "Sorry. Forget it for now. Did we order dessert?"

Pete and Mai glance up from their own conversation.

"No. Should we?" Pete says to Mai and me, the sweet tooths.

Mai glances toward me. "I'm nauseous. So your call."

I search Aiden's eyes. "No, I'm okay."

We wrap up our meal, signing checks and hugging goodbye, and when we're in the car, Aiden slips behind the wheel, exhaling heavily.

"What are you thinking?" I tell him.

Aiden sighs. "I don't know. I think I need to go see what he wants to talk about. It feels so out of left field. The only thing I can think of is that he's in trouble, and he needs a friend. I don't want to cut our night short, but—"

"He's your friend." I slide my hand along his arm. "Let's go."

Aiden grips the steering wheel until his knuckles are white. His jaw tics beneath his beard. He trimmed it, neat and close, not quite the scruff he's had for years, but shorter than it was in Hawaii. I can see the tight set of his mouth, the tension he's holding.

"Nice deep breath, Bear."

He exhales heavily and turns the engine. "Right. You're right."

As we pull onto the highway, I plug in my phone and set a quiet acoustic playlist running. Gently, I rub Aiden's neck.

"I'll catch an Uber back," he says, "so you can drive home. At least you can go home and relax. I don't want you waiting in the car for me. Who knows what he needs or for how long."

I set my hand on his thigh. "I don't mind waiting, Aiden."

"It's just . . ." He sighs. "I had this whole night planned."

"I know," I whisper, crossing the console and giving him a kiss to the cheek. "And that's the gift to me. I feel loved and thought of. Now, let's go. The sooner you talk to him, the sooner you're home for snuggles and my favorite flourless chocolate torte that you hid in the fridge."

Aiden narrows his eyes but keeps them on the road. "It's hard to hide a cake. You're supposed to pretend like you didn't see that giant white box behind the kale."

"Oops." I smile. "C'mon. Get driving."

TWENTY-EIGHT

Aiden

Playlist: "River," Leon Bridges

After I see Freya safely into the driver's side and shut her door, I enter my building, taking the steps like always—because fuck elevators, also known as office building death traps—up to my floor. When I push open the door from the stairwell, I pull up short.

Tom sits in a chair in the floor's common area, elbows on his knees. Without his regular ball cap, I wouldn't recognize him. He's not in his janitor's uniform, instead wearing a crisp, blue button-up, rolled up to his elbows, betraying tattoos I've never seen before, dark jeans, and boots.

He stands, eyes on the ground as always, scrubbing his neck. "Thank you for coming."

The door thuds shut behind me. "Of course. Your message sounded urgent."

He nods. "Yeah. It is. And uh—" He clears his throat roughly. "You mind if we speak in your office? It's private."

The hairs on the back of my neck stand up. I stare at the brim of his cap as he coughs discreetly into his arm, another wet smoker's cough.

"Sure," I finally answer, stepping past him toward the hallway that leads to my office. Once I'm at the door, I pull out my keys, unlock it, and let us in. Tom wanders in behind me, stepping aside so I can shut the door behind us.

"Please," I tell him, gesturing to the sofa. "Make yourself comfortable." Tossing my keys onto the small plate I keep next to Freya's and my wedding photo, I stare at her picture, her beautiful, smiling profile as she stares up at me like I hung the fucking moon. I feel what a gift she is, and not for the first time lately, my thoughts circle back to the exciting, terrifying, incredible possibility that soon we could be expecting a new gift. A little person who's part of Freya, part of me, and entirely part of our love. A baby.

"I'm going to try to be direct," he says roughly, clearing his throat and drawing me back to attention. "But that's not really my strength. I'll do my best. I just ask that you let me finish."

I lean on the edge of my desk, ready to hear him, a posture I've assumed thousands of times for office hours, students, friends. "Okay. I'm listening."

"On my two-year anniversary of sobriety, I felt confident enough that it was going to stick." He adjusts his ball cap and interlaces his hands again. "It was the longest I'd lasted. Ever. It felt like a lifetime. In the best way. So I called the only woman I'd ever loved, and I asked her for another chance. Just to see her, to talk. I had no hope for anything else, much as I wanted more."

I shift my weight, leaning farther on my desk and folding my arms.

"She said no at first. But I'm . . ." He laughs hoarsely. "Well, I'm a persistent kind of man, and as I told you before, I've learned the hard way what backing down cost us last time. I failed her when she and I were young, and I wanted to prove to her that I was better than that now. So I wrote her letters, tried to tell her how I felt, what I'd done and gone through to be where I was. She finally agreed to meet me for a cup of coffee.

"Sorry," he says. "I'm trying to be quick. I promise I'm getting there."

"That's all right," I tell him.

"So we met for coffee, and then . . . she started having me over for dinner on Sunday. It was nothing romantic. Just . . . friendship—cautious friendship. She opened up a bit, told me more about her life. Things were good." He sniffs as his hand disappears under the brim of his cap, as if he's pinching the bridge of his nose, pressing against his eyes. "And then I betrayed her trust."

Air gusts out of me and disappointment sinks, heavy in my chest. I bite my cheek to keep quiet, so I won't push or ask how or why. I wait. And the silence grows.

"She told me about her son. She trusted me with that knowledge, believing me a changed enough person to be happy for him without asking anything else from the person I'd failed so horribly when he was . . ." His voice breaks, and he takes a long, steadying breath. "When he was just a baby. *Our* baby."

A cold sweat breaks out over my skin. My arms drop, my good hand gripping the desk for stability.

"But I was so desperate to see him," he whispers. "Just a glimpse. So I did something I shouldn't have. I got a job where he worked that was only supposed to be a temporary fill-in. I swore to myself it would just be for those few weeks, that I'd never let him see me, that I'd be a shadow who kept his distance. I'd get my glimpse, a small precious chance to see who he'd become. I swore to myself that I'd never speak to him, never do something so dishonest as try to know him without telling him who I really was."

My ears ring, air sawing in and out of my lungs.

"But then the man I'd filled in for just got sicker. He wasn't coming back to work, and I had a choice to make. The night before I had to commit to a permanent position or bow out," he croaks, burying his face. "I finally saw him up close, heard his voice. And . . . it was incredible, realizing who he was and what he knew and how he worked, just in a single encounter. I couldn't give that up. So I stayed, and I did the cowardly thing. I talked to him, got to know him in this way that I could, never telling him who I really was."

The world swims.

"I was afraid," he whispers. "And weak. I took the easiest way to him, and like the addict I am, I was hooked. I couldn't stand the thought of losing him."

Finally, he peers up. "The thought of losing *you*."

I stare at him blankly, shock turning my hands cold, my body far and distant. Observing every minute detail, I see Tom fully for the first time. The shape of his neat salt-and-pepper beard, the deep lines at his eyes, etched into leathery tan skin. A strong, sharp nose, and the last thing I thought I'd ever see:

A pair of blue eyes, as vivid and striking as mine.

The world tips. "Who are you?" I whisper.

His eyes are red-rimmed, wet. "Thomas Ryan MacCormack, but to everyone here, Tom Ryan. A man who doesn't deserve to call himself what he is to you."

I stare at him. This man who said without saying . . . he's my dad. Tom Ryan? I can't . . . I can't process it. It can't be him.

But it is. I know it's him, searching his face, seeing so much of myself. It makes my stomach roil. And as if he senses my absolute revulsion, he blinks away.

"I can't tell you how much I regret this. How sorry I am. I took the coward's way," he says, almost as if to himself. "Rather than ask you for another chance to know you, I stole it. Because every time I tried to work up the courage, I—" His voice breaks. "I admired you so much. I knew I'd disappoint you. And you spoke to me like you saw me as your equal, not some nobody, like so many people around here do, putting on airs. You spoke to me like you saw something in me. Like you respected me, and . . . I couldn't lose that."

Finally I find my voice, a surge of anger bursting inside me.

"That's some twisted shit, Tom. Infiltrating my workplace. Dropping your paternal advice. Being a 'friend' to me. Seeing me at my . . ." That day I sat beside him on the bench outside, drowning in my anxiety, flashes through my mind. I swallow roughly and take a slow, steadying breath. "At my fucking worst. You took away my choice," I tell him through a clenched jaw, tears thickening my throat. "You lied to me."

"I know," he whispers. "It was wrong."

"You had no right to do that." I push off the desk, standing to my full height. "You didn't earn that privilege to know me. You left, and you lost that."

He blinks up at me, his expression the portrait of miserable regret. "I know."

"Then why the hell did you do it?" I ask hoarsely. "And why did you have to show up *now,* when I'm finally not ripping at the seams? When I'm trying to build a family of my own, when I finally have a prayer of not being an absolute fuckup like you were?"

He makes a low, pained noise and buries his face. "I'm sorry. I wish I'd never done it. I never meant to hurt you."

"Never meant to hurt me!" I walk toward Tom, where he's still seated on the couch.

"You abandoned your family!" I bite back the break in my voice. "And now you have the balls to show up and try to claim something you never earned—the chance to know me. You broke my mom's heart. You made my life so *fucking* hard. Do you have any idea?"

A tear slips out of his eye.

"You made our lives hell. She broke herself, exhausted herself, cried every damn night for *years,*" I whisper angrily. "Because of *you.*"

"You think I don't know?" he says finally, standing up and meeting my eyes. "You think I didn't hate myself, day after day for what I did, how I failed you both? I meant what I said that night, when I told you how much I regretted not fighting my demons harder, failing to do whatever it took to earn your mother's trust and a place in our family. You think I don't hate myself for screwing up *again*?"

"I don't give a *fuck* what you feel," I tell him, right in his face. "I learned not to care about you a long time ago. And still, it managed to nearly rip apart my marriage, to punish the woman I have only ever wanted to protect, to poison the one good thing I've *ever* had!" I slam my fist over my heart. "You shouldn't have that power! You don't deserve it."

"I'm sorry," he says. "I can't tell you how sorry I am, Aiden—"

Hearing him use my name cuts like a knife through my heart. I pull back. "I don't want to hear another word. No more of your empty words. No more lies."

He blinks away, staring at his feet. "I understand."

A long heavy silence holds between us.

"I need you to know something," he mutters.

"Jesus," I groan, dropping to my desk. "What?"

"I quit. I won't be here anymore. So I'll be out of your life. As much as . . . as much as I'd give anything for the chance to try to earn your forgiveness, to have anything with you, however little you were willing to give me, I know I don't deserve it."

My heart aches, a hot, sharp pang in a place so old and hidden, I set a hand on my chest, where it hurts so deep, I can barely breathe. But I do breathe. I breathe through the pain, the depth of my anger and disgust and disappointment in him . . . and the terrifying truth that the strongest, newest part of me doesn't want to be ruled by any of that. The part of me that's healed in his marriage, that's grown in his capacity to feel and fear and love through it, *that* part of me wants to heal more than to burn in righteous anger.

"You're right," I tell him roughly. "You don't deserve a second chance. You'll never be able to make up for what you've done. It's all much too little, too late."

"I understand," he says quietly. "It's why I needed to tell you. Even though, what I did . . . I don't expect your forgiveness for it."

"Good. Because you shouldn't." I stare at him, each breath tighter, more difficult. "But that doesn't mean *I* shouldn't, either."

His eyes snap up and meet mine. "What?"

"Had you done this a mere month ago, I would have thrown you out. I would have shut that door right behind your ass and buried the pain you caused deep inside me, next to everything else you fucked up."

Tom's expression, so much a reflection of mine, searches my face. "But?"

I lift a shaking hand to my throat, where Freya's chain used to sit, warm against my skin. My courage. My reminder of her love. But I know now I don't need a chain to have her with me. Her love's with me, in me, always. It's changed me from the foundation of who I am, so that now I can look Tom in the eye and honestly say, "But I love someone who's shown me that love doesn't give second chances because we've earned them. Love gives second chances because it believes the best in who we are. And for some godforsaken reason, whether it's the fact that after all these years you went right back to my mom but not until you felt worthy of her, or that in your warped-ass way, you tried to be good to me, I want to believe the best in you. So . . . consider this your second chance, Tom."

I watch his eyes fill. "Oh God." He buries his face.

My grip on my desk tightens as my pulse pounds in my ears, as my chest tightens further. "But let me make myself clear. If you *ever* hurt Mom again, I will write you off forever, do you understand me? If she doesn't know about this, she has to. No more lies, no hurting her—"

"She knows," he says quietly. "Marie knows. And she's livid.

That's why this was urgent. I fucked up plenty, but you weren't hearing this from her or anyone but me. I had to tell you. I needed to face this and let you tell me what I deserved to hear."

The boy in me who always ached for his dad wants to lean toward Tom's heartfelt words and grasp their promises. To take his confession as a sign that I really mean something to him, that he cared enough to face me and own up. But I have to guard my heart. I have to take this one slow, cautious step at a time.

"Fine," I grit out. "You told me, and I've said what I need to say. Consider this my poor, shitty attempt to say somehow, eventually, I hope I can forgive you. But sure as shit, it isn't today. Now get out of my office and don't call me. I'll contact you when and if I'm ready. In fact, see yourself out. I'm leaving."

I snatch up my keys, storm out, and head straight down the stairs.

Halfway down, I crumple on the landing, tugging in rough gulps of air, as my throat tightens and burns. Stars dance in my vision as I fumble for my phone, dialing the only person I have in my favorites. Because I love my mother, and yes, I have friends, but there's only one person who's earned that place, and I need her right now. I need her so badly. And thank fuck, I'm no longer afraid to own that.

The call connects. Rings once. Twice.

The third ring echoes in the stairwell. The fourth is closer. I startle, dropping my phone to the floor with a clatter.

"Aiden?" Freya yells.

"Freya," I answer hoarsely.

I hear her pace quicken, her feet fast as she runs toward me. Her hair glitters like a halo of stars in the night sky, sparkling wet from a rare, cool summer rain as she sinks down, so impossibly beautiful, and wraps me in her arms.

"Freya." Her name leaves my lips like a prayer as I lean into her. I clutch her to me, my voice breaking on a hoarse sob.

"Shh, Aiden, it's okay," she whispers. Her arms hold me steadily, her hands sweeping over my back. "I'm here."

"Oh God." I bury my face in her neck and cry. I cry tears I've been holding in since . . . always. Since I was a boy who felt incomplete and wrong and unlovable, who believed that his dad hadn't wanted him. Since I was a teen who saw his mother hurting, struggling, barely surviving, thanks to someone whose ghost still could inflict pain that he felt helpless to protect her from. Since I was the grown man who promised his life to the woman he loved, so afraid he'd become just like the man who'd hurt him most, so unsure he could ever be worthy of her vows to him.

"Aiden. Breathe, Bear. Slow breaths. In . . . then out. Good." Freya presses a soft kiss to my temple and holds me tight. "I'm here. Whatever it is, I'm here. I'm not going anywhere."

"Y-you didn't leave," I say between sharp gasps of air. "I'm so glad you didn't leave."

"Me too," she whispers. Her hand cups the nape of my neck as she presses another kiss to my face and breathes me in. "Me too, Aiden."

I walk into the house, dazed. Exhausted.

So much for recovering our date night.

Fucking hell.

I turn toward Freya and catch her watching me carefully, like she's waiting for me to explode. "Do you . . ." She sets her keys on the key hook for the first time in the history of the world. You know something's up if she does that. "Do you want to talk about it?" she asks.

I shake my head. "No. We can put on the movie, have some cake—"

"Aiden," Freya says gently. "I think we should call it a day. Dinner was wonderful. And we can have cake with coffee in the morning—"

"No." I throw open the fridge, knowing I'm pushing and I shouldn't. But I feel like Mom's and my old clunker. Herby, we called him—sometimes Mom joked she was nervous to turn him off because then she wasn't sure he'd start up again for her. If I stop, I don't know what's going to happen. Whatever it is, I don't want to do it right now. I can't handle anything else. I need Freya in my arms. I need to close my eyes and smell her lemon-sunshine sweetness, the sharp clean scent of fresh-cut grass. I want to picture summertime in our backyard and disappear from this place that hurts so fucking badly.

"Bear, please," she says softly. "Let's just—"

"H-he's my dad," I blurt out, setting down the cake. My hands are shaking, and my knees nearly give out as I brace myself on the counter.

"What?" she asks disbelievingly. "Who, Aiden?"

"Tom. He got the job to see me. He's my fucking dad."

Freya's eyes widen as she sinks onto a stool at the kitchen counter. "I . . . Oh my God, Aiden."

A wash of cold nausea rolls through me as my shock begins to dissipate, as the truth sinks in. I'm going to puke. Turning, I rush down the hall, through our bedroom, to the comfort of our bathroom. I make it just in time, emptying my stomach, wave after wave. At some point, my eyes are wet not just from vomiting, but with tears. Damn tears.

Freya's close behind me, dropping to her knees. She presses a cool washcloth to my face, like she always has when I've thrown up. More tears come as I rake my hands through my hair and tug.

"Shit, Freya. He . . . he . . ."

I dry heave, then spit, feeling the nausea finally start to fade.

Her hand travels my back softly. "One breath at a time, Aiden. One breath at a time."

Dropping the lid, I fall back against the sink cabinet and sigh heavily. "I'm sorry," I whisper, my eyes blinking open and meeting hers.

"Why?" she says quietly. "Why would you be sorry?"

Crawling up to the sink, I turn on the water and splash my face, rinse my mouth. "It's just a mess, Freya. After all we've dealt with the past few . . . months . . ." My voice dies off as I stare at something my mind refuses to admit my eyes are actually seeing.

Freya's makeup bag sits, a chaotic, colorful jumble of containers and brushes, spilling out onto the bathroom counter. And inside the open bag, a shiny foil packet catches the overhead lights. Birth control. Two pills popped out. Gone.

I blink, stunned. "Freya, what is that?"

Freya rises to her feet, stepping behind me, and following my line of sight. Her body goes unnaturally still. "Aiden, it's not what you think—"

"Then what is it?" I glance up at the mirror, pinning her eyes. I take in her stricken expression, the guilt filling her gaze. The second person in the last hour who's looked at me that way. "Answer me," I say quietly.

"Birth control," she whispers, palming away a tear.

It's so sharp and painful, hearing her say it. Understanding not only is there no baby, but she doesn't *want* one, either. When? Why? How did so much change?

"Why didn't you tell me?" I grit out.

She swallows nervously. "I was going to tonight. I just . . . didn't want to hurt you."

"And you thought keeping it from me wouldn't hurt?"

Tears spill over and slide down her cheeks. "I was trying to find the right words. I was worried you'd think the worst."

"And that would be?"

She wipes away her tears. "I thought you'd be worried that I was second-guessing us, or you'd blame yourself somehow, but I just want time with you. Finally, after these shitty months, we're close again, reconnecting. When my period came, I was shocked when I realized I was relieved. So relieved. Because all I could think was that we were doing so well. And now we'd have some time to enjoy that. If I got pregnant right away, that time would get cut short before a baby turned us on our heads."

"You did it behind my back."

Freya bites her lip. "It's only been two days. I was going to tell you tonight."

"Tonight. Really, Freya?"

"Yes. I swear—"

"This whole fucking fiasco started because of how miserable you were, how cut off you felt when I didn't tell you *every* single thing rattling around in my brain, and this is what you do? You can't tell me you don't want a baby anymore—"

"No," she says quickly, her eyes meeting mine. She steps closer, but I move away, my back thudding against the wall, desperate not to be touched. Freya seems to sense it, and steps away, giving me space. "Just not right *now*. I want a baby with you, Aiden. So, so much, and if we'd gotten pregnant, of course I would have been happy. But I just realized, once we're parents, that's it, forever, no turning back . . . I grew up with a big family, I know that shit is *hard*. It seemed like it could be so good for us to have a little more time before a baby happened."

"But you couldn't tell me. You couldn't ask how I felt and talk to me?"

Her shoulders slump. "Aiden, I didn't want to . . . hurt you." Her voice is weak. Her explanation weaker. "Can't you understand?"

"Oh yes. I understand it very well. It's the exact same motivation you gave *me* hell for." I push off the wall and stalk toward her. "What do you think I've been doing the past six months? Hm? Harboring difficult truths for shits and giggles?" I lean in, until our noses nearly brush, and my voice becomes a harsh, unsteady whisper. "Welcome to my side of things, Freya. Take in the view. You understand now, don't you? How easy it is to convince yourself that lies of omission are worth it to protect the person you love. To bide your time until you find the 'right' words, until you can get it *just* so. When really, all it is, is fear. Pure, unadulterated fear."

Another tear slips down her cheek. "Yes. I . . . do."

"But that's not what we promised each other. In Hawaii, at counseling, we made these grand vows of vulnerability and honesty, then this is what happens? Two weeks later, you can't trust me to hear you, to handle a tough truth?"

"Two days, Aiden!" she yells hoarsely, wiping her eyes. "You lied to me for six months."

"And you lied, too!" I yell back. "You were fucking miserable."

"We both were," she says through tears. "And now we were finally happy—"

"And you didn't trust that I could handle the first test of that happiness without fucking it all up." I search her eyes. "What do you think of me?"

More tears track down her cheeks. "Aiden, that's not what . . ." Her eyes slip shut. "I screwed up, okay? I should have told you, right away. We should have talked about it together—"

"I called you, crying in a fucking stairwell tonight because my alcoholic absent father just admitted to stalking me at my work. Do you know how humiliating that is?"

"No," she whispers. More tears. So many tears.

I'm building momentum, like a hurricane at sea, raw unbridled energy churning it wider and wilder. I want to stop. I want to shut up and let her apologize and let us talk, but all I am is *hurt*—one big bruise, from my heart out. And I needed her, just now, tonight, of all nights, *not* to be someone who added to that.

"I called you because I needed you," I say through the painful well of tears in my throat, "because I *trusted* that we're both leaning into this, Freya, that we're both vulnerable. And you hide it, why? Because you don't really think I've grown or changed, do you? You still see me as a fucked-up mess. Well, congratulations, you're right."

I brush by her, storming through the bedroom to my closet.

"Aiden! What are you doing?" she calls.

"Exactly what you told me to do a month ago, Freya. Getting the hell out of here."

I shove shit into my duffel bag, not paying attention to what it is or how much of it I'm throwing in there. I'm a blur of anger and pain, heart pounding, lungs tight. I wipe away tears, throwing my meds and a phone charger in the bag. That's as far as my brain can think. I don't want to care about plans or preparedness or promises or a damn fucking thing except getting away from all this shit, from the woman I just stupidly boasted to Tom believes the best in me, when really, clearly, she sees the worst.

I drag the zipper shut. "I'm leaving. You can have your space and time to think."

"Aiden," she yells, following me down the hall. "No. I don't want that. Please stay. Cool off. I'll sleep on the sofa, we'll sleep and—"

"I can't fucking think, Freya! I can't even get my head straight. I lied, you lied, he lied, Mom lied, we all fucking *lied*. And I thought we were going to be different, that's what we promised. It was going to be different. But none of it is . . . ." I shake my head. "Just . . . move aside, please."

Freya stares at me, her back to the front door. "Aiden. Don't go."

"Move. Freya." I hold her eyes, willing her to do what I ask. "Please."

Tears slip down her cheeks. Her hand grips the doorknob. But finally, she steps aside. And for the second time, I walk out the door, lost.

Absolutely lost.

TWENTY-NINE

Aiden

Playlist: "Grow as We Go," Ben Platt

I drive and drive. No music. Windows down. The wind biting and cool. I drive until my hand hurts from white-knuckling the wheel and my mom's apartment is in sight.

When I knock on her door, she opens it like she was expecting me. She takes one look at me and sighs. "He told you."

Pulling her close, I bury my head in her hair. I breathe her in, squeeze her tight with my good arm. "Mom."

"Aw, honey." She kisses my hair and pulls me inside. "Come in. Sit down."

Dropping onto the sofa, I fall sideways, against the cushions. "Why?"

She sinks down gently next to me. "Why what?"

"Why are you seeing him? Why did he find me? After all this time, when he left us, Mom. He hurt us so badly."

Sliding her hand gently along my back, she sighs. "Because he was sick. Because addiction is terrible, and I had to protect you. I told him not to come back until he was cleaned up. And he . . ." She swallows tears and shrugs, her voice whisper-thin. "He didn't. Until now."

My hand clasps hers. "I'm so sorry."

"What are you sorry for? You were a baby, Aiden. You were a gift. And I know it wasn't fair to you, how hard things were, but you were so damn resilient. You were my light in some very dark years. Even when you grew up looking just like that beautiful asshole. Just as smart and charming, with that smile that reminded me, even though he'd hurt me and you, he'd given me you. I could never regret that. And after all we went through, look what we have. Comfort. Stability. Happiness. We didn't let it bring us down."

I sigh. "It was fucking hard, though, Mom. It cost us both."

"You're right. And I do regret *that*. I just . . . couldn't make it any better than I did."

I squeeze her hand and hold her eyes. "You were so brave and strong when you shouldn't have had to be. You're my hero. You know that, right?"

She smiles at me. "I do, yes. I wish it had been better, but I have peace. I did my best."

"And after all that pain he caused, you've taken him back?"

She peers at me intensely. "Taken him back? Not romantically, no. He hurt my baby. He left his son. I don't know . . . I don't know if I can ever forgive him for that. Maybe one day."

"Then what . . . why did he say that you had him over, that you talked?"

"Tom had to go through me to get to you." Mom squeezes my hand. "I care about him of course. I wanted to see him, to know how he'd grown through sobriety. But most of all, I gave him a chance with me so I could know if he was worthy of a chance with *you*."

I rub my face in the cushions. "God, it's so . . . it's so fucking painful. I told him I wanted to be able to forgive him. That maybe one day I could. But . . . not now. Right now it just hurts. It *hurts*."

"That's because it's complex. Because love doesn't just stop or start because we want it to. He hurt us in a way that *should* be unforgivable, but love makes it messy. You'll figure it out in time. And if you don't want to see him, if you can't forgive him, that's okay. That's what's right for you."

"And you? What's right for you?"

Mom's gaze meets mine. "I'm not sure, Aiden. After everything he did, coming to your work, that broke our trust. Again."

I sigh, lacing my fingers with Mom's. "I'm hurt that you kept this from me, that you were seeing him without me knowing. Why didn't you tell me?"

"Because I had to protect you," she says sharply. "Because I wasn't sure yet if he was safe, if his sobriety would stick. I couldn't stand the thought of bringing your father into your life again, just to see him fail you and relapse. When I started to consider talking to you about it, once I felt confident he was going to stay sober, the timing was all wrong. The last thing I was going to do was throw your absentee, recovering-alcoholic dad at your feet when you were drowning in work and your marriage was on the rocks."

My hand drops hers. "You knew?"

"Of course I knew, Aiden. I know my memory isn't what it was, but I have eyes in my head. Freya was sad. You were distracted and stressed. Before you left for Hawaii, I could have cut the tension between you two with a knife. And the months before that, whenever you both came by to fuss over me, it was clear things weren't good."

Mom frowns at me tightly. "So, no. I didn't tell you that I was talking to your father. Not until I could be sure you could handle it, and more importantly, that he deserved for you to know. And then, what did he do? He told me he'd gone and broken his promise to leave you alone, that he'd gotten a damn job at the college.

"That was a week ago. I told him he'd flushed all the trust we'd built right down the drain. I ignored his calls while I tried to figure out how to tell you, what to say, without unraveling everything and upsetting you, especially with all you were going through. I certainly wasn't bothering you in Hawaii . . ." She exhales shakily. "I told him he had to get a new job immediately. I couldn't let him keep doing that to you. I had every intention of telling you once you and Freya seemed better. I counted on him keeping it from you. But it seems I underestimated him."

"*Under*estimated him?"

"What? You think he wanted to tell you that? That it was easy for him? To crush whatever tiny chance he had of earning your trust by admitting to what he'd done?"

"I don't know, Mom," I sigh heavily. "I'm so confused."

She sets her hand carefully on my back and rubs in soothing circles. "You don't have to have answers right now, not for yourself or for Tom. Take your time and take care of you." She drops her hand and smiles gently. "At least you have Freya."

I laugh emptily. "Yeah."

Mom stares at me. "Why are you saying it like that?"

I tell Mom about my epic blowup back at home, face buried in my hands, miserable with myself. "You don't have to tell me I over-reacted. I already know."

"Good," she says curtly. "Because that was pretty top-rate catastrophizing. She's two days into her pills and suddenly she's decided you're a hopeless mess and all the trust you've built is shattered?"

I groan and thump my head against the sofa's arm. "It hurt, Mom. I wanted her to trust me with the hard stuff, to believe that she could tell me, and I wouldn't freak the fuck out."

Mom leans in, saying out of the side of her mouth, "And then you freaked the fuck out anyway, didn't you?"

I groan again. "Yes."

"Instead of empathizing with how Freya's felt, hoping you'd trust *her* with your worries all these months?"

My stomach seizes. "Yes."

"Mm-hmm." Mom sniffs. "Now listen here. You wouldn't have reacted like that if Tom hadn't blown up your evening. I'm sure after you saw him, you had one of your attacks?"

I nod.

She pats my side affectionately. "Poor kid. So that set you off. Your anxiety is a wily thing, Aiden. And it spins you like a top. When you're panicked and, hell, even afterward for a while, you don't think clearly. You're shaky and reactive, for good reason, honey.

"Freya's been with you over ten years, and she knows that. I'm sure she understands exactly why you were upset, even though I bet she's also worried about you and hurting, too. In the morning, drive home. Tell her you're sorry. Fix it, in your Aiden way."

I rub my forehead, regret and sadness twisting my heart. "Some things aren't easily fixed."

Mom squeezes my hand. "I never said it was easy, sweetheart. This is how it goes. People who love each other hurt each other, too. What matters is that they learn and they try their best not to hurt each other that way again."

I sit up, my heart pounding. Mom's right.

I have to go home. I need to tell Freya that I'm sorry, to reassure her that this little way she hurt me isn't insurmountable, not at all. I stand, fumbling in my pockets for my keys. "I have to go back. I have to apologize—"

Mom stops me as she stands, too. "Aiden, you're exhausted. It's an hour drive home. Stay here, sleep. Wake up early tomorrow and drive back then."

"I can't, Mom. Not when she's alone and hurting. I have to go home."

Smiling up at me, she clasps my hand and squeezes hard. "You always were stubborn. At least let me make you a cup of tea for the road."

———

I let myself into the house as dawn starts to lighten the sky, closing the door quietly and watching for Freya's shoes. But they're stacked neatly on the shoe organizer. I almost pick them up and set them in the middle of the floor, right where they belong. Because the messy, beautiful woman I love is home.

Walking softly down the hall, I set my bag on the floor and cross our bedroom. Freya lies curled up in bed, the comforter tucked under her chin. Easing cautiously onto the edge of the mattress, I watch her steady breathing and slip a soft, blonde wisp off her forehead. It's impossible to miss the signs of crying. The tip of her nose is still pink, her eyes faintly swollen. I want to kiss them. I want to kiss every hurt away. Especially the ones I caused.

Careful not to rock the bed, I lift the comforter and slip inside, close to Freya, wrapping my arm around her. In her sleep, she sucks in a breath, then exhales heavily, burrowing closer to me. I run my hand through her hair, smoothing it gently back from her face.

"Aiden," she mutters in her sleep.

I press a soft kiss to her forehead. "Freya."

She sighs and smiles faintly in her sleep.

"I'm here," I whisper against her temple, planting another kiss.

Her eyes blink open slowly and meet mine. They stare at me, unblinking, until suddenly they're brimming with tears.

"Freya, I'm so sorry, I shouldn't—"

"*I'm* sorry," she says over me, her hand clasping mine and tugging it to her chest. "I'm so sorry. That was a horrible way for you to find out, let alone after your . . ." She swallows tears and wipes them away.

"Dad," I finish for her. "Yeah. It wasn't great timing. But what Tom did wasn't your responsibility, and you shouldn't have been in the crosshairs of my response."

"You were hurting, Aiden," she says quietly. "You had a panic attack, and when you came home, my pills blindsided you. I understood. I felt terrible, but I understood."

I pull her close and hold my forehead to hers, breathing her in.

"I wish I hadn't overreacted. I said the worst things I think about myself and put those words in your mouth, and that was unfair. To be angry at you for struggling to tell me something difficult was . . . wildly hypocritical. Forgive me."

She smiles tearily. "Of course I forgive you. Forgive me, too?"

"Always." I kiss her gently. Freya kisses me, too.

And then it's more than kisses. It's whispering touches and quiet, careful movements, taking off each other's clothes, warm skin, and cool sheets. My hands wander the beautiful swells and dips of her body, everywhere she's soft and dimpled, smooth and silky. I kiss her deeply and hold her close.

"Freya."

She smiles against my skin, stealing a soft, sweet bite at the base of my throat. "Yes, Aiden."

"I need you."

A quiet smile tips her lips. "I need you, too."

"Come here," I whisper.

Freya slowly straddles me but lies close, our chests brushing as I kiss her dimples, her smiling mouth, the curve of her jaw, each full, soft breast and tight rosy nipple. With steady strokes against her, every slick, hot slide of our bodies, I bring her close until she's tugging at my hips, urging me for more.

"I want you," she says faintly. "I want you inside me."

Easing into her, I whisper, "I'm yours."

Tears slip down her face.

"Freya, tell me you know."

"I know, Aiden," she says through tears. "God, do I know."

On a deep hard kiss, I seat myself inside her and earn Freya's cry. She wraps her arm around my neck, fusing our bodies, and I rock into her, steady, patient, even as Freya writhes.

"Faster," she begs.

"Slow," I tell her.

She laughs through tears, kissing me hard. "Even when you're torturing me, I love you."

"I know you do," I tell her quietly. And then I give her what she's waited so patiently for—everything.

"Aiden," she gasps as I fill her in deep, fast strokes, again and again.

My release blinds me. I'm lost in Freya's touch, her words and kisses, as I spill, calling her name. Rubbing her gently where she needs it, I stay inside her, connected, close, until she comes on a sharp gasp. I soak up every cry, the tight, powerful waves of her orgasm as she holds on to me.

When I can finally speak again, I sigh heavily, pressing a kiss to her forehead. "Thank you."

Falling softly to my side, Freya snuggles in. She tips her head up at me and smiles, a vision of sated beauty. "Thank you? For what?"

"For wanting just me a little longer. I'm going to be so happy when we have a baby, but you're right. I want to enjoy you first, just us, together. We have time, Freya. Years and years. We're just getting started."

Her eyes search mine and her smile deepens, just as dawn crests the horizon, spilling through our windows. "You're right. We are."

Bending over her, I kiss Freya tenderly. "There's no one else I'd want to face this with, but I'm sorry it's been so hard. All I've wanted since the day I married you . . . I've just wanted to give you your happily ever after."

She slides her hand through my hair, then tenderly along my cheek. "I thought I wanted that, too. So much so, I put it on your pendant."

"I miss that pendant."

"I don't," she says quietly.

I pull back to better meet her eyes. "What?"

"Because of that damn 'happily ever after.'"

My stomach drops. "What are you saying, Freya?"

"I'm saying 'happily ever after' doesn't exist. Not because life-long love is impossible, but because, as we've learned, no couple can live '*happily* ever after.' People whose love lasts, whose love grows and endures, choose each other in the unhappily ever after, the dark moments, not just the dazzling ones.

"We can't possibly hope to always live 'happily.' But 'ever after'? *That* we can hope for and choose. Because 'ever after' isn't an idea. It's a person—an imperfect person who's perfect for you." Her eyes search mine as she gives me one soft, tender kiss. "*You're* that person, for me. You're my ever after."

My heart glows as I stare down at her, the woman I love more than anything in this world. I clasp her face, wiping away her tears, blinking back my own. "You're my ever after, too, Freya. Always."

She wraps her arms tight around my waist and smiles up at me. "I like that. Ever after *always*."

"Bit of a redundancy, of course," I say through the lump in my throat, "but a poetic one—*mphm!*"

Freya kisses me hard as I pull her close, tucking her inside my arms. I kiss her back, reverently, slowly, and breathe her in.

"It's not redundant," she whispers against my mouth. "It's a choice, a belief. I choose you, my ever after, believing our love will sustain us, always. Ever after *always*. So there. Take that logic, Mr. MacCormack."

I whisper back against her sweet, soft lips, "Consider me schooled, Ms. Bergman."

She smiles as she kisses me again and again. And after that, under a brightening sky, the world collapsed to the breath and touch we share, words aren't necessary at all.

THIRTY

Freya

Playlist: "C'Mon," Kesha

Aiden flops onto our bed with a groan. Horseradish and Pickles jump up on the mattress in tandem, kneading him with their paws and meowing loudly as they lick his chin. "You two," he mutters, running both hands down their backs. "Such lovers."

"They learned from the best," I tell him, plopping onto the bed next to him. I turn on my side and slip my fingers through his hair. "That was impressive shower sex acrobatics, sir."

He grins. "Same to you, madam."

I shake my head, showering him in water droplets. "Excited for your first-ever anniversary party with the whole Bergman brood?"

He smiles, still petting the cats. "I am. Your family, Freya. They're . . . a gift. Really."

"I know. That's what I want with you."

His head jerks my way, startling the cats. "*Seven?*"

I laugh at his horrified expression. "I meant the dynamic. I like my job too much. And my sleep. Seven kids would be tough."

Relief clears his expression. "Phew. I was thinking maybe three."

"I can picture three. We'll see, won't we?"

"Yeah, we will." He tucks a wet wave behind my ear, his hand gentling the curve of my jaw. "I love you."

Leaning in, I steal a kiss. "Love you, too."

Our kiss deepens, Aiden shoving the cats off him as he turns toward me and slips a leg between mine. Then he suddenly pulls back. "Whoa. Getting ahead of myself." He sits up, and drags me upright, too. "I almost forgot."

"Forgot what?" Crawling beneath our sheets, I watch Aiden stand and rake a hand through his wet hair, then stroll toward his closet completely naked. Long, muscular legs. A tight, hard ass. The taper of his waist widening to his broad shoulders. They flex as he rummages around his closet, then turns, bearing a large rect-angle wrapped in brown paper and an ice-blue velvet bow.

Sitting on the bed, he sets it in my lap, then joins me beneath the sheets. "Happy anniversary, Freya." He holds my eyes. "I love you beyond words and time and space. I wish I could articulate how grateful I feel each morning, to wake up and see you next to me. Even when life's shit and the world feels heavy, I look at you . . ." He sighs. "Knowing I have you . . . that's everything I need."

"Thank you," I say through tears, kissing him gently. "I feel the same way about you, Bear. Should I open it?"

"Please."

I turn it over gently, ripping open the paper where it's taped. When I turn it around again, I stare in wonder at a framed print of a constellation, cut into a wide circle, black and sparkling against white matting. Below, stamped in tin:

> *"This dark is everywhere" we said, and called it light.*
> —JEAN VALENTINE, "ORPHEUS AND EURYDICE"

Tears spill down my cheeks. "Aiden."

His fingers brush mine, until our hands are braided together. "You remember?"

I nod, wiping away tears. "Our honeymoon."

"And the world's most depressing story of Orpheus and Eu-rydice," he says teasingly.

I laugh through my tears. "Because there was . . ." I slide my hand over the constellation, the night sky from our wedding night frozen in time. "Lyra." Peering back at the engravement, I stare at the words. "I don't know that poem."

"Neither did I." Aiden tips my chin until our eyes meet. "But I liked that in this version of their story, it's a better ending for Orpheus and Eurydice—no denial about the world's darkness. Just the beauty of two people finding a little light, making their way through it together."

"I love everything about it," I tell him, lifting up the print, admiring it. "It's so beautiful. And thoughtful." I set it down and wipe away tears, which fall fast and heavy. "Feelings," I groan. "So many of them."

Aiden pulls me into his arms. "I love you for those many feelings," he whispers against my hair.

"I know." I sigh inside his arms and smile as he kisses my tears away. "My turn now."

Leaning past him for my nightstand, I pull out a small box. "I love you, Aiden." I set it in his hands and hold his eyes. "There isn't another soul I'd want to share life with. Happy anniversary."

"Thank you, Frey." He steals another kiss before fumbling with the box. I watch him tear off the paper, then turn it over and open it. He stares and exhales roughly. "You made another one . . . another pendant."

"Yes and no." I kiss his cheek gently. "Look closer."

He lifts the chain and its thin, rectangular pendant, reading it silently.

Aiden + Freya =
3,650 days
520 weeks
120 months

10 years
1 ever after always

"Freya." He hugs me so tight, it makes me squeak. His nose brushes mine as he steals the softest kiss. "Thank you. This is beautiful. I'll treasure it forever," he whispers, kissing me deeper, promising more. So much more. "Almost as much as I treasure you."

"Good," I tell Aiden as I pull him over me, warm beneath the covers. "Because treasuring you forever is exactly what I had in mind."

"Where are they?" I ask my mother.

Mom leans back from behind the refrigerator door. "Who, *sötnos*?"

I glance up from the vegetables sautéing in the stock pot and give her a look. "My husband. And *all* my brothers."

"Oh." Mom shuts the door with her hip. "Outside. Talking. The boys had something to give Aiden."

"For what? It's my anniversary, too."

"Your *tenth*," Mom says, smiling at me. "Tin is the gift you give. Or aluminum. They represent the flexibility and durability necessary to sustain your marriage. You remembered, yes?"

"Mother." Tapping the spoon on the side of the pot, I set it down. "Do you know me? I'm obsessed with that shit." I smile to myself, remembering our gifts. And the glorious sex we had after exchanging them.

She shoos me aside so I'm out of her work area. "I figured you'd remember, but I also know you're back to working, and you seem very busy these days."

"I am busy, but not just with work. I do karaoke twice a month now, and Aiden and I started playing on a co-ed rec team again. It's a lot, but it's good. And even juggling it all, I remembered my husband's anniversary present."

"Well, I am glad you're happily busy, but don't forget about your mama. I'm here, you know. I feel very useless these days."

I wrap an arm around her waist and set my head on her shoulder. She kisses my hair, then starts chopping fresh parsley. "I know the feeling," I tell her. "I come by it honestly. But you're not useless to me one bit. I love you. And I know I have you in my corner."

"Do you?" she says.

Slowly, I pull away. "What?"

"How are you since vacation?" Mom asks, eyes on her task.

I frown in confusion. "Fine. I mean, good. Honestly."

"Hm." She slides the parsley aside and runs the chopping board under water in the sink. "I ask because it must have been hard to celebrate our marriage when yours was being tested."

I stare at my mother in alarm. "What?"

I'm going to kill my brothers.

"Your brothers didn't tell me anything," Mom says softly, intuiting my thoughts. "You're my child, Freya. I've seen your sadness. I wanted to ask sooner, but I thought it best to wait until things settled with Aiden's father before I brought it up."

Aiden hasn't seen Tom yet, but he's been talking about it in counseling a lot, and he's considering it. When he's not at therapy or the office, he's been home sharing the couch with me while he takes calls with Dan and, when all the work is done, watching movies and touching and talking. I've been completely absorbed in us, in making my life the balance of work and play that I need, until I forgot I never told my mother what I so deeply needed to. Guilt sits heavy in my stomach.

"I'm sorry, Mom. I didn't want to burden you with my marriage problems during your anniversary celebration. And since we got back, life's been nonstop."

"You don't need to apologize, Freya. From now on, you tell me, though," she says, pinning me with her pale eyes, the color of ice and winter skies, just like mine. She closes the distance between us and hugs me hard. "You don't protect me, because I am your *mama*," she whispers. "Mothers protect their children. As you will soon know."

I freeze inside her arms. "I'm not . . . We aren't—"

"I know," she says quietly. "But it's coming. And when you are, you will be a wonderful mother." She pulls away and cups my cheek softly. "Even more than you are, to all the people you love, a wonderful mama bear."

A burst of male voices draws our attention to the back deck, which I can see through the sliding glass doors. All the brothers, including Axel and Ryder, who flew down, are here because Aiden said he wanted us to start the tradition Mom and Dad have, celebrating our anniversary with family.

Squinting, I try to make sense of what they're doing out there. Aiden's laughing, all the brothers huddled around him.

"What's going on?" I ask.

Mom shrugs. "I don't know."

Willa, Frankie, Rooney, and Ziggy peer up from the couch and look out, too.

Eyes on the guys outside, Rooney smiles. "What's that about?"

"Don't know," Ziggy says. "Do you?" she asks Frankie.

"Uh. Yeah." Frankie grimaces. "But I'm not supposed to blab it. So I suggest that Freya gets out there."

Willa nods and grins. "Yep, go see."

Making my way around the kitchen island and toward the deck, I drag open the door. All of them glance at me, stepping back and parting the way, so I can see Aiden. "What is it?" I ask.

Aiden shakes his head and slides his hands beneath his glasses, wiping his eyes. "Your brothers . . ." He shakes his head again, a laugh leaving him.

Viggo steps up and says, "When things were hard for you two, we tried to tell Aiden we were there for him. And in our ass-backward way, we tried to show him, too. But we've realized through . . . you know . . . everything that happened since vacation, Aiden needed to know that truth not just our way, but his way, too."

"So," Axel says, "we pooled resources."

"And did a little reading," Ryder adds.

Ren smiles wide. "And we are now proud to join as tiny but still technically—"

"Angel investors," Oliver says brightly, handing me the envelope that Aiden held loosely in his hand. "Meaning the Bergman brothers now have a vested interest in our brother's work. God help you, Aiden."

"First time anyone would ever use 'angel' and 'Bergman brothers' in the same sentence," Viggo points out.

"You guys . . ." I open the envelope and read its contents, smiling to myself. Aiden's not hard up for money for the app anymore. He and Dan secured their principal investor, so this is . . . this is a gesture. Not a hefty financial investment, but rather an investment of love and belief and pride. I sniffle as I stare at the paper, understanding exactly why Aiden's laughing *and* tearing up. "You guys really are too much."

Aiden drops his hands, meeting my eyes. His are bright and shining, wet with tears.

"Why are you crying?" Oliver asks, his gaze ricocheting between us. "What's wrong?"

I move to Aiden's side and lock hands with him. "Nothing. You're just . . . knuckleheads, all of you. Lovable, impossible knuckle-heads."

Aiden takes the envelope from my hand, running his fingers over his name written on the outside. "You didn't have to do this, guys, but . . . it means a lot." He peers up at them and smiles tearily. "Thank you."

"Ah, shit," Ryder mutters, wiping his eyes. "I'm crying."

Viggo wipes his eyes. "Damn. Me too."

"Group hug!" Oliver yells.

Axel groans. "Guys, do we have to—"

Ren smashes us all together in his massive wingspan.

"Love you guys," Aiden says quietly.

A chorus of *I love you too*s echoes around us.

"Hugs!" Willa yells, throwing open the sliding door. "I love hugs. Let me in on this."

The pile of people grows, until Aiden and I are surrounded by every Bergman and the people we love. I hear my dad's booming chuckle, Ziggy's shriek when someone nudges her tickle spot, Frankie's grumbling about personal space, and Mom's smoky laugh.

As Aiden's eyes meet mine, I smile. And in the heart of the chaos, he steals a slow, quiet kiss.

"Let's go!" Dad calls when we break apart. "Mom's got soup on. Games until dinner."

Everyone trundles in, spreading over the massive sofa we have in the house that seats all of us. And the smell of Mom's cooking, the sounds of laughter as we play rounds and rounds of increasingly ridiculous charades, the pure joy of sharing all of this with Aiden nearly overwhelm me.

"How you doin', Frey?" he whispers from our spot on the sofa.

I peer up at him. "Wonderful. You?"

He smiles down at me, running his hand along my side. "Great." He flexes his arm, which is now out of its cast. "A healthy body. You in my arms. It's a good life."

Leaning close, I press a kiss to his lips. "It is."

"Okay," Willa says, accepting from Oliver the basket full of folded papers we're using for clues. She performs an impressive sleight of hand, extracting a paper from her sleeve that she almost convinces even *me* she's chosen from the basket, before she hands it to Rooney. "You're up next, Roo."

"How about my air guitar?" Aiden mutters, sneaking a soft kiss behind my ear.

I laugh and slip an arm around his waist, resting my head on his shoulder. "Nailed it."

"See?" he says, a warm grin brightening his face. "I'm getting better."

"Yes," I whisper, before we share a quick kiss. "But even if you never did, I'd love you, just as you are."

"Okay." Rooney stands and shakes out her arms. Her honey-blonde hair is in a haphazard ponytail, her blue-green eyes sparkling and feisty, her cheeks flushed pink. She's at home among the Bergmans—wildly competitive and way too invested in games.

"Okaaaay . . ." Viggo drags out the word, poised with the timer. "Go!"

Rooney opens the paper and stares at it. She scrunches her eyes, then snaps them open. Urgently, she stares at us women, tapping her lips.

"Lips!" Ziggy shouts.

Frankie gives her a *What the hell?* look. "Uh . . . mouth?"

Rooney shakes her head and claps her hands in irritation.

Willa frowns at her. "Talk? Blab?"

Rooney throws her head back on a mute groan.

"It's *kiss*," Aiden whispers in my ear.

I grin. "Oh, I know. We all do. You and the Bergman brothers aren't the only ones who can meddle."

"Damn." He whistles quietly. "I'm impressed."

"Time's almost up!" Viggo yells.

Growling in frustration, Rooney swivels and faces Axel where he stands, leaning against the threshold, watching her. She marches toward him, throws her arms around his neck, and crushes her mouth to his.

"Kiss!" I scream, right as time ends.

All the men gape in shock.

Rooney jumps back, as if hearing the word made her realize what she's done. She stares up at my brother, bringing a shaky hand to her lips. "Axel, I—I—I'm sorry. I didn't mean . . . That is, I shouldn't have . . . I'm just viciously competitive and I . . ."

Axel stands, silent, staring at Rooney's mouth. Then, slowly, he takes a step closer, his hand a whisper away from touching hers. She holds his gaze, breathless, wide-eyed.

"I think . . ." he says hoarsely.

Rooney leans a fraction closer. "You think . . . ?"

Ax swallows roughly as his fingertips brush hers. "I think . . . I have a new appreciation for charades."

Laughter erupts in the room.

"Hey," Ren says to Frankie. "Want to guess my charade, too?" He taps his mouth.

Frankie rolls her eyes, but her grin is wider than the moon outside as she pulls him close.

"Me too!" Willa yells, launching herself onto Ryder.

When I turn to Aiden, ready to demand my own charades guess, he springs up from the couch and hustles toward the sound system. There's a moment's silence before the catchiest damn party song hits the speakers. Aiden dials up the music, then turns to face me, hand out.

I laugh as I stand and take his hand before Aiden sweeps me into his arms, straight to a dip, and kisses me thoroughly.

"Aiden MacCormack," I say on a smile. "You would take our meddling and run with it, you incorrigible matchmaker."

"I'm a man besotted. Can you blame me for wanting to spread the love?" He lifts me upright and twirls me close.

Mom dances her way in from the kitchen, then pulls Dad to his feet. As everyone joins in, music fills the room, jostling elbows and bumped knees, twirls and dips and shrieks of laughter echoing around us. Running to the lights, Oliver dims them as Viggo stands on the coffee table, pulls two handfuls of glitter from his pockets, and sets them on the ceiling fan. Ollie flips the switch to turn it on, bathing us in a sea of rainbow confetti, which sparkles in the soft glowing lights.

Everything around us glitters, iridescent and magical, but I hardly notice. All I see is the man I wrap my arms around and kiss like my world is the space between us, this moment, loving him.

There's nowhere else I'd rather be.

Aiden

Playlist: "Never Tear Us Apart," Vitamin String Quartet

Four months later

Not for the first time, I'm reminded how damn lucky I am that Freya Linn Bergman is my wife, that all those years ago, because I said yes to a pickup soccer game, I met a fiery, powerful, bighearted woman who cracked a soccer ball straight at my face and bought me an apology beer, who fell in love with me, even in all my brokenness, and loves me as I do the hard, ongoing work of healing.

I watch Freya chatting it up with one of our investors, Gail, who's seated beside her at this swanky dinner to celebrate taking the app's development to its next successful phase. Ice-blue fabric that matches her eyes hugs her lush body, draped across those strong, full shoulders, snug at her waist. Even though it's hidden beneath the table, I see her dress in my mind's eye when she put it on just a few hours ago, a waterfall of winter-blue chiffon spilling down those wide, soft hips that I love to drag my hands down and grip possessively.

She smiles at Gail as she speaks, throwing her head back with a laugh that would fool anyone into thinking she's as happy as can be, not a care in the world.

But I know otherwise. I know *her*.

I see that her wide, bright smile stops short of its truest, fullest expression. I notice that her throat works with a swallow when Gail turns and tells the waiter she'll have another glass of wine. I sense Freya's hesitation as the waiter asks her next if she'd like another nonalcoholic cocktail—a precaution she's resumed since she went off the pill last month—before I read her mouth saying, *I'm fine, thank you.*

My heart squeezes in my chest, and I know, mindful of her cycle, even though she wasn't due to start her period for another two days—it's happened. She's where she was before she went back on the pill this summer: another month, and no baby.

"So what I told Margie was . . ." Phil's voice dies off. "Aiden. Everything all right?"

I turn toward another one of our investors, Phil, and force a smile. "Sorry, Phil. I'm listening. Go on."

I listen to Phil talk about the ongoing kitchen remodel debate he's having with his wife, an ear trained on what he says while every molecule of me strains toward Freya.

I count down the minutes until dessert is served and plates are cleared. I nudge her foot gently under the table and earn her eyes briefly, a tender smile just for me.

I love you, I tell her with my gaze. *I'm here.*

Her smile deepens. She swallows again, like a lump's in her throat, like tears aren't far behind her eyes. *I love you, too*, her expression says. *I know.*

Finally, it's handshaking and backslapping hugs goodbye. Valets jogging off with keys, bringing back cars and waving good night.

And then it's just us—Freya and I in the quiet dark, driving home. No music on the stereo, no windows down or hand surfing the wind, another sign that her heart is heavy. I hold Freya's hand in mine and drive with the other, softly stroking her knuckles with my thumb.

When we get inside, I step past shoes my wife's left strewn in the hallway, a collection of half-decimated cat toys. Horseradish and Pickles dash toward us in greeting, their collars jingling. Freya scoops them both up and they let her squish them to her chest, purring, luxuriating in her love. I don't blame them—I'm the same way when Freya opens her arms to me, more than ready to fall into the affection she gives so generously.

Following her to the bedroom, I step right behind her when she stops at the foot of our bed and sets the cats down. They scamper across the mattress and tangle into a tumble of sibling roughhousing. Horseradish knocks Pickles off the bed's edge, then leaps off, too, and a small laugh leaves Freya. That sound, it makes me smile as I reach for her zipper and start to drag it down. Freya glances over her shoulder, her eyes searching mine, as if I've surprised her. "May I?" I ask.

She smiles faintly. "Of course. Thank you, Bear."

I tug her zipper down the rest of the way, then press a soft kiss to her neck, breathing her in—the smell of summer sunshine, lemonade, a fresh-mowed lawn. The fabric slips down her arms. She shivers a little as I kiss her bare shoulder, too.

"It came tonight," I say against her skin. "Your period. At dinner."

She freezes, her face in profile. Slowly, she blinks up at me. "You noticed?"

I turn her until she's facing me fully and hold her eyes. "I noticed. You went to the bathroom and came back looking . . . like something had changed."

Tears well in her eyes. "I shouldn't be so disappointed—"

"The hell you shouldn't, Freya. Whatever you feel, that's valid. There are no *should*s here."

She bites her lip as a tear spills down her cheek. "It was unreasonable to expect it to happen right away. These things take time, especially with how my hormones are shifting after coming off the pill. It's just . . . at Christmas, it was so beautiful, it felt so special. I wanted a baby to come from that." She shakes her head. "Just sentimental nonsense—"

"Hey." I pull her close, cupping her neck. She wraps her arms tight around my waist. I breathe deeply, then kiss her temple. "It's not nonsense. I felt that way, too. I hoped what you hoped." She chokes back a sob, like hearing that's what she needed, like my bittersweet admission has given her the permission she needed to feel. "You need to cry, you cry, baby. Just let it out."

Freya lets out a sob, then another, as I hold her tightly in my arms. She squeezes me hard around my ribs and soaks my shirt collar with her tears. I stroke her hair, kiss her temple again and again, grieving with her.

And yet even in that grief, I am grateful. I feel how this is different from where we were the last time we faced this reality. This time, I had my eye on her from the day she went off the pill and the countdown to her next period began. I've had my heart ready for this and my focus where it should be—her. This time, she's leaned right into me, she's squeezing the hell out of my ribs, sobbing into my neck, because she knows I can hold this, *her*, everything she's feeling.

In the bitterness of our pain, there's a sliver of hope, a magnitude of love. We're stronger than we were, closer than before. We'll get through this.

I tell her that, whispered against her ear. "We'll get through it, Freya. One way or another."

She nods. "I know." Pulling back, she wipes away her tears, and I wipe them, too, tender sweeps of my thumbs across her cheekbones. "I'm so sad it didn't happen yet," she whispers, "but I'm so glad this . . . *us* . . . it's not nearly as painful, now that we're where we are. It's just . . . a lot of emotions, all tangled up."

I nod, smiling gently. "It is." I stare down at her, holding her eyes, knowing I can't fix this, can't predict what lies ahead for us on our path to becoming parents. But I know I can be with her, feel for her and for myself. I know that we'll make it through.

And I know my wife. I know what she needs. I know what I need, too.

"Say," I tell her quietly, "what do you think about heading up a weekend early to the A-frame?"

She frowns, confused. "And come home earlier?"

"No."

Freya's eyes widen. "But my work . . . I'd need to get coverage. And your classes, they're starting Monday, you'd be gone the second week of the term—"

"You have an amazing team who'll cover you. And Lourdes is an incredibly competent instructor. She's been chomping at the bit to teach this class since she started her PhD program under my mentorship, and she'll be thrilled to have me out of her hair sooner rather than later."

My wife searches my eyes, relief filling her expression. Relief fills *me*. I was right. This is what she needed. It's what I needed to give her, what I need, too—more time, just the two of us, tucked away at the A-frame, nothing but snowfall and cuddling by the fire, cooking and eating when we want, sleeping in, connection, rest. Comfort in each other.

"Okay," she whispers, and finally I see what I haven't since she came back to the table at dinner, and I felt the shift inside her—a full, beautiful Freya Bergman smile.

I adore the Bergman family—my in-laws, Freya's siblings, and their partners—but *damn,* is it nice to be here without them. The past five days have been a flurry of adjusting schedules, the logistics of moving up our flight, settling Mom in to watch the cats, with Elin offering to pop by daily and make sure everything's going okay, packing and grocery ordering for our stay up in Washington.

And finally we're here, Freya and I, hand in hand, crunching through the snow as we walk the gentle one-mile loop around the house, weaving beneath bare-branch trees heavy with snowfall, the world dimmed to moonlight and lung-burning, bracing cold air.

I stare down at Freya, remembering the last walk we took through the woods, just a few weeks ago when we were here for Christmas with her family, how a kiss became kisses, gloves tugged off, jackets torn open, how I had her pinned against a tree, fumbling for the zipper of her jeans so I could touch her, feel how she responded to me, make her feel good, the way she deserved, before a Bergman brothers summit text from her damn brother blew it all up.

Now there are no interfering siblings, no one needing a thing from us.

I have Freya all to myself to love and take care of. And I want to, so much. I have something to give her that I wanted to over Christmas so many times, but board games and cooking, charades and family hikes came between us over and over, dashing moment after moment. Finally, I have it. Time to do what I've wanted for weeks, but really years.

Freya smiles up at me, confusion knitting her brow as I draw us to a stop. We're at the back of the A-frame, warm light spilling from the kitchen through the sliding doors, twinkly lights strung across the deck, glowing softly.

"Aiden?"

I stare at her as I drag off her left glove with two quick tugs. "Freya."

"What are you doing?" she asks. "My hand will get cold—"

"Giving you something I've wanted to for a long time but couldn't."

Hand shaking, nerves coursing through me, I tug off both my gloves, stash them in my back pocket, then pull out the velvet box from inside my coat.

Freya's eyes dart down to the box. Her eyes widen. "What is that?" she whispers hoarsely.

I set the box in my open palm and say, "Open it and see for yourself."

Freya bites her lip, her eyes welling. Staring at the box, she bites off her other glove, then pockets it, before she steps closer and picks up the box.

When she opens it, her mouth drops open, too. "Aiden," she breathes. "What the hell have you done?"

"Given you the engagement ring I always wanted. The one *you* wanted."

Tears spill down her cheeks. "You . . . terrible, wonderful man. It's exactly what I wanted, but how . . . ?"

"You really should lock down your Pinterest board privacy if you don't want your nosy husband snooping around those pins of teardrop rings."

She laughs, thick and hoarse. "Aiden, it's . . . perfect."

Gently, I lift the ring from its case, a teardrop diamond haloed by dozens of tinier diamonds, and snap the case closed. Taking her hand in mine, I slip the ring down her finger, sized the same as her wedding ring, the perfect fit. "Timing hasn't always been on our side," I tell her quietly. "I didn't have the money to give you this, the way I wanted to, when I proposed to you. We've worked so damn hard for years, building a life from the ground up, healing and growing as people, chasing our dreams, some of which have been a long time in coming true. Some, which we're still waiting for."

Freya lets out a soft, sweet cry-laugh. It's so her, I barely hold myself back from kissing her. But I have to, because I need to say this. This, I need her to hear:

"If I've learned one thing in all my years of loving you, Freya Linn Bergman, it's that I might not always like how timing goes, I might be angry and scared and sad and frustrated, but I'll never regret a single moment, even in all its hardship, because I get to make it through with you. I get to love you, live with you, grow with you. And that is more important, more beautiful, than any perfect timing I could hope for." My eyes search hers as I clasp her hand in mine and bring it to my heart. "I hate that we've hurt and been hurt along the way, that we've been disappointed and struggled, but I love that we've made it through together, Freya. I love that even in all I don't know, I *know* I have you and you have me. That's . . . everything. I hope when you look at this ring, it'll remind you of that—that we can do this, that it's you and me, always, forever."

Freya draws closer, two crunched steps in the snow, then brings her hands to my face. "I love you, Aiden Christopher." She draws me in for a soft, slow kiss. "And I love this ring. But just so you know . . . even if the day never came that you could give me something like this, I would know and feel and remember who we are, what we can do. Our love . . ." She draws my hand with hers, from my heart, to her own. "It's here. *It never* has and never will be something that capricious, frustrating life and timing will touch."

I sniff, fighting tears. "Capricious. That's a good word."

A smile brightens her face. "I know it is. Which is why I beat your butt at Scrabble regularly."

"Woman—"

"Take me inside," she whispers, her arms twining around my neck.

I wrap my arms around her waist, drawing her close, kissing her deeply. "I think first, we need to get something straight. You might *occasionally* beat me at Scrabble, but who has the highest winner record in the family when it comes to Trivial Pursuit? Oh, that's right, me."

She laughs against my kiss. "Just check that ego, MacCormack, or I might have to deflate it for you."

"And just how would you do that, Bergman?"

Freya lunges toward the mound of snow beside her, sweeps up a handful into her fists, and packs it into a quick, brutal ball. I'm scrambling back, reaching for my own fistful of snow, when the first one hits me right in the back, icy and cold. I yell in shock, and Freya squeals happily.

I pelt her with a snowball that hits her in the ass as she bends to make another snowball, then she turns, winds up, and nails my glasses with a rock-hard snowball.

I hear the crack in the frames, feel the sting of my nose.

Freya's eyes widen. "Oh my God, Aiden. I'm so sor—"

I let out a whooping war cry and sprint toward her. Freya shrieks, spins, and sprints, rounding the house.

I chase her the whole way inside until we fall, a tangle of snow-soaked limbs and flushed cheeks in front of the fire. Feverish kisses and cold hands.

My wife in my arms, heart to pounding heart, I am the happiest man on earth.

Freya

I'll always love Aiden in his glasses, but there's something special about seeing him without them. Backup contacts in, he's crouched outside on the back deck, fiddling with a pizza in the portable woodfired oven he set up.

I smile, watching his profile, the furrow of his brow, the absent way he tugs his lip between his teeth. I love him so much, it hurts.

Aiden glances up and catches me staring at him. His expression clears from concentration to sweet adoration. I blow him a kiss. He mimes catching it and brings it to his cheek. We're sickeningly in love, but I'm not going to apologize for that. Not after all we've been through. I'm going to wrap my arms around this joy, this connection, this . . . renewal, and hold it close.

Aiden turns back to the fire and fights a shiver. Stubborn man, freezing his ass off to make me woodfired pizza. Deliberating about what to do, I turn and root around in the freezer for pints of ice cream, open the drawer to grab two spoons, then shut it with my hip.

I walk out onto the deck in slippers and drag the door shut with my elbow.

Aiden glances up, then does a double take. "Why are you outside in your pajamas? It's freezing. Get inside!"

"Nope." I set the ice cream and spoons on the edge of the hot tub. "You're out here. I'm out here."

"Freya." The fire pops, drawing his attention, giving me his back as he swears under his breath and spins the pizza inside the oven.

I grin. I love how he sighs my name, exasperation and love twisted together.

"Aiden." First I wiggle my joggers down my hips, lifting off my slippers and socks one at a time, stepping into the hot tub with one leg then the other. I tug my sweater off next, leaving it puddled on the steps of the tub.

"Baby, please go insi . . ." His voice dies off as he glances over his shoulder, as he drinks me in as I stand naked in the hot tub, bubbling water lapping at my legs. "Jesus Christ," he croaks, blinking rapidly.

I smile. "Finish up that pizza already, would you? I'm hungry. In more than one sense of the word."

Aiden seems incredibly torn between tending the pizza and ravishing me. It makes a blush heat my cheeks. I sink into the water and pop the lid off the pint of salted caramel. Digging a spoon into the ice cream, I watch him, still distractedly turning the pizza, his gaze wrenched my way again and again. I slide the spoon inside my mouth and suck.

His jaw clenches. "Goddammit, Freya. I'm gonna burn the pizza."

"So take it out already."

He sighs. "It's not as crispy as you like it, yet—"

"Bear, I don't mind. I just want you in the hot tub with me. Bring that half-baked pizza and get in here."

Aiden deliberates, but finally he pulls the pizza out onto the oversize plate he had at the ready, sitting near the fire to stay warm. Strolling toward me, he smiles, his eyes raking down my body, the bubbles dancing over my breasts, barely covering my nipples. I hold out a hand. "I'll take that."

Aiden sets the pizza plate carefully in my hand, holding my eyes.

I rest it on the corner of the tub that's flat and hold his eyes, too, riveted as he unzips his coat, then shrugs it off, adding it to my pile of clothes. Next goes his midnight-blue hoodie, dark gray sweatpants, the precarious dance like I did of tugging off socks and shoes, dipping one leg, then the other into the tub. As soon as he's in the water, he crawls over me and kisses me hard and deep, his tongue lapping at mine, hands gripping my hips. "That was quite the tease," he whispers.

I smile against his kiss. "You like it when I tease you."

"I do," he says, a smile tugging at his mouth. He reaches past me for the pizza plate, brings it between us, then groans. "Dammit, I forgot to cut it into pieces. I'll—"

He's standing, but I tug him by the hand back into the water. "You'll do nothing."

"Freya—"

I lift the pizza by its crust and take a bite. A moan of satisfaction leaves me. "It's perfect."

Aiden's eyes darken. "I think you should have another bite."

I smile, then take another bite, letting out another moan, overly dramatic this time to make him laugh. He does. But he also slides closer to me in the water, pulling my leg over his, his hand splayed high across my thigh. "Feed me?"

I do. I lift the pizza and he bites it. And then I set the plate down and reach for the ice cream again. Aiden opens his mouth and takes the spoonful. When I pull it out, he grips my wrist, ducking his head, his tongue, cooled from the ice cream, dragging up the hot, sensitive skin of my inner wrist. "There was a drip," he murmurs before he bites softly.

I suck in a breath and arch reflexively in the water. Aiden sits back, picks up the pizza, and offers it to me on the plate to bite again. "I think we should be done with pizza," I mutter. I'm squirming, turned on. All I can think about is that tongue right between my thighs, bringing me to orgasm.

Aiden grins wickedly. He knew exactly what he was doing when he licked my wrist. He knows I'm suffering. "I've got plans for you, Bergman. Better eat up so you'll have your strength."

I glare at him playfully, then take the biggest bite of pizza I can. Aiden laughs, then he leans in and takes an equally comically large bite. We sit there in the tub, cheeks full as chipmunks, half choking on our pizza, chasing it with spoonfuls of ice cream that "drip" onto more parts of my body—the curve of my breasts, the edge of my shoulder, the slope of my neck, more gargantuan bites of pizza that taste like woodsmoke and happiness.

When the pizza is gone and the ice cream is half melted, Aiden stands abruptly, leaving nothing to the imagination about how this little flirty dinner of ours has affected him. I reach for him, but he grips my wrist again, gently tugging me up. I stand in the tub, naked as he is, hot bodies pressed together, cold air cutting in around us. Aiden rubs his hands over my ass and tucks me close. "Get inside."

I raise my eyebrows. "Awfully bossy, MacCormack—*eek!*" A yelp jumps out of me as he swats my ass.

Aiden grins, then kisses me hard. "You like when I boss you. Now get inside and warm up. I'll be right there."

"Oh, I'll be warmed up all right," I call over my shoulder, making sure I bend and give him a full, generous view of my backside as I step out of the tub.

Aiden swears under his breath, clumsily stacking the ice cream pints, slapping off the bubble mode in the tub, grabbing the pizza plate.

I laugh, running inside, slipping a little on the wood floors as I dash toward the fireplace, wrenching blankets and pillows from the couch as I go. I hear the sliding door slam shut, the plate and ice cream spoons clatter in the sink, the pounding of Aiden's feet as he runs after me.

I'm half tackled, half spun onto the plush landing pad of pillows I've dropped, sprawled across Aiden. He smiles up at me, chest heaving, heat on his cheeks.

I stare down at him and slide my fingers through his dark waves, thickened to near-curls from the humidity of the tub. I hope, one day, if we have a baby, that they'll have his hair. That I'll scrub it gently in a bubble bath full of toys, brush it into soft, smooth waves, braid it down their back.

But even if we don't, I have him. I have this. My heart is full. And in that moment I feel so keenly the truth that you can ache for something with your whole heart and also feel overwhelmingly complete, all at once; that love like ours is big enough to hold all our longing inside it.

Gently, I lean in for a kiss, teasing, grazing his jaw, the corner of his mouth, a gentle tug of my teeth on his bottom lip. Aiden groans low in his throat, his hands rubbing over my ass, moving me against him, where he's hot and hard, thick between us.

"Fuck, you're wet," he mutters into my neck, biting me, lapping the echoing sting of pain-pleasure with his tongue.

"Aiden," I murmur, scandalized and delighted as I always am when he talks like that.

He laughs, then rolls us so I'm on my back, Aiden up on his elbow, his thigh pinned over mine. His hand parts my legs with the sure, sensual confidence of a man who knows what he's doing, who knows my body, its desires and every secret. Two fingers right over my entrance, drawing up wetness, rubbing at my clit. His free hand tugging gently at my nipple. I moan, rocking my hips against his touch.

Aiden eases off as he feels my pleasure build, making me wait.

I glare up at him. He grins.

"No teasing," I growl.

"No teasing?" he says, eyebrows lifted. "No teasing, says the woman who stripped down while I was handling *fire*."

I roll my eyes. "It was a portable woodfired oven—" A gasp cuts me off as he works me with his fingers suddenly, firm and expert.

"God, Frey, feeling you like this." He shakes his head, bends, and kisses me. "Fucking undoes me."

I sigh against his kiss, feeling my orgasm begin—sweet, aching pulses between my thighs, in my tender breasts. He lets off, and as I whine in response, Aiden grips my hips and flips me over, before wrenching me up onto all fours.

His hand slides between us again. "Dripping. That's how wet you are for me, Freya."

I bite my lip, blushing, then nod.

Aiden leans over me, his fingers stroking me deftly, teasingly circling my clit. "This pussy, Freya?"

I gasp as he rubs my clit in earnest. A nonsensical *nnngghhh* leaves me.

"This pussy," he growls, "whose is it?"

"Yours," I breathe.

"And this . . ." He pulls away so he's up on his knees, gripping my ass, spreading me wide before he slides every inch of him deep inside me. "Whose cock is this?"

"Mine," I moan as he fills me, then pulls back, agonizingly slow.

"That's right. God, you feel . . ." He grunts as I squeeze my muscles around him. "You feel so fucking good, Freya, so tight and wet, baby." He curls around me, his chest to my back, his breath hot on my neck. "Feel me, filling you up, giving you what you need?"

I nod frantically.

"I'll always give you what you need, Freya. Always."

He reaches around me, one solid arm planted by my side, the other rubbing softly at my clit, quick, light circles that make my breath catch in my lungs, stick in my throat, until it rushes out in broken gasps of air, pleas for more.

Need knots inside me, harsh, hot demand for release. I drop to my elbows, unable to hold myself up as he strokes into me, sure, powerful thrusts of his hips, grinding in mesmerizing circles when he's seated inside me that build up an orgasm so deep within my body, I can barely take the desperation it winds tighter and tighter inside me.

"Aiden," I cry as the ache inside me tips into the first promise of relief. I press back into him. "Don't stop."

He pulls out, shushing me gently as I cry out in frustration. I'm rolled onto my back, and he sinks into me, sending me sliding up the blanket. "Freya." His breath is ragged, his hand gliding up my arm until our fingers lock. Our gazes hold as he stares at me, openmouthed, wide-eyed, as lost to me as I'm lost to him, to the beautiful relief and pleasure our bodies give each other.

Emotion bursts out of me in a cry—joy, need, aching want, love, so much love. Aiden sinks into me and pins his groin against mine, grinding, thrusting, until I don't even know where his body ends and mine begins, only that we're close, close as we can be, and it's undoing me, wrenching my body toward release that's a white-hot riptide, fierce and furious, a powerful surge that finally culminates, sends my hips careening into his, my fingers gripping his shoulder as he cries out my name and spills into me again and again.

We gasp together and collapse, Aiden on top of me, then rolling me with him, tangled limbs and chests heaving for air.

I shiver and let out a shuddering exhale as he wraps me in his arms, so tightly against him, I can barely breathe. I love it. I love nothing more than feeling this man hold me to him like this is all there is—all he needs.

Slowly, tenderly, Aiden ducks his head, kissing me, closed mouth and sweet at first, then a languid, delicious flick of his tongue that makes me sigh, boneless, blissful.

We lie there for a while, simply looking at each other, firelight dancing over our bodies, in our eyes. We're a mess of sweat and sex, flushed and breathless still, as Aiden tucks me inside his arm, propping us up on pillows.

I wrap my arms around his waist and sigh contentedly. "Read to me?"

I feel his smile, his cheek lifting against the crown of my head. "Gladly." A little clumsily, he paws around for his phone on the coffee table and finds it, then opens up his reading app. "Now where were we? Ah yes." He clears his throat and begins to read.

I let my eyes fall shut, lulled by the rich, warm timbre of his voice, the sound of his heart pounding beneath my ear. I must fall asleep for a while, a light doze, in and out, half awake. I'm pulled to full alertness when he sets down his phone.

I peer up at him, frowning. "I drifted off. Wait, how did it end?"

Aiden smiles down at me. "As all good romances do. With lessons learned and a happily ever after."

"Hmm." I kiss him, my hand curled tenderly around his neck. "Well, that's a good ending, but not the best."

He cranes his head. "And why's that, wife?"

I smile. "Because husband, *our* ending is the best. One with space for all that life brings—not just happiness and hope, but waiting and wanting—with love to see us through. Our ever after."

"Our ever after," he says softly, "always."

ACKNOWLEDGMENTS

True to its subject matter—a marriage in crisis—this book was a challenge. It took much longer than its predecessors. It required faith and patience and a number of good cries and harsh bouts of anxiety. But it's here, and I'm grateful. I'm proud of it.

I'm particularly grateful to the community of writers who buoyed me up when I felt like I was about to go under, and to Jen and Katie, whose wise insight strengthened the authenticity and compassion that shaped these characters' nuances and journeys.

Through this story, I've tried to honor the complexity and difficulty of long-term partnership and marriage, of deciding when and how to expand a family, particularly in a relationship when mental health struggles are at play. I've tried to honor the people who will open this book and whose marriages have teetered on the brink of plummeting, who continually work hard to keep them safe and alive. I tried not to sugarcoat the work of marriage, because I know personally just how hard it is. And I feel I would be remiss if I didn't also say:

To those who read this book and wish they'd made it through like Freya and Aiden, to those whose committed relationships have ended, I'm sorry it hurts. I'm sorry it didn't unfold the way you hoped the day you promised each other everything. But please know you haven't failed. You've learned. You've grown. It just so happens you didn't grow *together* and what you learned took you to new and separate places. Let yourself grieve. Let yourself feel relieved. Release your guilt and shame. Be gentle with yourself, and when you're ready, accept nothing less than deep friendship and kindest love.

To those whose long-term partnerships are suffering: loving someone, sharing partnership with them, should never *ever* come at the cost of your true self; healthy sacrifice and compromise are essential, but if you're staring in that mirror each morning and you're looking at a ghost of yourself, something has to change— and that change has to be your partnership, so that you recognize yourself again, so that you thrive once more and live truthfully. You will always be worth more than preserving a system that oppresses and hurts you. Loving someone should never make you hide; it should never break you. You are worth it—your joy and authentic life are worth it.

To those who have traversed dark valleys and climbed to stunning heights, you have my deepest admiration, and I'm happy for you. Know that you have done something incredible: You have found a way to be you, for your partner to be them, for you both to be an "us" that fits and shares love, together. That is a gift. A hard-won gift. I hope you soak it up, the wonder of that hard-won gift— your ever after always.

The Bergman Brothers series, continuing with this book, portrays a big messy family, found family, and friends—imperfect people trying exceptionally hard to love one another well. There are rough patches and plenty of struggles along the way, but ultimately, their love is accepting, affirming, and profoundly safe. Some might say this isn't very realistic. To which I say, I'd like it to be, and this is why I write. As Oscar Wilde said, "Life imitates Art far more than Art imitates Life." I believe stories affirming everyone's worthiness of love and belonging have life-changing power—to touch us, heal us, and deepen our empathy for ourselves and others. Stories have the power to reshape our hearts and minds, our relationships, and ultimately the world we live in.

I hope by now that, as it has been for me, this Bergman world is a haven for you, reader, where these intimate relationships with oneself and others, platonic, familial, romantic, and beyond, affirm the hope for all of us—that we can be curious not judgmental, open-minded and open-hearted; that we can welcome and embrace one another, just as we are, and become better, wiser, kinder, for having experienced all that is possible when we do.

Keep reading for a preview of
Axel Bergman's story . . .

WITH YOU FOREVER

Rooney

Playlist: "Cowboy Blues," Kesha

My eyes are on the road, but my head is in the clouds. Windows cracked, cool autumn air spilling in as Seattle-Tacoma Airport fades behind me and a cozy cabin staycation lies ahead.

Thoughts drifting, I soak up the view: sapphire sky, emerald evergreens mingling with burnished bronze leaves, an onyx asphalt ribbon paving the way. My rental car blasts Kesha because, hello, I'm a woman on a solo trip, figuring out her shit—of course I'm listening to Kesha. There's just one of her songs that I avoid. Because the last time I heard it, I did A Very Terrible Thing.

I kissed Axel Bergman.

Which isn't the end of the world. I'm over it. It's not like I fixate on it. Or daydream about it. Not about The Charades Kiss or Axel, who I haven't seen since.

Who I'm definitely not thinking about now, as I drive through his home state, that song filling the car before I can skip it, while a rainbow whooshes across the sky.

Ohhhh, Rooney. Liar, liar, palazzo pants on fire.

My mind isn't on the road or in the clouds. It's in the past, in the moment after our kiss . . .

The clue—kiss—scrawled on a piece of paper, flutters to the ground. My lips tingle, my cheeks are hot as I stand with my head back, staring up at Axel, who I've just kissed.

Maybe "mauled with my mouth" is more accurate.

A rainbow gale of confetti whips around the room, spun off the ceiling fan blades that whir overhead. In a haze of soft, warm lights, the air thumps with that upbeat song's opening bars.

But it all fades as I look at him. Six feet, many inches of grumpy gorgeousness. An unreadable, dangerously kissable mystery.

Who I just crushed my mouth to for the sake of a charades clue.

I bring a shaky hand to my lips. "Axel, I—I—I'm sorry. I didn't mean . . . That is, I shouldn't have . . . I'm just viciously competitive, and I . . ."

He stands, silent, staring at my mouth. Then, slowly, he takes a step closer. For once, he doesn't leave like he always seems to when I get close. He doesn't run.

He stays.

"I think . . ." he says hoarsely, leaning a little closer.

I lean a little closer, too. "You think . . . ?"

Axel swallows roughly as his fingertips brush mine. It's the faintest touch, but it seismic-booms through me, in tempo with the music, as if it's the soundtrack to this tenuous, almost-something-moment.

"I think," he whispers, "I have a new appreciation for charades."

My mouth falls open in surprise. The silent giant just cracked a joke.

He takes a step closer, placing us toe to toe, and his gaze settles on my mouth. He bends his head toward mine. He's close. A little closer.

And just as I realize he might *be on the verge of kissing me back, sharp, warning spasms clutch my stomach, punching the air out of my lungs.*

In the world's worst timing, I'm the one who pulls away. *I'm the one who runs from the room. The moment stolen from me before it was even fully mine.*

That's where it always ends, where the daydream leaves me, wondering, *What if?*

What if I hadn't had to run off without a word of explanation?

What if, when I finally came back, Axel was still there, waiting for me?

My daydream *what-ifs* spin cotton candy sweet but dissolve just as easily when my phone's ringtone overrides the music. I glance at the screen, my throat tightening as I see my best friend's name: *Willa*.

The only sound in the car is the call's rhythmic ring. It's suddenly quiet—too quiet—and my thoughts have backpedaled to what I came up here to escape.

I wish I could say that kissing Axel Bergman in a moment of overzealousness for charades, then having to bolt for the bathroom in gastrointestinal agony, was the low point of my recent existence, but I can't.

Because since that night, my health nose-dived to the point that I had to take a leave of absence from law school, and when I came back to the apartment after finalizing said leave of absence, defeated, exhausted, so fucking lost, I couldn't stay one second longer.

So here I am, directionless, doing something I haven't in . . . ever. I'm trying to take care of myself.

Willa is still calling, each ring chipping away at my resolve. I take a deep breath, push the right button on the steering wheel, and accept her call.

Finding my upbeat, *I'm okay* voice, I holler, "I'm here!"

"You're here! Just got your text that you landed. Where are you exactly?"

"Whoa now, no need for an interrogation."

"You're lost, aren't you?"

"I'm not *lost*." Squinting, I glance at the GPS on my rental's display screen and the winding trail of my directions. Then I peer up at my surroundings. "I'm . . . heading . . . west."

"Uh-huh. You know you have nothing to prove to me, right? You're a biochem geek who's at Stanford Law. It's okay to have a weakness and admit that you're directionally challenged."

"I admit that I have many weaknesses and that I am directionally challenged. I do not, however, admit to being lost."

I swear I can hear her eye roll. "The property's entrance sneaks up on you. I can't tell you how many times I've missed it. It's easy to drive past, so go slow when you come to that hairpin turn."

I grimace as I stare at the directions. I have no idea what she's talking about. "Will do. I can't wait to see it."

"Oh, Roo, you're gonna love it. It's so beautiful. I wish I was there to welcome you and watch you take it in. I would absolutely reenact an epic *Chariots of Fire* run to your car if this professional soccer gig weren't so damn demanding. Crummy World Cup Qualifiers. Crummy flight. Crummy soccer."

"So crummy," I tell her. "Crummy dream come true, crummy playing for the U.S. Women's team. Crummy honor of being a rookie who's on the starting lineup."

"Okay, fine, it's not crummy, and I'm very excited. I just miss you." After a beat of hesitation, she says, "How are you holding up?"

"I'm . . . okay."

I set a hand on my stomach, which has started making warning twinges that I'm all-too-familiar with, especially since my old meds stopped working a few months ago. Thankfully, my new treatment has finally started giving me relief from my most serious ulcerative colitis symptoms, so I'm relatively much better—meaning I'm not incapacitated at home or in the hospital for dehydration and pain—but I have lasting damage to my intestines. Even while I'm in clinical remission, some symptoms are a permanent fixture in my life.

But Willa's not asking about my GI troubles. She's asking about everything else. Because this is the one thing I keep from her.

She and I have most of the West Coast between us these days, but we talk all the time, and she knows I've taken a leave of absence from Stanford Law. She just doesn't know the medical reason. Because Willa doesn't know I have ulcerative colitis. She knows I have a sensitive stomach and make more bathroom trips than most, but not why, not the worst of it.

When I told her I was taking a leave of absence, I explained that I was stepping back to assess if law school was still the right path for me, which isn't a lie. It's just not the whole truth.

I know. I hate keeping secrets from her, but I've had my reasons, and I believe they're good ones.

We've been best friends since we met, which was as freshman roommates and newbies on the women's soccer team at UCLA. It wasn't long into our friendship that she shared her mom's past battle with breast cancer and her new diagnosis of leukemia. That's when I knew the last thing Willa needed was someone else to worry about. With the right medication and sheer unreliable luck, ulcerative colitis is one of those diseases that can behave itself for years. Mine did through college, with only a few minor episodes that I managed to handle without raising Willa's suspicion. I hate lying, and I never wanted to keep it from her, but I simply felt in my heart that she didn't need one more thing weighing on her. The wisdom of that choice was confirmed when her mother died our junior year.

In the past few years since we've graduated, I haven't known how to tell her. I've been afraid to worry her. I haven't wanted anything to change between us. And the longer my lie of omission continues, the harder it gets to tell the truth.

That's why she doesn't know how sick I've been recently. That's why she thinks I've just been crushed by law school, and once again, it's not a lie—it's just not the whole truth. Law school *has* been stressful. I've loved it some moments, hated it others, and it's unequivocally the hardest thing I've ever done.

And then that stress, hours of studying, late nights, anxiety about doing my best, caught up with me, and I just couldn't do it anymore. *Your health or your studies*, my doctor said. *Pick one.*

"Rooney?" Willa says. "I think you cut out for a minute."

"Sorry." I shake myself and snap out of it. "Can you hear me okay?"

"I can now. I didn't catch anything after I asked how you're doing."

"Ah." I clear my throat nervously. "Well, I'm doing . . . okay. Just really ready for this time away. Thank you again for offering the A-frame. You still haven't told me what I can give the Bergmans for rent, though."

"I told you that you're not paying rent. You'll never hear the end of it if you even try. You're practically family to them."

Willa's boyfriend, Ryder, is the middle child of the seven Bergman siblings, a boisterous, close family that's welcomed me into their fold. His mom, Elin, is a Swedish transplant whose hugs and homemaking are the stuff of dreams. His dad, who goes by Dr. B, is one of those people who instantly makes any gathering a party. While Willa and Ryder met when we were at UCLA, and Los Angeles is where the Bergmans now call home, their family's early years were spent here in Washington State, often at their getaway property, the A-frame.

The Bergmans are the chaotic, tight-knit family my only-child soul always wanted, and they've done nothing but make me feel welcome. Since Willa is as good as theirs, and I'm hers, now I'm as good as theirs, too. At least, I was, until The Charades Kiss with Axel, the oldest Bergman son.

Not that *they* made it awkward. Apparently only Axel and I were traumatized by my rogue charades move. Nobody seemed remotely fazed afterward. Sure, they gasped when the kiss happened—

I mean, it shocked everyone, including me—but by the time I came back from the bathroom, and found Axel pointedly absent, they'd moved on. Laughing, teasing, setting the table for dinner. Like it was nothing.

They're either incredible actors or they weren't terribly surprised that I'd finally flung myself at Axel after nursing a long-standing crush I've tried very hard to hide—Axel, who threw me a rare bone of humor when he made that crack about "a new appreciation for charades," but who was clearly scared away by my antics. The whole situation was mortifying.

I felt sick. I was embarrassed. So that night I made my excuses, and since then, the past six weeks, I've made myself scarce, which hasn't been hard because I've been sick as a dog.

Do I wish I could figure out how to smooth things over? Yes. Do I wish I knew how to reengage without dying of embarrassment? Yes. But I have no idea where to begin, and I can't deal with that right now. I don't have the spoons to think about the Bergmans, especially Axel. I have the spoons to stay at their empty A-frame for the next few weeks, hiding from reality while figuring out how I'm going to eventually face it again.

It's an escape I desperately need. Which is why I really want to give the Bergmans something for my time here.

"Willa, I don't like the idea of staying at the A-frame for free."

"Too bad," she says. "It's there. Unused. Ryder said it should be empty until New Year's. That's when Freya and Aiden have their turn, so stay as long as you like up until then."

"Willa, seriously, I couldn't—"

"Listen, Roo, the place is paid off. It's there simply to be enjoyed. Ryder's parents barely bother coming up, so it's free for the siblings to use how and when they want. There's no need to pay when none of us are paying. We just do the minimum upkeep."

"I can do upkeep!"

She sighs. "You're *not* spending your staycation replacing lost shingles and resealing the deck."

"Don't tempt me. I love DIY projects."

"You're supposed to be *relaxing*."

"Fine. I'll settle for scrubbing the bathroom grout with a tooth-brush."

Willa snorts a laugh. "God, I miss you. Do you think you'll stick around long enough for us to catch up? I'm back in two and a half weeks. I'd be home sooner, but after we play, I've got to do a bunch of press and sponsorship shit—aka the stuff that actually pays the bills."

I glance in the rearview mirror at my reflection. I still look like I'm sick. Pale skin, shadowy half-moons under my eyes. Well, at least when we meet up, and I finally find the courage to tell her I'm sick, I'll look the part.

"I should still be here." Technically I don't have to be back un-til a few days before Christmas, to celebrate with Dad, then meet up with my advisor to discuss how I plan to proceed at school, but I'll probably come home at the end of the month for Thanksgiv-ing. The holiday is always a bit of a bust, since it's just Dad and me, but it feels odd to consider spending it apart from him. Even though I bet if I weren't home, he'd probably be happy working in his office or on set without feeling guilty about leaving me alone.

"Yay! I can't wait," Willa says. "But listen, no worries if plans change. If you head home before I'm back, we'll make it to Thanks-giving. We'll eat. Then nap. Then play board games. Then there's the soccer tournament in the backyard . . ."

A wave of guilt crashes through me. Willa assumes I'm coming to the Bergmans for Thanksgiving, like I did last year, after Dad's and my brief, early meal. I don't want to tell her how unsure I am that I'll make it, if I'll feel well enough, because I just never know when it's going to be a rough day and home is the only place I can handle being. If I can stand the embarrassment of seeing Axel since Kissgate.

Willa's still talking happily, planning our day. ". . . You better brace yourself. I'm going to tackle-hug you. I'm going to squeeze you so hard, you squeak like a puppy chew toy."

That makes me laugh. "You're disturbing."

"But you love me. All right, I have to get going. I just wanted to catch up quickly before I had practice. Love you! Text me when you're safe at the cabin?"

"Love you, too. I will."

"And text Ryder for help when you're ready to admit that you're lost."

"I'm not lost!" I yell right as she hangs up. Then I refocus on the GPS.

Okay. Maybe I'm a *little* lost.

Photo courtesy of the author

Chloe Liese writes romances reflecting her belief that everyone deserves a love story. Her stories pack a punch of heat, heart, and humor, and often feature characters who are neurodivergent, like herself. When not dreaming up her next book, Chloe spends her time wandering in nature, playing soccer, and most happily at home with her family and mischievous cats. To sign up for Chloe's latest news, new releases, and special offers, please visit her website and subscribe.

VISIT CHLOE LIESE ONLINE

ChloeLiese.com

Ready to find
your next great read?

Let us help.

Visit prh.com/nextread

Penguin
Random
House